ELEPHANT BOUND

NIKKI
SWINFEN

ELEPHANT BOUND

Elephant Bound
by Nikki Swinfen

First published 2022

Cover design by Jane Dixon-Smith
www.jdsmith-design.co.uk

Book interior by Eleanor Abraham
thisisthestory.co.uk
Typeset in Adobe Garamond Pro and Bembo Std.

ISBN: 979-8-8347-0625-0

The **Sheldrick Wildlife Trust** has saved nearly three hundred elephants, and a further fifty have been born to those who have been reintegrated into the wild.

You can support their crucial work by sponsoring a baby elephant, rhino, or giraffe at www.sheldrickwildlifetrust.org

Dedication

In memory of my mother, Ann, the matriarch of our family.
And for my father, David, with love.

PROLOGUE

TAITA HILLS, KENYA 2012

IT is waiting for them. A majestic baobab – ancient, all-knowing – towers over other, lesser trees. From a distance, the copse seems anointed by the morning sun, steamy heat rising from its leaves, tipped by golden light. The recent good rains have transformed this landlocked island from skeletal brittleness to dense bush so picturesque it is as though it has been scooped up and placed here by gentle, green-fingered gods.

They have driven silently through miles of scrubby grassland. Above them, the morning crackles into life; below the vertiginous road, the green circle breaks mirage-like into view. Thin, spidery lines trail out from it like lightning scars. These paths have been gouged out by the slow, rhythmic tread of generations of elephants. Their pursuit of sustenance has forged dozens of sinuous lines, bringing a cycle of life and energy to the copse – the trees and water providing life and energy in return.

The baobab beckons them to enter. They park the Landcruiser in its shade, Hamisi jumping out first, instructing the others to stay in the car. Satisfied there is no longer any danger, he signals them to join him. Gigi gets out, but stands stock still, her limbs floppy, as though she has a fever. She tries to steady herself with a deep breath, but a thick ferrous smell hits her nostrils making her retch.

Fenella starts to run towards the trees, but Barbara grabs her granddaughter's shoulder and she stops momentarily, looking back into Barbara's eyes. There is a warning in them. What she will see will not just be dreadful, it will pluck out a memory, long pushed under her skin; tweak at it until it resurfaces.

'Come.' Hamisi can only manage a single word, his mind

racing at the speed of his heart. He pushes forward through the scrub, hacking a rough trail with his panga. Then he stops.

The silent scene lying before them will be etched on Gigi's memory for the rest of her life. She has a weird passing image in her mind of the bodies at Pompeii. The way that the people seemed frozen in the act of some ordinary daily pastime. The elephants are gathered around a waterhole. Some have been drinking and lie face down in a cruelly comical fashion, back ends high in the air. A baby lies at the edge of the water, muddy from play. Some still have clumps of grass in their mouths, half chewed. One leans with its trunk laid over the head of another, giving the impression it had been nuzzling into it – a greeting or a goodbye? In the centre, the waterhole, its shimmering surface unbroken, lies utterly still, not its customary russet brown mirroring the land, but a thick, magenta red.

Gigi gags and has to push Hamisi aside to be sick.

Hamisi stands stunned. 'Bastards.'

Barbara and Fenella are the last to arrive, hands held. Her forty-five years in the bush have steeled Barbara for most things, and she has seen many animals killed at the hands of humans, but this carnage is so at odds with the surrounding utopia, that she cannot take it in. Her legs give way from under her and she falls to the ground, still clutching Fenella's hand, yanking her down too.

'Hamisi?' she whispers.

He understands her question. 'Yes, Barbara, it's her.'

PART 1

CHAPTER 1

TAITA HILLS, KENYA 2011

'HAMISI, Hamiseeee!' He could hear the shrill voice ricocheting around the camp; hear the insistent slap, slap of the woman's sandals on the hard earth. The trouble with being out in a small camp in the bush was there was nowhere to hide. Well, there was if you were a civet or a snake, even an elephant – elephants were surprisingly good at concealment. But, as a cumbersome six-foot human, hiding was impossible, even for one as experienced as Hamisi. No, he'd better just get it over with. He unzipped his tent and stepped out, startling Lydia who had been standing right outside.

'Hamisi, it's my shower.' Lydia's querulous voice was both demanding and disturbingly flirtatious. 'There's some sort of frog in there and I just can't abide frogs. Please have it removed.'

Hamisi wondered why Lydia wanted to be here at all. She was scared of spiders, snakes, scorpions, ants, she couldn't take the heat of the day, and found the quiet of the night too unnerving to sleep. She got bored waiting for animals to appear at the waterhole and simply could not keep quiet. In none of this was she unusual. She was brash, rude and selfish – a cliché of wealthy Western tourists, but clichés existed because they were, more often than not, true. 'Of, course, Lydia. Lead the way.'

Really, such housekeeping issues were not his job. There was a legion of staff at the camp, but Lydia would have absolutely no idea of their existence, given the opulent standard of the camp, and it was just easier to do it himself. On entering Lydia's luxurious tent, the smell of her expensive perfume hit him in the back of the throat. At the bottom of her shower was the 'frog' (actually, gecko). Miraculously, as the little creatures normally zigzagged like quicksilver, he caught it unawares, quickly covering it with one hand and slipping his other hand under. He kept the tiny gecko cupped until he reached the mess tent. 'Here you go, little friend. Lots of tasty flies and bugs around here.' Hamisi smiled to himself. Lydia would be helping to feed this creature with all the flies on the food scraps around this bit of camp – paradise for geckos. Lydia was following behind him, so he made all the necessary reassuring noises to her, and she could now return to her evening of being served hot food and sundowners in the comfort she expected.

Now he was out of his tent anyway, Hamisi made his way to the bar to steel himself with a cold bottle of coke and to shoot the breeze with Fikiri, the camp manager, who was writing out his weekly food order for the kitchen. 'Jambo, Fikiri. Good evening, my friend. What's cooking?'

Fikiri acknowledged the pun with a laugh despite, or perhaps because, Hamisi made the same joke every week. 'Slow-cooked elephant researcher,' retorted Fikiri. 'Done to a turn – nice and crisp!'

'Okay, okay, I deserved that!' Hamisi laughed. 'Can I have a coke, please?'

'Help yourself, I need to go through this grocery order before I send Sammy out with the van in the morning. Do you need anything from town?'

Hamisi joined Fikiri behind the bar and reached to get a coke from a small battered drinks fridge which sat precariously on a pile of crates and hummed as loudly as a swarm of locusts. 'A couple of notebooks from Nagi's store would be good, thanks. What time are the new lot getting here tomorrow?'

'Late afternoon. They won't be in time for lunch, but we need to give them a good evening meal as they're driving down from Nairobi, not flying. They'll be hungry.'

'Good, okay. I have a few hours in the middle of the day to catch up on things then.' He took a large swig of coke, then mumbled,

'Here we go again,' and headed over to the campfire where the tourists would shortly gather following their dinner.

The evening meal of chicken and rice and fruit salad had been polished off with gusto; the conversation had been polite and good natured. The assembled guests remained oblivious to the staff, who scuttered around like backstage crew, making the whole scene seamless. Cushions and rugs in earthy shades of copper and ochre adorned the chairs and polished concrete floors of the low-walled dining room. Swooping voile drapes of raspberry and apricot hung from the high beams. The campfire area had been set up just outside the dining room. Soft blankets, edged with tassels and tiny bells had been artfully swathed over the camp chairs, ready to embrace any occupants who felt the slight chill of the evening. Fairy lights twinkled, and a small clearing on one side of the fire had been swept to create a makeshift stage for the 'spontaneous' Maasai dancing beginning at precisely 8:00 pm.

Hamisi was to be on call this evening, as every night, to be the resident storyteller. He always had a knack for recounting tales from the bush with enough flair to keep his audience enrapt, but enough restraint to make the stories seem real. Many of the tales had not happened directly to him, but he told himself that it was simpler and more exciting for his audience to believe that his life was one long catalogue of amazing adventures, rather than a life of study, paperwork and bookkeeping. He spotted Barbara, the owner of the camp and surrounding game reserve, seated at the head of the large refectory table. 'Penny for your thoughts, Barbara?'

Barbara was jolted from her contemplation. 'What? Sorry… oh, they aren't worth a penny. I was just remembering things. I seem to be doing that a lot lately. I don't know why. It's like a scab I'm picking at. I can't help feeling something is afoot. Do you ever get that? Like something important is happening out there and any minute it is going to have something to do with you. It's coming at you. Oh, I don't really know what I'm talking about!' She shook her head briskly and topped up her gin and lime. 'Sit down here with me, old friend. How are you?'

'I'm fine. I just got off the phone to Angel and the girls. Grace came top of her class in a maths quiz today. She is very pleased with herself!'

'So she should be. A chip off the old block, heh?'

'Well, yes from her mother. Maths wasn't ever my strong point. I've always hated that part of my work – the data reporting. In the past, I was terrified of getting things wrong. I'd get Angel to check my work!'

'Quite an admission, Doctor Gitonga!'

'Well, I always got it right, I just needed her reassurance!'

'Hmm!' Barbara smiled at him. 'Shall we?' She pushed back her chair, stood up stiffly and tipped her drink towards the assembling guests.

'If you say so,' Hamisi gave her a knowing smile and took her arm as they went to join the others round the fire.

* * *

'I was disappointed not to see rhino, today.' A middle-aged and rather corpulent man leaned forward wheezily and grumbled into his whisky sour.

'Rhino,' thought Hamisi. Not 'a rhino' or 'some rhinos'. The man talked like an old-fashioned game hunter, or at least tried to. Did he think that was how he was supposed to talk?

'Now, that time we were in Botswana in '99... Do you remember, Janice?'

'It was very quiet all day,' agreed his wife. 'In fact, there has been very little of interest all week. The brochure seemed to promise more exciting, rare animals. Wouldn't you agree, Hamisi?'

'Well, I'm afraid that they *are* rare. So, by definition, it can be very hard to see some of them. We just can't control where they will be or even if they are around. This isn't a safari park; they are *wild* animals, after all.'

'You're right, of course, but I just hoped we would see *one* lion,' said Janice.

'Well, we certainly heard them. I couldn't sleep on that second night. It sounded like the lion was right outside our tent!' Lydia's comment seemed accusatory, like she blamed the lion for her bad night's sleep. But perhaps that was just Hamisi's imagination. He needed to snap out of this mood.

Hamisi tried to revive the flagging conversation. 'Did I ever tell you about the time I was collecting elephant urine for an academic paper and got completely covered in elephant poo?'

'Yes, you did,' said Janice, flatly.

'Tough crowd,' Hamisi muttered to himself. He was relieved to see the Maasai dancers drift over to the swept ground, singing softly.

The dancers took their places, facing the guests in a half moon. They made a soft thrumming noise and began rocking rhythmically backward and forward, knees slightly bent, backs hunched. An occasional yell or thump from the spear of the leader of the group prompted the movement to quicken and voices to get louder, then return back down to the rocking thrum. Each man, dressed in traditional crimson-and-purple finery, seemed to sing his own part and think his own thoughts, but the sound was unified in a collective harmony. The chorus built up to its crescendo and the rocking became jumping, the dancers pogo-ing higher and higher, until they seemed to double in height. The shouts became more hypnotic and insistent. The warriors became one pulsing mass of shining black skin, spears and beads; their limbs taught and sinewy. Every time they rose into the air, their hair, styled intricately into ochre-stained braids, rattled softly like rain on a tin roof. Their performance wasn't hostile but forceful and utterly mesmerising.

Hamisi had watched the Maasai dance enough times to allow

himself ten minutes' wistfulness, whilst swishing his now warm coke round and around in its bottle. Despite the inauthentic circumstances, the rhythm of the drums and the animalistic thrum of the singing always had a nostalgic effect on him. It was the rhythm of his childhood – the voices of his friends.

Looking about him, Hamisi could see that, as usual, the dancing served merely as background noise to the guests who, losing interest in the performance, continued to chatter throughout. What had once been a proud and joyous ceremony had now been reduced to pantomime, he mused. There was half-hearted applause when the guests realised the spectacle had finished and the dancers shuffled off to grab a surreptitious drink from Peter in the back kitchen.

Barbara, however, never took her eyes from the dancers; she never tired of watching this spectacle. She knew all the young men individually – proud warriors who fought hard to maintain their way of life against increasing antagonism. There was Joseph, a quiet man, whose grandfather had helped to build this camp when Barbara inherited it forty years ago. Dipo, the tallest of them all had, for many years, been a sickly child. His mother, Lupito, had fought to get him proper medical attention and now he was as strong as a lion. Lupito had been a kind friend to Barbara in her own hour of need and they still met regularly for tea and gossip. Dipo turned to Barbara at the end of the dance with a smile and a nod and blessings from his mother.

'So, Barbara—' Lydia whispered loudly up close to Barbara's face, her breath garlicky and hot. Barbara tried not to stare at the slick of lipstick on Lydia's teeth. 'You don't really have enough game here to be impressive. We've seen far more animals in Botswana and in the Kruger, but you have a good location for a retreat. This place could be a goldmine. You could develop the camp to accommodate far more people. Make it a bit more luxurious, put in an infinity pool, spa. You'd get far more of the "right" sort of people, if you know what I mean?' Lydia sat back in her chair, pushing her glasses up with a well-manicured finger, satisfied that, having shared her genius with Barbara, she was about to be thanked for her insight and wisdom.

Barbara wasn't sure what an 'infinity pool' was, but she did know what Lydia meant by the 'right sort of people' and felt her hackles rise. 'I'm sure that sort of camp would be very lucrative, yes, Lydia, but it's not really what we're about.'

'What *are* you about, then?' snapped Lydia, clearly affronted at Barbara's lack of enthusiasm. But she didn't wait for an answer and turned to continue gossiping with Janice.

Barbara moved to sit next to Hamisi, letting out a deep sigh as she collapsed into her chair.

'Oh, Hamisi,' Barbara whispered through gritted teeth, 'I do appreciate my lot, really I do. I love my country and wildlife and I love showing it to other people. But God, why are they always such thumping bores?'

Hamisi smiled and nodded slowly, swinging his coke bottle between his fingers. 'Just keep smiling, Barbara. Tomorrow, they will be gone and some *completely* different people will take their place!'

Barbara sniggered. 'Yes, of course. Right, I'm off to bed. Tomorrow is another day. Lala salama, Hamisi.'

'Goodnight, Barbara.'

Barbara made herself a cup of ginger tea and took it upstairs to her room. Cupping her mug, she stepped out onto her balcony to watch the night sky for a few minutes. Now that she was no longer in front of the fire, the chill night air nipped at her bare skin. She wrapped a throw from the chair around her shoulders. There were still clattering noises coming from the kitchen: the last of the cleaning up from tonight's dinner, and Peter and his team would be getting things set out and ready for an early breakfast. The current party of Americans was breakfasting early as they had to reach the airstrip by 8:00 am. There would be a bit of a lull before the next guests were due to arrive in the mid-afternoon.

Barbara tried to clear her mind of the next day's plans and enjoy the sounds of the evening; the chorus of nightjars, cicadas and frogs replacing the chatter of people. Below her, the dying embers of their campfire glowed silver and pink. In the very far distance, a single light marked out the location of a mosque, nestled in a blanket of seemingly endless bush. This mosque, like all the places of worship in the area, was large, elaborate and well maintained. The churches had no shortage of funds, but the ordinary people who attended them were living in deep poverty.

Barbara no longer held youthful indignation about this, but the injustice still rankled with her. She was quite proud of her safari camp, and felt she had been a good employer. They had taken on many local people over the years in the kitchens, as drivers, cleaners and askari. They had also helped a handful of the most promising young people become guides, funding them through their exams and awards.

It wasn't enough, though. This wasn't what Barbara had hoped for the camp when she took it over. For years, it had been a research hub and they had been doing important work, monitoring the local wildlife and flora. Her sister and brother-in-law, who had entrusted her to manage the camp many years earlier, had recently died, one soon after the other, and had bequeathed the camp to her. Perhaps her ownership of the camp should have motivated her more, but life had veered off course and she hadn't the energy to pick up that work again. It was easier to just pander to guests who simply wanted to sit and watch animals from the comfort of their Landcruiser, eat well, drink sundowners, and take endless photographs which they would bore their friends with when they got home. For them it was just another holiday, a 'bucket-list' entry; something to impress the folks back home.

'What *are* you about, then?' Lydia's sneering words buzzed round and round in Barbara's head, mirroring the night sounds.

The woman's views weren't important, and Barbara shouldn't let them get to her. But she couldn't stop their incessant echo.

From her chair, she could see the photograph on her bedside table of Rob and his family. She had taken it on her birthday, over a decade ago. They had all just come back from an early game drive, checking Makena's herd, and had been about to get lunch, when she had persuaded the others to pose for a photograph. The baby was fractious after the long drive, but her other granddaughter was very excited after having spotted a leopard. She had been first to see it, lolling in the high euphorbia branches, and had nearly burst with pride, pointing it out to Clive, her beloved 'Babu'. Clive had gone to fetch something from the jeep and returned, making faces at the children to try to get them to keep still for the picture. It felt like yesterday, and a thousand years ago. So much had changed. One incident could change the course of so many lives so quickly.

The sadness of her losses was always there. Even now she talked to Clive. Just after it happened, she would see something or meet someone and think 'wait till Clive hears about this', but moments later she would remember that he wasn't there anymore and another fragment was chipped off the wall protecting her fragile heart. As the years went by, though, she embraced these thoughts and talked to Clive, in her head at first, then out loud when she was alone. It gave her comfort to imagine what he might make of a situation, what advice he might give her. He was always so calm and balanced.

Barbara felt a tenderness at the back of her jaw and her eyes prickled. In recent months, memories she had managed to entomb under layers of busyness and distractions seemed to be fighting to reach the surface. She was a positive person by nature, but angry thoughts were emerging, and more often she was allowing them in, letting them fester and taunt her. Why was she so lazy? Why had she gone for the easy option and dropped everything they had believed in, just to keep afloat? There was no point to the camp if it did not serve a useful purpose. What was she keeping it afloat for? She could live well enough without its income and she really hadn't anyone to pass it on to. Not after what had happened.

Why had she stopped caring?

Enough now. She coughed, stood up, straightened and returned to her bedroom. She had never been one to wallow. Tomorrow she would discuss her feelings with Hamisi. He had been her constant through everything that had happened – a loyal friend and the cleverest person she knew. Together they could come up with something.

CHAPTER 2

TAITA HILLS 2011

THE next morning, after they had waved their smiling goodbyes to the Americans, Barbara asked Hamisi to stay and talk to her for a while. 'I know you've got things to do, Hamisi, but I want to pick your brain. It's important.'

'Of course. Let me get us a big jug of lemonade and some of Peter's flapjacks,' said Hamisi. 'This sounds like the sort of chat that requires snacks.'

He fetched their provisions, and joined Barbara into the office, placing the tray of drinks on her desk. Barbara liked to be tidy, and the office, or at least her half of it, was well-ordered and clean. Hamisi's desk had once been shared with her son Rob and, although the research data was filed away professionally, the desk itself was buried beneath an explosion of correspondence, invoices, books and general detritus. It was as if Rob were still there, so similar were they in their habits. Barbara unlocked a cupboard, knelt to reach a file at the very bottom – only slightly nibbled by rodents – and thrust it at him.

'Right, do you remember this, Hamisi? Your and Rob's proposal?'

'Of course,' he said, taking the report from her and flicking through the limp, dusty pages. 'We worked really hard on that. It was such a buzz finishing it.'

'But it's not finished, is it?' said Barbara. 'You never actually put any of your ideas into practice.' He looked at her, bewildered. 'Sorry, I didn't mean to sound accusing. I just meant, why don't we do it, or at least try? I am so tired of grinning like the Cheshire Cat at people I dislike, quite frankly, explaining all about our lives and environment here, knowing they don't actually care, and will have forgotten most things I've said to them. I'm tired of pretending to be interested in their problems back home and, most of all, I'm tired of pretending that we are waiting for Rob to come back and make it all alright again, because he isn't coming back, is he?'

She sat down suddenly, tearful and looking shocked at her own outburst and at his puzzled expression. Hamisi's face gradually softened as he looked back down at the report clutched in his hands. He smoothed it out on the desk and slowly turned to the contents page, running a finger down the lines, stopping now and again, smiling to himself in remembrance.

'This work meant everything to me back then,' he murmured. 'We barely slept for months, but it was such a happy time, do you remember? Rob, Jo and I took turns monitoring and counting the species, talking all night about things we had seen, the life stories we put together for the animals. We were so positive that our findings were going to make a difference; that there was real hope for the future.' Hamisi sat up straight and turned the report face down, his palm lingering on it a moment, feeling the memories flood back.

He looked through to the living room at the long trestle table. These days it was pushed up against the wall, covered in an oilcloth and laid with neat stacks of magazines and tasteful coffee table books. Back then it had always been at the centre of all their days, piled high with folders, scraps of kikoy cloth, old snares removed from the bush, a dik-dik skull, well-thumbed copies of *Nature* and *National Geographic*. On top of the general detritus, Jo would lay out her drawings of the animals, Rob and Hamisi would couple their scribbled notes and polaroid photos to the drawings – a game of mix and match. Barbara would scold them for discarding forgotten plates of half-eaten sandwiches which would be coated with ants within minutes. Their children – his daughters and theirs, would play crouched beneath the work, age differences irrelevant in their world of imagination and giggles.

'Do I think he's coming back? No, I don't, Barbara. And he was really the force behind this work. I had more training, but he had the fire in his belly. Well, he and Jo. Without that, I don't know if we can put it into practice.'

'Surely, it's worth a try, though?'

Hamisi felt the familiar fug of apathy hover over him and he trotted out the customary excuses – the ones he told himself every time the guilt intruded. 'I don't know that it's so relevant these days. People have other priorities. Lack of work, this seemingly endless drought we're going through, politics, illness. The fate of wildlife seems almost unimportant compared to the urgent problems people here are facing day in day out, doesn't it?' The question went unanswered as they both sat silent for a moment. Hamisi looked back down at the report, then at Barbara. It was pointless saying these things to her. She knew how hard life was out here; besides, that wasn't the real reason he had given up on their dreams. 'I used to care so much, you know I did, we all did, but well, after… after what happened… I suppose I couldn't get excited about anything anymore.'

His words hung in the hot, gritty air between them. An eagle screeched overhead, breaking the silence.

'I know,' said Barbara. 'I've felt the same. For years, nothing mattered any more, but… I don't know. Something in me is stirring. I feel agitated – annoyed at myself all of a sudden. We are so privileged to live here, to work here… all this beauty. But it's fragile, and all we have really done in the last ten years is make it easier for those who already have it so easy. We provide a comfortable base for people to sit back and watch animals from a safe distance. It's amusement. We are an amusement park. We feed them the beautiful views and the dramatic anecdotes, then they head up to Nairobi and stop off at The Carnivore for crocodile steaks and impala burgers before getting their flights home. Meanwhile the animals are dwindling, the local people are desperate. If we don't try to make things better, doesn't that make us complicit?'

'Bad men need nothing more to compass their ends, than that good men should look on and do nothing,' said Hamisi.

'John F. Kennedy.'

'John Stuart Mill. Perhaps… but where do we start?'

'We get back that "fire in the belly" feeling you mentioned. Not just from us, but from other people. We need to attract people here who can see what we see, not just people who want a photo opportunity and a pretence at authenticity. We need people who already care, but can be made to care more by giving them a real chance at making a difference.'

'How do we get them here?' asked Hamisi.

'Well, some of them are already here. There are young people in the area who never get a chance to know the wildlife on their doorstep as anything other than a nuisance. And we could attract volunteers from further afield.'

'How would they be different from the tourists who already come here?'

'Okay. Here's an idea. We run a competition. We ask them to put together an essay on why they have what it takes to work here. It doesn't have to be Hemingway, it's not the quality of the writing that's important, but the knowledge they have gleaned and the ideas they come up with. We should be able to judge their conviction by what they submit.'

'And what is the prize for this competition?' asked Hamisi, slightly warming to the idea.

'We offer free accommodation for, say, a month. Open to individuals, families, whoever. We just need a bit of new blood here.'

'And what about the old blood?'

'We get local people involved too. Run competitions for the local schools, get some of the joint initiatives up and running that we wanted to put in place. Get emotional investment in place. That's the most essential thing.'

'Well, yes,' said Hamisi, 'your volunteers will go home, feeling they've done something amazing, but it won't be amazing if it doesn't benefit the people and the wildlife they've left behind.'

'Of course. So, the ethos has to come from that, from what

local people need and what will protect the environment and its animals. Who do you know who would be a good person to co-ordinate meetings with a few of the local villages?'

'Probably Fikiri. Before he went off to university and travelled around with that safari company, he was born and raised down the road in Kilenga. He came back here to be with his family.'

Barbara clapped her hands together, smiling. 'Yes, Fikiri would be ideal. He has such a great way about him as well. Everyone loves Fikiri!'

Hamisi poured them both another glass of lemonade and browsed through the report once more. He turned to a chapter about the local flora. 'We knew that trees would be a big part of the solution. Planting trees. Jo was just back from planting trees outside Nairobi with Wangari Maathai, you know, when she had taken on the powers-that-be over deforestation. Jo was like a crazy person after that, bursting with ideas. I remember thinking at the time how cynical I had felt when I first met Jo, how many times I had seen middle-class Westerners come here and try to change things. Religious zealots, gap-year students, corporations dodging taxes through apparent good deeds. But Jo was like a thing possessed. She was so angry about injustice and apathy. I was so in awe of her energy and she was so bossy, I did whatever she told me to!'

Barbara laughed in recognition. Hamisi continued. 'Do you remember the different funding ideas we had, the educational sponsorships and the environmental ones? They were really simple ideas, but so great, because they invited people to be part of something, even if they couldn't get here. And they didn't have to cost much for any one individual.'

'There's a word for that now, isn't there? In these modern times – crowd backing?' said Barbara.

'Crowdfunding.' Hamisi smiled.

'Yes, crowdfunding. It really wouldn't be hard to get that off the ground, particularly if we had some technical help.'

'Fikiri's the man for that too. He's a bit of a geek,' said Hamisi. 'I love it, Barbara. I do need to run it by Angel first, though. If you're talking about reducing income from paying guests, that will affect all of our jobs here. We still need to pay people.'

'Yes, there will be income. I'm just talking about getting things off the ground first. We have to honour the bookings we have taken and not do those visitors a disservice. They have signed up to what we have always offered. But in the long term we attract people to pay to come and volunteer here. They will pay a lot less, of course, so the provision will be a lot more basic. We can make savings on lots of things without affecting salaries – on the type of food we have here, on the distances we drive … on the alcohol for goodness sake!'

Hamisi pushed back in his chair and smiled across at her. He saw in Barbara's face a look that had vanished from it a decade ago – optimism.

CHAPTER 3

TAITA HILLS 2011

IT was too late to turn back now. Many times over the last few months Barbara had doubted the wisdom of her proposals; each day had brought problems: the bedding arrived with too many double sets and not enough single; the main water pump running from the generator broke down time and again, as it always had done, but now more demands were being put on it, it had to be replaced, at vast expense. Some wood for the roof frames went missing, but miraculously reappeared after Fikiri went to investigate in a couple of nearby villages.

But these were all minor setbacks. There was a sense of purpose which had not been felt in the camp for years. Women sang, men hammered, radios blasted out joyful, rhythmic music.

Barbara walked through camp with a tray of sweet chai and some biscuits. She chose a prime viewing spot, so that she could survey the new accommodation area, then set about making herself a makeshift table from a plank on top of a tree stump, and a stool from a box of supplies from the ironmongers in town. Fikiri, tall and broad-shouldered, had his back to her as he ticked off something on a clipboard.

Fikiri had worked for Barbara in the early days, before taking a job with a safari company. He was of indeterminable age, but had lines only where his face had set into its constant smile. His mouth was always slightly open, like he was about to tell you something, comment on what you had said, or philosophise about the world – something he did often, fancying himself as a bit of a poet.

'Fikiri, come and join me.' He nodded and squatted down beside her. She poured him a cup as he got comfortable. 'I just heard from the magazine. They were just confirming that the competition will be in next month's issue. The deadline for entrants is a month from now, so the volunteering project will definitely be in February. That gives us six more months to reorganise the camp. Tell me how things are progressing. It certainly looks like the buildings are growing fast.'

Fikiri had designed this new accommodation set half a mile from the main camp. Several men were putting the finishing touches to the makuti thatch on a large concrete rondavel.

'Well, as you can see,' said Fikiri pointing at the structure, 'we've put the kitchen and bathrooms into the main building and we've made a start on the bandas.' At this he indicated the foundations of what were to become the six smaller, round dormitory buildings. The bandas ran in a line, perched over a deep ravine. Guests currently stayed in sturdy canvas tents with solid roofs. These would remain, but be simpler in their décor. No more 'Out of Africa' touches like pith helmets hanging on the walls or brass telescopes and compasses artfully placed on writing bureaux. The new look would be modern, unfussy and functional.

Sleeping in these bandas would be done in basic camp beds, so it was a little less comfortable than the main camp tents, but Barbara knew that the bandas had a fantastic view of the conservancy. A long refectory table had already been set alongside the bandas, also looking down at the landscape below. She imagined how much fun it would be for young people to come out here and chat into the night, under the milky sky, putting the world to rights.

'Well, it looks wonderful so far. How do you think things are going, Fikiri?'

'Oh, Barbara, I sing in my heart! Can you hear the women singing?'

'I can. But they sing so often, I don't think I really hear it anymore!' Barbara laughed.

'Yes, they do sing all the time, but this singing does not just reach the ears, it reaches the heart.' Fikiri clutched his heart in a dramatic gesture, smiling broadly. 'We've had some difficult times around here – terrible – and the villagers have felt powerless to control their fate. They are always at the mercy of the weather or governments or large landowners. No offence, Barbara.'

'None taken.' Barbara smiled.

'We can't live the lives of our parents and grandparents here anymore. I myself went to the city and got work with a cousin.'

'But you came back. You wanted to come home?' asked Barbara.

'I did. I wanted to teach my children the ways of my childhood, before they lost all that knowledge living in the city. It's a beautiful place, and there is still a strong community in my village. I still have my aunt here and some of my brothers and sisters. I wanted my boys to know them properly.'

'I can understand that.'

'A good strong family is very important to children.' They fell silent for a few minutes and Barbara dwelt a little on this remark.

Fikiri continued. 'But the days of running little farms and selling your wares at the market – those days are gone. Children now have to get a good education to get jobs in the towns. The elders are very sad about this, they don't want to lose their children, but they know that education is essential. Whether the children leave to get jobs in the cities or stay to make life better here, they need to learn much more about the world. With employment here at the camp comes income, from that income we can improve schools. So, it's a good thing we are all doing here – very good.'

'Can we help more directly, do you think?'

He thought for a few moments, then nodded and pointed eastward. 'I tell you what. In Kilenga, we have built a school, but, so far, we have had to educate our children with little help or funding, and it hasn't been easy. The school is very basic and there is only one teacher in charge of about forty children, all of different ages. We built it so that the children would not have to walk miles to the nearest school, but it really isn't adequate, and certainly is not well enough stocked with paper, pens, books, you know

– all the ordinary things that make a school function. We need a longer-term solution. To maintain the school and give the children a good level of education so they can go off to high school and get a diploma.'

'Can we go to visit it this week? I'd like to take a look.'

'Of course, I'll go this afternoon and see what would be a suitable day. It would be good to meet with some of the women too, not just the elders. I know that it's the women who have done most of the work on the school.'

'You do surprise me!' laughed Barbara.

Later that week, Barbara accompanied Fikiri to Kilenga, which, at an hour's drive, was the nearest village to the camp.

'Fikiri! Welcome!' John – a slender young man in a checked shirt – greeted him with a firm handshake. Fikiri returned this with a hand on the man's shoulder.

'Good, to see you, John. This is Barbara, my boss. She is the owner of Bibi's Camp over that way.' Fikiri indicated west with typically exaggerated gesticulation. 'John is the schoolmaster here, Barbara.'

'And let me introduce Michael, Phyllis and Freda,' said John.

'Good morning,' said Barbara as she clutched the hand of one of the women. 'Of course, this lady, I know. Phyllis works at Bibi's Camp in the kitchens. You are famous for your baking, Phyllis!' Phyllis looked down at the ground, her face was slender, with wide eyes, quick and nervous, but her delight at the compliment was written in her quiet smile.

'Good, good. So, you know Phyllis. Michael has four children at the school, no less!' added John. 'Lastly, we have Freda. Freda is the powerhouse behind the school. What she doesn't know about fundraising from local businesses isn't worth knowing. Freda, Barbara.'

'Good to meet you.'

Freda took both of Barbara's hands in hers and squeezed them firmly. 'Likewise. We would love to show you around. But first we shall have tea and some of Phyllis's famous cakes.'

The group walked from the car to a large low building, dust billowing around their feet. This was the primary school. The children had finished their work for the day and were playing outside. A playing field had been created from a patch of bare earth, cleared of large stones and vegetation – the ground compacted by so many football matches, group songs and school plays over the years that it was as solid as concrete. The children played with old crates and bottles, a metal hoop, a set of skittles made from tin cans and a cricket ball. A piece of canvas tossed over the long horizontal branches of a yellow fever tree served as a playhouse and several of the smallest children were play-acting at being shopkeepers. Barbara smiled and joked with some of the children who skittered past them as the group weaved towards the building.

'Please sit,' said Freda. John gathered up a few of the thin metal class chairs and put them around his desk, then bundled up several piles of papers.

'Oh, John. I hope we aren't messing up your things,' said Barbara.

'It's nothing, please,' said John. 'I have a system, it's all fine!'

The room was stifling and dark, but the joyful sound of the children playing outside the window cut through the gloom. Phyllis nodded to two other women, who came through with trays of doughnuts, fruitcake and a pot of hot sweet tea. Thanks and pleasantries exchanged, Fikiri directed the conversation to the matter of the school.

'Okay, so I have brought my good friend Barbara here. We've been working on some new ideas at her camp and we thought we might combine efforts. We were hoping you could talk about your wonderful school and discuss what we might do as a partnership to make improvements, or help the children in some way. Freda?'

'Yes, thank you for coming, both of you,' said Freda. 'It's lovely to meet you, Barbara. I am sure it is a very busy time at the camp.' Barbara and Phyllis smiled and nodded to each other.

Freda tilted her head towards the window. 'So, you can see we have a lot of children here learning at the primary school: thirty-eight at present, ranging from five-year-old Cherish to thirteen-year-old Jonathan. Jonathan should really be away at secondary school in Kasigau – he is very clever – but his father is sick, so he is still here, helping to run his shamba. He also helps John with the younger children.'

'That is a pity for Jonathan. Do you think he might get to go away to school at some point?' asked Barbara.

'Perhaps, but without his help on the farm, his parents can't afford to send him. A 'catch 22' unfortunately,' replied Freda.

'Indeed. Sorry, please carry on, Freda.'

'Well, like I said, we have thirty-eight children, but only one teacher, one classroom, one cook – that's all. We also have very few schoolbooks, so the children have to share. They have a rota for their homework, passing the books around, so every piece of work takes a long time. Also, this room has no floor, just mud, which gets very difficult in the rains; and no doors, which means we get a lot of unwelcome visits from unattended goats!' Freda gave a bubbly, girlish laugh, but quickly returned to her point. 'We need these things, Barbara. We need a floor, doors and schoolbooks. We have done our best so far, but we started building this school eight years ago, before even Jonathan first came, and we still need to do so much. But we have to work on our farms and in the markets, and some of us work away and our parents take care of the children. There is simply not the time to put any more effort into this building. We would really appreciate some help. Do you have any suggestions?'

'Well, first of all, I congratulate you on what you have achieved.'

'I won't tell you how I acquired those schoolbooks, I might be arrested!' Freda's bubbly laugh again.

'Your secret is safe with me!' Barbara replied. 'It looks like you need some manual help in the short term and some longer-term fundraising help, am I right?'

'Yes, yes. I have exhausted all my contacts for now, so when Fikiri said you were happy to help, we were very pleased.'

'Well, I think I have a perfect solution.' Barbara sketched out her hopes for the camp and the possibility of tying in the work with local projects. 'You see, this was how we started our business. I came here with my son, just to do secretarial work for the previous owner. I've now been running the camp for forty years, many of those with Fikiri's help. We have become a tourist camp, which has done very well, but my Head of Conservation and I have taken stock and we realise that the camp is not doing the most it could for the area in terms of conservation and the local economy.

'We've decided to change direction and return to being a research camp, so we will have facilities for scientists and researchers to carry out monitoring and reporting. We will also be inviting people in for volunteering holidays. These are very popular these days. People actually pay to come and work!' This raised a laugh with the group.

'Of course, they aren't really – they're paying to have an amazing experience. Something they cannot possibly get back home. Because we're lucky to live in this wonderful country. And we can share that with people who want to give something back.'

Michael, who had been quiet up to now, raised his hand tentatively.

'Michael, you want to say something?' asked Fikiri.

Michael began nervously. 'I'm sorry, I do not want to appear rude, but do we really need help from more Westerners? We have always seemed to have been a sort of exhibit to visiting tourists. I know that we have done well from this sometimes, selling trinkets and clothing at our stalls, but it can be a little... well... patronising. I don't mean you are patronising, Barbara, please forgive me, I just mean that Africa has had decades of people coming over and volunteering and having their photographs taken with our smiling children, and they are very pleased with themselves. But we need real help from people who hold knowledge or resources we don't have.'

Fikiri looked uncharacteristically troubled at this remark, but Barbara smiled. 'Michael, I do know what you mean, and I'm not in the least offended. You are quite right. You have a wonderful teacher in John, you don't need the place running over with gap-year students, attempting to teach the children, then leaving and passing on to another one *ad infinitum*. What we suggest is this: that we begin a volunteer programme initially to get our camp and your school up and running properly. This will require brute force and simple administration, mainly, so we do not need any specific skill set. We're running a competition to attract those people and to begin promoting the idea more widely. I think we could do something about your school building and get you some books and jotters, perhaps get the help of a local supplier – a marketing campaign, so that they have an agreement with you to continue to contribute those things over a longer period. There always has to be a bit of "you scratch my back, I'll scratch yours" in these matters.'

'Okay,' Michael nodded.

'In the longer term, we want to do some actual useful research at the camp, something that will help to make a difference to the environment around us and the wildlife here, whilst also working with you to protect your livelihoods, your farms, your jobs, opening out to other villages and farms in the area. Now, that will mean exchanges of ideas. We want to bring in scientists, marketing specialists, researchers. This will not be a half-hearted thing, a side-line to make the camp look good. We want to actually *do* good. That will mean we need your help too. We need jobs doing at the camp, as we still need to feed people, and do the usual maintenance jobs. We will also need mechanics, cooks, drivers, computer operators, beekeepers, animal specialists. These people need to be permanent, so need to be local. We can help with training programmes, sponsorships, it could be wonderful for all of us.'

This was the first time Barbara had really articulated her ideas and she was getting more and more excited herself, almost breathless with each idea as it occurred to her. She hadn't actually discussed this many details with Hamisi or Fikiri, but they were good men who liked a challenge. The details would just work themselves out, she was certain. She felt a physical sensation, a quickening of her heart, and her brain was fizzing with ideas. This was it – 'a fire in the belly'.

PART 2

CHAPTER 4

NAIROBI, KENYA 1963

THE room was filled with swirls of colour, as Barbara and Sheila tossed skirts, tops and dresses out of their wardrobes. Then they turned to the patchwork of items strewn across the bed and laughed.

'Not exactly Biba!' said Sheila as she grabbed a pink and orange swing dress from the pile. The pattern was quaint, rather than cutting edge, the capacious dress had been expensive, bought for boarding school dances, but its stiff fabric was fit only for damp, cold climates. She made a face as she held it up in front of her and considered her reflection in the long mirror.

'I'm sure we can sort something out from this lot.' Barbara was more sanguine and positive by nature. 'Now, pass me that tulle skirt and that yellow day dress.' The Kings Road had yet to reach the Delamere Avenue, and the sisters, like their contemporaries (and their mothers) had dresses in almost the identical shape, just slight variations in prints – ranging from small pink rosebuds to large yellow paisley swirls. 'Right. There is so much fabric here,' Barbara flung the dress flat out onto the bed. 'We just need to trim the bulk out of some of these and add plain sections to the sleeves and waists. Look, pass me the scissors.'

Sheila watched with her fists balled up against her cheeks. 'God, what will Ma say?'

'She hasn't been in our rooms for years; she won't even notice. Look, I cut the sleeves like this, so they are straight up on the shoulder, then we sew in some of that tulle, gathered into a sleeve.'

'But the tulle is purple!' exclaimed Sheila.

'Contrasting colours are just the thing! Alright, now we undo the seams on either side of the dress, and resew them in tighter, and take six inches off the length.' Barbara ran the scissors around the dress with a flourish. 'Voilà – an instant shift dress, straight off Carnaby Street! We can even use the off-cuts for hairbands and scarves. We just need to be a bit cut-throat and use a bit of imagination!'

'We could dye stuff, too,' suggested Sheila. Barbara's exuberance was infectious.

'Of course, I think there's a packet of green Dylon in the bathroom that was the wrong shade for bush wear!' laughed Barbara, affecting a Brigitte Bardot pout in the mirror as she smoothed a skirt over her hips. 'See, it's going to be fine. Just think, you and me in the city, by day, learning how to be independent working women – by night, party!'

'Oh Barbara,' said Sheila, diving onto the pile of clothes. 'I don't know what trick you pulled to persuade Ma and Papa that we should live together in Nairobi, but I will be forever grateful. I don't know how much longer I could have stood Aunt Hilary's preaching over the breakfast table. And she was always trying to set me up with some pink-faced bore at those church am-dram horrors.'

'You're welcome! I just got them to see sense – that there wasn't room at Hilary's for me too, but that I needed to be with you so that I didn't fall in with the wrong company! The YWCA is very 'proper' with their curfews and their 'no-men-in-the-room' policies.'

'Quite right too!' Sheila laughed. 'Never mind that the YWCA is also close to some of the best nightclubs.'

'They don't need to know that. It's close to work for both of us.'

'Oh my goodness, did I tell you it took me two hours to get to work on Friday? The bus from Aunt Hilary's was always bad enough, but this time there was a huge jam because a fight had broken out, right in the middle of Government Road! Apparently a cow had got lost – I don't know… fallen out of someone's truck or something – then, when they found it, it had given birth in a pothole. Then there was some heated dispute about ownership of the cow, which everyone seemed to get involved in, even the commuters on my bus. We sat waiting for absolutely ages for the police to break it all up, by which time, all the cars and buses had overheated and were all bumping into each other. When I finally got to work, I needed to sit down for half an hour with an aspirin and a flannel on my head.'

'And you don't know how much I was bursting to get out of there,' said Barbara. 'A whole year, Sheila, an entire year of them without you to smooth things over and only me to focus all their disappointment on. Well, I say a year, but I think they have purposely spent as little time in Karen as possible. They claim that all the 'best' people have left the suburbs, which is why they've been upcountry with the Simpsons since January and they stretched that trip to England last May out to a full four months. They'll be glad to get the house to themselves.'

'You're forgetting our brother. He's still there,' said Sheila.

'Oh, golden-boy Nigel doesn't count. They don't even notice him. And he's always at the office, buttering the directors up, ready for when he inherits the kingdom. No, it's me they can't stand to be around. Even three years at English boarding school with that Alistair Sim lookalike headmistress didn't seem to produce a sufficiently acceptable daughter. The first thing I did when I got back here was strip down to a kikoy and run down to the lake for a swim!'

'What about "deportment, enunciation and manners", Barbara?' teased Sheila. 'Wasn't that the headmistress's motto?'

'Well, that's all very well if you want to impress the High Commissioner's wife at the ball, but not for cocktail hour at the Sombrero. You know they didn't pay all that money for our education to make us clever, don't you? Just more marriageable. Well, more fool them missing out on our potential. Anyway, they're going to get a huge shock when they find out that Nigel can't even add up, let alone run a multi-million-pound hotel chain.'

'Harsh, but yes, I think Nigel would be better employed as a... well... I can't think of what exactly,' said Sheila.

'Precisely. Whereas you and I are going to be sophisticated and respected working women.'

'With allowances.'

'Well, yes, but I won't need mine for long. I am going to make my mark, Sheila. They think that this is just yet another instalment of the great husband-search, but I have bigger plans than that.'

'So you don't want to meet men.'

'I didn't say that. I love men!' Barbara punctuated her statement with a pout of her lips, smiling at Sheila's expression of mock-horror. 'I just mean that I am here to do something important, something new. The world is changing Sheila, it's exciting. Don't *you* feel excited?'

'I do, yes, but I also would like to meet someone nice. That just hasn't been possible under Aunt Hilary's regime. Not unless they come with their own parish.'

'Or possible in these clothes,' said Barbara surveying the room. 'What on Earth would we look like amongst all the smart cool city women?'

Barbara and her sister ached for the new fashions and freedoms that seemed to be quite normal in the West and were beginning to trickle into East Africa. For the sisters, life in the city seemed worlds away from their stuffy, privileged home life. Nairobi was thriving – the 'Garden City' – full of young people and anticipation, change and contrasts. Nairobi had seen unspeakable horrors and glimmers of hope as national rebellion was beginning to settle into national Independence or 'Uhuru'. The words of the charismatic leader of the new movement, Jomo Kenyatta, echoed through the city's offices and markets, clubs and stores. He called for 'Harambee' – a pulling together. Barbara in particular, breathed this all in and felt exhilarated. Contrary to her parents' objectives, her head wasn't simply full of typing speeds, schedule planning and social politesse. There was change in the air and she found it thrilling.

Tonight, the sisters had been invited to the birthday party of Barbara's work colleague Peggy. They shared a superficial, rather than close friendship, but Barbara liked Peggy a lot. She was a tiny, elfin woman, but held any room in thrall to her pronouncements, and was a master at introducing people to new friends. They always had fun at any party at which Peggy held court.

'Leave your coats in the spare bedroom back there,' shouted Peggy as she backed away from the door, inviting them into the smoky hallway. Party guests lined every wall, squeezed into every corridor. Whispering trysts were held in dark corners. The Rolling Stones' 'Come On' bounced around the flat, the lyrics melting into the thrum of chatter and laughter. Barbara removed her coat and smoothed down her dress. She had been so pleased with it yesterday; she had taken a plain black crepe dress, shortened it to high above the knee and sewn in large triangles of yellow fabric, making the skirt swish out. Then she had added an oversized bow in the same spotty fabric to the neck and finished off the outfit with a black, baker-boy hat. It had felt so fun and modern, but now, looking around her at the women she felt overdressed, ridiculous. Everyone here seemed so effortlessly chic – Audrey Hepburn-esque in their simple black shift dresses and long cigarette-holders. Barbara tried to tune into the voices and scanned the room for familiar faces, but Peggy already held her elbow and was guiding her towards a small group of men and women she only vaguely recognised.

'Darlings, these are the gorgeous Dunbar-Watts sisters. They could be sipping gin slings in a dhow, floating around the Indian Ocean, but instead they are here, chez Peggy, happy to chug down cheap wine and listen to you lot. I shall leave them in your capable hands while I go and check the salmon mousse.'

A large man took a step towards the sisters, a half-step too close. His face was flecked with broken veins and he had the beginnings of flabby jowls – already a committed drinker's face, thought Barbara, recognising the signs. 'Hi, I'm Tim,' he boomed, holding out his left hand to Sheila, not relinquishing the red wine in his right. 'That's Toby. We work together at a shipping company. This is my girlfriend, Linda. Toby is unattached and very acquiescent, so if either of you lovely ladies is short of a date, he'd happily oblige.'

Toby looked embarrassed, but smiled and offered to fetch the girls a drink. Barbara stepped away from Tim, turning instead to Linda, who she realised worked on another floor of her own office, and she occasionally saw her in the office canteen. 'I love your outfit!' Linda shouted in Barbara's ear. 'You look like Pattie Boyd.' Sheila was left to make conversation with Toby, who, having returned with a glass of champagne each for the sisters, was attempting to ask her questions about her views on Independence.

The clamour of the party forced the group to talk to only one person at a time, taking turns to shout in their companion's ear. After a few minutes, Barbara looked over to Sheila, eyebrows raised, but Sheila signalled back that she and Toby were heading out to chat in the courtyard, away from the noise. Barbara and Linda gave up on conversation and mutually decided to join a small group of women who had kicked off their shoes and were dancing in a tight circle. Tim was left, clutching his girlfriend's drink and looking desperately around the room for someone to impress.

When the sisters met up again it was in the kitchen, a few hours later, hot and in need of a cold drink, Barbara because she had not stopped dancing, Sheila, because she had not stopped talking.

'You seem to be having fun!' goaded Barbara.

'I am, actually. He is really nice. Most of the men here seem just like that awful, smug Tim, but Toby is really interesting. He works for his father's firm.'

'Urgh,' groaned Barbara.

'Yes, okay, but he isn't going to do that forever. He promised his parents he would work there for a few years before they sell the business on and his father retires. His family have land down south he wants to use as a tourist resort. He has all these ideas about taking tourists out on photographic safaris.'

'That does sound interesting actually,' conceded Barbara. 'Do you want to leave yet or stay a bit longer. Personally, I need to put my aching feet up. Also, I didn't do such a great job on this side seam, look.' She twisted to show a gaping hole in her dress.

'Very Mary Quant, I must say,' laughed Sheila. 'Just let me tell Toby we're off. I'm sure he will see us home.'

Toby had parked his car not far from the flat, so, saying their goodbyes and thanking Peggy, the three headed outside. The air was cool and damp, a lingering smell of rubber and cement in the air from the city's factories. The car journey was short and quiet as they adjusted to the contrast from the noisy party. Toby was first to speak. 'Are you two going to the Independence Ball?'

'I think our parents got an invitation, but they are torn about going. On the one hand, lots of their cronies will be there and it's the sort of event that's good for business,' said Barbara, a note of sarcasm in her voice. 'On the other, the prospect of Uhuru terrifies them, and they are rather in denial about it all. Are you going?'

'Yes, I am. I'm all for it, actually. Independence I mean, Harambee and all that. I think the days of imperialism and the interference of Western countries in Africa are done and dusted.'

'Perhaps a little hypocritical considering your family has presumably done very well out of Africa,' Barbara teased, though only half joking.

'I know, that sounded so pompous and, yes, we have done very well. Your family has too, I think. We can't undo that, but we can be part of the future. It's like a chance to show what a modern country can do if everyone pushes forward.'

'You're right,' said Barbara. 'It's partly why Sheila and I are here, in the city. I wouldn't want to be anywhere else right now. Especially not being holed up in Lamu with Mama and Papa!'

Toby stopped the car outside the hostel and ran round to the side of the car to help the sisters out, Barbara first from the back seat, then he opened the front passenger door and held his hand out to Sheila. Barbara noticed that something about the way he did this made Sheila smile coyly.

'Well, I look forward to seeing you at the ball, even if your parents bow out. Perhaps we could meet up before that, though?' This question was directed squarely at Sheila, who had stayed silent throughout the ride home.

'You know where to find me,' she said quietly as she slipped her hand from his and walked to the door of the hostel.

'She's just trying to act aloof and enigmatic,' said Barbara with a wink. 'Give me your card and I'll make sure she calls you.' She followed Sheila's scowl into the hostel, shoes dangling from her fingers.

CHAPTER 5

NAIROBI 1963

'CAN I borrow your blue dress, Sheila?' Barbara called through from the bathroom when she heard the dorm room door shut.

'And "*Hello,* and *how was your day*?" to you too!' Sheila answered as she threw down her bags and plonked down on her bed. She removed her shoes and rubbed at her heels. 'Oh, my poor feet. I got us some fabric and hair grips from Ahmed's.'

Barbara emerged from the bathroom. 'Great, thanks. I was down to three Kirby grips! Sorry, I'm just panicking a bit about what to wear tonight. It's the end of the students' exams this week, so there's going to be a big night at the Bonanza. We're meeting up with Helen and Deborah there at seven o'clock.'

'Oh, you go. I just haven't got the energy. Borrow the blue dress and the bag that goes with it. I'm going to stay in, soak my feet and read a nice book.'

'Don't be like that, Sheila. Look, after tonight the students will all be gone for the summer. Then it's back to bumping into slimeballs from the accounts office or fighting off bloody Maurice and his entourage of sycophants.'

Sheila growled. 'I was so looking forward to a night on my own.'

'That's my girl! Come on. Have a shower, then I'll do your hair like Sylvie Vartan.'

'My hair's twice as long as Sylvie Vartan's.'

'Well, your eyes then. And I can still backcomb your hair and flick it, so it looks like hers.'

'Okay, okay, you got me. Just let me get freshened up. And you owe me one!' Sheila headed for the shower.

* * *

Barbara and Sheila pushed through the swing doors, the piercing sound of a trumpet heralding their arrival; the performer was no Hugh Masekela, but he was giving it his best shot. Club Bonanza was a world away from their parents' fussy, sophisticated dinner parties, and they revelled in its chaotic exuberance and energy. Here young Whites, Blacks and Asians talked and danced together. The house band promised an evening of music from the Beatles, Chuck Berry, Gerry and the Pacemakers and Cliff Richard. Posters on the wall celebrated London's Soho, Andy Warhol, art house movies and ironically displayed kitsch advertising campaigns.

Tonight, as most nights, the club was heaving with heat and colour and chatter. There was a distinct end-of-term buzz in the air, most of the students having gone straight to the club after their final exams. The students' relief at finishing their studies was palpable – the atmosphere reckless and silly. At the far end of the room the house band was playing 'House of the Rising Sun'. In one of the booths, a group of young women had built a precarious tower of champagne glasses and a man in a silver suit was bent, limbo-like, at the foot of the table, drinking the wine as it cascaded out of the glasses. A rather overweight Indian man, wielding a chicken drumstick, was chasing his female friend around the dancefloor. The girls spotted their friends in a booth, giggling over cocktail glasses.

'Hey, Sheila, over here!' One of the girls stood and waved them over, dozens of silver bangles jangling on her wrist. Helen worked with Sheila in the typing pool of an engineering firm. The girls squeezed past clubbers dancing wildly on the checkerboard floor.

'Hello, ladies!' laughed Helen. 'We were just talking about you! I was telling Deborah about that awful Mrs Sneddon from the purchasing department.' Deborah looked up past the friends, distracted by something. 'Hey, everyone.' She said in a low voice.

'Look at this bunch, just beside the stage. Don't they look pleased with themselves?'

A group of male students was walking towards them. Identifiable from their long-sleeved shirts and heavy twill trousers, they carried the air of those with assured futures – serious and confident. One of them, a tall Indian man with long, glossy hair was looking straight at their group, grinning and holding out his arms, swaying comically to the music. The band were playing a Ronettes song and the young man was mouthing the words.

He held out his hand to Deborah and dragged her to the dance floor. Behind him, his blond friend nodded at Sheila and she grinned back and got out of the booth to dance. There were two men remaining and Helen and Barbara sat awkwardly, waiting to see what happened next. When the pause became uncomfortable, Helen stood up and faced a stocky young Italian. 'Oh, for goodness sakes. You, come with me. Let's dance.'

'I suppose you're stuck with me.' The last man was quiet and well spoken. He was Black, with tight short curls and Buddy Holly glasses.

'That's a bit of an assumption,' said Barbara, stiffly. 'I'm quite happy on my own, actually, just watching.'

'Oh, s-sorry.' The man looked genuinely upset. 'That was very rude of me. Please, I didn't mean...'

Barbara laughed. 'I'm sorry, I was only teasing you. Would you like to dance?'

'Erm, yes. If you'd like to. I'm not great at it. I don't dance very often. My name is Clive, by the way.'

'Well, Clive, just follow what I do, and you'll be fine. I *am* great at it!'

Clive wasn't lying when he said he couldn't dance, but he persevered and before long, the two of them were gyrating and twisting and doing the Watusi with the rest of the dance floor. Clive was at least a foot taller than Barbara and his limbs seemed to have no connection to each other. Every time he turned in a circle, he seemed to kick out the wrong leg or flail an arm out towards her. She had to keep ducking to avoid being slapped. His face showed deep concentration, but it was hopeless.

Clive bent down to talk into Barbara's ear. 'Can I buy you a drink?'

'Yes, please!' Relieved he was giving up, and desperately thirsty, Barbara replied, 'A Gimlet, please. I'll go and sit down.'

Clive returned to the booth with Barbara's cocktail and a Tusker beer for himself. 'I think the other dancers need a break from me!' he laughed. 'You don't mind?'

'Not at all. Gives me a chance to catch my breath. Are you studying at the university?'

'Yes, until today – law, but I want to get into journalism. I have a job lined up with a small local newspaper, but I hope to get a job at the *Daily Nation*, or the *Star* eventually. What about you, are you studying or working?'

'I'm a secretary at the Ministry of Agriculture,' replied Barbara, but I've just been offered a job within the Game Department.'

'Does it look like a good job? Will you take it?'

'I don't know. I think so. It's actually a bit less money, but it's a new department and there might be more chance of promotion. The job is mainly writing up reports for the department to take to central government.'

'What sort of reports?' Clive was looking straight at her, genuinely interested.

'It's data gathering, really. Well, at the moment, there is a lot of talk of there being too many elephants in some of the National Parks. The government needs to establish what the numbers really are and what they might grow to, as they need to decide whether they have to cull them. Although, personally, I think that's just wrong. That's why I'm struggling a little with deciding about the job. If I am part of the team producing the data which is used to argue that elephants should be killed in large numbers, what does that make me?'

'Yes, I see. But it wouldn't be your data, you would just be compiling it.'

'I know, but I'd feel complicit.'

'You talk as though a cull is inevitable. Is it?'

'From what they have told me so far, I think so.'

'Well, it's your decision and I'm sure you'll give it a lot of thought. Let me say just one thing, though. If you feel strongly about the ideas that the government has about elephant culling, what good can you do from your job in the Ministry of Agriculture?'

'None whatsoever.'

'Well, perhaps you'll find a way of influencing things if you're there, working with these people.'

'I'm just a secretary.'

'That's your job title, but it's the way you do your job that matters, the way you conduct yourself. Do you think it's been easy to get to university and get a job with my background?'

'No, of course not, I'm sorry. I'm don't mean to be glib.'

'I'm not trying to get your sympathy; I just use myself as an example. I've had to overcome people's first impressions of me, as I'm sure you have. Now, my first impression of you, in this club with your friends, is of a fun, happy city girl. But I've talked to you for a few minutes and what I already know is that you are a serious, intelligent, principled person, who wants to get on in her career, but who has her own ideas. Yes?'

'Flattering, but keep going!'

'Well, perhaps you and I can't control the world we live in, the prejudices, the assumptions. But we can control our responses to them. And eventually, people see past their assumptions, they really do. I think you should go for it and do it your own way, make yourself visible and your viewpoint important to them, just for what it's worth.'

'Wow. Well, I wasn't expecting quite such a philosophical discussion on a Friday night at the Bonanza!' Barbara sipped at her Gimlet, discretely taking in more of Clive's features. He had high cheekbones and deep brown eyes. His fingernails were short and ragged – a general nervous habit or nibbled while studying for his exams? His clothes were inexpensive, but immaculately clean and pressed. His glasses had been mended at the hinges, clearly a homemade repair but done carefully.

It had been such a short conversation, but for Barbara, it was heavy with significance and she would run through Clive's words over and over in her mind. The world had slipped a little on its axis, giving her a totally new perspective. There would be a before and after to this moment that would be forever delineated in her mind. Before and after Clive. The way she lived before and after Clive. The way she viewed the world before and after Clive.

Clive looked straight at her and she shook her head a little, jolting herself back to reality, embarrassed, just realising that the music had stopped. The band leader announced they were taking a rest break and the rest of Barbara's group came back, joined by their new male friends. The girls shimmied into the booth, fanning themselves, pink-cheeked and laughing.

'What are you two whispering about?' asked Sheila, noticing the flush in Barbara's cheeks.

Barbara sipped her drink pensively, oblivious to Sheila's question. Sheila nudged her for an answer, eyebrows raised in curiosity.

'I was just telling Clive about the job offer. He thinks I should take it.'

'I've been telling you that, but you never listen to me.'

'That's not true!' Barbara was almost grateful for a little filial ribbing to deflect from her blushes. 'Anyway, his reasons just made more sense than yours.'

'Charming, I must say!'

The party continued to dance and drink and laugh for the rest of the evening. As the lights came back on and the noise changed to the clatter of plates being gathered up and the musicians packing away their instruments, Clive accompanied Barbara to the cloakroom.

'Will I see you again?' he asked, coughing the high-pitched tremble out of his voice.

'Just call the Game Department – I'll be there!'

'I'd really like to continue our chat. How about a coffee in your lunch break next week? I start at the *Herald* on Wednesday and the offices are only a couple of streets down from Moi Avenue.'

'I'd like that. How about the New Stanley on Friday?'

Barbara and Sheila said their goodbyes and made their way back to their hostel.

'You're quiet,' said Sheila. 'What's going on. You're never quiet!'

'I just had a nice evening, that's all. And now I'm tired and need my bed.' Barbara was twitchy. Her sister knew her too well, perhaps better than she knew herself, and the evening chatting to Clive had unnerved her.

There was no need to speak further. Sheila put her arm around Barbara's shoulder and gave her a squeeze.

'You've met your match, I think.' She said quietly.

Barbara just smiled.

CHAPTER 6

NAIROBI 1963

GRATEFUL that he had decided to sit out on the hotel veranda instead of the packed restaurant, Clive couldn't stop his knee from juddering and knocking the table. He kept moving his leg, but it was as though his body was betraying him, making his nerves as obvious as possible. His forehead glistened and his throat was dry. She was only three minutes late, but he was convinced that she wasn't coming.

He read and reread the menu, just to force himself to look down, instead of scanning the streets for any sign of Barbara. Finally, he caught a glimpse of her, making her way past a flower stall on the other side of the street. Her blonde hair was artfully pinned back with a large blue clip; she wore a smart wool *eau de nil* two-piece suit and a matching scarf. He felt even more awkward and gauche in his cheap nylon shirt and a rather dull mud-brown tie. She walked with such confidence, he noticed, chatting to stallholders and smiling at passers-by. He spotted a waiter who was also watching her, almost dropping the teapot he was placing on a table. What had he been thinking asking her to meet up with him? He started to lift himself out of his seat ready for escape. He should just leave and pretend he had forgotten.

No, too late. By standing up he looked as though he was trying to be noticed. She waved, and he affected a small wave back. As she neared the veranda, he observed several men lift slightly out of their seats and nod to her; Clive remained standing as she approached.

'Hello. Glad you could make it. W—would you like a drink?' Clive stuttered.

She was helped into her seat by a waiter in a long white jacket and red fez who had been noticeably absent until that moment. 'A coke, please, Clive. Are you eating? I'm starving. I would love a sandwich or something. Sorry, my mouth is running away with me. I had to run most of the way. I got stuck finishing off a report my boss needs this afternoon.'

'It's fine – it's so good to see you. Please, here's the menu.' He fumbled for the menu, thrusting it at her. 'A coke, please,' he asked the waiter, who had remained hovering beside Barbara.

'Yes, madam.' The waiter directed his answer to Barbara.

'Water for me, please,' said Clive. The waiter made a low sound but did not look at Clive. Was he imagining it: the waiter seemed very sullen, almost disapproving?

'I'm ready to order food too, thank you. I'll have a chicken sandwich, please. And a side salad,' said Barbara.

'A ham sandwich and potato salad for me, please.' There was a slight delay before the waiter acknowledged the order.

'So, you listened to me babble on about my job when we met at the club,' said Barbara.

'You hardly babbled. You had an important decision to make. Did you make it?'

'I did. I took the job. Thank you so much for the advice,' Barbara said, straightening her skirt and settling into her chair. 'But I'll tell you all about that later. Now, I want to hear about you. Tell me about yourself, please! Spare no details.' She flicked her napkin and spread it on her lap.

'Well, there's not much to tell. Like I said at the club, I've just graduated from University College in Law.'

'But you aren't going to be a lawyer, isn't that right? You said you are going to be a journalist.' She nodded thanks to the waiter as he placed the coke in front of her. He put Clive's water down a little heavier.

'Yes, but I couldn't study journalism here in Nairobi, so I thought I would learn about the legal profession, about how the law works in this country. Of course, it's always changing. Kenya hasn't yet found her feet under the new administration. But I'm interested in what's going on – who the movers and shakers are, what rights we have as citizens. What the new political freedoms and machinations will mean for all of us in this modern age.' Clive stopped himself. 'I'm sorry – that sounded rather pompous.'

'It didn't at all. You just sound passionate. Are you optimistic?' she asked.

'I am, yes. I think we've come a long way already. Kenya has moved very fast to become a world player in some of its industries, like tourism and some imported crops. It's obviously been very hard won, but I think we can move on and become a wonderful example of modern Africa.'

Their food arrived and they began to eat silently. Clive could hear the low whispers from a neighbouring table as a group of middle-aged ladies glanced furtively at the two of them. Barbara seemed oblivious to them.

'So, what's your own story, Clive. Are you from the city?'

'No, not at all. I was born in a small village near Naivasha. My father had had a small farm on the edge of the lake.'

'I bet that was beautiful. What did he farm?'

'Oh just beans and sorghum; maize sometimes. And we had goats and a few cattle. Just enough for the family, really, and a little bit over to trade at the market.'

'Are your family still there?'

'Not there, no.' Clive shuffled in his seat. 'We lost the farm.'

'I'm sorry,' said Barbara. 'That's awful.'

He had made her uncomfortable, which was the last thing he wanted to do. 'It's okay now and my family do still live in the area. There were eight of us and I am the only one to come to the city.'

'And do you go back there at all? Or do they visit you?'

'One of my brothers came to stay with me once. And my youngest brother hopes to go to the university. But they like it back home. None of them wanted to move out to the city like me. I love to visit them, but I'll never go back to live there.'

'I've been to Naivasha before. My parents have friends there with a house on the lake, but it was a long time ago and we never stepped off their property, so I don't really know the country there.'

'I could show you it if you like. We could take a boat out.' Clive blurted out the invitation, then immediately regretted it.

'I'd love that. How about next month?' Barbara laughed and Clive realised he must have looked horrified. 'Or not, sorry. I'm being impetuous. My sister is always telling me off for it. I don't like to wait around. You're shocked, I'm sorry.'

'Not at all. Next month is a good time to go. The dry season brings a lot of animals and birds to the lake.'

'How wonderful. My parents own a hotel right on the lake. I've never stayed there and, to be honest, I'd rather avoid that and word getting back to them.' A short silence followed, then she continued hurriedly. 'Oh, gosh, that sounded wrong. I just mean I like to be left alone, to do my own thing without them knowing my business. And I don't ever stay in their hotels if I can help it. I'm trying to be independent, you see.'

'I do see. So your parents own hotels. Have your people been in Kenya long?'

'Well, no, only a few generations. My grandfather Ernest arrived in Africa in the 1890s. Earnest he was not, though! He was a thoroughly disgraced third son of an earl, whose gambling debts threatened to ruin his family's fragile reputation. So when they were selling off Africa cheap, he invested the last of his allowance into a parcel of land and controlling shares in a railway company.' Barbara stopped to eat her sandwich. Which, Clive noticed, she did with a sort of brisk delicacy. 'Unlike several of his compatriots, who threw everything into the infamous Lunatic Express, his modest investment steadily grew. He ended up with enough profit to risk investing in large-scale property. So, he went into the hotel business and built some of the swankiest hotels in Nairobi.'

'Well, he was enterprising, I suppose,' laughed Clive. 'Being a gambler paid off in the end!'

'Indeed, it did, though I think timing was everything. People came to make a new life and build the colony up and they needed places to stay. And he benefited from financial handouts from the British government. Anyway, his sons took over the business when his insalubrious past inevitably caught up with him and his liver, and the family continued to increase their fortunes as the Empire's hold increased.'

Clive realised that he no longer felt nervous and that he was enjoying just listening to Barbara speak. She was clearly at home in these surroundings; if he was to continue to make his way forward in this world, he needed to be just as relaxed.

'So, does your family still run the business day to day?'

'Yes, well they own it, whether they run anything is a matter of opinion. They have very little to do except entertain or be entertained. They are nominally in charge, but they don't really have to do what might be considered "work". They give parties.'

'Ah.'

'They do have something of a reputation for their parties. They make a point of buttering up any visiting dignitaries. Before the move to Independence, their dinner parties were legendary, some might even say, notorious. There were still people in their circles, both residents and visitors, who hankered after a piece of the old "White Mischief" glamour of Kenya. My mother always managed to ensure that just the right amount of scandal infused her parties, alongside the cocktails and floor shows.'

'I am intrigued!'

'Don't be, they were revolting. I hated those parties. When I was little, my mother would dress me and my sister up in lacy frocks and get us to hand out canapés. Women would profess to my mother that we were adorable, but as soon as her back was turned, they would sneer at us. These people were supposed to be paragons of good breeding, but I have never met people more uncouth and ridiculous. I couldn't wait to leave and live my own life. I was determined I was never going to be like my parents and become one of those buffoons.'

'And how about now? Do you think Independence will affect them?'

'No, they're untouchable. There were White people killed in the struggle, of course, but my parents have a protective shield of money, that's the bottom line. Their privilege protects them.'

'So, what did you do to get out?' asked Clive.

'Well, I went to Kenya High School for Girls, as my sister had done. She's about a year older than me. She was there at the Bonanza, you remember?'

'Yes, indeed, she seemed lovely.'

'She is, and very well behaved. I was less so, so they sent me off to boarding school in England for the last few years of school, but I kept skiving. Well, absconding, actually!'

'Very naughty.'

'It was naughty; very childish. How very spoiled I was. You must think I'm awful, wasting my education like that.'

'We're both products of our upbringing. You were hardly going to say to yourself "I must value everything that is being taught to me because so many people aren't so privileged." It's just not realistic to expect children to think that way. All you can do is weigh up how you feel now and act accordingly. You have to pay attention *now*. Learn from what you hear and do your best to do the right thing.'

'You're right. But I suppose it was my own little rebellion. I hated the life I was born into. I realise now how lucky I've been, but I couldn't have stayed in that environment and lived off the fortune my family had made by exploiting other people. I was supposed to receive a good education, meet and marry the right sort of man and continue in the family business. And, basically, do what I was told.'

'But you don't like to do what you are told.'

'Not if I fundamentally disagree with it, no!' Barbara laughed. 'By the time I was, um, "released" by my boarding school and was back home, things in Europe were changing, getting more exciting. In my life, it seemed like the same rules of White society had remained unchanged here since the turn of the century. Our housekeeper, Rose, had a sister who cleaned in one of our hotels and would collect discarded magazines for me. They'd been brought in from England and Italy via the hotel guests, who then went upcountry or to the coast and left such surplus extravagances behind in their pursuit of the "authentic" safari experience.' She raised her eyebrows at this. 'Something I'm sure they tired of by about day three, by which time they would turn tail and return to the comforts of the city's hotels.'

Clive laughed. 'You're probably right!'

'I treasured those magazines. They gave me a glimpse of a modern world. Young people making their mark in business, fashion and music. They were throwing out the rules and being brave and independent. My parents and their cronies seemed to escalate their privileges in defiance of the change that was taking place in the world and right on their doorstep. They hunkered down further behind the safety of their gated communities, armed askaris and high concrete walls, in denial at the inevitable. I wanted to run away and get swept up by change.'

'And how is it working out for you, this new lifestyle?' asked Clive.

'It's alright. I used to get an allowance, but my mother said that if I insisted on working, I shouldn't need it. I think she expected me to live way beyond my means, concede defeat and go back home. But I'm too bloody-minded for that!' she laughed. 'Turns out I'm as frugal as Ebenezer Scrooge. I make most of my own clothes, Sheila and I share a room at the YWCA, I cook and I'm very organised.'

'That education wasn't wasted then?'

'Hah – yes, we were being taught how to be useful wives and

we have become self-reliant city girls! They didn't expect that, did they?'

They continued to chat about siblings and politics and books they liked and music they hated, until Barbara suddenly exclaimed that she had to get back to work. Clive smiled and beckoned the waiter over for the bill. 'I can't believe the time; can we do this again?' he asked.

'I'd love to. Next week? Thank you for lunch, Clive. I've so enjoyed it. I start the new job next Monday. All because of you.'

'Goodness, I hope it turns out well, for my sake!' he laughed. 'I'm sure it will though. You will make it good. And I'll call you about Naivasha. We can stay at my sister's house. I'll sort it all out.'

They stepped out from the veranda and into the full sun of the afternoon, kissed cheeks lightly and walked their separate ways back to work. A few hundred yards on, Clive dared a glance back in Barbara's direction. Just as Barbara did the same.

CHAPTER 7

NAIROBI 1963

THE bus door slid open with a hiss and there was Clive, right in front of her on the road, ready to take her hand to help her to step off.

'Hi!' Barbara said, smiling as she took the proffered hand. He led her across the dusty road to a row of shops. These formed a long, white concrete boulevard, a wide overhang sheltering the walkways from the strong midday heat.

'Here!' He hopped up to the pavement and stopped beside a drinks stall. 'What would you like?'

'A lemonade, please. Hot journey!' She noticed how completely relaxed he seemed and almost childishly pleased to see her.

'Two lemonades, please.' Clive paid the shopkeeper and passed Barbara her bottle. A homemade bottle opener jutted out from the counter and, in one swift move, Barbara flipped the lid from her drink and swigged it back. Clive stared at her.

'What's wrong?'

'Nothing. You're just so…'

'So what?' she laughed.

'Unladylike is the wrong word.'

'I should hope so!'

'Unselfconscious. Cool, I suppose.'

'I'll settle for cool,' she shrugged. They turned to leave the stall, nodding their thanks to the shopkeeper. 'So, how far is it to your sister's place?'

'Not far. And I have borrowed my brother's van. It's just over here.' Clive led her over to a row of cars which cut diagonally down the middle of the boulevard, took her suitcase from her and helped her into the passenger side of the van. When he got in himself, she noticed that he had to drive hunched forward with his knees either side of the steering wheel. 'No air-conditioning, I'm afraid," he said. 'And if we open the windows, your hair will get full of dust!'

Barbara laughed. 'Don't worry, I'll pop on a scarf. Let down the windows!'

'So, what do you think of my home town so far?' said Clive as they turned down the main street, shouting short sentences to each other above the noise of the open van.

'It looks just like Nairobi, or like it a few years ago,' Barbara yelled back. 'How many of your family will there be at the lunch?'

'All four of my sisters, me, my brothers Frederick and Godfrey. And all the husbands and wives and children. So – a few!'

'Goodness. I've never done this before, you know – been invited to meet someone's entire family. What do I need to know first?'

'Well, they all know that you are, well... European.'

'You couldn't really have got that one past them!' Barbara scraped a curl of hair from the lipstick she had applied carefully on the bus, now gritty with dust.

'No, indeed.'

'And we are meeting at your sister Njeri's house?'

'Yes, she is the eldest after me.'

'So you're the eldest? Of how many again?'

'Of eight. I wasn't born eldest. I had an older brother, Christopher, but he died of malaria as a child.'

'I'm so sorry.'

'Thank you. To be honest, I don't really remember him. But it did change things for me.'

'An eldest son is quite important in a Kikuyu family, is that right?'

'Yes, as an eldest son, I outranked my mother. I was very aware of this as a boy – it was a privilege, but a responsibility too. But my mother was a very strong woman and so we respected each other. My father wasn't at home very much, and she came to depend on my help with the rest of the children.' Barbara nodded sympathetically. 'It was mostly a happy time, though. We all got along very well. And my parents were very forward-thinking. They wanted us all to have a good education and get good jobs.'

As they continued along the palm-fringed, dusty road, the landscape around them had changed abruptly from whitewashed concrete to miles of flat, empty scrubland. The openness of the landscape made Barbara tingle with exhilaration. She felt a strong connection to this wild, untamed country; she never felt like this in the city or in her parents' well-kept gardens up-country. Throwing back her head, she turned to smile at Clive who seemed to un-hunch from the steering wheel.

'So where did you all go to school?' asked Barbara.

'We'll pass it shortly. Would you like to see it?'

'Very much.'

After a few miles, a small township came into view. Clive slowed the van and turned down a track between some wire fencing.

'Here,' he said, shutting off the engine.

At first, the building they had stopped outside looked rather dilapidated to Barbara, but as they walked around the side of it, they could hear a teacher asking questions and the unmistakeable sound of excited children clamouring to answer.

'This is it.' Clive opened out his arms towards the building. 'It's not where we started off, though.'

'No, why was that?'

'Well, my first school was a small Christian primary, run by missionaries. It was basically just a clearing with a bit of a roof over it. It was all very well; my parents recognised that Christian schools were adequate and that the teachers generally had good intentions, but their emphasis wasn't on academic education. As Kikuyu, we had never really been expected to carry out work beyond blue-collar jobs in either agriculture or in the administrative offices, as subordinates to the British.'

'They wanted to keep you in your place,' added Barbara.

'Yes, so you see, our parents wanted us to be modern – to get good jobs and be able to look after ourselves – as the old life of farming and fishing, of living as part of a community was ending. But they also wanted us to understand and respect our traditions, to go forward with our own culture. They were very radical, very intelligent. Our father was very passionate about his Kikuyu traditions and history. He felt – like a lot of his friends – that we were in danger of losing our heritage and customs under colonial rule. We'd already lost our farm and our community was breaking up. So, he became a member of a couple of the anticolonial groups that were springing up everywhere in the provinces. This was before Mau Mau.'

He turned to the school and stood pensively for a moment. 'You know, it might not look like much, but my parents and their friends physically built this school with their own hands as well as collecting money to pay for supplies. They were so determined to provide us with a broader education than the mission schools.'

'Good for them. You should be jolly proud of them. It must have been hard. And dangerous, I should think,' Barbara said quietly, lightly touching his arm as she walked towards a bench under a yellow fever tree. She sat in the shade, facing the school.

Clive sat next to her and continued. 'It was, and in ways you might not expect. The colonial government obviously wanted to limit our ambitions and keep us out of political and economic matters; but we had pressures from extreme anticolonial groups too.'

'Really? I'm afraid I have so little understanding of the situation. My parents rarely talked about the Emergency when I was growing up, and even now they never discuss any politics that they don't feel matters to them.' Barbara felt a pang of guilt. She was blaming her parents for her lack of education, but it would have been perfectly easy to learn these things for herself. 'And I suppose that in the city, and in my job, everyone is trying to look forward and forget about everything that happened in our past. I'm rather ashamed of that. There's no excuse.'

'Don't be ashamed. At least you're asking the questions.'

'Hmm…' She looked at him apologetically. 'Sorry, please carry on.'

'So, schools like ours became central to the whole political maelstrom. Some independent schools had been used for Mau Mau oathing ceremonies, so the government became suspicious of them, but at the same time, the Mau Mau saw the schools as being associated with colonial rule.'

'Why would they think that?' asked Barbara.

'Well, if we were going to have an education that was recognisable in the wider world, we had to follow a standard curriculum, not just make up our own syllabus. We were doing subjects we could not have studied in the Christian schools, and our exams had to be recognised and assessed by a central body – an English body – and that caused problems.'

'Ah, I see. It's very unfair, though – what else could the new schools have done?'

'Exactly – an impossible paradox. So, by now, Mau Mau was growing in popularity and numbers, and they were recruiting from our village and the surrounding area. It split my family. I had an uncle who was an active member of the Mau Mau.'

Barbara turned to the school and got up to walk around. 'I hadn't realised how difficult it was for your community. I always thought it was just the Mau Mau against the British.'

'No, it was very complicated and very emotive. Schools like mine became pawns between Mau Mau supporters who saw the schools as agencies of colonial government, the British who doubted the motives of the Kikuyu and saw the schools as Mau Mau hothouses, and those, like my parents who just wanted us to have a rich and useful education. The Mau Mau began a campaign against schools like ours and threatened to burn them to the ground.

'I kept going to school, but it was very dangerous. We had armed Home Guards outside the school to protect us. Can you believe, our teachers were armed? One day they actually shot into our classroom while we hid under our desks.' Clive shook his head. 'These were members of our own community.'

They stopped talking to listen again to the children talking.

'In my last year at the school my father was killed.' Clive said this so quietly, Barbara barely heard him.

'Killed? By whom?' she asked, shocked.

'No one really knew. They found him hanging from a tree just through there.' Clive turned to point to a patch of acacias. Each side blamed the other. There was never a proper investigation. They were incendiary times and death was commonplace.'

'Your poor mother.'

'Yes, but she didn't grieve. She just got more determined.'

'I see where you get it from.' Barbara smiled at Clive. He turned away from the school and the acacia trees beyond and returned her smile.

'Yes, she was a force to be reckoned with! And you will see that in my sister Njeri too.'

'I'd better watch out, then!'

'Come on. Let's go.' Clive placed his arm lightly around her waist and began to lead her back to the van. She turned to face him and placed her palm on his cheek. Looking deeply into his eyes she could see the years of hurt and sadness; there must have been anger there too at such injustice, but she couldn't see it; Clive never seemed bitter, just focussed.

'I… gosh, I'm never lost for words,' she started, dropping her hand but still staring into his eyes. He held her gaze while she continued. 'I'm so sorry for how things have been for you. That's so easy to say, though, so glib... I don't mean to be.' She took a deep breath and continued. 'What I really want to say is how in awe I am of you. You seem so quietly strong and calm. I am full of frustration and anger with my parents, and I can never hold it in, I have to shout back and slam doors and weep. But what you have had to endure, I just can't imagine and I am so… so… I feel so childish.'

'Well, you aren't and I don't really think of my life like that. I have been angry, of course. You should have seen me at seventeen. I was not a nice person.' He chuckled. 'But if I live my life full of remorse and vengeance, they will have won. I could lower my expectations and just grumble and shout, but then I wouldn't achieve anything. You might think we are very different, but I think we have two very important things in common. We love this country and we are excited by the future. You are bright and positive and you want to learn and help and progress. I want to challenge injustice and bring about change. We are the future, don't you see? Separately and together.'

Barbara looked down and clasped his hands in hers as if to steady herself. Then she tipped back her head, leaned into him and began kissing him. She had expected him to stiffen, to resist at least for a moment, but he responded as though he had expected this – that it was so natural and he had always known how perfect they would be together. She released her grip and moved her hands up to hold his body closer. She felt his hands gently embrace her around her waist. Those long elegant fingers she had watched as he wrote furiously or pushed up his glasses or opened a door for her. Now those hands were stroking her back, her face. He cupped her head gently to pull her in closer to his mouth. She felt excited but safe in his arms. Her face glowed with the heat of the moment, but Clive's skin was soft and cool. A few lost moments later, she clutched him around his broad back, and what had started so suddenly melted away in a sprinkle of gentle kisses as they laughed with happiness. She nuzzled into his chest and the children in the school began singing.

CHAPTER 8

NAIROBI 1963

THEY arrived at Njeri's house a short while later. The house was large and surrounded on all sides by a garden bursting with vegetables and fruit trees. What seemed to Barbara like dozens of children ran out towards the car and jogged next to them, smiling in at the windows, as they trundled down the track. Clive told them off brusquely but with a wide smile.

'Happy to be home?' asked Barbara.

He nodded. 'I will always love it here. I've got so much to show you. But first, we'll need to get the interrogations over with. You feeling strong?'

'Do I have any option?'

'No!' he laughed.

'Clive, my dear brother!' A man ran towards them as they got out of the car and shook Clive vigorously by the hand. 'And this must be Barbara, so nice to meet you. I am Clive's favourite brother, Frederick. But I'm sure you know that!' Barbara laughed and returned the brisk handshake. 'Pleased to meet you, Frederick. As his favourite brother, you must know all his best secrets, so I will be quizzing you later!'

Frederick roared with laughter and, sweeping up their bags, marched ahead towards the house. The children continued to run around them asking questions as Clive fended them off. One little girl slipped her hand into Barbara's and looked up at her with big shy eyes, asking, 'Are you Clive's girlfriend?' Barbara caught Clive's eye and smiled back at the girl. 'I think I must be, yes.'

The family were seated in the back garden around a long table under a wide makuti roof. Barbara gulped as at least twenty faces turned to watch them approach. One of the women, tall and angular and unmistakably a sister, left the table to greet them, holding out her arms. 'Welcome, brother, welcome. It has been too long; we have missed you. Godfrey?' she called over to a teenage boy. 'Bring your big brother and his friend a drink.' Njeri took Barbara's hands in both of hers and squeezed them. Barbara felt both welcome and intimidated.

'Njeri, this is my friend Barbara,' said Clive. 'Barbara – Njeri, our eldest sister.'

'And wisest!' said Njeri, in a tone that seemed only half-joking. She pointed at the other people around the table. 'Our sisters Kioni, Inira and Jata are at the end there with their husbands. Over there is Frederick's wife, Mercy. And,' she opened her arms towards the garden and the playing children, 'all our nieces and nephews. I won't tell you all their names now!'

'My name is Blossom,' whispered the little girl who was still clutching Barbara's hand. Barbara knelt down to speak to her.

'Hello, Blossom. Who are your parents then?'

'My Mama is Jata – the pretty one over there – and my Baba is Matu. There in the blue shirt. He is very funny!'

'Will you take me over to meet all your cousins, Blossom? But you will need to tell me all the names very slowly, so that I can remember.' Godfrey returned with their drinks; Clive went to greet his bothers and, after leaving the children to their games, Barbara returned to the table to join the women. 'Lovely to meet you all,' she said, smiling at the group of eager faces. At the far end of the table a few more children sat whispering together; Barbara noticed one little girl picking pieces of dried fruit from a bowl and dropping them under the table.

'Please, Barbara, sit down here under the roof where it's cool. Let me pour you some more water.' Njeri instructed one of the children to refill a water jug, then sat down herself. 'Now, I'm sure Clive has warned you about us.'

'He calls you "The Committee",' admitted Barbara, initial nerves easing as the warmth of the family shone on her.

Njeri and the other women laughed. 'He is quite right. That's what we are. Not the men,' she made a dismissive gesture. 'They do nothing but sit back and moan about who has the hardest job, who has to fire one of his workers, who has to stay in the office the latest. But we are the ones who run things around here.'

'Except for Clive,' interjected Inira. 'He doesn't complain. He is a very good man. Did you know that after our father died, he worked and worked to put us all through school, even the girls? He's still paying towards Godfrey's school fees.'

'No, he didn't tell me that.' Barbara looked over to Clive who seemed to be fixing something for a sad looking little boy.

'He took part-time jobs, and sold bread and cakes that we and our mother made at markets and in cafés.'

'And he got work on one of the fishing boats,' added Kioni.

'Until Mama found out and put a stop to it,' said Njeri. 'She was furious – consorting with the enemy *and* not going to school – a terrible sin.'

'Clive told me that your family lost their farm. I'm so sorry. It must have been hard for your parents. To lose their land and their way of life. Hard on all of you,' said Barbara as Njeri handed her a plate piled high with food. Barbara was alarmed at the size of the portion, but tucked in. 'And there are a lot of you.'

'Eight of us – four boys, four girls,' said Jata. 'It was bad for our Baba, as he was very proud and very angry about what had happened, but he and our mother were determined to provide for us and get us a good education. So, inevitably, Baba had to take a job as a supervisor at one of the big fisheries,' said Jata.

'And most of us work at the fisheries now,' said Inira. 'We didn't want to, after what happened to our father. But the fishery jobs are the best in the area and we love living here. Only Clive wanted to get work in Nairobi. He's still the most ambitious of us all. Except perhaps Godfrey, but he is still young.'

'Do you work, Barbara?' asked Njeri.

'Yes… I…' Barbara started.

'Wanjiku... are you feeding that warthog again?' Njeri stood to tell off the little girl who had been stealing fruit. The girl froze with one arm under the table.

'Wilfred is so hungry, Mama. Since you stopped him coming in the house, he has no food.'

'Has no food, what nonsense, child. He eats grubs from my compost pile all day long. Go on now, take him away!'

'Sorry, Barbara. You were telling us about your job.'

The family chatted until well into the evening, Clive and Barbara exchanging occasional glances in between the affectionate teasing, family stories and interjections of advice. That night, a sense of peace and happiness overwhelmed Barbara as she drifted off to sleep.

They drove east towards the silhouetted trees, myriad birds and monkeys performing shadow plays in front of the cinnamon and gold sky.

'I can't believe you prepared all this and left me to sleep. What time were you up? Your sister must think I'm a terrible lazybones!' Barbara rummaged through the knapsack Clive had brought and pulled out the flask of coffee.

'Don't open that yet. I just want to get to a kopje on the right here. We can get out and climb up it to see the sunrise properly.'

They parked under a tree, Clive took the knapsack from her and led her to a flat kopje. 'Just walk behind me. It's quite smooth and safe, honestly. You won't trip, just follow my feet. I have been climbing this rock since I was four years old.'

Barbara did as he said and kept her eyes firmly on his feet; he climbed quickly, but she managed to keep up, following him step for step. As they got higher and her eyes adjusted, it got light enough for her to feel safe looking up. As she did so, Clive looked down at her from the top of the rock, looking rather angelic, she thought, her heart flickering.

'Well? Worth the early start?'

She grabbed his outstretched hand, steadied her feet, inhaled, then took in the scene around her. In her concentration, she had not noticed the cacophonous noise. All manner of birds – pelicans, go-away birds, cormorants, cranes – were greeting the dawn with gusto, overlapping with the calls of the night creatures, the frogs and owls.

'Come, sit and we can open that flask.' Clive shuffled to a ridge that served as a perfect lookout point. 'Hang on, take this first.' He handed her a bundled up kikoy to wrap around her shoulders, then poured them both a coffee from the flask.

'Now.' He took a quick gulp and pointed ahead. 'Can you see that clearing on the shore?' She nodded. 'And can you make out the big lumps on the grass?'

'Oh, my goodness – hippos? Grazing? But I've only ever seen them in water. I don't think I've ever even seen their feet!'

'They graze at night, when it's safer. If you get up early enough you can see them.' The hippos' brown forms became more distinct as the light rose.

'Look there!' exclaimed Barbara. 'Giraffes – a whole load of them. There must be thirty or forty. The steam from their breath – it's like they are all smoking cigars!'

'This is my favourite place in the world and my favourite time to be here,' said Clive, obviously pleased at her excitement.

'I don't blame you. It's magical. Look, look – warthogs and a hyena!' She hugged her knees in glee. 'And that tree over there in the lake. Gosh, the trees are so strange, sticking out of the water like that in the mist. That one has every branch covered in cormorants drying their wings.'

A soft pink glow revealed a flock of pelicans swimming in formation on the edge of the lake, as synchronised as a corps de ballet.

'I don't think I've ever seen so many birds in one place. No wonder you love it here.'

'I do. I have to come back now and again when I've had too much of the city. As a boy, I spent all the time I could down here at the lake. My family was pretty noisy, so I would come here for the peace. I'd get up early to sit and listen to the birds, then come back after breakfast with our goats and draw dung beetles, starlings, tortoises, anything I could, in a little sketchpad I carried around. My father gave me a pair of binoculars; they were not the best – I had to keep mending them – but they are very special to me.' He reached into the knapsack again. 'Here.'

'These are the same ones? How wonderful! Oh, I bet he was so pleased to give you these.'

Clive smiled as he watched Barbara point the binoculars at the cormorants. 'Find the object you want to look at, don't move, then bring the binoculars to your eyes. That way you don't lose sight of your subject.'

'I see. You're right! Well, I never knew that!'

'Sadly, the fact that there are so many birds is perhaps not such a good thing.'

'What do you mean? Surely it is healthy?'

'It's not that. Yes, the lake is healthy, but it is full of non-native species – tilapia mostly, for commercial use, and people like to come here to fish, so they have been put into the lake to breed. The tilapia are overbreeding and the lake is actually very shallow, so water levels are an issue. I worry that it's just the beginning. The lake was even used as an airport for a while. It's become a resource – lots of opportunity for exploitation. Fresh water, fertile land, temperate weather. It's already changed a lot since my childhood. Our farm was just behind that line of trees.' He pointed behind them.

'You haven't told me how you lost the farm.'

'Compulsory purchase. Well, I say purchase, but no actual money changed hands. We had farmed the land for generations, but didn't own it in the modern sense of the word. Our community was offered work on farms and fisheries, but we had to live in tiny houses, taxes got higher, wages lower. My father got a job as a supervisor at a fishery and continued to work there as we were growing up. I knew he hated it, hated giving in to the fisheries, but there were a lot of us to look after.

'I wanted to show you this because it is so special to me, but also because it is changing. I fear that all the so-called progress we have witnessed has not just had a human cost. As long as places like this are commercially profitable, people will suck them dry – quite literally here, I'm afraid.'

'What can we do?' Barbara looked again through the binoculars at the cormorants and pelicans.

'Keep vigilant. Educate people. Care.'

They stepped down from the rock. A soft warmth was rising as the sun spilled light over the water. A lone sea eagle flew from its perch in a naked tree and, in one smooth movement, scooped a fish from the surface. They turned and climbed back down the rock to the van.

* * *

On the way back to Njeri's house, they stopped at the market to buy provisions for their host. Barbara was paying for a loaf of bread, when she heard her name being called.

'Barbara, is that really you? What on earth…?'

She turned to face the voice. 'Nigel? I... I… I'm here with a friend. Why are you here? And it's a bit early in the morning for you, surely?'

'I'm here with our new French chef, Jean-Michel. I wanted to know how much we are paying for our groceries.'

At that moment, Clive came over and stood beside Barbara. 'Clive, this is my brother Nigel. Nigel, this is Clive.'

Nigel nodded but said nothing. 'So where is your friend?'

'*This* is my friend,' said Barbara holding her hand out. 'Clive.'

Nigel scoffed, then his face fell as he realised what she meant. 'Oh, I thought that…'

'That what? Clive was my driver? My 'boy'?'

'Well, yes, I suppose. Where are you staying?'

'With Clive's family nearby. We've just been to visit the lake.'

'What? Why stay there, when the hotel is right here?' Nigel pointed across from the market at a large brick building.

'Oh, of course, I hadn't really got my bearings yet. Well, we were invited to Njeri's, so why would we stay at the hotel?'

'You might have stayed there as it might have been more... appropriate,' said Nigel through gritted teeth.

'Ah, I see, well don't you worry about it, Nigel. I'm perfectly alright at Njeri's – you know I have an actual bed and a shower and everything,' she replied with no attempt to hide the sarcasm in her voice.

'I really think Ma and Papa would be most displeased. What if some of their guests see you with the company you keep?'

Barbara gripped her shopping basket, twisting her hands around the handle. She waited for Clive to say something, but he stood there, looking impassive. 'Nigel, Clive is my friend and you are being extremely rude.'

'I don't really care. What I care about is our reputation and your lack of consideration. Now, I insist that you pack whatever things you have at this person's house and come immediately to the hotel.'

Barbara scoffed. 'I shall not. Who the hell are you to tell me what to do?'

'I am your elder brother and if you do not come back with me I shall have to tell our parents.'

'I think perhaps you ought to do as he asks,' said Clive.

'He has no authority over me. I'm a grown woman.'

'A grown woman who is running around Kenya with a native. You could bump into any of our friends here, Barbara. What would they think?'

'It is of absolutely no consequence what they think!'

'I think you will find there would be very grave consequences.'

He stood for a moment, waiting for a reply. 'Have it your way. I shall see you at Christmas. You are coming home for Christmas, I presume. Alone?'

He turned and walked towards the hotel. Barbara stood staring after him, still gripping her basket. 'Why didn't you say something? How could you let him talk like that, as if you weren't there, as if you were nothing?'

'That I should even need to explain that to you says so much about you and how sweet you are. Come now, let's get back.' Clive took the basket from her and led her away.

CHAPTER 9

NAIROBI 1963

BARBARA had been working at her new job at the Game Department for a few months. It had been a busy time, with all government departments being overhauled and reorganised, ready for the change from a colony to a republic. Every department vied for its rank among the others and Barbara's colleagues had been hastily putting together reports on tourist numbers, species decline, issues between farmers and the National Parks, and she could not take much time away from the office. Nevertheless, in exchange for not leaving the office all week, she had negotiated a long lunch break every Friday, so that she and Clive could meet up. Both ambitious and independent, they thrived on the busyness of their jobs, but Fridays were sacrosanct – they marked the beginning of their weekends and they would cram as much time together as they could into those few days.

Barbara was late as always, and could see Clive from across the street, at their usual table on the terrace. Rather than looking anxious, like he had on their first date, he seemed purposeful and focused. He had papers spread out on the table and was frantically writing, never looking up. He sat hunched, knees raised, his right arm crooked over the page, as if hiding the answers from covetous fellow examinees. The scene made her feel suddenly maternal. She wanted to protect this man. He looked both wise and vulnerable. Cherishing the sight of him so absorbed in his task, she took her time walking towards him, but as she got closer she mumbled apologies and excuses. For a moment he seemed to be surprised to see her, but quickly registered and hurriedly swept up his papers and stuffed them into his battered cowhide satchel.

'Sorry, sorry, sit down.' He stood until she had made herself comfortable. 'I ordered you your usual, I hope you don't mind.'

'Not at all. Saves time. How was your week?'

'I just got back from Mombasa this morning; I've been there since Friday.'

'Why was that?'

'Well, it was a bit last minute, as a colleague got ill. It's the first time my editor has trusted me with a big piece.' Clive was attempting to exude an air of solemnity combined with nonchalance, but Barbara could tell from the way his mouth turned up minutely at the corners that he was trying to suppress a boyish exhilaration. 'He liked the articles I submitted about local issues – opening factories, schools getting ready for the Uhuru celebrations, that sort of thing. I told him I was really interested in investigative work – looking into dubious business dealings and such. Well, I told him that the most obvious place to start was Mombasa – that's where most commodities arrive and leave Kenya, so he sent me off there for the week and told me to just sniff around.'

'So, did you find anything?' asked Barbara, intrigued and a little concerned. 'And what did you do to "sniff around"? What does that even mean?'

'Well, I started off by researching trade routes and possible incongruities. Quantities not looking right, odd-looking business links, that sort of thing. I wanted to gain people's trust primarily. I – quite truthfully, sort of – said I was writing about success stories in the build up to a "new" Kenya – and could I come and see them? So, I spent a lot of time being shown around factories, ports, warehouses. Obviously, they want to show themselves in the best light, but sometimes you just get a glimpse of something that doesn't fit – something not right – and you can follow a trail, a disgruntled employee, a deal gone wrong. People will talk to you if you just ask them in the right way. The deadline for the first article is Tuesday, so I was just collating my notes and I'll need to run it by our legal department.'

'I bet your degree has come in handy now.'

'Yes, it has. I know how to report things without being too inflammatory. The thing is that there is a lot of criminal activity amongst import/export bodies and the authorities turn a blind eye. Someone needs to say something. That's the point of journalism, surely, to stand up and say something?'

'You didn't put yourself in any danger, though?' Barbara shivered a little; an almost imperceptible sense of foreboding caused her heart to quicken.

'No, of course not.'

Their food came and they ate for a while, not speaking.

'So, was there a particular thing that you could follow through – an exciting lead?' Barbara knew he wasn't going to give too much detail about what he had done in Mombasa straight away, but she was still curious to know what had caused this palpable excitement.

'Ivory smuggling,' he replied in a whisper.

'Do you mean iffy trade deals, bribing customs officials, that sort of thing?' She returned his whisper.

'No, more than that. I mean actual poaching to order. From the US it seems, mostly.'

'Oh, God. I know that hunting without a licence is on the increase. Graham at work reckons that everyone's eyes have been off the ball with Independence looming. The British haven't cared enough about poaching in recent years to put money into protecting the reserves and the animals within them, and for Kenya herself, it is too low down in the priorities. The chaps I work for are just banging their heads against brick walls. Taking the law into their own hands a lot of the time.'

'I know. Mismanagement everywhere. Double standards too – hunting licences are only issued to Whites and Asians, because we native Kenyans are not allowed to own firearms. But the poachers get their guns from somewhere. And it's worth the risk for them. The money they get from ivory smuggling is beyond what they could earn in a lifetime farming or working in a factory.'

'Will your paper publish this, do you think? It's not really a time for recriminations, is it, with Independence round the corner?'

'If it were a big national paper, probably not. They'd be too worried about their reputation. And I agree, with all that's gone on, people need to feel positive about change. But our paper is small but serious. We all feel responsible about telling the truth. And we're not owned by a big hot shot who has to suck up to the right people.'

'Well, I know about them!'

They carried on eating for a while. Barbara was anxious about what Clive had told her; she knew that the world he was dipping his toe into was bound to be dangerous. But she also knew that his experiences growing up had left him with a strong sense of morality and justice. He could not abide duplicity. He had seen members of his own family turn against their community in the name of political ideology. Added to that, he loved his country, its wild places and extraordinary animals.

'You know what?' said Barbara as she finished the last of her sandwich. 'You should come up-country with me next month. I'm going to stay with Sheila and Toby at Taita Hills. Do you remember – he was going to jack it all in and start running his parents' farm as a tourist camp? Well, they're doing a recce next month to see what wildlife is in the area, where best to set out the camp and so on. They hope to move there themselves once they have a better idea of their plans. They'll be speaking to some of the neighbouring farmers to get the lay of the land and so on. Perhaps you could tag along and see if there's been poaching activity around there?'

'Do you think the farmers would speak to me?' asked Clive.

'Yes, I do. For one thing, Toby knows them all and would give you an "in", and for another, you could charm the birds off the trees, darling!'

* * *

A few weeks later, they packed some clothes and met up with Sheila and Toby at the city's Wilson Airport to fly down to Taita.

'Good morning, chaps.' Toby stood beside the six-seater Cessna and helped the pilot with Clive and Barbara's bags. 'Go on, Barbara, you get in the back with Sheila. Clive we're in the middle. How are you at flying?'

'Well, we'll soon see!' Clive clambered in and braced himself as the plane began its ascent.

The party wordlessly watched the landscape from their windows, as the plane followed the contours of the Athi River, over long-spent volcanoes and snaking tributaries. It was Clive's first flight in a plane and the trip was simultaneously thrilling and vomit-inducing. In between vomiting episodes, Clive got a view of his country that he'd never had before. After the messy scatter of warehouses and hangars, the outskirts of Nairobi were edged with neat, continuous lines of crops – pineapple, bananas and beans. This suddenly gave way to wide ochre plains, peppered with scrub, stretching for mile upon mile.

The land of his boyhood had been increasingly reduced by commercial development and encroachment, but here the panorama was astonishingly gigantic, prehistoric, untameable. Small villages and towns clung to the river's edge; the lives of their inhabitants synchronised with the river's moods. He felt inordinately proud of this land – this 'cradle of mankind'.

Toby passed him a wet cloth. He nodded his thanks, wiped his face and took a sip of water. Toby had to shout above the engine noise. 'Better now?'

Clive sat back in his seat and nodded. 'I think that's it now. I feel a bit steadier. I've always dreamed of flying, but I didn't reckon on the sickness.'

'You'll be alright now that we're at height – much smoother flying now and then the descent will be quicker.'

'Not too quick I hope!'

Toby laughed. 'So, Sheila tells me that you are hoping to work on an article while you're down with us.'

'Yes, I don't want to upset anyone, but I'm hoping to follow some leads I've traced backwards from my research in Mombasa.'

'Fishy?'

'A bit, yes.'

'Well, it does make me think.' Toby took a swig of his water bottle. 'We have this chap working for us – Johan du Toit. He's never put a foot wrong, actually. Has run the ranch very well for six years. But… well. You know when you just feel something isn't right?'

'I'm beginning to get that a lot!' laughed Clive.

'I've heard a few rumours; lots of gambling stories – often a pretty girl on his arm. And that he's been seen driving a nice new Mercedes around town which I've never seen at the farm.'

'Perhaps he is a lucky gambler.'

'Perhaps, but the stories are always of him flying off the handle after a big loss, fights, threatening the staff, that sort of thing.'

'He sounds charming.'

'Hmm… Anyway, my father has asked me to nose around a bit while I'm down. The farm is fine, the books show no signs of strange goings on, but… well, truthfully, I've never liked him, so perhaps I just want to find something. Also, we won't need him much longer with the plans I've got. But, well, I'll tell you all about it later.'

'Sure.'

'Anyway, I also understand that you're not really a city-type, that you're from up-country. Is there anything in particular you would like to do or see?'

'I'll be happy with anything. Birds, bugs even!'

'Plenty of those!'

They arrived at an airstrip, crudely cleared from low, scrubby bush. Met by a young man in a Land Rover, they continued on to the house where Toby's family had lived, on and off, for fifty years.

'Please, make yourselves at home. Barbara, yours and Clive's bedrooms are through there, Sheila and I are over on the right. This room is where we all eat so if you'd like to get freshened up, we can meet back here for dinner and sundowners.'

The group settled into their rooms, then having washed away the dust of the journey, met up for a simple supper of bean stew and bread. They ate in silence at first, enjoying their meal, until Toby, clearly a fast eater, laid down his cutlery, stretched out his legs and gave a loud sigh.

'Oh, it's good to be back. I do love it here. What do you think, Clive?'

'It's a great place, from what I have seen so far. Will you take us for a tour?'

'In the morning, yes. Let's get up early – it really is the best time. I want us to drive around the edge of the conservancy and talk through the possibilities. I'd really value your ideas.'

'Very happy to. Sheila, what's your plan? Are you going to move here soon?' asked Clive.

'I've given notice at the firm, so I can get down here properly in about six weeks. Toby will be going back and forward to Nairobi, meeting money people, suppliers and things. I want to pass my job on to my replacement, sort out our belongings, then move everything down. I'm so excited. And it's been Toby's dream his whole life.'

'You know, Barbara,' said Toby 'I think Sheila has mentioned this to you – there would be a job here for you if you'd like it. I need someone to build our relationships with the local land-owners and discuss any overlap of responsibilities with the Game Department. You must have learned a lot in your job, and you're great with people!'

'Thank you, Toby. I'll think about it, but of course I do want to be with Clive as much as possible, and this is a bit remote for him in his job.'

Toby handed a small tot of whisky to each of the group and they continue to chat around the table for a short time about Toby's schemes, before heading off to bed.

CHAPTER 10

TAITA HILLS 1963

THE next morning, after a breakfast of kedgeree and coffee, the group set out to survey the land.

'My family have owned this section of land since just after the Great War,' explained Toby, as the group headed west to the furthest end of his farm. 'My grandfather applied under the Ex-Soldier Settlement Scheme. They began farming cattle, then added maize. There's a cluster of large cattle farms here, all owned by the same families dating back to that time. Thousands of people might have left Kenya lately with the political changes, but the farmers down here stay on, just getting on with things, away from the commotion.'

Clive winced a little. 'What about the local people?'

Toby was unembarrassed. 'Well, of course, there are many local people here, all farming their little shambas. In the old days, the settlers tried driving them off – pushing them out of the markets with cheaper produce, and pulling them off their land to work on the big farms.'

Clive saw Barbara flick him an anxious look. After all, this was just what had happened to his family. Nevertheless, he knew that Toby's intentions were honourable, even if he was rather oblivious to his perspective. So as not to embarrass him or Barbara, he carried on politely. 'You say the "old days". 'Do you mean that things are different now?'

'We're trying to do things differently, in the main. But it's been difficult for my family to manage this from a distance. My father didn't want to farm, he went into shipping, so he's left the management of the place to the man I mentioned to you on the plane. So now I want to make big changes – I want to make better use of the land and integrate better with the community. I have been itching to take it on!'

Toby sat forward in his seat, rolling his glass between his palms. 'You see, this land is full of wildlife, or at least it could be. We've one of the best concentrations of wild animals outside the parks. It's a battle to keep the hunters and poachers away, but my idea is to set up a camp and run safaris. To do away with the cattle farm altogether. I'm looking at a long-term project, combining social and environmental development with tourism.'

'That's an ambitious aim,' said Clive.

'Yes, but what better time to be ambitious than now? It's just the sort of project the new regime should be interested in – more work and prospects for native Kenyans, international money coming in, the protection of our wildlife.'

'I can't argue with that,' replied Clive. 'I can see how passionate you are about this land, and I am very grateful for your hospitality, so I don't want to cause you any issues with your neighbours, but, as we discussed, there is a very real likelihood that a trail of quite serious wildlife crime is regularly running backwards from Mombasa to this part of Kenya. It's not just low-level poaching, there's something more organised going on. Like you said, the people here live a little under the radar, and I have contacts who have pointed me in this direction. I know this might be uncomfortable for you, as someone who knows the land and people here, but is there anywhere you think I could make some discreet enquiries?'

'Of course. I want us to start business with a clean sheet, so you have my support to try to flush out any criminal activities,' said Toby. 'Let me have a word with a couple of the chaps up north a bit. And I suggest that we pay a visit to Mr du Toit tomorrow. But for now, I propose we follow this road south. I've packed some sandwiches; we can head off to one of my favourite waterholes and see what we can find!'

* * *

The following day, Toby and Clive drove to the estate manager's cottage. It was a small, two-storey house, rather shabby, with a large barn to the side. As they drew near, a man came out of the barn, holding a large canvas bag. Even from a few hundred metres, Clive could see from the strain on the man's face and the way he shuffled that the bag was heavy. He began to walk towards the house then, appearing to change direction, shoved the bag under the tarpaulin of his pick-up truck.

'Is that him?' asked Clive.

'That's Johan, yes.' They pulled up behind the pick-up and the man quickly fastened a rope, stepped in front of their Land Rover and raised a hand in greeting.

'Good morning, Toby. You… you just caught me. I was just heading out to check the small herd over by Kilenga.'

'Good morning, Johan.' Toby wound down his window and reached out to shake Johan's hand. 'Do you have a few minutes before you set off? I'd like to introduce a friend of mine… well, you are almost my brother-in-law now, aren't you?'

Toby nodded towards the beefy blond man. 'Clive, this is Johan who has been running things here for, what, about six years?' He smiled at his passenger and leaned back to give the men a chance to greet each other. Clive noticed a slight look of, what was it? Revulsion? No, perhaps not quite that, but certainly confusion on the other man's face. It was a familiar reaction, and one that he had learnt to buffer his feelings to, but there was something deeper in this man's expression, something that made him shiver.

'I… I… good to meet you, Clive. What can I do for you, Toby?' Clive noticed him glance several times back at his cottage. Perhaps he was imagining it – he had decided that he didn't like this man, but he was a journalist, he was supposed to be impartial.

'I'm giving Clive here an idea of what's what, you know, as regards my new plans. I was hoping we could all have a meeting this week to discuss things. Could you come for dinner on, say, Thursday?'

'What sort of meeting?' Johan snapped, then seemed to right himself. 'Erm, Thursday… yes, yes, I suppose that will be okay. Is there anything specific you want me to talk about or bring? Do you need the accounts? What plans exactly?' His manner was brusque and, Clive thought, a little annoyed. Perhaps he was just an anxious type, being out here alone so much of the time, but he did seem reticent.

'That's a date then. No, don't worry about bringing anything. We'll see you at 7:30? Good man. See you then.'

They drove away, nodding their goodbyes, and Toby said, 'That was a little odd. He seemed a bit put out. Don't you think? I only asked him for a meeting and he behaved as if I didn't trust him.'

'He did seem a bit bad-tempered, but I don't know him.'

'I always find him a rather intimidating chap. Don't know why. He's South African, obviously, and very butch, which I am not!' He laughed. 'And another thing – there are no cattle near Kilenga anymore. We moved them six months ago. He knows that of course, so why lie?'

The men carried on driving. Clive pondered his own reaction. He must learn to temper his views, be more open-minded. It didn't matter that the man had made his skin crawl. What mattered was facts, wasn't it? Du Toit had done nothing really unusual, perhaps he was just over-analysing the man because of Toby's warnings. He decided to change the subject. 'How will you get animals to come here, to settle on your land?'

'Well, they already do, here and there, but obviously the cattle are fenced off in quite large areas. We shall sell most of the herds – I have a buyer already in Laikipia. Then the fences will come down to allow the wildlife back in. There is also a small dam which was put in to redirect a river. We can remove that and get things back to more like how they were fifty years ago. Nature has a way of reclaiming things, but it will need a bit of a nudge from us first.'

'Has everyone around here been in favour of your plans?' asked Clive.

'On the whole, yes. Our promise of improved roads has helped sweeten things a bit. We need to improve the roads to allow for more comfortable experiences for tourists, and to get supplies through more regularly. And there is enough space around us for it to not really affect the other big farmers.'

'And the small ones?'

'What? Oh, I see, the locals and their shambas. Well, I haven't heard any complaints.' Toby looked a little embarrassed as he realised his tactlessness.

'It might perhaps be wise to speak to some of the elders in the neighbouring villages. It'll affect them too, you know,' said Clive.

'You're quite right, of course. I'll do that. I know who to see first – Chief Masengo. He's a good man… heads up a large Bantu village to the north of here. He'll be a good ally. He'll think I'm quite mad, of course. What sane man in Africa sells off his cattle, especially good, fat cattle, to allow the land to take over and wildlife to thrive!'

They drove to the first of the cattle posts and Toby pointed out where the dam stood, and what type of vegetation was likely to take over once they had removed the cattle. They returned to the house and, as the four of them sat down for a glass of lemonade, Toby explained their dinner plans for later that week and the nervousness of the estate manager. 'I just got the feeling we had caught him in the act of something.'

'It may just have been me,' suggested Clive. 'I do tend to illicit that reaction in people.' He smiled, but Toby was clearly dismayed.

'My dear chap, I don't imagine it was that. There was something shifty about him.'

'Well, you know I don't like him,' Sheila retorted. 'He's a boor. He never addresses me, even if I speak to him directly. He replies to you.'

'Does he? I haven't noticed.'

'Oh, Toby, I really do despair of you sometimes.' Sheila got up and placed a kiss on the top of Toby's head as she led Barbara to the veranda where lunch was laid out. 'You're so naïve. You think every man is a jolly nice chap. You're going to have to harden up. Not everyone is as likeable as you.'

'Isn't it good to see the best in people?' Toby replied, weakly, turning around in his seat to face her.

'Not always, no. Sometimes people hold their own interests above anyone else's. Please just be careful.'

The men got up to follow the women through to the lunch table.

'Well, if I'm such a bad judge of character, what did *you* think of our friend, Johan, Clive?'

'Well, I don't really have anything to base it on, but there was something about him I didn't like. I think that he sensed that from me. Perhaps it wasn't just my colour that unnerved him. Anyway, let's see what he has to say for himself on Thursday. Does he know all about your plans?'

'Some. He knows about the cattle sale, of course. He's the one organising their transportation in a couple of months. But I haven't really discussed his role in things. He's just been left to his own devices here really.'

'Do you think he resents your sudden appearance and all your changes?'

'Perhaps. He hasn't said so, but I suppose you wouldn't when it's your livelihood. I'm ashamed to say I hadn't given it much thought.'

'What will his role be?' asked Clive.

'Well, that's just it, I suppose. His area of expertise is cattle farming. That's how he came to us and that's what he's always done here. He gets on well with the other farmers here too, so he's been left to do all negotiations over land, discussions about boundaries, water issues and so on. We've really depended upon him for all that.'

'Will there still be a need for him to do those things now that you're here?' asked Barbara. 'Surely you'll want to discuss matters with your neighbours yourself and, without the cattle, you don't need a cattle specialist.'

'Absolutely. His job is redundant. I can ask around if any of the other estates need a manager. Perhaps that would be better for all of us than trying to shoehorn him into a role that isn't really needed.'

They ate the rest of their meal in contemplative silence.

Thursday evening arrived and Johan appeared, precisely on time, clad in a slightly too tight linen suit and garish orange tie, hair lacquered, but face characteristically unshaven. He produced a bunch of flowers for Sheila and a bottle of South African white wine for Toby.

'Good evening, one and all,' Johan boomed as his giant form entered the house. 'Hello, Sheila, good evening, Clive – we met the other day and, I'm sorry, I don't think we have met.' He took Barbara's hand and kissed it.

'I'm Barbara, Sheila's sister. And Clive's girlfriend.' She smiled over at Clive, who smiled warmly back at her.

'Indeed, indeed.' Johan's ebullience was at odds with his previous mood and, as he entered the sitting room and made small talk with the others.

Dinner began quietly, but the uncomfortable silence broke once Toby mentioned South Africa.

'Best country in the world. Best farming too,' said Johan, tipping back in his chair. 'The beef there knocks this into a cocked hat.' He pointed down at his meal.

Clive squirmed as he saw the hurt on Sheila's face. She had insisted on cooking the beef herself, the staff having only been allowed to prepare the vegetables for this important meal. He watched as she cleared her throat, sat up straight and smiled at Johan.

'Do you miss it? South Africa I mean?' she asked.

Johan looked down at his plate, took a huge mouthful of potato, then turned to direct his reply to Toby. 'It's the discipline I miss – the structure.' He tapped a finger on the table. 'A man knows his place there. We have a long history in the Cape. My people have been there for generations. We made the country great, made the land productive. It's too unpredictable here – the climate, the politics, everything is so disorganised.'

Johan continued in this vein, not allowing for much interjection as he compared his country favourably against theirs with tales from his time in the defence force and on his family's farm. Eventually, the plates were removed and replaced with coffee and *petit fours*.

'Sheila, these are just divine!' said Barbara, nibbling on a chocolate truffle. 'Are they made from *Kenyan* chocolate?'

'Indeed they are. From Kilifi!' Sheila returned Barbara's question with a wry smile. 'Johan, please help yourself.'

Johan reached for the plate and took three truffles, tossing all three into his mouth whilst continuing to talk. Clive remained quiet, and instead watched as Johan's initial joviality gradually gave way to agitation, presumably oiled by the large quantities of South African wine he was drinking.

'The cattle on our farm were always healthy too. Not like here. We have just had to deal with yet another breakout of rinderpest. We had just got the cattle clear of the last bout, and it all starts all over again.'

'Well, obviously, that will not be our problem very soon,' interjected Toby. He continued, turning to look him in the face. 'See here, Johan. My family has given me *carte blanche* on the management of things here. Pop knew I was unhappy at the firm; he gave up running the farm for the same reasons – it just wasn't for him. He's done well in the shipping line and no longer needs the income from the cattle, so he would have just sold up. But I persuaded him that I could run things, but put the land to better use.'

'What makes you think removing the cattle is putting the farm to better use?' Johan replied stiffly.

'Well, by *better*, I suppose I don't really mean more profitable. I mean better for the land. I've seen what over-grazing can do to land and we've been at risk of doing that here. We've had some really dry years, and times when disease has spread between our cows and the local cattle and wildlife. I rather think we are tinkering with nature a bit too much. And this is…'

Johan interrupted. 'I have to disagree. Yes, the natives' cattle bring disease – they never inoculate them, then blame us and come crying to us for compensation when they lose animals.' Clive noticed Johan shuffle further forward in his seat, with the effect that he towered over Toby. He continued to boom, spittle collecting at the corners of his mouth. 'But we have good, healthy animals, plenty of medicines, dips and feed supplements and we have always done well at market. There is enough land here to rotate the herds to the more abundant grazing. We leave the grass to regrow when we rotate, and we regularly burn the old pasture to renew the soil. It has all worked for many years, despite the occasional drought.'

'I'm sure it has, but the bottom line is, as the owner of the land and the farm, I have made the decision to change what we do here.' Toby's voice had risen for the first time in the conversation and it surprised Johan so much, he stopped talking over him and listened.

Toby continued. 'We've done well here, we all have, and we're extremely grateful to you for your help, but now things will be changing. Given your skills and, I should think, your preferences, I believe it best if we part company. I shall make sure you are properly recompensed and, of course, I'll provide excellent references. I've spoken to some chaps I know up north and there is more than one likely opportunity for you which we can discuss later.'

Toby stopped talking and the two men just sat looking at each other. Clive noticed Toby slowly lower his juddering wine glass, as he seemed to calm down from his uncharacteristic outburst. Johan, on the other hand, was quickly proceeding to fury.

'You are FIRING me? YOU are firing ME?' Johan's slurred voice spat out the words. 'I have worked for your father for all these years. Pulled his herds up from scrawny, pathetic creatures into fat, healthy beasts, for what? I have not had a raise in over three years. I live in that shitty little cottage, while in your absence your native staff live in your big house in luxury. You didn't know that, did you? I keep the land free of pests and disease and you want to bring it all back? You have never worked here. You went from your fancy school to your fancy university and then to a job given to you by your daddy, all the while never setting foot back down here. What the hell do you know about any of it, huh? I have given you my best years and you are just throwing me aside.'

'Nevertheless, Mr du Toit,' Toby kept his composure, despite the man's rage. 'You are in the employ of MY family, and as the representative of MY family I am bringing that employment to an end, as it is no longer required. You must have realised with the sale of our cattle that this was a likely outcome.' The two men continued to glower at each other over the table, both unyielding.

Clive, watching from his seat next to Johan, had noticed the manager's body language change. At the beginning of his outburst, he was bolt upright, red in the face and stabbing a finger at Toby. He now slumped slightly in his chair, and he rubbed his hand on his leg. This leg was trembling uncontrollably under the table.

'He's not just angry,' thought Clive. 'He's anxious about something.'

'Yes, well… I…' Johan stammered, lowering his voice a little, 'I thought you would still need me.' There was a slight plaintive note in his tone now.

'I think it best if you leave now, Mr du Toit. It is late and the ladies want to get to bed. So, if you don't mind, I shall see you out.'

As Johan stood to leave, he stumbled and knocked over his wine glass and the bottle from which he had been drinking steadily. He made no effort to clean up, but lurched towards the door and strode wordlessly out of the house, without a backward glance at his hosts.

'Well, I'm glad that's over.' Sheila laughed nervously, bursting the silent bubble and the others let out a collective sigh of relief.

'If you don't mind, Toby. I think I might just keep a watch on Mr du Toit for a day or two,' said Clive.

'Why it that?' asked Toby. 'Do you think he will do something?'

'Just call it a journalist's hunch,' said Clive absently.

'Well, then, of course,' Toby replied, then brightened. 'Right, I very much need a small snifter before bed. Anyone else?'

* * *

The next morning, Barbara woke and peered into Clive's room to find his bed empty. He was always quite tidy in his habits, but his bedcovers looked like they had been hurriedly thrown back. She wandered through to the kitchen and found Sheila already up and drinking a cup of tea.

'Is Clive about too?' Barbara asked.

'I haven't seen him and the Land Rover's gone, so I suppose he's gone out. Perhaps he's left you a note.' The women searched the kitchen but found nothing. There was nothing to do but wait.

'I'll leave Toby to sleep a bit longer,' said Sheila. 'He was really quite agitated last night. I could hear him moving around very late.'

'I'm not surprised. What a to-do! You don't suppose Mr du Toit will do anything nasty?' mused Barbara, pouring herself a cup of tea from the pot.

'I really have no idea what he's capable of. Toby never spoke about him much. I suppose he was the sort of person one takes for granted. They didn't have much to do with each other.'

The sisters continued to prepare breakfast and chatted about mutual friends in Nairobi. After an hour or so Toby joined them, he was clearly tired – his face puffy and pale, but he was fully dressed.

'No Clive this morning?' he asked.

'No. Vanished. Taken the Land Rover,' said Sheila, brushing his face with a light kiss. 'He's been gone for ages. We might as well eat breakfast now. Let's put some of the eggs and bacon in the oven to keep warm for him when he gets back.'

Barbara divided the food onto plates then refilled the kettle and set it on the stove. As it began to whistle, the noise overlapped with the sound of a vehicle approaching. The group moved to the veranda and watched as Clive turned off the engine and jumped out.

'He's gone!' he shouted up at them as he made his way towards the front door.

Clive joined them at the table on the veranda and Barbara fetched his plate from the oven. The three waited patiently for Clive to take a few bites of breakfast before continuing. Clive sat back and wiped his mouth with a napkin. 'I got up early to drive over to his cottage. I walked the last few hundred yards so that he wouldn't hear me and thought I might poke around a bit outside. I hope this is all okay, Toby.'

Toby nodded his assent, and Clive continued. 'Well, the jeep was gone, so I reckoned I could snoop around without being heard. I tried the outbuilding first as there was something odd about it. The door was open and there was a… well, a smell. What do you think I found?'

'I dread to think,' said Toby, rubbing his eyes.

'Snares. Lots of them. Used snares. And a lot of blood everywhere. And the worst thing.' He fumbled in his cowhide satchel and pulled out a bloodied rag. He then placed the rag on the table beside the salt and pepper and proceeded to unwrap its contents. 'This.'

The group leant in to examine the object. It was about six inches long, butter-white and caked with dried blood. Barbara gasped and threw her hand to her mouth. 'Oh God, it's a tusk. A tiny tusk!'

'This is from a young elephant,' muttered Clive. 'Not a baby, but a young one. There are no nicks or grooves or yellowing. This is the first growth of a young animal. He must have dropped it without realising. I would guess that by dropping this and not missing it, he had far bigger, more valuable specimens. And I would guess he has gone a long way from here with them.'

'God, the bastard,' exclaimed Toby. 'I knew he was a disagreeable man, but I never took him for a crook. What can we do?'

'Alert the authorities, I suppose,' answered Clive. 'He may be over the border into Tanganyika by now. Although, my feeling is he will need to shift his cargo, so he might have risked Mombasa. I should think he has contacts there who would take it off him.'

Barbara stared, frozen, at the little tusk. It was such a small object but it represented so much. A young elephant had been killed, most likely in a brutal fashion, to provide it. Its loss had not even been noticed by this horrible man. Its fate had been decided by his greed and by the desires of people far from here who cared nothing for the majesty of the creatures they were destroying. She realised now why Clive had become so embroiled in this business. How these animals needed champions, or their slaughter would go on unabated. She made a silent pact with herself. She would take that job that Toby had offered. She needed to be part of this. She and Clive could work this out somehow.

CHAPTER 11

TAITA HILLS 1963

BARBARA helped Clive to pack a bag. 'Are you sure about this?' she asked. 'Why not just leave it to the police to track him down? You don't know what sort of people he might be involved with; he's an angry armed man.'

'The police will take too long, if they even do anything at all.'

'Clive, please, you're not just chasing a story, you're chasing a criminal!'

He held out his hand and pulled Barbara onto the bed. 'You know we have to do this. Anyway, Toby has called the border police at the various Tanganyika crossings and at the port at Mombasa. And he's spoken to his father in Mombasa too, suggesting he make some calls of his own.'

'Do you really think you'll find him, in this huge country?' Barbara was crying now. Clive squeezed her hand.

'Of course the chances are slim, but we both agree that Mombasa is worth a shot, after we've made another stop at du Toit's cottage. He may have left something there that could help us track him down.'

Barbara nodded. 'I can't stop you, I realise that. You're too principled and, frankly, pig-headed.' She wiped her eyes and exhaled. 'Is this what life is always going to be like for us? You running off into the lion's mouth, me waiting?'

'I can't make any promises, although I'm sure that life as a journalist won't be this dramatic every day!' Clive tried to sound jovial and dismissive, but Barbara wasn't fooled. It was as if she could see through to his bare bones. He was grateful for this most of the time. She was a fine judge of character and held no truck with superficiality. In a country where the way you looked on the outside absolutely defined your place in it, she was exceptional. It was one of the things he most loved about her – her total honesty and the way she would home in on the truth of something; but it meant he could keep no secrets from her.

'Just take care. I can't ask more than that,' she whispered, kissing his cheek.

* * *

Clive met up with Toby in front of the house and they set out in the Land Rover. At du Toit's cottage, they parked up and called 'Hodi!' but there was no answer. They entered the house with keys Toby held on a large ring.

'I told you I was looking for connections here to the ivory poaching trade,' said Clive. 'I'm sorry it was so close to home.'

'Don't be. If it had to be anyone, I'm glad it's someone I always disliked and not one of our neighbours who we need to keep on side. At least I hope they're not responsible.'

'Well, we have no proof of that either way at the moment,' replied Clive. 'For now, it seems indisputable that Mr du Toit is very actively involved.'

'Perhaps he was desperate. Perhaps we didn't pay him properly.' Toby seemed contrite.

'No offence, Toby. But a well-fed, White, middle-class man like that would not be desperate. At least not in terms I understand. Perhaps he is heavily in debt or something; there were stories of a gambling habit, weren't there? But desperately poor? Mouths to feed? Sick children? No. He is simply greedy.'

'You're quite right, of course. But, God, what a start to our new endeavours. I wanted to bring back the wildlife for everyone to visit and enjoy and he has been slaughtering it.' After a cursory look around the front entrance, Toby turned to say, 'Let's go back out to the outhouse first.'

Clive had pushed the door shut earlier. Now he opened it again and the full force of the smell hit them as they entered the gloomy shed. Snares, used and unused, sat in untidy piles. The former identifiable from the clumps of matted fur and streaks of blood slicked across the surface of the knotted metal. A bucket sat in the corner, overflowing with blood and other indeterminate matter.

'God, it's horrific. How many animals has he had in here?' said Toby. The men wandered round the shed picking up tools, inspecting tarpaulins. 'He can't have done it alone, can he?'

'Sorry, I need some air.' Clive rushed out and was sick, Toby followed him out and sat down heavily on a canvas chair, a dazed look on his face.

The two of them said nothing for a few minutes, then Toby turned to Clive. 'He's clearly been storing ivory and such, but I can't believe he was single-handedly poaching everything himself.'

'I doubt it,' agreed Clive, who crouched, leaning on the wall of the outhouse, and wiping his mouth. 'Like he kept going on about last night, his skills are as a farmer. He strikes me as completely uninterested in the wild space around him, only in farming. To poach on this scale, you would need a lot of knowledge of the land and wildlife – their habits, the effects of weather and other animals, following tracks and detecting spoor, that sort of thing.'

'I think you're probably right. Oh dear, then it is a bigger problem than just him,' Toby said despondently.

'Yes, but not insurmountable. He let this happen but now he's gone and you can get on with things now. You'll be present to keep an eye on things. He had no one to stop him for miles around, so there wouldn't have been much need for secrecy and subterfuge. The men in his employ can have been quite openly killing elephants and he could cover it all up. With the right threats and bribes, one can achieve a lot.'

'So how do I stop it, now that the cash cow has gone?' Toby smiled sadly at his own pun.

'You can offer employment as rangers and trackers; reward men for news of possible poaching in the area, that sort of thing. You can turn it around by offering positive inducement to help grow the farm your way.'

'I suppose. Okay, let's look inside the house. I don't suppose he'll have left anything obvious, but it's worth a look.'

'Of course, it is.' Clive headed back up to the front door. 'He'll have been in a terrible hurry and his priority was getting his stash out of here, so he might have been careless.'

They went back into the house and started on the ground floor. The sitting room was spartanly furnished with only a few personal belongings – coats and boots, a fishing bag and rods. There were no ornaments, no paintings or photographs.

'I'll look upstairs,' said Clive and headed up to the single bedroom.

The room was stuffy and grubby. A clothes rail was the only furniture apart from the bed, and it had just a few pairs of trousers, shirts and threadbare jumpers thrown over it. In this room of khaki and brown, only the bedspread stood out. It was white and covered in delicate cornflowers.

'Pockets,' thought Clive. 'That's the best place to start.' He lifted the heap of trousers and shorts from the clothes rail and threw them on the bed, then sat down and began to rifle through. Every pocket contained something – a piece of wire, screws, coins, a small ratchet and a doorknob – everyday detritus. In the third pair of trousers he found, inside a large crusty handkerchief, a neatly folded piece of paper. His heart stopped and he wiped his now clammy hands on his own fresh hanky. He caught the edge of the paper with his nail and peeled it open.

A few lines were scrawled on the paper:

> *St. Saviour's Pr Schl, Francis Ave MBA.*
> *11:00 15th Sep.*
> *Ask for Mr Ali*

'Toby, come look at this, I might have found something,' Clive called down. Toby ran up the stairs to join him. 'Look at this – an address. It's a school. He has no children, has he? Why would he be interested in a school?'

Toby took the scrap of paper from Clive. 'That's tomorrow. Looks like he has a date to keep. A school.' Toby pondered this, then looked Clive squarely in the face as the thought occurred to him. 'Who would search a school?'

'Very good point. Should we look for anything else?' asked Clive.

'There's not much here. I vote we leave now and try to get to this school before he does. Come on.'

They locked the house back up and jumped into the Land Rover. Careful not to sacrifice the car to a flat tyre before they reached the highway, Toby drove gingerly through the bush until they got to the Mombasa road, then they sped off in search of their quarry.

Mombasa was buzzing with life and traffic, which, as a contrast to their few days in the bush, came as a bit of a shock. People and donkeys drifted along the road in front of their car, the sound of the muezzin calling for prayers from a high minaret drowned out all the chatter and rumbles from the street. The air was sticky and filled with the scents of spices and animals.

'Do you know where you're going?' asked Clive.

'I think so. I think Francis Avenue is in Old Town, near the port. I seem to remember seeing it before. Let's do a circuit, then if we don't find it, ask. If we get really stuck, we can bob into Pop's office. It's in the port district too, and Pop knows every street around there.'

It wasn't long before they found the street, and they managed to park the Land Rover around the block. Out of sight, but near enough to feel safe.

'Now what?' asked Clive, as they stood outside the entrance to the school. 'We have a bit of a problem. What do two young men, one White, one Black want at a school? Do we just walk in? Who do we ask for or say we are?'

'Ah. You're right. I think the most believable thing, and what will get us in to snoop around, would be if we were here to mend something or inspect something. Any ideas?' asked Toby.

'In the films, people have this all sorted. They turn up in costumes and are just let through without question!' laughed Clive.

'They do. But perhaps we just need to do that – act with supreme confidence. Tell you what. Let's go to my father's offices after all. There will be janitors' uniforms and things there, and we can cobble together some ID. Come on.'

'Well, if we do that, why don't we come back here in the morning? Du Toit is apparently due at 11:15. We could try to catch him in the act,' suggested Clive.

'A sting operation?' Toby smirked at his friend. 'I think you're rather enjoying this!'

'It beats reporting on garden parties and matatu accidents!' laughed Clive.

* * *

A few minutes later, they were in Mr Spencer Snr.'s office explaining the situation. Toby's father listened gravely, then spoke up.

'So, you've followed him here because of a piece of paper. Do you still have it?' Toby nodded and handed the scrap to him.

Mr Spencer turned the paper around in his fingers. 'Well, yes, I know the school. But you're right. We will look very stupid reporting this to the police if we end up wasting their time. But, perhaps you could just have a look, to make sure it's nothing, strengthen your case and whatnot?'

Clive was amused by this man – tall, handsome, but rather stern-looking, discussing the matter as though it was utterly normal.

'Let me get my assistant, Jane, in here. She's bound to have some ideas.'

* * *

They returned the next morning at 10:30, Toby in a suit, a clipboard tucked under his arm, Clive in a grey boiler suit carrying a large holdall. They both sported badges, typed out by Jane, declaring that they were from the municipal water company.

'You'd better do the talking,' said Clive, as they pushed through the small door into the school office.

'Wish me luck,' Toby whispered back.

'Good morning, Miss Jenny is it?' Toby read her nameplate and employed his most charming smile as he flashed his ID card at the young receptionist. 'We've been sent here by the council on an urgent matter – a blocked sewage pipe under the road at the back of your building.

The receptionist looked startled. 'I'm sorry, why do you need to come in if the problem is under the road?'

'Well, this pipe runs out from under your school, see? If we don't get to the pipe urgently, the contents will back up under the school and burst open – we're talking raw sewage, Jenny. We can only reach it from here in order to flush the contents through and mend the pipe. Can you please let us through now to inspect it?'

'Um… I'm not sure I can do that. I don't have the authority to let anyone in and Mrs… my boss is out today. So…'

'I know this seems irregular, but I assure you, it is urgent. Listen. Why don't you call my superior? His number is on my pass, here.' Toby held out the card for the woman to dial the number.

A few moments passed, then someone picked up at the other end and spoke to the school receptionist.

'Yes, hello. You are the water department, then…' the woman turned away from Toby and Clive as she spoke to the person on the other end, 'Yes, that's good… I have two men here at St Saviour's claiming they need to inspect a sewage pipe urgently... Oh, it is... alright... Excuse me?... Evacuate... are you sure?... Oh, I see, of course. Yes. I'll sort it. Thank you... Goodbye.' The woman's eyes had widened and she stood up suddenly and grabbed a folder from under her desk. 'Follow me, I have to alert all the teachers and evacuate the building. It could be highly dangerous, she said. Noxious fumes or something!'

'Absolutely, you lead us down to the back of the building and then let us know once everyone is out.' Toby said authoritatively, then turned to whisper to Clive. 'Nice touch, Jane. That'll make it easier.'

A few minutes later, the building was abuzz with children's excited voices and the stern commands of nuns as they marched through the corridors. One of the nuns turned to the men and said, 'We shall take the children to the park around the corner. If you would be so good as to find us and tell us when it is safe to return, we would be most grateful.'

'Of course, Sister. We hopefully won't be too long.'

'Okay, then,' said Clive, looking at his watch. 'It's 10.51. Let's have a look around the school for large closets, basements, that sort of thing. You go upstairs, I'll go down. Meet back here in ten minutes then, if we find nothing, we'll hide out and wait to see if something happens.'

The men separated and began their quest. The school building was a couple of hundred years old, damp and crumbling. There seemed to be no cupboards or other large storage in the classes, so Toby continued to scale the stairs to check if there was any sort of attic above the schoolrooms. On the top floor, all he found was a small hatch in the ceiling. When he pushed this aside and peered in, it was clear that this was too small an area to hide anything of any size, and items like large tusks would never fit through the hatch. He gave up and ran back downstairs, passing down through the main floors until he heard the noise below of footsteps on a stone floor.

He carried on running, expecting to find Clive in the basement below. He reached the bottom of the basement stairs and his eyes were drawn to the corner of the pitch-dark room, where torchlight picked out Clive's face. Toby called over, but then registered the other man's anxious expression and froze. The torch being shone at Clive was being held by another man who stood behind him in the shadows.

'Who are you?' snapped the dark figure. 'Why are you snooping around here?' The man spoke slowly and Toby could tell from his voice that his teeth were gritted, as though he was straining to grip something.

'Excuse me, sir, there's been a mistake. We're just engineers. There's a problem with your sewer which we've been sent to investigate and it might cause terrible damage.'

'Don't lie. I've worked in this building for years. The sewer doesn't run anywhere near here. Who are you really?'

'It's true, we're council engineers. Perhaps someone made a mistake, yes, that must be it...' Toby was gabbling and trying to work out what to do. 'Please let go of my colleague. We haven't done anything. If you don't believe us, call our office.'

The man loosened his grip a little, which was enough for Clive to break free and run towards Toby. The man yelled after him; as he did so, a door opened in the opposite corner and light flooded in from the street above, outlining the large silhouette of a man. It was Johan du Toit.

'What's going on, who is in here?'

Du Toit could not make out the identity of the figures in the gloom and Toby and Clive took the opportunity to scramble back up the basement stairs.

'Oi! Who are you?' du Toit shouted again, but the men had managed to escape and were running for the front door of the school. They pelted through the corridors, adrenaline pumping. Toby caught sight of a bookshelf perched on a low table and pulled it with all his strength to the floor behind him. The contents scattered, creating enough chaos to slow down their pursuers and they made it to the front door. The sun outside was blinding, so, as they tripped out onto the pavement, they could not at first make out the scene that awaited them.

'Toby, over here!' a voice shouted.

Toby shielded his eyes as they adjusted and he could make out his father waving him over to the other side of the street.

'Pop!' Toby and Clive ran over to him. As they turned back to face the school, they saw the two men emerge, similarly blinded, into the waiting arms of the police.

'Foolish man parked his pick-up right here!' Mr Spencer smiled. They turned around to where Toby's father was pointing, and saw a large group of men in uniforms lifting out the contents of the pick-up. 'When I called the police to report it, they told me there had been suspicions that something was going on in that school. Something about a bribed policeman being caught out. Looks like quite a haul. Well done, chaps!'

Piece by piece the policemen removed the items from beneath their tarpaulin shroud – two dead lions, several monkeys, a pangolin and around half a dozen large tusks. Toby felt his knees give way and he slid to the ground. Clive was bent forwards, catching his breath and trying to stop his uncontrollable shaking. They watched as Ali and du Toit were handcuffed and led to a police car and driven swiftly away to their fate.

'I won't forget this!' Du Toit suddenly yelled over to the men. 'You can count on it, you bastards, you haven't heard the last of me.'

'Never liked the fellow. Hope they throw the book at him,' scoffed Mr Spencer. 'Now, chaps. Fancy a Tusker after all that?'

CHAPTER 12

NAIROBI 1963

BARBARA sighed as she pressed the final clasp of her suitcases and took a last look around the room she had shared with her sister for nearly two years. Christmas was approaching and, along with it, the inevitable family obligations. Their parents were sending a car to take them back to their house in Karen. After the break, Sheila was due to leave her job, which would naturally mean a change of accommodation for them both.

Barbara left her cases stacked up in a corner of the foyer and went to join her sister in the common room for a last cup of tea. Surrounding them were photographs of celebrations and familiar faces from their days at the hostel. They had been some of the happiest times of Barbara's life – her first taste of freedom and of making true friendships, of learning about the world outside her cloistered youth. She was ready for change – she was always ready for change, but it was still a sad day.

'All set?' asked Sheila, looking up at Barbara and laying down the magazine she had been reading.

Barbara smiled, but she was very uneasy about returning to their parents. 'Yes, all ready. How are you feeling about it?'

'Well, I'm not going alone, am I? I've got Toby coming up for Christmas too.'

Toby and Sheila had been inseparable over the last few months and, as his family had gone to spend Christmas with relatives in England, he had been readily invited to join the Dunbar-Watts' celebrations.

'I'm going to tell them about Clive. I've decided,' said Barbara as she sat down hard opposite her sister.

'Are you sure that's wise? You haven't been seeing him for very long.'

'Well, it's as long as you've been seeing Toby. Anyway, I don't care. They keep foisting that awful Maurice on me and it has to stop. I'm not marrying him, no matter how much they might wish it. It's my life and they really aren't all that interested in me anyway.' She picked at the skin around her fingernails, avoiding any eye contact with Sheila.

'They just won't have it though. If you decide to throw your lot in with Clive, that will be that.'

'So what? I'm earning my own living now, such as it is. I didn't even rely on their holy connections to get the job, I've done it all myself. What difference will it make to them who I marry? They'll just continue having their parties, and carry on gossiping and judging.'

'Yes, you're right, but listen to me, please. Now, you know I will always be here for you. I think Clive is just the nicest man. After Toby, of course!' She smiled at Barbara. 'But it's not just about them, is it? It will never be easy – you know that, no matter how determined you are. How many people do you know in mixed-race marriages?' She didn't wait for an answer. 'None. It is completely unheard of here. Completely taboo. As far as Ma and Papa are concerned, you couldn't do a worse thing than marry a Black man, and a Kikuyu at that. You know how they feel about the Kikuyu since Mau Mau.' She reached over and took Barbara's hand. 'I just worry that, through it all, you've forgotten what you'll be giving up. Because you will have to.'

'Well, that's their issue – they can never see past the colour of a person's skin, or their parent's job, or how things will look to other people. I've had enough of that,' said Barbara. 'So it happens that the man you love ticks all their boxes and my man doesn't. But I won't give him up. Life in their world doesn't make me happy, so why would I choose it over the man I love? And I do really love him, Sheila. He's the most gentle, intelligent, honourable person I know, and I want to spend my life with him. I want to have adventures and make something good with my life, our lives. I feel excited, not worried. Can you understand that?'

Sheila eyes were rimmed red, but she smiled at her sister. 'I do, sweetheart. And you will always have a home with Toby and me, no matter what. Well, why not see this holiday as a bit of a last hoorah? Have a lovely time, don't pick a fight with them. Go to the parties, pass round the canapés. Then tell them gently, before you come back to the city. No drama – just tell them and go.'

'I'll bear that in mind, but do you really think there will be no drama?' Barbara smiled.

She came downstairs at the last possible moment before her absence would become noticeably rude. Her parents' parties always followed the same sequence of events. She could tell, even before going downstairs what stage it would be at now. Her father, Douglas (or 'Punch'), would be holding court over a sea of fawning faces. Her mother, Felicity, who could drink the most hardened man under the table, would be directing proceedings, ensuring that the people she considered the most interesting or provocative would be put together and then plied with alcohol.

Strains of their favourite samba music were floating through from the terrace, incongruous at this New Year celebration in the heart of Africa, and slightly out of tune. Familiar faces that Barbara remembered from all the parties in Karen, in Lamu, filled the rooms. If not the exact same people, they looked the same: flawless tans, skinny women with prim coiffured hair, men in expensive linen suits. The only Black faces belonged to the staff and the band. The food was the same as always – elegant, French or Mediterranean, nothing native.

Barbara stood on the veranda with her back against the cool concrete wall, nursing a large gin and tonic. Her father and mother were surrounded by a semi-circle of their old cronies. She loathed them – the men's hearty laughter and pawing hands, the women giggling coquettishly and over-acting their amusement. All of them drunk on their own fabulousness.

She saw her mother stiffen as she cast a sideways glance in Barbara's direction. Perhaps it was her outfit. Barbara couldn't resist a little rebelliousness and was wearing a dress she had adapted from a Vogue pattern, using a bold orange African fabric and trimmed with Maasai beading. She finished off the ensemble with an oversized beaded choker. The rest of the party wore flowing organza and chiffon, with delicate and expensive jewels. She returned her mother's disapproving look with a raise of her glass and turned to go back into the house. She wanted to chat to Ethel who worked in the kitchen, she could reminisce about childhood mischiefs while helping Ethel with the dishes. From nowhere, her father appeared at her elbow.

'Come now, Barbara. You're being very neglectful of Maurice. Why don't you fetch him a glass of wine and come with me?'

'Let go of me, Papa.' Barbara wriggled out of his grip. 'I will bring him a drink, but then I am going upstairs. I have a headache coming on.'

'Don't be ridiculous. You know how much trouble your mother has gone to with this party. You haven't been home for months. You need to show a little respect. So, you'll come with me, smile and be polite. Your sister can manage it, why can't you?'

Barbara fell into step with her father, swiped two drinks from a proffered tray, drank from one swiftly and held out the other to Maurice. 'Maurice, darling! Please have a drink. How have you been. How is the banking business?'

Maurice, either too shocked or too self-absorbed to read the sarcasm in her voice, readily replied. 'It's all good, actually, Babs. We are in the middle of a merger with an Indian firm, actually, so busy, busy.'

'Are you? Actually. *Morry*. What is the purpose of this merger, then? Is it going to bring economies of scale to both parties, resulting in fewer costs and thereby benefiting your borrowers and their businesses? Or is it just going to make you and the shareholders oodles of money?' Barbara stared at him challengingly, over the top of her glass. Maurice looked back at her, face suddenly pale and perplexed, then at the floor, then he turned to Toby for masculine support.

'You didn't answer me, Morry,' she tapped him on the shoulder.

'Oh, um, yes, sorry. I didn't realise you were serious,' he stuttered.

'I'm quite serious. After all, what is your motivation? You seem very pleased with yourself, so I thought it must be a very altruistic thing, this merger.'

'Barbara,' interrupted Toby, 'I think Sheila wanted to talk to you. I believe she is over near the pool, if you come with me, I can take you to her and she can say whatever it was she…'

'Smooth, Toby. Very smooth.' Barbara took a last slug of her drink and followed him to find Sheila. 'I'm sorry, Toby, but that man brings out the worst in me. I can't look at him without resorting to sarcasm. It's like I'm allergic or something.' There was a giggle in her voice.

'Yes, well, for the sake of good form and Sheila's feelings, I thought it best to break it up.'

'Why Sheila's feelings?'

'We are about to make an announcement, and I didn't want you buggering it up, alright?'

'An announcement? Oh, Toby, I'm thrilled. Good for you. Right, I need to talk to Sheila. Now!'

Barbara was grateful for the change of atmosphere at the party. The mood of the guests shifted from self-conscious cool to genuine delight at the announcement of the engagement. With one more swift gin, and judging the jovial mood of her parents, Barbara felt bolstered enough to share her own news.

She took her mother aside and whispered. 'Ma, I'm glad you're so happy that Sheila has found love. I am too. She deserves nothing less. But you see, I have too. Found love, I mean. His name is Clive, he is a journalist in Nairobi and although there is nothing official to announce yet, I plan to spend my life with him.'

'But Maurice, does he know?'

'Ma, I don't know why you persist with this. Maurice and I have never even gone out properly together. Since childhood, I only ever see him at your parties or those of your friends. I'm sure he has much bigger prizes than me in mind anyway.' She had seen Maurice a few minutes earlier with a freckly brunette, the heiress to a transport firm, quite absorbed in her conversation.

'Well, this Clive. Where is he from? Karen, Westlands, or is he from England, is he based out here? Do we know his people?'

'No, you don't. He is from Naivasha. And he doesn't work for the *Times* or the *Telegraph*. He works for a small local paper. But he has an interview with the *Daily Nation* next week. Anyway, his full name is Clive Chege.' She waited a moment for the significance of this to sink in. It only took a split second.

Without taking her eyes off Barbara, Felicity said in a commanding voice that homed in on her husband, 'Punch, come here please, your *other* daughter has something to tell you.' Felicity bundled her daughter into the study, joined moments later by Punch and Nigel. The three of them encircled Barbara as she stood against the wall. 'Right, young lady, explain,' her mother spat the words.

'You didn't tell them, then?' Barbara asked her brother, who smiled smugly, drawing on a cigarette. 'I thought you'd have enjoyed telling them about our meeting in Naivasha.'

'Oh, I'm enjoying this much more,' said Nigel, perching on the side of an armchair. 'Go on, spill.'

'Alright. The man you saw me with in Naivasha, Clive Chege, is the man I love.' The words tumbled from her mouth in a rush and she felt both fear and relief at saying them. 'I am not going to marry Maurice. I am going to marry Clive. We love each other.'

Her family stood in silence, so she ploughed on. 'We will get married in the summer and live in the city. Clive is very focussed and ambitious and, believe it or not, the rest of Kenya is moving on and changing with the times. And we are…'

'You are disgusting,' her mother said, her face truly horrified.

'Disgusting? How can we be disgusting? Clive is a good man. He's noble and hard-working. He practically brought up all his brothers and sisters...'

'Oh, I bet there were hordes of them. They breed like rats,' said her father. 'Has he had his way with you yet? Have you actually let him touch you?'

'They… they what? Has… he…? I can't believe you would say something so utterly horrid. Well, that's made everything easier. I thought perhaps you would trust me to know my own mind; to give him a chance, but I can see what's important to you and it's not me. Excuse me.' She pushed past her mother and aimed for the door.

The rest of the night was spent in muttered fury, the senior Dunbar-Watts attempting to retain a measure of decorum at their party while chasing Barbara around the house with questions and accusations. They flitted adeptly between party chat and angry recriminations. Barbara had never had any illusions about what affect her announcement would have. She only felt regretful at spoiling the evening somewhat for Sheila and Toby. But Sheila was phlegmatic and Toby was kind as they helped her to pack and leave the house.

'Where will you go?' asked Sheila.

'To Clive, of course. It's all planned. It's not as though I expected anything different.' Barbara found herself feeling quite calm – an almost ethereal peace enveloped her now that she had made her choice.

'But where will you live? You can hardly live with Clive.'

'We'll get married. Like I said, it's all planned. He's bound to get this job at the *Nation.* He's found a new apartment outside town which I'm sure I can move into and I can carry on at the

Game Department. Really, we are not doing anything revolutionary.'

'You know that's a very naïve thing to say and you don't actually believe it,' said Sheila sternly. 'Have you thought how this will affect Clive? He has family, a reputation, a job. They will all be affected.'

'Of course, I have. Neither of us are under any misapprehensions. But we're happy in each other's company. Really, truly happy. You know me better than anyone, Sheila. You can see how I feel, can't you?'

'Yes, I can. But I can also predict how hard this will be for both of you. But you have my blessing, such as it is. I love you dearly and I think Clive is a wonderful man. You are both always welcome at Taita Hills. But please be cautious. The world – especially this world – is not kind to rebels.'

Barbara kissed her sister and took her bags out to the waiting taxi. Only once she had waved a cheerful goodbye to Sheila and Toby – arm in arm on the front porch – and driven down the long drive and out of the gates guarded by askaris, did she allow herself to cry.

Barbara was waiting for Clive when he arrived back from Naivasha. His sister, Jata, had just had another baby, so he had spent the Christmas break with her and her family. His flat was in a new gated complex that had been designed for office workers. The askari at the gate was under strict instructions not to let any non-residents without passes into the complex, but this kind young man sympathised with Barbara's plight and let her sit in the cool of his office until Clive's arrival. When he did arrive, his old cowhide satchel over one shoulder, he looked taken aback at the sight of Barbara and her luggage waiting for him.

'Has something happened, Barbara? You look awful,' he said,

picking up her suitcase and nodding his thanks to the askari. He led her through a courtyard and into the building.

'It's fine. I'm fine. I've just come from my parents'. I'm afraid I stormed out.'

'Oh dear.' Clive opened an internal door for her to pass through.

'And of course, I'm homeless since Sheila and I left the hostel. I am meant to be taking rooms in Westlands next week, but for now I haven't anywhere to go.'

They reached his apartment. Barbara had never been in it before. It was as tidy as she had expected, and tiny – only two rooms, but immaculately clean and sparsely decorated. The only picture on the wall was a large painting of an African landscape. She recognised it as Lake Naivasha and remembered their time together there with a pang of nostalgia. Why couldn't all their days be like that – perfect – just them and the wildlife?

'Did you paint that?' she asked.

He nodded with a look of slight embarrassment. 'It's not very good.'

'I knew it the moment I saw it. The view from your kopje.' She continued to stare at the painting.

He changed the subject. 'Alright. Well, I tell you what. I have a colleague on the paper who lives alone. She might be able to put you up for a while.'

Barbara nodded, biting her lip. She was almost hoping for a racier suggestion, she ached for Clive. She wanted nothing more than to throw herself at him and for the world to leave them alone. 'I couldn't live by their rules any more, Clive,' she said, in a voice more determined sounding than she felt. 'I know I should be grateful for my good life, my education. But do I have to show my gratitude by being their idea of a model wife? They don't care if I'm happy, just so long as I marry the "right" sort of person, a person who makes them look good and benefits them. It's all so mediaeval. My God, it's the sixties!'

'You don't need to convince me. I believe in you and I think you'll succeed in whatever you choose to do, but they are your family and family rifts cannot easily be healed.'

'I'm sorry, I know that your family had a terrible time during Mau Mau. But I'm not doing anything awful to anyone. I love you and my country and I love working. Most of my friends left Kenya as soon as they could once Independence was confirmed. I'm not actually doing any harm by being with the man I love and trying to carve out a life of my own. Why can't they understand that?'

'They don't know you like I do. They don't know how good and determined and special you are. But I don't want to cause a wedge between you and your parents.'

Barbara looked at him, shocked. 'You're not the cause. My God, Clive, if you have caused anything, you have caused me to be a better person. I'm more thoughtful, more ambitious, more sympathetic because you are and I admire those qualities. The things I want are the things we have together. I don't want money and parties. I want to be part of this exciting new world they keep promising us.' She shook her head, shaking out her frustration at this world which promised change, but didn't account for people like her parents who railed against it.

'Come here.' He pulled her close and kissed her. They stood for a while, just holding one another, feeling the warmth of each other's bodies. Then Clive said quietly. 'This isn't the big romantic scene I would have planned, but… will you marry me?'

Barbara heard his voice deep through his chest where she rested her cheek. She stood quite still for several moments, then looked up at him, her chin pressed against the knot of his brown tie. Still, she said nothing.

'I… I'm sorry…' stuttered Clive. 'It's too much to ask. It's impossible. I know that. It's just that I… well, I love you very much and… sorry, no of course not.' He started to push down on her arms that were still tightly wrapped around his waist, but she held fast.

'Clive, I thought you would never get up the guts. I nearly had to ask you myself, for goodness sake!' Her face flushed and she launched herself at him in giggly kisses.

CHAPTER 13

NAIROBI 1964

BARBARA and Clive focused on their jobs over the next three chaste months as they waited for the marriage certificate to be authorised. Clive's position at the *Daily Nation* started to take him abroad, causing more delays to a wedding date. As a reporter for science and nature issues, he managed to persuade his editor that it was important not only to report on what was happening in modern-day Kenya, but also to draw comparisons with other countries in Africa. The paper was keen to promote the message of Kenya's forward-looking attitudes and aspirations, so his editor acquiesced.

For Clive, this meant an opportunity to look at issues from a broader perspective. He wrote a piece on the effects of the fashion industry on animal welfare, and had met with Joy Adamson, author of the hugely popular memoir *Born Free*. The Adamsons' work had begun to have an effect that stretched beyond Africa, and Clive could sense that conservation issues were beginning to gather momentum. As Toby had thought, old-style hunting was becoming passé. More and more filmmakers and photographers were coming to Kenya, and in their wake, increased numbers of tourists were beginning to take an interest in Africa's unique and extraordinary wildlife. The more his investigations revealed about the current state of his country's wild animals and places, the stronger his feelings became for the need to expose their exploitation and need for protection.

Barbara's job at the Game Department was demanding and fulfilling, and she enjoyed the company of her colleagues who, as rugged ex-military types, were a world away from her family and their social set. Nevertheless, at the back of her mind was the offer that Toby had made her and the possibility that she could be right on the ground, helping to revive an area to its full potential. As a privately owned estate, Toby's farm would not be subject to the same frustrating regulations and inter-departmental dogfights which plagued the game parks. And, in particular, there would be no sweeping culls.

* * *

'Well, come out, let me see!'

Sheila sat on Barbara's sofa with Clive's sisters Jata and Njeri. Barbara entered the room, unable to stop grinning. Sheila was staring at her, her hand at her mouth.

'What? What is it? Do I look ridiculous? Was it a mistake? You see I wanted the dress to represent both our cultures. Does it work? Oh, Sheila, say something!'

'Oh, Barbara, it's amazing! You are so clever and it's just beautiful!' Sheila wiped the tears from under her eyes, blotting the running mascara. She stood to give Barbara a squeeze – gently, so as not to crease the pale-yellow silk.

'I copied it from a picture of Jean Shrimpton in *Harper's Bazaar*! But Inira is clever too.' Barbara turned to face Clive's third sister who had followed Barbara into the room, wielding a pair of scissors. She gave a delighted nod of thanks. 'Inira hand-dyed the fabric for my headband and cuffs using traditional Kikuyu techniques. And look!' She patted her neck. 'You see all the tiny cowrie shells? We were up until midnight sewing these on!'

'It does work, the burnt orange and the ochre are the colours of Africa. And such happy colours. Oh, Barbara, I'm so happy for you!'

'Well, for heaven's sake, stop crying then!'

* * *

Barbara had no desire to cry. As she sat in the car with Sheila and Toby, taking them from Westlands into the city for the ceremony, she realised she had never been so happy. Despite the obstacles, here they were.

'You're remarkably calm!' Sheila laughed.

Barbara nodded. 'I am, because it's right. It's just so completely right. Being married to Clive is all I want. Obviously, the wedding's not a big society do like yours was, I'm afraid.'

'So what, we're different people. I loved our wedding of course; I felt like a princess.' She squeezed Toby's hand and they smiled at each other. 'But what matters is the promise you make to each other in front of the people who love you.'

'Clive loves you; I wish he could have been at your wedding.'

'So do we and you know that I tried, but Ma and Papa wouldn't have it. It was just too soon. They'll come around.'

'They won't. You know that. Do you think they'll be there? At the registry office?'

'I don't know, sweetheart.'

It was too much to hope, Barbara supposed. She knew that they were angry at her choice of husband, but she was still their daughter. She had sent them an invitation, made all the arrangements. Would they come?

'At least I've got Toby to give me away!' She smiled at Toby who blew her a kiss.

'You know I'll want you right back again, we need you at Taita!'

* * *

The registry office was bustling with people; a baby was crying in the Registrar of Births office and a large party of wedding guests came running down the stairs, cheering as they spilt out into the street. Toby headed up the stairs to find Clive, and Barbara and Sheila were ushered into a small anteroom. Inira joined them, handing them each a small bouquet, before helping Barbara to straighten her dress.

'They're the colours of the new Kenya, do you see?' Barbara said to Sheila as she smoothed her hand over her bouquet. 'Red roses for the blood shed, green leaves for the land, white lilies for peace and the black ribbon for the colour of the people.'

Sheila gave her a kiss and whispered, 'Every happiness, my darling sister.'

There was a knock at the door and a smartly dressed young woman entered holding out a telegram. 'I'm sorry to interrupt,' she said, 'but I was told to give you this right away.' She handed the telegram to Barbara and left. Inira crept into the ceremony room next door.

'Do I open it now? Do you think it's urgent or just a well-wisher?'

'Well, she said she had to give it to you right away,' said Sheila. 'I suppose it must be important. But it's up to you.'

Barbara tore at the paper and read the contents. She could feel her heart beat faster and her arms felt weak.

'What does it say?' asked Sheila taking Barbara's elbow.

'Here. Read it. It's from Papa.' She handed the note to Barbara and fell into a chair.

Sheila read out loud. '"Barbara STOP there is still time to end this STOP go ahead and you can never come home STOP". Oh Barbara,' she passed back the telegram. 'I'm so sorry. I knew they wouldn't come; it would be too much to expect that, too public. But I did think they would send their love.'

'Well, that's that then.' Barbara stood and patted at her hair. 'Don't look at me that way, Sheila. I'm quite alright. Right, shall we go?'

Strength had returned to her limbs, but inside she felt shattered. She had never lived up to her parents' expectations; indeed they seemed to barely notice her. Nigel was every bit like his father and Sheila had always been so sweet and good and had never given them cause for confrontation. Barbara had always felt like a misfit – the interloper of the family destined to drift away from them.

The music started and an official opened the door which led to the ceremony room. Toby entered and slipped Barbara's arm through the crook of his elbow, giving her shaking hand a squeeze. Sheila turned towards the room and began the procession; Barbara, holding tight to Toby, walked straight and tall towards her beaming bridegroom.

A few weeks later they drove, in a car borrowed from Toby, down to the coast for their honeymoon. Barbara had made the booking – rebooked twice because of two work assignments in a row which had taken Clive to Southern Africa. The day was perfect – clear blue skies, warm not hot, and a gentle cool breeze wafting over from the azure sea held the humidity at bay. The hotel was very fashionable and Barbara had often met up there with friends, although had never stayed there, as her parents' hotel was further up the beach. Nevertheless, the concierge recognised and welcomed her as she and Clive walked into the lobby.

'Miss Barbara, how nice to see you. It's been a few years since we saw you here.' The concierge helped her with her case. 'I must tell Mr Huntley that you're here. He will want to pass on his regards to your parents. Please just wait here for a moment.'

'Oh, William, there's really no need…' Barbara called futilely as the man disappeared into the office. He returned a moment later, accompanied by a small, wispy man in his sixties, dressed in linen shorts and a loose pink shirt. 'Why Barbara,' he said. 'I didn't know you were visiting. Why do we have the pleasure of your company? Is the Flamingo full up? Surely not for you!' He smiled and shook her hand effusively. 'And who are you with?'

Clive had been standing beside Barbara and held out his

hand to the man. 'Sir, my name is Clive Chege. I am Barbara's husband.'

The man seemed not to have noticed Clive's presence until this moment. He gasped and looked bewildered. 'But... you are...' With sudden realisation, the man's expression changed from effusive to furious. 'But Barbara, are you trying to make a fool of me? What is this?'

'What is what, Mr Huntley? Clive is my husband. We were married last month and I have booked us a chalet for the week.'

'I'm afraid that is quite impossible.'

'Mr Huntley, I hope you are not refusing us a stay. Kenya is independent now; Clive has every right to...'

'This is my hotel and I decide on the clientele. I'm afraid your Kenya is more modern than mine or that of my clientele. I'm going to have to ask you to leave.'

'But we've paid, you can't do this. Clive I'm so sorry, I had not realised Mr Huntley would be so ignorant or so racist.' Barbara's tone was rising.

'Barbara, it's alright,' Clive said, calmly, taking her hand to lead her away. 'Let's just get our money back and stay somewhere else.'

'It is not alright! How dare he?' By now she was shouting.

'Miss Dunbar-Watts, if you continue to make a scene, I will have to call the police,' Mr Huntley said sharply, without raising his voice.

'My name is *Mrs* Chege, and you can call the police, we are not doing anything illegal.'

'You are causing an affray in my hotel. Again, I ask you politely to leave.'

'Come, Barbara. It will only spoil things to persevere. I don't want to remember our honeymoon like that. Let's go and we'll sort something else out.'

Defeated and furious, Barbara took the cash from William and they headed back to the car. She was overcome with fury and embarrassment and once back inside the car she burst into tears.

'How can you bear it? How do you not go mad when people are like that to you all the time? In your own damn country, for God's sake!'

'If I let it affect me I *would* go mad, so I try to remain polite, passive, and I suppose I box it away somehow. But I try to think of the bigger picture, of what I want to achieve and the best way to get there. Sometimes that means just biting my tongue.'

Barbara sniffed. Her indignation wasn't going to help Clive or find them somewhere to stay.

'I have a suggestion,' said Clive after a few moments.

'No one can stop us from pitching a tent on the beach and sleeping under the stars. Are you game?'

Barbara burst into tears again, but nodded and threw her arms around him.

After a week of camping on the beach, cooking crabs and red snapper over an open fire, swimming and sunbathing. They headed back onto the Mombasa Road, but veered off at the Voi turning and headed off to see Sheila and Toby at Taita Hills.

'Welcome, both!' Toby had seen the car arrive and came outside to greet them. 'How are you? How was the coast? Come, come, let me help you with the bags.' Toby and Clive each dragged a suitcase from the boot, and Barbara gathered up a pile of gifts from the back seat. 'Sheila's prepared a feast fit for Dionysus, but perhaps not so debauched. We have become very tame despite our wild surroundings. Bed by nine, up at five. Come on in!'

The house had clearly benefited from Sheila's artistic and practical touches, and the resulting atmosphere was much more tranquil and comfortable than at their visit the previous year. Sheila hadn't quite shaken off the habit of surrounding herself with the finer things of life that she had grown up with, and Barbara spotted a few expensive paintings and ornaments purloined from their parents' homes.

'Sheila, this is beautiful, what a lot of work you've put into it,' exclaimed Barbara as she looked around.

'Let me show you your rooms.' Sheila took Barbara's arm and led her to the east wing of the house. 'They will be let out to our paying guests soon. We have our first booking coming up next month.' They reached the guest bedroom which opened straight out onto a veranda and an astonishing view beyond. 'Just imagine the sunrises as you sit here with your binoculars and your first coffee of the day! We've made everything terribly nice, but then we're hoping to attract people who will be paying us handsomely for a wonderful experience, and those sorts of people are accustomed to things being a certain way.'

'You can take the girl out of Karen…!' teased Barbara. 'Sorry, it is just stunning. You've done a wonderful job. I am going to enjoy the luxury after I shake all the sand out of my clothes!'

'Oh, you love roughing it, don't kid me!' laughed Sheila.

'I do. In fact, the city is starting to get to me, rather. But let's not talk about that now. I want to hear all your stories of married life, then I might tell you mine!'

Toby and Clive had been talking together at one end of the table and the sisters at the other, but now they had finished eating and the conversation turned from catching up with news, to thoughts of the future.

'So, Barbara, any more thoughts about the job here? I can't offer to pay you much, but your experience and your famous organisational skills would be very much valued here.'

'I have – well, we both have – been thinking about it a lot. I do enjoy my job, and Clive's paper is in the city, but it is getting harder to live there in other ways.'

'In what ways?' asked Sheila.

'Well, there is the small matter of our marriage. It seems that for all it professes to be a groovy, modern city,' Barbara smiled at Clive as she said this, 'Nairobi struggles with the concept that two people of different colour might actually not just be friends, but lovers.' Her expression darkened. 'They are just not very nice to us. We don't often get invited to parties, and if we do, we seem to be the subject of astonishment – a sort of exhibit. We are both rather tired of it – of having to be pioneers for interracial marriage. Sometimes we just want to be seen as an ordinary couple.'

'I'm so sorry to hear that, chaps,' said Toby softly.

'There is another reason that our current domestic arrangements will not suit us for long.' Barbara looked up at Sheila, who immediately read the cryptic look in Barbara's face.

'Oh, Barbara! How thrilling, when?'

Toby was a little slower to catch on, then realised and immediately reached over to shake Clive's hand. 'Oh, old chap, that's fantastic news!'

'It's due in April. I have told them at work and given notice. Beyond that, we don't really know what to do.'

'Well, you must move here. It's perfect!' said Sheila, throwing her arms around her sister. 'I can help with the baby. And there is much more room for you here.'

'Slow down, Sheila!' said Barbara, gently pushing her away. 'It *would* be perfect to have the baby here, but it would mean Clive and I seeing even less of each other.'

'Yes, it would, mpenzi,' said Clive, reaching for her hand. 'But it would be much better for you to be here than alone in our flat with a new baby. I'm away from the office so much anyway, I can ask if I can be based here some of the time. It's worth asking, isn't it?'

'Yes, of course it is. Do you really think they might let you?' Barbara smiled. The issue had been niggling away at her throughout their holiday, but now she looked at the three encouraging faces smiling at her, she let the worries float away.

She loved this place. Even though she had visited only a handful of times, it had got under her skin. It was as though the natural world outside made the clocks stop and all worries about work, politics and other people become superficial and trivial, as something more primal enveloped you. Life here could be simple and real. Throughout her life, Barbara had felt a gulf between her parents and upbringing, and the person she felt she truly was; here was where she could be herself. Loving her man and her child, doing something productive and important without battling provincial attitudes. Despite her privileges, and because of them, she would always be judged for not taking the path expected of her. This would be a wonderful place to raise a family. It was wild and exciting but also peaceful and nurturing. There were children and other mothers in the village nearby. They would be far from the city and its prejudices and the lonely and stifling existence of living in a municipal apartment.

'But the job?' Barbara, directed this at Toby. 'How could I do it? I'm sorry, I feel like I'm letting you down.'

'Not at all. If you are up for the challenge, you can start when you like. Why not combine working with us with bringing up baby? I'm sure one of the local girls would be able to help with some of the less exciting parts of motherhood to help free you up a bit. It seems pretty perfect to me.'

'Go on, then, if it's alright with Clive, then yes, I'll do it!'

'Of course, it's alright with me. And thank you, Toby and Sheila for making it possible. I think you'll make quite a team!' The group raised their glasses and toasted to the future of the farm.

* * *

On their return to the city, Barbara and Clive spent the next few months preparing for the birth. Barbara worked out her notice, then moved with the first of their belongings to the farm. Clive had to travel to Mozambique in the spring, but had agreed some leave in April to finalise arrangements and to join Barbara for the birth. Sheila clucked around Barbara like a mother hen as the birth got closer.

'I feel bad that we have taken over the "royal suite!"' Barbara half-joked, as the sisters sat on the floor of the guest bedroom sorting baby clothes.

'Don't be silly.' Sheila gave her a squeeze on the arm. 'I want you to have it. There are plenty of other rooms for the guests, and Toby has big plans for building a suite of luxury huts over by the escarpment. This will just speed things along. It was never going to be ideal having guests staying in our house. And I am so excited thinking of you sitting up here, nesting with your baby, looking down on Africa like some beautiful bird.'

'Like a vulture!' laughed Barbara.

'No! Like an eagle! Oh, I don't know.' She tossed a bonnet at her sister. 'How long until Clive gets here?'

'About three weeks, I think. He is in some remote part of Mozambique at the moment, and will stop in Dar es Salaam on the way back, to report into the Tanganyikan office before heading here. He needs to submit his article before he can take the time off.'

'It's all so exotic. But I bet you can't wait to see him.'

'I miss him so much when he's away, but it will be all the easier being here with you. When are you going to start a family?'

Barbara caught an almost imperceptible wince on Sheila's face when Toby walked in and reminded them that lunch was on the table.

CHAPTER 14

TAITA HILLS 1965

ROBERT Maina Chege (Maina for his paternal grandfather, as was Kikuyu custom, Robert just because Barbara liked the name) slipped into the world oblivious to the controversy which surrounded him.

Barbara had awoken early to a wild slapping noise and rose to close the shutters. Stopping to watch the restlessness of the weather outside, she twitched with agitation. She knew this was the day. The baby wasn't due for another week, but she knew. An electric sensation bloomed from her abdomen to the back of her shoulders, making her stand straight and firm, feeling both apprehensive and inexplicably calm. She could wake Clive, who had arrived home the morning before, but for now, solitude was what she craved. This would be her last time completely alone and she wanted to cherish it.

She tiptoed across the house to the kitchen and prepared herself a little tray, neatly set out with a cup of ginger tea, a plate of toast with honey, a glass of orange juice and a banana. Settling down to eat at the dining table, ready to devour her breakfast, she suddenly lost her appetite. An urge to keep moving overcame her, so she headed downstairs to the staff quarters to rouse Rosa, the housekeeper, taking a piece of toast to nibble as she did so.

'Rosa,' she whispered as she gently rapped on her bedroom door. 'Are you awake?'

'Yes, Mama, are you alright? Is it the baby? Oh dear, Mama.' Rosa jumped out of bed and put on her housecoat, opening the door as she tied the cord. 'Please, Mama Barbara, sit down here on my bed.'

'I'm fine, but I'm sure it's coming. Can you send someone to the town to get the midwife? I'd rather she were here sooner rather than later.'

'Of course, you leave it with me. Do you want to stay here, or can I help you back upstairs?'

'I'd like to go back up, if you don't mind. Please get dressed, though. I'll be alright for a few minutes.'

Rosa dressed then lifted Barbara off the bed with a practised arm. 'There, now. Pole pole. We shall go up. I shall get Mama Sheila and I will send Issa to get the midwife. You just take your time, mpenzi.' Rosa was much smaller than Barbara, but took her weight without flinching, as Barbara leant into her with the first grip of pain. They stopped on the stairs and Rosa stood back while Barbara clenched the thin wooden banister, knuckles white, back arched, dropping her toast. The contraction passed and they continued.

'There we go,' murmured Rosa as they reached the sitting room. 'Sit here. It's dark and cool. You rest awhile and I'll sort everything out.' She left the room, but returned with Barbara's tray. 'You've already been busy this morning!' she laughed, as she set the tray down. 'Now you try to eat some more. You will need it for strength. If you need to walk around, walk around. Your body is very powerful and it will tell you what to do, alright?' Rosa left quietly, closing the door behind her.

Barbara went to take another slice of toast, but felt bile rise in her throat and put it down again. This time the contraction hit her with the force of a punch, and she slipped forward, losing her grip on the arm of the settee, landing down on the floor. She crouched face down and found her balance, placing her hands on the rug and her knees on the floor. As the contraction subsided, she had the sensation that she had climbed a tall hill and her ears had not yet popped; sounds were muffled and distant. Through the fug, she could make out noises around her and sensed a hub-bub; people were entering the room and saying things to her, but they seemed far away, calling to her from the land as she bobbed about at sea, stranded. Many voices filled the room now, and the air of concern rose to one of panic. Someone mentioned blood. An arm across her back steadied her and she allowed her head to drop forward, screwing her eyes shut to focus. An urge to rock took her over and she began to swing back and forward. In the far distance she could hear the sound of singing nearing her and her rocking fell in time with it.

'Here we are, Mama.' Rosa's gentle voice was followed by a deeper Scottish brogue which approached her.

'Keep going Mrs Chege, you're doing marvellously. Now, Daddy, is it? You just go out of the room and keep out of the way for a little while. Go and fetch us lots of cloths, big and small. Mrs Chege and I will be just fine.' Barbara sensed a cool hand on her forehead and felt the woman adjust her nightie to examine her.

'Good, good. All is well, my dear. I'm Miss Stewart. The baby is crowning already. There will be no time for you to finish your breakfast, I'm afraid!'

Barbara was soothed by the woman's brusqueness, but couldn't reply, she could think of nothing but this moment, this task, eyes clamped shut, willing away all the chatter. Again, she heard the singing. It was closer now, just below the windows. In the song were thousands of years of strength, love, sisterhood; grandmothers, mothers and daughters. It was the song of lions and birds, of the wind in the trees, rain and rivers, of wise mother elephants and the fierce love of cheetahs. Barbara reached into her pocket and pulled out a tiny lapis lazuli elephant which Clive had given her on their wedding day as her 'something blue'. She rocked and swayed and clutched the elephant, squeezing it with each contraction, the sweet voices from outside filling her with power and courage. She let out a roar, and in its echo came a tiny but determined cry of protest.

Clive ran into the room, just in time to see his son emerge. Tiny, curly-haired and, Barbara was certain, smiling.

'A boy, Mrs Chege! You have a son. Well done, you clever girl.

Congratulations, Mr Chege! Now that you are here, would you like to cut the cord?'

Clive nodded shyly, took the proffered scissors and cut where the midwife pointed at a clamp. 'Yes. There? Thank you, thank you.'

'He's a beauty. Here.' Miss Stewart passed Clive his new son. 'You hold him while we get your wife comfortable. Turn around slowly Mrs Chege. Rosa has made a nice little nest for you over here on this rug. You just lie down and rest for a moment while I do the necessaries.' The midwife skilfully swept the baby out of Clive's arms, wiped him down and laid him out on a set of scales. 'Eight pounds, two ounces. That's a lovely weight. I'm sure you are rather glad you didn't go another week!'

She passed the baby back to Clive who laid him down into Barbara's waiting arms. 'Here, my wonderful girl. Look what you did. He's a miracle.' She took the baby from him gently and opened up her top to let him feed. Clive kissed her forehead, then went over to the window. The singing had stopped at the baby's first cry, but as Clive shouted down 'Ni kijana!' to the waiting women, a whoop resounded and the women ululated in celebration.

Clive turned to face Barbara. 'Five ululations for a boy. That is the tradition. They are full of joy for us.'

As he returned to wave his thanks at the window, two women stepped forward, holding out a large parcel. He lifted it from the women and looked at them questioningly. The elder of the two women waved him back inside, which he took to indicate that they wanted Barbara to unwrap it. Checking she was comfortable; Clive explained the parcel to Barbara as he placed it beside her on the floor. Her eyes filled with tears as she picked at the thin fabric strip which held the bundle together. It fell open to reveal dozens of little treasures. There were neatly folded, bold-printed fabrics, some left large, as kangas, some cut to a foot square, as nappies; there were beaded bracelets and tiny carved animals, cups and bowls and even a tiny, but sturdy, carved wooden stool.

'Oh, how kind!' exclaimed Barbara, exhaling all the tension she had held. She beamed, but her face was pink and damp from tears and sweat. 'They have made all these things. For us. How absolutely lovely.' She began to feel overwhelmingly tired and let go of the bundle.

'Shall I let the others in, or do you want to be left alone?' asked Clive.

'Could I have a little while, just me and him, please, then I will be ready to receive my adoring public!' Clive chuckled and stroked Barbara's hair from her face. 'Is that alright, nurse?' asked Barbara.

'I just need a bit of time with you to finish things off, but then I can leave you alone for a little while.'

'I'll bring the others in an hour, with some sustenance.' Clive kissed Barbara and the baby.

Final ministrations over, the midwife helped Barbara to lie on the settee – wrapping her and the baby snugly in blankets – and tidied up the room. As she readied to leave, she laid a cool hand on Barbara's shoulder.

'Good girl, look at you, you're a natural. I shall pop in again tomorrow to check on you, but let me know if you need me sooner. I am just at Dr Morgan's surgery in Kasigau, so you can reach me on the telephone. Now rest, love.'

The room was finally empty and Barbara looked down to study her new son. 'Oh, my darling. What a life we are going to have. We have big plans – adventure awaits!' She bent her head to kiss him and felt the downy curls on her lips; the soft, warm angles of his body nudged into hers. He finished feeding, but continued to make suckling faces which looked to Barbara like kisses. His eyes opened slowly and he turned to face her. She said nothing more but gazed into his clear, deep, brown eyes, flawless and knowing.

'You are very special, my darling. You have come from such love. No one will ever take that from you.'

* * *

Clive was able to stay at the farm for a week before returning to Nairobi, then had to travel on to Uganda. From now on, his work abroad became more frequent and for longer periods but, as they had hoped, his paper allowed him to take the occasional break to come home to spend time with Barbara and Robert. After a few months of concentrating on the baby and establishing a routine with him, Barbara gradually worked up to fitting some work in every day. Barbara, Toby and Sheila settled into their roles at the farm. Toby took charge of matters financial and technical; Sheila oversaw bookings and design and décor and Barbara took care of marketing and research. Each morning, she would feed and change Robert, have breakfast, then sit at the large wooden dining table with Robert's Moses basket beside her. This was wedged into a large chair, so that he could always see her face. He spent much of the morning sleeping like this, or batting at a mobile that one of the local children had made for him from wire, string and bottle tops.

Using her experience at the Game Department drawing up reports, Barbara correlated statistics from published articles on wildlife issues with reports from Toby and his team of rangers who made daily recces of the farm. From her contacts within the world of hospitality, she pulled together likely target customers. She organised her findings into a large folder and presented Toby one afternoon with a synopsis, laying out the best people to target as potential visitors to the farm and what they might be likely to see. They knew that there were very few wildebeest but many different antelope in the area. There were several types of giraffe and, importantly – the big draws – elephants, rhino and buffalo. They were not on a major migratory path here, so what they had to offer was not guaranteed epic views of large shifting herds, but rather the joys of small, surprising and unique wildlife experiences.

'This is great, Barbara,' said Toby as he thumbed through her report.

'I think we really need to focus on our birdlife,' stated Barbara. 'Not to the exclusion of everything else, but we have an abundance of birds and the bird-watching community is especially passionate, almost obsessive, really. They correspond internationally, so word spreads quickly if there is something special to see. So, I think they would be an ideal group to target.'

'We certainly have some unusual and beautiful specimens to boast about to the discerning bird-watcher!' agreed Toby. 'And they're happy to sit and wait for wildlife to appear. They won't expect drama at every turn.'

'I've started the ball rolling by contacting some old friends in Nairobi. We could have a bit of a launch party for some of our old friends to get things moving.'

'Good idea,' said Sheila. 'I can organise that.'

'Then I thought we could get some leaflets printed to leave at hotel lobbies and at the airport,' Barbara continued.

'Definitely. Thanks for this, Barbara. Great stuff. Let's do it!' said Toby, closing the report.

Barbara smiled and left the room to collect Robert from his nap. He was already awake as she crept in, and stared smiling at her.

'Hello, Bobby,' she whispered as she scooped him up. Rosa had put him down and, as always, insisted on putting a cap on his head. It had become almost a game between them – Rosa would put him down with a cap on and Barbara would remove it the moment she didn't risk waking him. Sometimes, like now, she would return and the cap was back on. 'Come my darling, let's get this off and pop some nice fresh clothes on you, then why don't we take a little walk?'

She swaddled him in a kanga, facing her, and headed out to see how Sheila had been getting on with her latest project. With the help of some men from the village, Sheila had converted some old farmworkers' quarters into smart and clean lodges. They would continue to use the house for dining, but the lodges would be sleeping and washing accommodation, and Sheila had made them beautiful. Toby had ambitions to build larger chalets as well as a large and impressive house to serve as the main building at the farm, but they agreed to start small, continuing to live in the farmhouse, and would eventually develop the site when they knew they'd have regular visitors.

Sheila had just sent the men home to get their lunch, and emerged from one of the lodges.

'Ooh, Barbara, do come and see what they've done. I'm so pleased with it!' Barbara followed Sheila into each lodge – it had been the first time she had been inside them, as Sheila had wanted to surprise her. Each one was different, each with a theme – birds, exploring, the sea, and, Barbara's favourite, elephants. Each bed was swathed with layers of coloured muslin to keep out mosquitoes, although they were at a high enough altitude for these to not be much of a problem. New concrete floors had been poured and polished and the bathrooms had been completely gutted and refitted with proper plumbing and expensive fittings. There were shelves packed with books, and the men had painted murals on the walls pertaining to the theme – a large colourful elephant, outlined thickly in black; a tree full of birds – lilac-breasted rollers, superb starlings, egrets and, soaring above, vultures; a beach with palm trees and tiny hermit crabs and large friendly turtles making their way back to sea; and a map of Africa, peppered with images of wildlife, trains, camels and surrounded by dhows and large sailing boats. Barbara was astonished at the skill.

'Oh, Sheila, they are simply marvellous! I think Bobby and I might move into the elephant one! What do you think, Bobby?'

Sheila laughed and they walked together back to the house, Sheila's arm slipped into Barbara's. 'It's all coming together, isn't it, sis? How lucky we are.'

CHAPTER 15

TAITA HILLS 1965

BUSINESS was slow for the first few months after the launch party, but as nature began to reclaim the farm, rewilding took hold and, a year later, they had an almost continual run of clientele staying in the lodges, and the farm had begun to turn a small profit. Their reputation for photographic safaris was growing, largely due to a couple of particularly knowledgeable rangers, Fidel and Jackson. Jackson had an encyclopaedic knowledge of his country's wildlife, especially of its birds, and Fidel had eyes as keen as a Verreaux's eagle and left tourists astonished at his ability to distinguish perfectly camouflaged, dun-coloured and stationary creatures from a distance of what seemed like miles.

December brought news, however, that would change their venture forever. Late one morning, an expensive car drew up outside the house. All the guests were out and Sheila and Barbara were taking the opportunity to drink tea and play with Robert on the veranda.

'Who can that be?' asked Sheila, shielding her eyes and feeling slightly panicked, mentally running through her bookings diary for anything she might have forgotten. A man stepped out of the driver's seat and turned to open the back door. From the car emerged their mother, Felicity. Normally an air of imperiousness surrounded her, utterly confident as she was of her own superiority. But here, she looked small and slight, dwarfed by the sprawling trees and blue open sky. She pulled a purple wrap tighter around her shoulders, then stumbled towards them in polished black high heels.

'Ma!' Sheila ran down to meet her mother at the front door. 'What a lovely surprise!' She reached to embrace Felicity and they kissed lightly. 'Please come in. Barbara and Robert are inside.' The two women entered and were met by Barbara, who held the baby in her arms.

'Ma. How are you?' said Barbara, leading her mother to the sitting room. 'This is Robert, or Bobby. Won't you sit down?'

Felicity had not said a word, but she nodded and sat down in an armchair, smoothing her skirt. The other women sat to face her as she sat utterly still. She slowly removed her sunglasses to reveal eyes red-rimmed and bloodshot, starkly contrasting with her pale complexion.

'Oh, Ma!' gasped Sheila. 'What's the matter? What has happened? Is it Papa?'

'I… I… wanted to come myself.' Felicity gulped as the words rushed out of her. 'I didn't want to send a wire or phone. It's your father.'

'What about him?' asked Barbara.

'He's dead. He died. It was so sudden. A heart attack. He wasn't even doing anything; he was just out fishing with James. They were up at Gura River and he stood up suddenly and then just dropped down dead.'

'When?' asked Sheila.

'The day before yesterday. I was up in the Aberdares with him and just had Angela with me. We'd only just got there on Friday, and well, the men were keen to get some trout, so off they went. I said it was too hot, but he wouldn't listen.'

Felicity had shrunk further as she sat poised on the edge of the chair, twisting a handkerchief and occasionally dabbing her eyes.

'Where is Nigel?' asked Barbara. They did not keep in touch with their brother.

'He's in Nairobi, at the lawyer's. There's so much to sort out, you see. And, well, he is in charge now, of course.'

'Yes,' said Barbara absently. 'Oh, Ma, I don't know what to say. I just can't believe it. I wish…' She left the sentence unfinished.

There was the sound of another car drawing up and Toby ran into the house, sensing that the incongruity of the black Mercedes might signal bad news. 'Felicity, my goodness, what…' He saw her expression, then looked to Sheila.

'Papa has died,' said Sheila, her tone incredulous and confused.

'What? Oh my God. Felicity, let me get you a drink. Sheila, Barbara?' The sisters shook their heads. The group sat in silence until Toby re-emerged with a small glass of whisky and put it into Felicity's gloved hand.

'The thing is…' started Felicity, pausing to take a large gulp of her drink. 'The thing is that Nigel is nominally in charge of the company, but he doesn't want to run it alone. In fact, he can't.'

Barbara shifted in her seat, bewildered by this change of topic. Her father had just died, what did the running of the business matter right now? She mumbled a rebuke under her breath.

'Sorry, Barbara, did you say something?' her mother looked at her face for the first time since she had arrived.

'No, it was nothing. Go on.'

'It's not only that he doesn't want to. Well, you see, the firm has been losing money – rather a lot as it happens. Your father made a few… well, ill-informed decisions, and it turns out that we are in trouble. The board have refused to keep Nigel in his role as CEO. They said that with Punch gone, they need someone else at the helm. Someone additional, I mean. They can't fire him, but they need a second person and they insist it has to be you, Toby.'

'What, why on earth? Toby sat down suddenly.

'They know how successful you were at your father's firm. How you oversaw those buyouts and kept all the jobs.'

'Well, that wasn't just me,' said Toby quietly. 'And, crucially, I don't know the hotel business.'

'Oh, it's all the same really.' Felicity's tone had become lighter, almost dismissive. 'You will be fine.'

Toby looked over at Sheila for reassurance. She gave a tiny nod, so, emboldened, Toby sat up and looked straight at Felicity. 'I'm sorry, Felicity, but I simply don't want to do it. I'm very flattered that you think me capable, and I am extremely grateful for the offer, but we're pulling something together here which I'm very proud of, and I can't leave it.'

'The thing is, Toby,' Felicity had stopped weeping. She tilted her chin towards him, her face now grey and hard. 'We, as a family, need you to do this. If you do not, there will be no business. We will have to sell, to break it all up and sell the pieces to pay back our creditors. If that happens, there is no property in Karen, or Lamu or Nyeri; no inheritance for you and Sheila or your offspring, should you have any.' She aimed the last statement pointedly at Sheila, ignoring Barbara.

'Now, Felicity. I think perhaps it is better that we discuss this another time. You've just lost your husband and Sheila and Barbara have lost their father. Why don't we collect your things from the car and we shall make up a nice room for you? We can discuss this properly when we've all had time to absorb what has happened.'

'No, thank you. I have arranged to stay with the Pritchards.' Felicity had regained her composure now and swept out of the room. 'They're expecting me.' She turned as she reached the front door; her driver was standing by her open car door, waiting. 'I need an answer by tomorrow, Toby dear. I'm sure that you will make the right choice.'

Sheila, who had been dazed by the change in the conversation, suddenly stood up and went to embrace her mother. 'Please stay, Ma. We have so much to talk about.'

Felicity froze and gently extricated herself from Sheila's arms. 'No, really, we don't. All the funeral arrangements are being taken care of and the solicitors are handling the business. All you need to do is turn up at the funeral. I take it that your husband is abroad, Barbara?'

'Yes, he's in South Africa until next month.' Barbara seethed. She knew why her mother was asking and she never referred to Clive by name. Then she added, knowing what the answer would be, 'I can ask him to come home sooner, if you like.'

'No, no. Don't trouble him. It's not *his* family, after all.'

The comment stung and Barbara gasped, squeezing Bobby tight. Felicity had taken no interest in her only grandson; had not even looked at him. She stayed in the room, while the other two saw Felicity to her car. When they returned, the three of them sat silently for a while taking in what had happened.

'I don't think she cared about telling us about Papa in person. She just wanted to get straight to the matter of you running the company,' said Barbara.

'I think perhaps you're right,' replied Toby, 'but it doesn't alter the fact that I'm going to have to do it.'

'No, Toby, please!' said Sheila, 'Don't let all this go. We've all worked so hard on it. It's been your dream.'

'But, darling, think how many people it would affect if the hotels go under. The shareholders won't just find another buyer at short notice. They'll want their money, quick smart. They won't care about redundancies and letting down suppliers. No, it's not only your family who would lose out. Don't you see, it's hundreds of people. I have to do it, even if it's just for a couple of years.'

The reality sank in for Sheila. 'Of course, you're right. Oh, Toby, I'm so sorry.'

Toby walked over to where Sheila was sitting and crouched down on the floor to face her. 'Let's just do what she says, just for a couple of years. I can get someone to run things here, and then we can come back. They can't force me to stay on at the firm, but I can make sure things are more stable for the future and then pass it on. It doesn't have to be the end, darling.'

'Would you trust me with running things here, Toby?' The words escaped Barbara's mouth before she had time to think. 'And Clive too, of course. He'd be around for part of the time.'

'Well, of course, how perfect. And, Sheila, you could divide your time between the city and here, making sure everything is shipshape!' He looked Sheila in the face and kissed her. 'It will be fine. It's a setback, but we can make it work, alright?'

CHAPTER 16

TAITA HILLS 1967

'NATHANIEL, come and meet Barbara!' Clive called over to the foreman who was supervising the men laying the foundations of the main building. He was easy to distinguish from the other workmen, not only because of the clipboard in his hand and the tool belt with all manner of measuring equipment tucked into it, but because of his immaculate attire. This was definitely the boss, and he didn't get dirty. He was a thickset man in his thirties, dressed in thin chinos and a pressed blue cotton shirt. He wore what Barbara thought were remarkably smart shiny shoes for a man in the building trade, regardless of his seniority.

'Nice to meet you, Nathaniel.' Barbara offered her hand. 'And this is Bobby.'

'Good morning, Bobby.' Nathaniel bent down to shake the boy's hand, but Bobby was unsmiling and clutching something to his chest. 'What do you have there, Bobby? Can I see?'

After a moment, Bobby, feeling a bit more trusting, released his arms to reveal a small replica hammer.

'Well, I see I have to add another worker to the payroll,' chuckled Nathaniel. 'Are you good at banging things with your hammer?' Bobby gave a shy nod.

'Well, then. Can you see, over there, there are some stones?' Another wordless nod. 'Can you break some of them up for me? We need to fill these holes with small stones, to help keep the walls up. So, you would be helping me a great deal.'

Delighted, Bobby ran to the heap of stones, made himself a little seat from a couple of flat rocks and set to work. Clive stepped out of the house and joined Barbara.

'Thank you for that!' said Barbara. 'He's getting so bored in the tent. He's fascinated by all of you out here.'

'Not a problem. I have three boys of my own. I know they need to be kept busy. And he'll be quite safe over there. Would you like me to show you around and tell you about the build?'

'Yes, please. I've worked on the plans with Toby, but I can't really imagine it all complete. Clive, can you come?'

'Sorry, I just need to get on with some work,' said Clive. 'I'll leave you two to it.'

'Follow me and we'll go inside!' Nathaniel led Barbara to the middle of the marked-out area.

'After clearing and flattening the ground, we hammered in wooden markers, connected by wires to indicate where the walls will be. Can you see?' Nathaniel pointed to the four corners of the clearing. 'We used the Pythagorean theorem and diagonals to check that all the lengths are correct and that the walls are definitely ninety degrees to each other.'

Barbara raised her eyebrows and nodded, but had only the vaguest memory from school of what the Pythagorean theorem proved.

'We then drew lines with lime, and dug trenches where we marked out. We are going to fill the trenches with a layer of murram, which is what Bobby will be helping with.' Nathaniel winked. 'Iron bars go into the trenches which are first filled with a little concrete to prevent the iron rusting and to keep air out. We should finish that stage by Wednesday. As long as the rain holds off.'

'Is it going to rain, do you think?' asked Barbara. It hadn't rained for weeks.

'Very unlikely,' said Nathaniel, 'but only God really knows. Now, where we are standing here is going to be the main downstairs area. Off to the right there will be the kitchen and dining room, and over there on the left will be the offices. You will have a nice view from there, since that is where you will spend most of your days.'

'Yes, that was my idea,' laughed Barbara. 'In the city, I didn't even have a window in my office, so I made sure we planned a nice working area here. It would be such a waste not to, wouldn't it? Especially since we're going to be in the business of showing off our wildlife. We want to be able to see what is happening out there every day.'

'Indeed,' agreed Nathaniel. 'I have a big window in my office. My view is not so spectacular, but I can see trees and cows and people going about their day and it keeps me happy, like I'm part of the world outside.'

'Can I get you a drink?' offered Barbara.

'No thank you. It's nearly lunch time. We'll all stop for an hour soon and I'll have lunch with my men. We have all we need. You can leave Bobby here until then, if you like.'

'Thank you, that would give me a bit of time to do some work, I need to make a list of what furniture we are going to really need at first to send over to the timber merchant in town. Then some of your chaps can make a start on it.'

'If that timber can get here by late next week, we'll be waiting for the concrete to go off and won't need so many men on the build, so they can make some of your desks and shelving. We have a couple of really skilled guys here,' said Nathaniel.

'Yes, I'm hoping they're going to make our beds too. It'll be nice to sleep on something a bit more solid than a camp bed!'

'Yes, yes, Ahmed over there is from Lamu and is a master at carving Lamu beds. He'll make you something beautiful.'

'I've seen them a couple of times before – in some of the finest houses in Nairobi! So beautiful, and a good way of keeping insects away at night.'

'Well, when the time is right, I'll get him to talk to you about what exactly you want. He can make the spindles plain or twisted. He can even paint panels on the headboard – peacocks or flowers. Very romantic!'

'I don't think we need a romantic bed, but I would like it to be pretty!' laughed Barbara. 'And he could make a mini one for Bobby.'

'Definitely. Well, I'd better get back to the men. Kwa heri.'

'Kwa heri, Nathaniel. Asante sana.'

Barbara clambered down the hill from the building site and across to the tents, which had been pitched on a flat piece of ground opposite. There was a circle of tents around the campfire; seven altogether. One each for Peter the camp cook, his assistant Issa, the rangers Jackson and Fidel, and two which were shared between the two askaris and two young men who did general manual work. Barbara shared the last tent with Bobby and, on the rare occasions he came home, Clive. The mess tent was everything from kitchen, dining room and meeting room. There was one toilet, which was really just a long drop surrounded with canvas, with a basin on a table outside, which the staff kept clean and stocked. Then, finally, there was a makeshift office with one table, and chairs set facing each other where Clive and Barbara carried out all their work for the camp. Barbara stopped by the mess tent to make herself and Clive a cup of tea before getting back to her correspondence. Peter was already getting lunch ready. 'Sasa, Mama Bobby! Habari yako?'

'Nzuri sana, Peter, asante. What's going to be for lunch?'

'Lentil soup and sorghum bread, Mama. It will be ready in about an hour. I will call when it is all ready for you.'

'Asante, Peter. See you in an hour.'

Clive was sitting in his chair when Barbara came in with the tea.

'Peter has made gingerbread men!' Barbara said as she set the drinks and a plate of biscuits down.

'That young man is a magician' said Clive, grabbing a biscuit. 'Where on earth did he get the ginger?'

'Or the sugar for that matter!' said Barbara.

'Come over here, Barbara, look at these.' Clive had spread a dozen or so photographs across his desk. 'Toby sent us these.

He contacted Brian in the Masai Mara and he forwarded them. They've just finished building the first proper tourist lodges for their photographic safaris. They still run hunting safaris, but he agrees that the market for tourism is steadily increasing throughout the country. Air fares are going down and people with a bit more money to spend are coming here. Not to mention city types in Nairobi who want a break for a few days. We need to think about offering short- and long-term accommodation.'

'Do you think that the markets are the same? What is the income level of these people? Are they looking for luxury or an authentic experience?' Barbara fired questions at Clive.

'Well, I think we have to offer both. Gone are the days of the old White hunter. This is fashionable and modern Kenya and you are a very fashionable and modern girl,' laughed Clive. 'What do you think people want?'

'I'm flattered. I haven't thought of myself as modern and fashionable for a long time. Or as a girl, come to think of it! Well, you're right, the days of the hunting safari are thankfully numbered,' replied Barbara. 'I think Kenya owes a lot to the Adamsons and *Born Free*. People do want authenticity – to see the wild, red in tooth and claw. But middle-class Europeans won't understand how to rough it, will they? They'll need flushing toilets and regular meals at table; not beans in a bowl on your knees and a long drop. They want excitement, but not discomfort.'

'You're quite right. I think we need to expand our building project. Yes, we need the main building for us and to use as a research centre, but I think there's a business opportunity here. Instead of a tented camp, I think we should build small huts. They would still look somewhat like tents, but be more solidly made with wooden frames and thatched roofs, painted khaki.'

'Yes, I see. Can we get Nathaniel to help us plan something out?'

'Yes, well, we would use much of the same materials as for the main house. Come on outside with me.' Clive led Barbara out and stood beside the groundworks. 'Toby wanted to aim big, didn't he? I thought we could build five to begin with and see how that goes. They could be right over there, where we planned to put the tents, and have them all along this escarpment and down below too, so they all get a view over the land. The ground level ones would be right by the waterhole and up here they would look down on it. Each hut could have a little veranda with table and chairs. Somewhere to have a sundowner and take photographs. Everyone could eat together in the main house or in a large dining room, so the huts would only have to include a bedroom and bathroom. What do you think? Do you think Toby would approve?'

'I do, I think he'll be thrilled.'

'Barbara, Clive, come with me!' The ranger, Jackson, was running up the escarpment towards the couple, radio in one hand.

'What is it?' asked Clive 'Is someone hurt?'

'No, no, it is nothing like that. Something amazing. Come with me in the jeep.'

'Let me grab Bobby,' said Barbara. She ran over to scoop Bobby up from his stone-breaking. He let out a little squeal of protest, but quickly got caught up in the excitement.

The group piled into the jeep and Jackson sped off. A few minutes later, they were in deep bush and Jackson slowed right down, talking quietly on his radio to Fidel, whose jeep they could see a few hundred yards ahead. Jackson pulled up beside Fidel and they all looked ahead. The bush parted ahead of them, opening out to a large clearing. Within the clearing were close to a dozen female elephants, all adults, standing in a circle, some facing in, some out.

'Can you see?' asked Jackson in an excited whisper. 'Can you see what's happening in the middle of their circle?'

'No, it looks like a sort of dancc,' said Barbara. 'They're all shuffling and swaying.'

'It is a baby, Mama. There's a baby being born. Right now!'

'Oh, my goodness, really? Bobby, did you hear that? This is a very special day.'

'Is it really rare to see an elephant birth?' asked Clive.

'It is,' Jackson nodded. 'I've never seen it; Fidel has never seen it. He has seen a very young one – new, new. But never the actual birth. We're very lucky.'

The group stayed silent, watching the drama unfold. Even Bobby seemed to understand that he must not move, that they must be very alert and not cause the animals any worry.

'It's happening,' said Jackson. 'Can you see? Look between the legs of that front one facing us. There's a baby coming now!'

The large female moved sideways just in time for the group to see the baby drop from its mother. All the other elephants faced inwards now and were fussing over the pair, touching the mother's face and prodding the baby with their trunks. It lay on the ground for what felt to Barbara like an age, but with a little more nudging, it lifted its head, tested the air with its trunk, then scrambled to its feet. The group let out a collective gasp of relief.

'Can you tell the sex?' asked Clive. Jackson picked up his binoculars and focused. 'I couldn't swear to it, but I would say it is a girl.'

'A baby girl, Bobby! What do you think about that?' Bobby clapped his hands, sensing the glee.

'Can we give her a name?' asked Barbara?

'Of course,' replied Jackson. 'Bobby, what do you think?'

'Happy, happy, happy!' said Bobby.

'I think she should have an African name,' said Barbara.

'You know, where I come from, up near Meru,' said Jackson. 'Many little girls are called Makena; it means 'happiness'. Is that a good name, Bobby?' He turned to look at the little boy.

'Makena!'

MAKENA

TAITA HILLS 1971

THERE is a pile of berries on the ground by the big water. They were brushed from the shrub when my sisters barged through to take a drink. I watch them now as they are devoured by many insects. A flutter of bright green butterflies has gathered to feast on the juice before the hot sun bakes it to a sticky stain. Other crawling things have emerged too. But they must be quick. This heat is not good if you are small. I am small, but not as small as the creeping insects.

I am not even the baby anymore. Left Tip was born when the rains were at their strongest. He was nearly swept away by the river soon after his birth as his mother – my mother – tripped and kicked him in her pain as he dropped from her on the riverbank. But my grandmother was there, with her circle of sisters, watching over the new life. She caught him with her leg and flipped him up, his ears flapping open like the petals of a new flower to reveal a wet, hairy face. He stood as if he knew, as if he had just been standing all the time and fallen over. I was watching from a nearby thorn bush, watched over by my cousins Two Scratch and Birdie. I wanted to get closer, to see my brother being born, but they pushed me down, keeping me safe from the swaying bodies of my aunties and from the lions we could smell were not far away. They had tried to hide downwind from us, but lions are stupid. We do not only smell them. We see and hear and just know.

I am learning from my Grandmama – she is named Fierce and she is everything to us. She is our mother, leader, protector, teacher. Once my brother was born, the aunties all touched him with the tips of their trunks and, knowing all was well, called me and my cousins over to meet the new baby. He was named Left Tip after a little while, as his left ear has a point at the bottom that is quite different from any of the rest of us.

I am getting hot, lying here, but I have to stay. We have walked all morning to reach this water. It is the dry time now and water is far, far. Fierce knows where all the last good waters are when the smaller waters have dried up. We need to walk for a long time to each one, so we walk, drink, rest, walk, drink, rest. This is the rhythm of our days in this heat. We move mostly at night when there is some cool. Fierce knows to take us to the waters with the most shade in the strongest heat.

I should be sleeping, but I am too hot. I can feel Birdie's leg twitch. She is waking now. One by one my aunties, sisters, cousins wake from their slumber. Fierce stretches her trunk up and senses the air. We are to head towards the hills. It looks too dry, as if there cannot possibly be water that way, but Fierce is always right.

Left Tip seeks me out and tries to clamber onto my back before I can get up. He is whipping me with his trunk. To him, everything is still new and fun. I am the big sister, so I must tolerate his silliness and help him. But in this heat we must be slow and sensible, so I push him off. He nibbles at me as if he wants to feed, so I steer him towards our mother, Flower, grumbling to her as I do, alerting her to Left Tip's needs. He suckles for a few minutes while I, and the rest of my family, drink a little more to sustain ourselves for the long walk ahead.

We have been walking for a long time, when Flower stops suddenly and nods to Fierce. Everyone stops. I know that she has heard something. She is swaying her head, trying to clear her mind to focus on the sound. Then we all feel it. A rumble in the ground. I feel a little alarmed, but all the adults are calm, and a surge of excitement passes through the group. Then I understand. Family is close. We move again, keeping our course, and after a short while the source of the rumbling is in view. It is Fierce's sister, Cross Tusks, and her family. They come from the east, but are walking in the same direction as us, towards the hills. Cross Tusks also knows where to get the best water in the dry days. Our two groups merge and we become one happy band. We have not seen these cousins for a season or more, so it is very exciting. I look for my friend, Pink Tail, who was born in the same season as me. I soon spot her, trotting tightly alongside her mother, Dew Drop. At first, she is shy; she seems not to like the chaos of the reunion, but she sees me and runs towards me, all fear forgotten. We greet each other at first with a touch of the trunk tips, then we trumpet our greeting and run together, ahead of the group. Flower spots us and calls us back. We make more greetings with these cousins of ours, then move together. We all feel invigorated by this meeting and our group gathers pace. I walk with Pink Tail.

We reach the big water as the air is beginning to cool and the sun is lower in the sky. We do not have it to ourselves, of course. We are the only elephants, but there are many antelopes and a few zebras, even a troop of baboons. I hate baboons. They are bold and mocking. One day, when we were napping, I felt a heavy weight land hard on my ear. I got up and saw a sausage fruit lying beside me on the ground. Above me I heard the cackling of baboons – many, many baboons in the tree. It must have been their sleeping tree and they were cross at us for using its shade. The cackling woke my family up – the baboons seemed to be laughing at us and jumped from branch to branch, making more sausage fruit fall.

I get too close to a mother baboon now, her baby clinging to her back. She whips round to face me from the edge of the water and bares her teeth at me. They have teeth like hyenas. They even laugh like hyenas. They are like long-legged, tree-climbing hyenas. I hate them. I move to the other side of my mother and keep away from them.

Left Tip has been walking under our mother's stomach since we left, suckling a little, but he is becoming old enough to browse a few low, juicy leaves. My mother picks some from a shrub overhanging the water and passes them to him gently. He has trouble with the branch, flicking himself in the eye several times before holding it down with his front feet and gnawing the leaves off. The sight makes me happy – I remember being so clumsy; I still am sometimes.

We all take a good drink – we youngsters go first, then two of our grandmothers. They are slow but very wise and kind. They are followed by the rest of the group and, lastly, by Fierce, who has kept lookout while we drank. There is something strange happening at the high kopje. Funny creatures are gathered there; just a few of them, but they are making a lot of noise and moving things around. Strong smells waft over to us as we drink at the small water at the foot of the kopje, making our eyes smart and water. We do not linger, and Fierce insistently leads us on to another waterhole to stop at for the night. I turn to look back at the high kopje. I do not feel Fierce's trepidation, only curiosity.

I look harder at the funny creatures; they are too far away for me to see clearly but I can feel their noises. Two of them are separate from their group, facing us, one bigger than the other. I think they are looking down at us drinking. They remind me a bit of the baboons, but they are not barking and baring their teeth at us. They just quietly watch and mutter to each other in a funny high-pitched way, the small one, sitting on the big one. We take our time at the water, enjoying a cool bath after our long, hot day. I bathe Left Tip by sucking water up my trunk and squirting it over him. He flaps and wiggles in delight. All the while, I keep watching the kopje. The bigger creature has risen and put the smaller one on the ground, walking away. The small one has not stopped staring out at us. It sits there, legs outstretched, almost still.

The family have all had their fill of water, and Fierce gives the signal to head off. I give one last look at the creature on the kopje, nodding my head at it. I think it has seen me do this, as I just make out a movement, the slow lifting of a tiny leg. I feel no fear. Instead, I feel a connection with this little creature – a kinship.

PART 3

CHAPTER 17

OXFORD 2011

SHE had to ring the doorbell three times before Alex answered. Starting to panic a little and rifling through her bag for her own key, Gigi eventually saw his obscured figure through the stained glass of the front door, making its way towards the entrance hall. He opened the door with a smile, and exclaimed his delight, as though he hadn't seen her for weeks. Cleanly shaven and dressed, Alex was as always in a collared shirt; she had never seen him without a cravat, summer or winter. 'I was just gardening round the back. Didn't hear the door, sorry. Come on in, Gee. Let Ziggy through to see Suki. She's missed him. I can open up the back door and let them play in the yard.' Gigi removed her shoes, let the dog off his lead and followed Alex inside.

Although Gigi's mother had died the previous spring, her presence still pervaded every part of the house. From the paintings on the walls (some of which were her own), the innumerable books, the uneaten food in the cupboard. The house seemed to be holding its breath, waiting for Petra's return from an errand, soon to return to pick up her paintbrush or finish writing a letter. They walked past a large pile of unopened post and the answerphone flashed a warning of two waiting messages.

'How are the children?' Alex asked as they entered the kitchen. He opened the patio doors to release the scrambling dogs and turned on the kettle. 'Coffee?'

'Yes, please. Xander played his first gig on Saturday. I was so nervous for him, but he seemed so cool about it. They were really good, actually.'

'What sort of music do they play?'

'Not your sort of thing,' laughed Gigi. 'Nor mine, actually.

Nineties covers mostly – grunge – Nirvana, Gorillaz. Stuff they were playing when I was at uni. Wasn't my thing the first time around.'

'Afraid you lost me at 'nineties'! Still, nice that he's got a hobby, away from his A levels.'

'It is, although don't let him hear you call it a hobby. He's very serious about it. I'm afraid he spends more time rehearsing than studying. He still seems to get the grades, though. Infuriating. He's so clever.'

'And Annie?'

'Still wise beyond her years. She had her birthday party on Saturday.'

'Ten years old. Hard to believe.'

'I know. Anyway, she was blowing out her candles and the kids were saying the usual "Make a wish, what did you wish for?" – you know?'

Alex nodded.

'Well, she said "Wishes aren't magic, you know. They don't just happen. You have to make them happen."'

'She's not wrong.'

'I know. She's my new lifestyle guru. We should all be more Annie. Sometimes I wish she was a bit sillier, a bit more girlie, but she's got this old soul. Even her art is mature. Sometimes I think she's channelling Mum.'

Alex smiled, but turned away to make the coffee and said nothing. Her dad had always been funny, witty, great company. But, in his grief, his default mood had become melancholic. He occasionally asked her about the children, but Gigi knew he wasn't really paying attention, that it was just the polite and conventional thing to say. She was sympathetic – after all, her parents had barely been apart for nearly sixty years – but she was conscious of not having really grieved herself for her own loss. She often questioned herself about this numbness, this apparent lack of emotion, but she never figured it out.

'Oh, nearly forgot. I've brought us some biscuits. Annie made them at school, so – take your chances!'

'As long as they don't break my teeth! There are fig rolls in the cupboard too, just in case!'

Gigi laughed. 'Right, Dad. I've got precisely three hours. We can either walk the dogs then get some lunch or I can tackle the garage. What's it to be?'

'Walk and lunch?' Alex asked hopefully.

'Wrong answer. Well, at least, let me have an hour in the garage now, then we can have a quick walk and eat after.'

'Deal. I want to get some more weeding done anyway, so I can keep an eye on the dogs while you get on.'

They finished their coffee and went their separate ways, agreeing to meet up at 12.00, ready to go out. Gigi armed herself with rubber gloves, cleaning products, boxes and bin bags. The first sight that greeted her in the shambolic garage was a pigeon corpse in a far corner. Her father was perfectly aware of its presence but had claimed ornithophobia and ignored it.

'You're the first thing to go.' Gigi addressed the limp body as she picked up the bird in her rubber-clad hand. The bird's wing fanned out as she lifted it, giving the impression of suddenly coming to life, making Gigi gasp momentarily. She managed to plonk it unceremoniously into a plastic bag and took it outside to the bin. Much of the floor was strewn with back issues of academic journals, some of them over twenty years old. It was an easy and satisfying job, throwing them all indiscriminately into a box for recycling.

Gigi was the fourth child of five, and the only one not to have left Oxford. Thus, the unavoidable task of sorting out their mother's detritus after her death had fallen to her. It occurred to Gigi that, emotionally, a person can leave a huge gap in the hearts of their loved ones, but physically their possessions can leave an enormous burden. She was, by nature, emotionally attached to things herself, so found the job of sifting through her mother's bits and pieces heart-wrenching. Every item required a decision, and she was not decisive. She squirrelled away the thought that, one day, her children would have to do the same thing if she did not curb her own hoarding habits.

A large plastic crate on the floor was filled with children's books. The old puffin paperbacks were too dated for her own children. There was a full set of Dr Seuss, well-thumbed and torn. Gigi had bought her own new copies of these, considering them classics. As an American, Petra had instilled in her children an appreciation of the philosophy of Dr Seuss. And philosophy it was, not simply silly rhymes. The moral dilemma of *Horton Hatches an Egg*, the materialism questioned *in How the Grinch Stole Christmas* – Gigi and her siblings had all been expected to look beyond the obvious, to question motives and norms. When they read the Narnia books, Gigi was instructed to draw parallels with Christian beliefs and stories. It all rather spoiled the fun for her.

Nevertheless, she agreed about Dr Seuss – there were wise words contained within those silly rhymes, Gigi whispered to herself one of her favourite lines: the one about the importance of being you. You could look the same to everyone, but there could be lots of 'yous' underneath and you could be in control of that. The realisation made her feel a little lonely, but also powerful. She took the box out to the hall – she wouldn't even look through them – they would go straight to the charity shop for other children to love. Feeling energised by her own resolve, she turned back to the room and the task in hand.

Two old mirrored wardrobes faced each other in a corner of the garage where they were being stored until a home could be found for them. Their mirrors were dull and pockmarked with age. She stared back at herself in one of them. Her reflection was not just of one Gigi gazing back, but hundreds of Gigis, as the mirrors reflected each other countless times. Her image was multiple, ethereal. She swung her arms above her head and the prism-edged reflections followed, making her look pleasingly like a cross between a snow angel and a dancer in a psychedelic music video.

She giggled at herself. Being in her family home always made Gigi feel like a small child again. The mirrors seemed to throw her back to her childhood, stirring those old memories and comparisons with her siblings. She resembled her brothers – the same hair – toffee brown, small retroussé nose, large brown eyes. But her two sisters were so different from her, this separateness enhancing their almost divine status, already being older and having lives outside their home that a younger Gigi imagined were filled with sparkling conversations and sophisticated parties (but probably weren't, as she realised now). They had blue eyes, Roman noses. They wore their clothes with practised ease, and carried themselves with an elegance that Gigi knew even now she would never achieve.

She was as clumsy and absent-minded as she had been as a little girl. One of her eyes was slightly larger than the other, she was left-handed where all her siblings were right. She was a 'not-one-thing-or-another'. Her hair was neither straight nor curly, dark nor blonde, long nor short. Her sisters – one blonde, one dark – had long flowing shiny locks. Growing up, they had listened to avant-garde music, discussed books she didn't comprehend, debated adult issues in French with the rest of the older family members, so that Gigi and her little brother wouldn't understand (although secretly she did). They became all that had been expected of them – professional, highly educated, idiosyncratic – all cast from the mould their mother had formed, leaving Gigi to the role of not even a black sheep – more a sheep of an indeterminate beige.

* * *

Under some old blankets, she found a shoebox containing dozens of tiny folded paper parcels, each carefully labelled with a name and date. The names were those of Gigi and her siblings and inside the packages were baby teeth – seemingly all the baby teeth from all of their childhoods. Gigi herself had kept her own children's teeth in a little jewellery box, but to see that her mother had done it too... her remote mother who never appeared to do anything in the least sentimental – that she had taken the time and care and kept these little relics of babyhood for all these years and hidden them away just for herself. The incongruity of this find gave her a jolt and she sat for a few minutes contemplating it. Keeping baby teeth was such a raw, physical, motherly thing to do and she had never looked at her mother that way, as someone nostalgic for their babyhoods. She picked out one packet for each child and placed the rest with a little reverence into the bin bag.

The next job, she decided, was to clear out the drawers of a large dresser that was destined for her sister in London. Each drawer contained a random selection of pretty boxes of various sizes – the sort that Gigi only ever saw on old films when a woman received a fancy dress or a new pair of shoes. All of these were packed with photographs. There seemed no order to this filing system. Some photos were in colour, but the majority were black and white. Gigi knew that if she started inspecting them now, the hour would pass very quickly and she would have achieved nothing, so she piled up the boxes by the door to the house, for her and Alex to go through together another time, perhaps when he was feeling stronger. The lowest drawer was the deepest. She fumbled for the bottom of the pile of boxes within, when she felt that at the very bottom was not a box, but a book. 'Probably an album,' she said to herself. 'A singular attempt to be organised!' She lifted up the pile of boxes and left it with the others, then returned to the drawer. The book was not a photo album exactly, but a large fat scrapbook. On the front, in neat but immature writing was the inscription 'Petra Legrand – Private!!!'

Gigi felt a jolt in her chest and the prickle of tears behind her eyes. She clambered out of her kneeling position and carried the book gently over to a low bureau. This was also piled high with flotsam, but she managed to push a tower of papers to one side, giving herself enough room to open the book fully. She took a deep breath and opened the first page. The book had been neatly ordered into chapters as though it was a novel, but it was peppered with drawings and photographs of people and places Gigi knew were real.

Her mother barely ever spoke of her childhood. Gigi knew partly why that was. Her grandfather, her mother's father had been, by all accounts, a drunken boor and her mother had closed the story of her childhood and put it away like this scrapbook. Gigi had always wanted to know more about what seemed to her an exciting and exotic past that was part of her history too, but was an unspoken taboo. No one ever discussed Petra's childhood. But now here it was in front of her, fully illustrated.

She flicked through to gauge how old her mother must have been when she compiled it and what period it covered. The first page was dotted with photographs of Petra aged about ten with various pets, clearly the most important figures in her life at the time. Whereas a little girl of today might have decorated the pages with stickers or hearts or other whimsical touches, this book was set out very neatly, almost professionally, with footnotes and tiny explanations noted under each photo or drawing, which were numbered and referred to in the main text. Not all pages of the book had been used, so Gigi thought there perhaps wasn't another following on from it. It appeared to end when Petra was sixteen, so probably the time that her mother had emigrated to England.

There were photographs of her mother horse-riding, sailing, running in a school sports event, sitting in a tree, painting. She didn't often smile in the pictures, she had never been much of a smiler, but she had a sort of wistful, other-worldly look – a child whose thoughts were deeper and more considered than most of her age. There was a look of Annie about her.

Since her death, Gigi had come to feel a growing empathy and realisation that her mother's remoteness had been borne out of awkwardness, despite her intelligence and erudition. She had been self-conscious and shy and had never known how to relate to most people, cutting herself off increasingly from day-to-day activities that involved social interaction. But through her father's grief, and illustrated in this scrapbook, Gigi saw the young woman her mother been – precociously clever, beautiful, practical. The attributes that Gigi had always found hard to live up to herself, were things of which she was most proud in her mother, and now in her children.

What troubled her recently was that this exacerbated her own feelings of inadequacy. She had not fulfilled the family mantra, 'live your best life'. She had led a good life, had done no harm, but the feeling now occupied her thoughts every day that life is precious and should be valued and lived to the fullest. She was in danger of wasting what time she still had. Gigi had grown up not just wishing to travel the world, she had fully expected to do it. Her career ambitions were vague, but she wanted to see as much landscape, wildlife and culture as possible. She wanted to see the moon tip ever so gradually on its axis as she ventured further east. She dreamed of big skies full of stars, of giggling children, hot dusty roads and new friendships.

None of this had materialised. Gigi had graduated from her mediocre university, with her unexceptional business degree with no motivation other than squaring her debts and paying her rent. This was in stark contrast to her siblings who had followed lucrative careers in London, Boston and France. Her younger brother had worked all over Asia in some sort of cryptocurrency role, something she could not comprehend no matter how patiently and repeatedly Dan explained it to her. She herself had endured a string of lowly admin jobs, taking calls, making tea, letting her male bosses pass her ideas off as their own, eventually settling into full-time motherhood which, despite her protestations to her siblings, she loved. She was proud of her children and proud of her own job of raising them.

Staring back at the scrapbook, Gigi tried to think of the biggest risk she had taken lately. What had she done to lift herself out of her routine? She was always starting new hobbies, reading about new things, but as for actually doing something new and daring, she came up utterly blank. When she had recently (finally) organised a personal pension and undertaken a questionnaire on what type of pension to take out, the results showed that she was so risk averse, she should just stash her savings under her mattress. She was dismayed at this apparently comprehensive summary of her character.

Gigi jumped as she heard her name being called. Alex was ready for their walk. She realised she had been crying. They were not tears of grief, but what? Regret, frustration? She wiped her eyes and checked herself in the wardrobe mirror as she returned to the house to join her father.

'What's the matter, Gigi?' There was no hiding from Alex.

'I'm fine, really, I am. I just spent the whole hour looking at pictures of Mum. I found this really nice scrapbook. It just got to me a bit.'

'I'm sorry, love. I can get like that too. Let's go and be tearful over a nice hot lunch.'

CHAPTER 18

OXFORD 2011

THEY bundled the dogs into Gigi's car and set off for the park. It was too windy to talk, so they walked together, arms linked, in companionable silence until the dogs came back, panting and then headed off to a café. They found a table by a window overlooking the river.

'Dad. Do you think Mum had any regrets?'

'I know she wished she had started painting professionally sooner, but no, I don't think she did, not really. Why?'

'Oh, it's just an age thing, I'm sure. It was just that photo album. She did so many things, even as a child. I just don't think I've done everything yet, but there's no time now and I still don't know what I want to do. I love being with the kids, but it's like I've given "me" up and I don't know where to get me back.'

Alex passed her a tissue to tend to the rolling tears, and replied to her in his old reassuring style. 'If I've learnt anything in life it's this. You have to play the cards you are dealt, but you *can* shuffle them. You have a family to take care of and you can't forget them, but you need to find a way of finding your happiness or you can't give happiness back to them. You have all the elements of a good life right there, but you have to decide on the priorities.'

Gigi nodded and sniffed into her tissue. 'You're right, but I can't just make sweeping changes.'

'No, but you can't be unhappy. The children will go on to make their own lives. And you would never do anything to damage them, would you? Why not talk to the family about it? There must be ways for you all to fit in things you'd like to do with things you have to. You've given seventeen years to the family's needs, perhaps it's your turn to branch out a bit.'

Gigi agreed, but inwardly knew that this was just an outburst. She would go home and get on with supper, bury this conversation and go on as normal. The waitress came over to take their order.

Meals ordered, Gigi got up to look at a pile of papers left out on a side table for customers to peruse. She picked a wildlife magazine and brought it back to the table, along with a *Guardian* for Alex. 'I used to subscribe to this,' said Gigi, 'I always loved to read about the faraway places. But it just got too expensive to keep buying it every month, you know.'

'A treat like that is alright, now and again,' smiled Alex.

'Yes, I suppose so.' Gigi flicked through the magazine whilst Alex read the day's paper. An article caught her eye. 'Listen to this, Dad. Win a family trip to monitor wildlife in beautiful Kenya.' What do you think of that? Shall I enter?' Gigi laughed.

'Perhaps it's a sign!' Alex chuckled and squeezed her hand.

The article described the location of the reserve, including a précis about its owner, Barbara Chege.

'*She Swapped Kenyan Royalty for Life in the Bush*,' ran the title, and it was accompanied by several photographs of Barbara. One was of her aged nineteen at the Independence Ball in Nairobi in a cocktail dress – flicked, bobbed hair framing a mischievous face. Another was of her feeding a baby elephant. A group picture had the following explanation under it – 'Barbara's son, Robert Chege, an acclaimed wildlife biologist with his family at their remote home in Taita Hills.' A current photograph of Barbara was at the centre of the piece. Gigi felt an instant connection with this woman. She had a sort of warm elegance about her. She still had the full swept-back hairstyle of her youth, the blonde a little faded. Her face was slender but not severe, and her smile was that of someone who is truly kind – a smile that comes from the heart.

Gigi read about Barbara's life from when she first took over the reserve in the late 1960s; her battles to protect the area against developers, hunters and, above all, poachers; her raising her son there until he went to university; then the story of both of them running the reserve until he left in the early 2000s. For the last ten years, ran the article, the reserve had been run as a luxury camp and base for safaris, but the current poaching crisis had led Mrs Chege to switch back to her original ideas and develop the area for the future.

'That sounds so exciting. Imagine being part of that!' said Gigi.

'Nothing ventured, nothing gained,' said Alex. 'I mean it. What harm can it do to enter. And you know a lot about African wildlife. It could be your Mastermind specialist subject!'

'Don't tease.'

'I'm not. I am quite serious. What do you need to do to enter?' Gigi passed him the magazine. '*Write a 500-word report on the crisis facing East African wildlife today.*' You could do that standing on your head. You'd better do it quick, though. There's only a week until the closing date.'

Gigi flicked through the article again, pen poised over a blank sheet of lined paper. She had wanted to see Africa since she was a little girl, enchanted by David Attenborough documentaries and reading *The Flame Trees of Thika*. Over the years, she had collected elephant ornaments and read voraciously about the continent – its people, histories and wildlife. In Dan she had married a fellow-Afrophile. Year on year they had hoped to visit, but then work commitments, money worries and parenthood took them hurtling down a straight but bumpy road, passing turnoffs leading to adventurous travel time after time, until they forgot about that dream completely.

The childhood she had once fantasised of for her children – of running barefoot through the bush, befriending small animals, naming all the local birds, climbing trees and swimming with a gaggle of friends, wild and free – had never happened. They were a typical European family – computer games, takeout pizzas, sleepovers and trips to museums. It was a life of school gate politics, keeping up with the neighbours, exam tensions and car problems. A good life, but an ordinary one. She looked again at the picture of Barbara Chege. Perhaps it was because she had looked at the photograph a dozen times now, but Barbara had an air of familiarity to Gigi, of sisterhood. Now she not only wanted to go to Africa, she wanted to meet Barbara, to hear all about her life. She began to write.

A familiar soft, uneven slapping noise broke the silence as Gigi reached the bottom of the page. Annie flumped down the stairs and into the kitchen. Her face was pink and damp, her hair, with its cow's lick (which Annie hated) sticking up in ludicrous brown tufts. She nuzzled wordlessly into Gigi's cardigan, smelling warm and biscuity.

'Morning, monster,' whispered Gigi, kissing the top of her head. 'Good sleep?' Annie nodded and turned to Ziggy, all signs of sleepiness gone, kissing him liberally and making promises of breakfast and play.

The dawn spell broken, Gigi set about making porridge and toast, boiling the kettle, pulling packed lunches she had made the night before from the fridge. Her morning routine was almost balletic, so familiar was it. She had to go and wake Xander, who always slept through his alarm, always had to have a long shower and always rushed his breakfast.

Xander was seventeen, studying for his A levels and had just passed his driving test. So many anxieties bound up in one person. He had always been clever. Gigi joked that she and her siblings had inherited their parents' brains, but they had just shared them between the five of them. It was apparent, though, that her children had been gifted an academic aptitude that had seemed to bypass Gigi. They found schoolwork easy to the point of being dull, and were top of their classes for most subjects. They were popular, too, with both their friends and teachers – a double whammy that school-aged Gigi also had not pulled off.

Xander emerged, clean-shaven and smartly dressed in the power suit his sixth form college insisted on. 'Morning,' he boomed, as he gave Gigi a hug, kissing her on the top of the head – something he'd been able to do since he was twelve. Every time she caught sight of Xander she was taken aback. A boy with Botticelli curls and tubby physique had long been replaced by this man-child; Gigi often had the feeling that she had been whisked forward in time to view her future – here it is, look – and she would be whisked back any time now. Xander put two slices of bread in the toaster, blitzed a fruit smoothie in the blender, then spread his toast with a favourite combination of peanut butter, honey and Marmite. He stood to eat his feast, whilst making a cappuccino to take with him on the drive to school.

While the children ate, Gigi dressed. She had taken to deliberately wearing increasingly outlandish clothes. She felt, with the escalating invisibility of her years, there was no reason not to be a bit braver with her outfits. Today, she settled on a khaki jumpsuit and mustard scarf. She tied her hair up, crowning it with an embroidered headband and put on earrings she had treated herself to on her last birthday – abstract faces in thin gold wire. She grabbed the car keys, dog, Annie's PE kit and kissed Xander as they parted for their morning journeys.

'Morning, Honey.' Dan called at bang on 10:00 as usual. He knew that she would be in from the school run and dog walk, but not yet out to the gym. He would have completed his regular team briefing and not yet set off for his client meetings. It was a less frantic time for them to catch up than in the bedlam of the early mornings or the distracted fatigue after Gigi had finally got Annie to bed.

'How's your day going so far?' asked Gigi, bracing herself for the response.

'Oh, ok, I guess.' Dan's tone was resigned, distant. 'I'll be back earlier than usual tomorrow.'

Gigi tucked the phone under her chin and started to fill up the sink. 'Okay, why's that?' she asked. Usually Dan got home from his week in London after eight o'clock on Fridays.

'Well, now don't get cross… I know we talked about this and I was going to stick it out for another year, until Xander had left school.' He paused. 'Gigi, I've resigned.'

Gigi let this sink in for a few moments. She turned off the tap and dried her hands.

'Gigi, say something. Please, say something. I know it's not what we discussed. I know it was impulsive and, frankly, pretty stupid, but I just feel…well, I miss you guys. I have missed so much with all these years being in London all week. What if I go solo a bit sooner than we said? We've put away enough to see us through the next six months. I have a year left with Xander before he leaves home, if I stay home now I get the best of Annie before she grows up and lords it over us completely…'

'You think Annie's not in charge already?' Gigi finally broke her silence. 'You know what she would say, don't you?'

'That I should be more responsible?'

'That you should spend more time with her.'

'Actually, something she said was ringing in my ears all through my meeting. "Daddy, why do you go away from the family to look after the family? You being away just makes me sad. And that's not looking after me very well."'

'Harsh.'

'It was. And being away makes me sad too, Gigi. This wasn't how things were meant to be, was it?'

'Look. It's done now. It *is* done, right?'

'Yes, I handed the letter to Briggs this morning, ahead of the briefing. He said to tidy things up today and then I'd have to go on gardening leave for the next three months.'

'Well. You know what? I think it's great.'

'Really, after all we said about Xander's uni fees and the dog's vet bills and everything?'

'You know I went round to Dad's yesterday to help sort out more of Mum's stuff? Well, I got a bit emotional – finally!' Gigi laughed, brushing away a tear. She jumped onto the worktop and rubbed the dog's back with her feet as he lumbered over to be fussed.

'I'm sorry, love. I'm sorry I wasn't there.'

'But you will be. Tomorrow. Anyway, I found something that shook me up a bit, but in a good way. I think we need a reboot, you me and the kids. A break from the treadmill. I did a silly thing. I entered a competition for us all to take a volunteering trip to Africa.'

'Wow!'

'Wow indeed. I know we probably won't win, but it just made me think. We have been super careful over the years and you have been doing that crappy job with those horrible people to keep things steady. I've been at home, which I love by the way, but I just feel that I could be doing something more with my days. So, come home, let Annie tell you off and let's make some plans. Some fun plans.'

CHAPTER 19

NAIROBI 2012

THE seat belt lights pinged, and the passengers jumped out of their seats for the scramble to get their belongings and rush out of the plane. Gigi had never seen the point of this, as soon enough they would all be at that baggage carousel, glumly watching other people's luggage circling round and around.

'Right, have you all got everything? Phones somewhere safe? Zipped up your bags? Thrown away your rubbish?' She didn't wait for answers. The questions were rhetorical anyway, as she had already done most of this for the children, while they mouthed music lyrics and tapped at their phone screens. 'Stay together, guys, it's no joke, an airport like this.' Actually, the prospect of Jomo Kenyatta Airport did not panic Gigi anything like as much as Heathrow, but still. She checked the letter again, still hardly believing they were actually about to embark on African soil.

> Dear Mrs Wedderburn
> I am writing to inform you that you have been selected to take part in an amazing opportunity, helping us to rebuild our wildlife monitoring centre in Taita Hills. We were particularly impressed with your entry which demonstrated your obvious passion for Africa and her wildlife.
>
> Please find attached a detailed itinerary and contact details. You will be met in Nairobi by Fikiri Lekanai, who is the manager at Bibi's Camp. He will accompany you for a day in Nairobi, then drive you to the camp on Monday 6th February. Please let us know if you have any concerns or queries. We look forward to welcoming you to Bibi's Camp!
>
> Yours sincerely,
> Barbara Chege
> Proprietor

She tucked the letter back into her handbag and nudged her husband awake. 'Dan, come on. How you can sleep through this, I don't know.'

'Hmm, what? Yes, I'm all set. Are the kids ready?'

When they eventually reached the back door of the plane, the heat and light hit Gigi in the face with such force, she nearly stumbled. The hairs in her nostrils bristled as she inhaled, prickling the back of her throat. Above the airstrip, a murder of crows hovered and bickered, familiar, yet not. African crows living a parallel life to those back in England, but still behaving in the same way – opportunistic and ballsy.

'Look, kids – over on those telegraph wires – swallows. They've flown all the way from Europe, just like us,' said Dan.

'But without the onboard screens and complimentary nuts!' joked Xander.

They jostled through the various checks, gathered their bags, double, triple checked everything, then went to search the arrivals area for the promised Fikiri.

'Please, let me help you with those bags, madam.' A man smiled toothlessly at them, keeping pace.

'Come, come, my sister's shop is just here. She sells fresh lemonade and beer for good price,' another man shouted across at them amiably.

'Take my taxi, sir. Anywhere you like, I can take you there.'

Gigi and Dan were polite but firm as they pushed past the hawkers to reach the barrier. Annie pointed, giggling, to a man holding up a small sign with the word '*Weddybum*' scrawled in large green letters.

Fikiri was all smiles as he hurled the bags into the back of his open-top jeep. 'Welcome, welcome! Did you have a good flight? Are you hungry? Did you want to buy anything at the airport?' Fikiri barely paused for breath, not allowing for any answers to his rapid-fired questions. The family all chattered at once in reply and to each other. There was a nervous excitement and relief at completing the first part of their journey.

'How far to the camp?' asked Dan when the cacophony died down and they clambered into the jeep.

'Not far, not far. Six, seven hours,' smiled Fikiri.

'Ah. Okay.' This fact sank in and everyone was quiet for a few minutes as Fikiri began to negotiate the road out of Nairobi.

'But you know we don't go now, right?' Fikiri looked at Dan, confused. 'You are visiting the National Park here first. I take you now to the Norfolk, then pick you up at two o'clock for a drive around the park. We don't leave for Bibi's Camp until tomorrow morning.'

'Of course, great. Thanks, Fikiri.' Dan sank into his seat and the chatter resumed.

At 2:00 pm precisely, Fikiri was waiting in the hotel lobby in a crisp white shirt, chinos and a baseball cap, ready to take the family to Nairobi National Park. The journey seemed to take only a few minutes, but they were heart-stopping minutes, filled with constant horn-honking, yelling and loud music.

A minibus, known locally as a matatu, as Fikiri explained, had broken down on what resembled a roundabout, in that it was round – no other similarities could have been inferred with one in Europe. Scores of people seemed to spew from the van, which should surely have only accommodated about twelve. There was a lot of shouting from the surrounding drivers, but another matatu was quick to pick up the passengers and benefit from his fellow driver's misfortune. The process of transferring the passengers and getting back on the road was astonishingly efficient and everyone was soon moving again, if not exactly according to the rules of the road. One unfortunate lingering traveller appeared to have lost several scrawny chickens, which, not believing their luck, had scattered to freedom.

The park was just outside the frenzied city. They drove on the main Uhuru Road, past the national Wilson Airport and away from the thick, eye-watering smell of the tyre factories. Gigi looked out of her window at wizened marabou storks which seemed to inhabit every spartan tree in the city. They scoured and scavenged in the many piles of detritus strewn along the pavements, watched over by hovering black kites. Gradually, the gaps widened between the giant posters of smiling politicians and Omo washing powder, until there was more green than concrete. Once they passed through the security gates, guarded by armed rangers, the park was surprisingly quiet and tranquil, all traces of the city forgotten. On first impression, the park seemed rich with grasses, trees and water, but less abundant with animals.

Past the entrance gate, they drove up a small hill, where Fikiri stopped beside a large concrete cube. 'Before we go on, I wanted you to see this.' Fikiri let the party get out of the jeep for a few minutes to read the inscriptions on a brass plate fixed to the large monument. Annie read it aloud. 'This monument which commemorates the burning of 12 tons of ivory by HE President Daniel T arap Moi on July 18th 1989 was made possible by the generosity of the East African Wildlife Society and the World Wide Fund for Nature. Great objectives often require great sacrifices. I now call upon the people of the world to join us in Kenya by eliminating the trade in ivory once and for all.'

'But why did they burn it?' asked Xander. 'When you have so much poverty, couldn't the government sell it and use the money for good?'

'Some people would agree with you. The ivory was worth about $60 million,' said Fikiri. 'But we are very proud as a nation of our stand. We did it to show our intolerance for the ivory trade. We are a developing country, so it was a huge gesture. But the more ivory is acceptable as a tradable commodity, the more it will be desired and, therefore, poaching will increase, do you see? That is not good for our country. Poaching has sadly increased more and more since 1989 and we have had more burnings since then. The ivory market has increased because of decisions made by large international bodies to allow the sale by other countries of their stockpiled ivory. They wanted to do what you say – sell in order to bring money into their governments. But it stimulated the market and poaching has – what's the phrase? – "gone through the roof" now.'

'So, it was a pointless gesture,' mused Xander.

'Not pointless for us,' said Fikiri, sternly. 'We stand by our decisions. We have paid the price for other people's bad choices, but we will not sink to their level.' For the first time since they had met him, Fikiri was unsmiling.

'Kenya has been so brave,' said Annie quietly.

A little more sombre, the family got back into the jeep and drove on. The first creatures they saw were hartebeest – tall, chocolatey antelope, with ridged, twisted horns, bent to an outline that reminded Gigi of a Greek vase. They were both elegant and rather butch. She could understand why they didn't seem overly perturbed at the car's presence. These were not fey, jumpy creatures. They stood calm and proud.

The group seemed to drive for a long while before seeing anything more, until they reached a small waterhole where, opened up before them, was a tableau – apparently enacted just for their private enjoyment. Several types of antelope were gathered at one end. Fikiri identified them as impala and reebok. Two giraffes stood at the bank opposite their jeep. One nibbling contemplatively at a high branch of a eucalyptus tree, the other standing with all its legs akimbo to allow it to bend down far enough to reach the water.

Fikiri explained that there were officially three types of giraffe in Kenya – the Nubian, the Reticulated and the Rothschilds, but recently the Masai giraffe had also been declared a species on its own. 'There has been debate back and forward with the powers that be about how we should categorise our species and subspecies. It sounds boring, but it matters, you see. It makes a difference to how their numbers are counted and whether they qualify for further funding. The conservation world is a complex one, I can tell you, with many disagreements such as this, clouding the issues. Everyone is so passionate about their cause, but different bodies squabble over the importance of their project or species over others. These are desperate times.'

'Are giraffes in trouble?' asked Dan.

'They call the giraffe the "forgotten megafauna",' replied Fikiri in a quiet voice. 'There has been so much attention on lions, elephants and rhino, that people almost forgot about giraffes and they have been quietly declining at a huge rate for the same reasons as the others – habitat loss and poaching.'

This fact left the party quiet for a long time as they sat and watched. Like the closing scene of a play, the animals left in small groups, until all that remained on stage was a pair of young wart-hogs. Fikiri gently restarted the engine and they moved on.

The vegetation cleared to reveal an open dry area, only spartanly covered with scrubby bushes. A group of ostriches – one very haughty male and three females – skittered away from the jeep's path and seemed to vanish into thin air.

The scrub thickened a little and Annie piped up: 'Look – lots of bottoms – they look like cows!'

Fikiri laughed. 'Not cows, exactly. Buffalo. We need to drive carefully around the herd. They are very grumpy creatures.'

They slowed down to look at the buffalo and give them a wide berth. The tightly packed herd seemed to surround them in all directions.

'Can you see they are a mix of males and females? The males are easy to pick out – their horns form that saddle of solid bone which flicks out to the sides. It's called a "boss". Nothing can penetrate that,' explained Fikiri. 'Not even a bullet. Only after they are dead can burrowing ants eat away at the horns.'

The buffalos' confidence showed. They stood, quite unper-turbed, with only the occasional steamy snort indicating any an-noyance at the human presence.

Into the thicker trees, and there was less to see at ground level now, so they looked up. There on a high protruding branch was an owl, then behind it another, perched on what looked like a nest, but was set too high for them to see what might be inside.

'They are Verreaux's eagle-owls,' said Fikiri.

'I love their pink eyelids' said Gigi. 'Very Bette Davis!'

No one spoke for a while, and the rhythm of the jeep on the rough road, despite the jolting, had a soporific effect on the party. Their adrenaline had worn off and the tiredness from their flight had set in. Gigi's eyes even began to slow blink as her head bobbed up and down with each bump in the road. Suddenly, Fikiri gasped and slowed down quickly but gently. 'Look, look – there – just up ahead!'

Gigi sat up straight and tried to focus. There was a rhino right in front on them and, behind it, a tiny baby.

'A BBB!' laughed Fikiri with clear delight.

'A what?' Xander asked.

'Black baby behind! They are black rhino. The white rhino – they are not black and white – it was called "Weit" meaning "wide" because it has a wide mouth and that got misunderstood and the black was called "black", so as not to confuse it with the white. Anyway, the white rhino eats grass, more like a cow. They have their babies in front, so they can keep an eye on them as they graze. You see, black rhinos are browsers – they eat from bushes. The black rhino mother walks in front of her baby to clear the bush in front of it. BBB!'

The rhino and her calf disappeared like magic into the bush.

By now the light was nearly gone and they trundled out of the park. Gigi realised that they had not seen a single other vehicle since arriving through the gates. Now the scene was shockingly different. The traffic chaos of earlier was now exacerbated by the dark, and the sudden noise was hard to adjust to.

* * *

As they ate their dinner that evening, Gigi sat back and watched her family; they were buzzing with the events of the day.

'What was your favourite animal today, Annie?' Xander asked his sister.

'The baby rhino, no question. I've never seen anything so ugly and so sweet at the same time!'

'Hah, true. I liked the giraffes. I had no idea there were different species, I just thought a giraffe was a giraffe.'

Gigi smiled over at Dan; he gave her a knowing smile back, took a big gulp of beer and sat back contentedly in his seat. 'My favourite thing was the memorial. I found that really poignant. It just put a different perspective on everything we saw. When Fikiri said how far the trip to camp is going to be tomorrow, I was a bit horrified,' he said 'but actually, I think I want to make the most of everything, even the long drives. It's just like nothing else I've ever done.'

'How about you, Mum? Are you enjoying the trip so far?' Annie looked at her mother intently.

Gigi nodded, smiling and swallowed the scratchiness in her throat.

CHAPTER 20

NAIROBI 2012

'GOOD morning, everyone!' Fikiri was smart and cheerful as he met the family outside the Norfolk and helped them pack their luggage back into the jeep. 'I'll help you check out, then we're off to a rather special place this morning. We have a few spare hours before we need to head off and you are going to visit the David Sheldrick Elephant Orphanage.'

'That's where the orphaned elephants go first when they've been rescued?' asked Gigi.

'Normally, yes. It's the main hub for the charity, too. The centre near your camp is in Tsavo East and is for older, stronger babies where they are habituated with other eles and gradually released into the wild. The Nairobi centre is where they go as tiny babies to be nursed and treated. Sometimes they are very damaged.'

At the orphanage, Fikiri told them, the elephants ranged in age from one month to about a year – some were tiny, just the size of large dogs. Others seemed already huge to Gigi – shoulder high and very boisterous. Initial trepidation about the condition of the orphans was forgotten as the family became absorbed in watching them tumbling over each other and playing. Talking over the din as a group of elephant babies played a spirited game of football, a senior ranger, Edwin, explained the work of the charity. Edwin had an earnest face; his voice was gentle and slow, but he commanded the attention of all the visitors with his obvious affection for the animals in his care. He pointed out a few of the individuals and explained how they had ended up at the orphanage. A three-month-old male had been separated from his herd after a confrontation on a farm. Another had been found standing alone beside her dying mother who had probably been poisoned.

Annie was particularly taken with a very sweet female called Quanza – nine months old, a little clumsy and very determined. When she got hold of the grubby squashed football, she flung her trunk around it, posting it under her legs, and proceeded to sit on it, squabbling with the other elephants as they tried to push her off the ball. When Annie asked him what her story was, Edwin explained that she had been found at the bottom of a latrine pit by a group of passing children.

Edwin took the family to a little enclosure to the side of the main building. 'Come with me and see something, it is not only elephants that land up here. We take in all sorts of waifs and strays. People know we're here and know we care, so we get other babies.' Seemingly unperturbed by their presence, a huge adult black rhino stood a few hundred yards away, grazing pensively from a net bag full of green branches.

'Some baby!' Dan chuckled.

Edwin clicked his tongue repeatedly against his teeth. The rhino clearly recognised this gentle summons, and he ambled over to the group. 'His name is Rufus. He's seven years old. He first came to us when he was a baby and has returned to us now. He knows he's safe here. He did have a mate, also raised by the Trust, and we think she was pregnant. But she has been killed, probably poached. The authorities told us that she had been poisoned, so they burnt her carcass. They said they didn't want to risk poisoning other animals, but we suspect she had been shot.'

'Why do you think that?' asked Xander.

'There had been similar incidents in this area, but the authorities want to play it down, as they need the tourists to feel safe. And you are, of course,' he added, hurriedly. 'Poachers mainly operate at night and you would never be out in the bush at night. They are after the horns, of course, for the Asian markets. They can earn a year's salary in one night if they succeed in getting a horn.'

A woman standing by the sleeping pens waved over to Edwin, gesturing him to bring the family over.

'Let me introduce you to Daphne Sheldrick, our founder and matriarch,' said Edwin. 'I shall leave you to chat, while I get on with the morning feed.'

'Good morning!' Daphne greeted them with a smile and an extended hand. Daphne's kind face had the weatherbeaten ruddiness that was characteristic of those who had spent a lifetime in the tropics. 'I understand that you are off to Taita Hills today to work on a volunteer project down there.'

'Yes, we are. We're very excited about it,' said Annie.

'Would you be able to take some things down to our other centre for us? We have some paperwork and some meds to go there. If we know someone is going anyway, it saves us a trip.'

'Of course,' said Dan. 'Just speak to Fikiri, over there – he's driving us.'

'I will. Thank you so much. Now, what is your name, young lady?' She looked down at Annie who was not looking at her, but staring out at the elephants being corralled into the feeding pen.

'Oh, yes, sorry, it's Annie,' she broke from her daydream.

'And how old are you?'

'I'm ten.'

'Well, Annie, you are obviously very grown up, so you can help to feed them in a moment, but for now, would you like to see something rather special?'

'Yes, please.'

'Come this way. But you must be quiet as a mouse. Just in here, have a peek over the wall.'

Daphne stood back a little to let the family look into a small dark pen. 'He's a year old, we just picked him up last night,' whispered Daphne. In the corner of the pen a small elephant was lying, covered by a blanket, guarded by two wardens.

'He is sleeping off a tranquiliser for now. It will be a shock when he wakes up, so both Boniface and Ernest are here to calm him.'

'Poor boy,' said Annie. 'But he looks quite big and strong compared to some of them.'

'Well, yes he does,' Boniface answered, 'but at one year old, he might be more fragile than the other elephants, as he will have spent more time within his herd, bonding with his family.'

The elephant's breathing was steady and sonorous. He lay quite still, but occasionally, his trunk flicked, or his ear whipped up, as if he were dreaming. His skin was surprisingly supple and smooth, except for his trunk and he had a fuzz of baby hair running up the ridge of his back, just peeking from under the blanket.

'He was found near Mount Kenya,' Boniface continued. 'His family had been poached. We got a call yesterday and went up there and brought him back last night.'

'Will he understand what is happening?' asked Xander.

'Not at first,' said Boniface. 'And you know, sometimes elephants grieve so much that they just die from unhappiness and there is nothing we can do.'

Annie looked distraught but Daphne quickly explained. 'They are given so much love here from the keepers and the other elephants. They have the best possible chance. We'll let you know how he gets on. I have a good feeling about him.'

'Does he have a name?' asked Annie.

Gigi could see she was trying to be brave and grown up and it touched her heart.

'We normally give them a name that is to do with where they were found, but I think perhaps we can bend the rules today. Would you like to name him, Annie? No matter what happens to him, he will bear your name and you can be very proud of him.'

Gigi wasn't sure that Annie really understood, and worried that she would be broken-hearted if this elephant died. But she never sugar-coated things for her back home, and this trip was bound to teach them all some brutal lessons, cushioned as they had been in their life in England.

'Barbar,' said Annie without hesitation. 'Like in the books. He's a strong and regal elephant and I know he will be fine.'

'Very well, Barbar it is. Come now, you can help feed the babies which, believe me doesn't take long!'

Each member of the family was handed a bottle and told to thrust it into the mouth of an elephant. They had each been allocated one baby, while some of the keepers expertly fed two at the same time, juggling and passing each other fresh bottles when the first ran out after a few seconds. It was a joyful, frenzied few minutes of flapping trunks and concentrated guzzling. Within what seemed like moments, all the bottles were finished, and the family panted, clutching empty bottles, stroking elephants and taking photographs.

'Wow!' laughed Gigi. 'I feel like I've run a hundred-metre dash!'

'I know what you mean,' said Dan. 'My guy has no manners, he just kept nudging me for more, more, more!'

They followed the lead of the keepers and other visitors and returned their milk bottles to the crates they had come from. They chatted a while longer as they walked. Daphne told them of a female visitor to the orphanage whom the elephants had kept slapping with their trunks.

'It was the oddest behaviour. We had never seen them behave that way. They normally pay very little attention to the visitors and certainly don't get distressed like that. So, one of the keepers had to go over to the elephants and move them away from the woman. It turned out she was wearing an ivory bracelet. They knew what it was, and it really upset them.'

'Why on earth would she wear one, especially somewhere like this?' said Gigi.

'There's no figuring some people,' agreed Daphne. 'She just hadn't made the connection, I guess. She must have just thought, what do I wear to an elephant sanctuary. Well, this bracelet is elephant-y, that will be just the thing.'

'You must despair of humans sometimes.'

'I do sometimes, but you know, elephants are far more forgiving and empathetic than people. I heard about a man who had a car crash in the Tsavo area, you know, near where you are heading later. He was found by a herd of elephants. They buried him gently in leaves. Perhaps they took him for dead, as they will do this for dead elephants, or perhaps they were trying to protect him. Whatever it was, that action probably saved his life – protected him from predators.'

They were nearing the exit and slowed to a stop. 'So, what did you think of our orphanage?' Daphne directed the question to Annie.

'It was amazing,' said Annie. 'I think it is the saddest and the happiest place I have ever been, all at the same time.'

'I know just what you mean,' said Daphne quietly. 'It is very sad that we have to be here at all, that there is such a need. But here we are, and we try to help every animal that's brought here. We never turn anyone away. And between us we have years and years of experience and love. And hope – what we have more than anything is hope. And elephants sense that, you know. They trust us and we have a lot of success in setting them free. Please try to visit our unit down in Tsavo.'

'Yes, we plan to' said Gigi. 'We're staying near there, and we hope to spend a few days with your colleagues. I'm sure we'll have an awful lot to learn.'

'Perhaps,' said Daphne, 'but really, you just need kindness and patience. The very best of luck. Do get in touch if you need help with anything. Fikiri has my number here.'

They said their goodbyes and left to get into the jeep. Suddenly, Annie turned and ran back to Daphne, throwing her arms around her middle. Daphne knelt down to be level with Annie's face and hugged her back. The family got into the jeep wordlessly and waited for Fikiri.

'You okay?' Dan asked Gigi.

'What a lovely woman,' whispered Gigi. 'She just has a sort of glow about her, do you know what I mean?'

'I do, love.'

'Right, everybody.' Fikiri re-joined them in the car. 'Xander, can you put this behind you in the back? A few bits and pieces for us to take to the rehab unit. All strapped in? OK, Taita Hills, here we come!'

MAKENA

TAITA HILLS 1984

PERHAPS there will be rain today. Every time the sun rises, this is what I think. Today, perhaps there will be rain. We are lying in the shade of a cluster of fever trees. But they are no more than twigs and do not keep the relentless sun off our backs. I look around at my family. My great grandmothers are gone, long since. Fierce is still matriarch, but our family is much changed. Cross Tusks, matriarch of our fellow clan is dead, and her family scattered. Dew Drop, Pink Tail and her little brother, Muddy, have joined our family, but the rest of them are gone, we don't know where. We have lost Birdie, she got sick and we had to leave her in a patch of shade. She lay there for days, just breathing shallowly until she was taken. Fierce knew when her time had come, and we all gathered back at her shady spot and laid branches over her. When we did this for the great grandmothers, we laid good green juicy branches over their heads to nourish them, but we could only lay bare sticks over Birdie. I think about this – time and again. It was not right, but we had no choice. My little brother, Left Tip, should have left last season to make it on his own, but the time is not right. He still needs the guidance of Fierce and his sisters and aunties, or who knows what fate awaits him.

The bulls have become aggressive. Where they used to edge our group, drink with us, pass on news of further family, now they are filled with anger. We came across Treetop a few days ago standing stock still beside an upside-down tree. When he saw us, he ran straight at us. Fierce and Flower had to bellow back at him and stand their ground, with us behind them. We thought he would plough right through us, but something stopped him, and he turned and loped off. He did not look like the proud, regal bull he always was: he looked broken.

I have a baby of my own now to look after – Butterfly. She is named for the butterflies that I liked to watch when my family rested under the fever trees. She seems to flap her little delicate ears like they are wings, with slow, focused intent. I love all my family, but I love Butterfly fiercely and I worry every day now that she will not get food or water. She has lived through two long rains and she was strong and determined, but now I can see her weakening. Her legs are thin and I when I caress her face with my trunk, I can feel the small sharp bones under her fragile skin. She tries to keep up as we follow Fierce in her search for water, but she becomes tired and sleeps much more than she did. She was lively like me, restless when she should have been resting, playful and naughty. But now her spirit is leaving her, and I cannot help. I can only keep her close and give her any good leaves or scrub I can find, let her drink first, keep her warm with my body at night.

We have followed Fierce to a place far, far from anywhere we have been before. All the places we know have dried up. We have circled our lands over and over in ever increasing spirals, but now we need to move on. This land is where Cross Tusks used to walk. But Cross Tusks is gone, and we do not have her wisdom to guide us. We have only the knowledge of Fierce and the other older aunties. Now, Fierce has certainty in her stride. She has begun to march purposefully, and we must keep up. Butterfly is struggling to keep pace and holds back. I slow with her, following her loping, exhausted gait, despite my instinct to catch up with the others.

We are beginning to lag behind. Light Eyes turns to check us and sees how far behind we are. She must have signalled to the others as they turn, as one, to face us, lifting their trunks – questions in the air. I push Butterfly a little behind her rump to guide her towards the group who now wait patiently for us. But she, with a remaining spark of her old stubbornness, plonks herself down with a force I have missed in her. If only this wasn't the wrong time to be obstinate. She needs to move. I try to lift her up with my trunk, pushing at her bottom, but she shoves down, so I succeed only in driving her along the ground, in what might otherwise be a comical pose. I look back at my family imploringly and they come to us. They circle Butterfly. Directly in front of her is Fierce, who gently caresses her face and purrs soothingly. Butterfly tips her head into the caress and finds resolve in it. She rises to her feet, wobbly but determined, and we set off again, slower than before, but with a pervading sense of urgency. It is not long before we see in front of us the source of Fierce's premonition. Amid the baked dusty ground is a green patch. It is not as lush as the doum palms fringing the wide river, or the euphorbia forests full of vervet monkeys, but there is a sweet smell of maize and beans.

We approach softly at first, cautiously as we do not know this land, but then relief and joy overcome us and we run and run and throw ourselves into the tall straight plants. We gorge ourselves on the juicy vegetables, stripping the cobs from their stalks. Butterfly feeds on the dropped maize at my feet. There is trumpeting and snorting and joy.

Suddenly, there is a loud crack. Louder than a tree snapping. We stop eating and wait for two heartbeats. Then all is chaos. Fierce screams and backs into us, pushing at us with her bottom. Her gaze is fixed on something. There is a creature in front of us pointing something at us. I don't understand what it is, but Fierce, Light Eyes and One Tusk do, and their panic is immediate and pervading. We all turn to run away from the creature, but we get our legs caught up in the maize stalks and in some sort of tangled thing on the ground. There is another snap, we run hard this time, the babies keeping up as the fear drives them forward. We run and run until we find a small kopje and there we stop to catch our breath.

My head is bowed at first, but I lift it to check Butterfly. She is there hidden between me and the grey rocks. But as I look up at the rest of the group, I notice something – a stick jutting out of Fierce's side. She doesn't seem to have noticed it yet. She is checking two of the youngsters, dipping her trunk behind their ears, purring. I move towards her to check her. I sniff at the stick. It smells odd – sour and hot. Then I see that Fierce has blood coming from her side where the stick is jammed in her. She looks at me and at the stick as if she has only just noticed it. She tries to pull at it with her trunk, but the angle is wrong. The youngsters move away to give us room and I get hold of the stick and yank it hard. It comes away, but when I look at the wound, there is something stuck in it. I signal to Flower who has the strongest and most agile trunk of all of us. She takes her time, feeling around the wound, sniffing to calculate exactly where the object is, then with one swift tug, she pulls it out. Fierce screams, but composes herself as soon as the object is out of her side.

She fusses over the wound for a moment, but is suddenly alert. Something is wrong. Her eyes pass across us all, then she shakes her head frantically. It is not long before we all realise what has upset her. Pink Tail is not with us. A surge of panic fills me as I search all the faces for my friend, but she is not here. Fierce backs out of our cluster and turns towards the place we ran from. We copy her and look up the hill towards the green patch in the distance. Trunks aloft, we can sense a wisp of Pink Tail in the air, like she is passing by us in a thin dust cloud and is gone. Muddy lets out one shrill screech, but at this, another stick flies towards us, landing with a small thud on the ground at our feet. All we can do is run away. We have to leave Pink Tail and get to safety.

We don't stop running until we are far out of reach of the creature and its sticks. It is safe here and we can rest and Fierce and the aunties can tend to her wound. Dark is approaching, so we make the most of the cool and bed down. Not one of us sleeps, though. We are too full of fear and loss and worry for what the next day will bring.

PART 4

CHAPTER 21

EAST NEUK, SCOTLAND 2003

'IT'S so bumpy!' A woman perched across the aisle had been complaining since the bus set off. 'I don't know why they don't sort out this road. It gets worse every winter. All the snow and the tractors. The roads crack under all that strain and they only ever patch it up. And we have to be thrown around on this bus which is going TOO fast!'

She had raised her voice in the direction of the driver for that last statement. Fenella cringed. The woman was so ignorant and rude. It wasn't the driver's fault and he had to keep moving to get to the stops on time. The roads here were absolutely fine.

In Africa, the potholes caused you to be thrown around so much that you often feared you might bite right through your tongue. One day, when she was out driving with her mother getting groceries, they approached a hole in the road so big, a goat had fallen in and was clambering to get out. Luckily, her mother was always primed and ready for such surprise encounters and swerved, leaving the goat none the wiser of its potential fate. By contrast, Scotland's roads seemed a paragon of modernity and good maintenance. Fenella marvelled at the orderliness at traffic lights and roundabouts, the good manners with which drivers generally behaved, waving to acknowledge a fellow driver who had allowed them to pass through a tricky weave of parked cars. On Africa's roads, you took your chances and took no prisoners.

Fenella settled into the journey, finding the woman's constant droning and the winding road had a rather soporific effect on her. She always sat on a left-side window seat if she could. This way she could peer over the hills and tall fir trees at the sea below, the road tracing the curve of the coast. Sometimes the view was obscured as they detoured from the main road to drop off passengers, but as they picked up the road again, there would be a glimpse of deep blue, then a full view of the sea in all its glory. The waters of this coast reminded Fenella of a wild woman, whose mood you could never predict. She was a nurturer, feeding the local people and birds with a fecundity of fish, but she could become tempestuous without warning and many souls had been lost fishing these shores. The view was never the same two days running. In winter storms, the water was a boiling stew of bleak grey-green, indistinguishable from the low livid clouds. On calm days, the little two-tone, two-man boats bound for home, drifted leisurely into harbour, perhaps savouring the calm of the shallower waters, leaving behind them the squall of the Atlantic Ocean. A puff of sea birds wheeling above them as they brought their catch to port.

Today was dull, but the sea was still blue – not China-blue, more a deep indigo. The low tide revealed sharp, toothy granite rocks flanking the coast. These rocks formed the last line of defence between the sea and the land. Sometimes, as the sun's shadows played tricks on the rocks, they seemed more benign and you could swear they were gaggles of beached seals, until several minutes of staring at them proved you wrong.

Today had been another anxious day. Fenella's school was like those she'd read about in books – stiff and prim – but it lacked the awfully good adventures. The emphasis was on order and compliance, not learning and creativity. The uniform, something she had never had occasion to wear before, was mostly grey and made of a scratchy woollen fabric that was heavy as armour, and yet still not enough to keep out the cold of this damp Scottish climate. At least its anonymity suited her – this armour shielded her from the world. And she succeeded in staying fairly anonymous, despite her unusual upbringing and appearance. She was strangely ordinary or something. At first, when she had arrived in the middle of the school year the previous March, other students had been intrigued. But when the inevitable probing revealed nothing exciting, they had soon lost interest in her. Of course, her accent was unfamiliar and her physical appearance was decidedly unusual. Her hair was fiery red like that of her mother and uncle, but unlike them, and most Scots, it formed a puff of long corkscrew curls. Her mother had always told her to be proud of this striking feature which so embodied her dual heritage, but her desire to avoid the inevitable questions caused her to try, unsuccessfully, to scrape back her locks into a discreet low ponytail.

She was even more of an oddity because, although she had come from overseas, she didn't board. Many of the other pupils had come from other countries, or had parents who still lived abroad, but they almost all boarded. Day pupils tended to be from the local area, born and bred, the children of local doctors, lawyers, golf-course owners. These were two clans and, although there was no outward animosity between them, they were quite distinct. Fenella was neither one thing nor another; she had come from Africa, but lived locally with her aunt and uncle.

Her childhood had been remote and free, and she had never before attended a conventional school, which meant her chances to make proper friends of her own had been few and far between. She never talked about her parents and was vague if anyone asked. Her fellow pupils had more or less stopped asking and she had been accepted, if not embraced, by the school community. Her circumstances and her refusal to talk about them made it hard to make trusted friends, to find common ground with someone. No one was outwardly cruel or unkind to her, but she just didn't fit, so she kept her own company.

She had always buried herself in books and returned to the company of familiar characters. Her friends were Jane Eyre, the second Mrs de Winter, Cassandra Mortmain in *I Capture the Castle*. She felt safe, embraced by these women who were out of place, outwardly awkward and timid but, when the chips were down, rose to the challenge, emboldened by their circumstances.

For now, her solitude suited her. She went to school, did what was expected of her, went back to her uncle's house and otherwise spent as much time as she could soaking up the local landscape and wild places. Luckily her aunt and uncle were not only kind, but free-spirited and gave Fenella the space she needed.

Other differences were also evident between Fenella and her new contemporaries. She was much further ahead in her education than the rest of her class. Their ignorance and their apathy towards their education astonished Fenella. She'd had to curb her enthusiasm for learning as she had learned early on that to seem too keen was a serious social faux pas. Even the teachers seemed to be irritated by her precocity. Her first week had included a case in point.

'Who can tell me the origins of the story of *Frankenstein* by Mary Shelley? Fenella?'

'Erm, well, there are parallels with the Promethean myth from *Ovid* and Coleridge's *Rime of the Ancient Mariner* – you know, the whole making a man from the image of the gods and the revenge of the oppressed. And Mary Shelley was very interested in the ethics surrounding scientific breakthroughs of the time – in chemistry and physics.'

When she had stopped talking, Fenella could tell from the silent gaping of her classmates and the teacher's pinched expression that this was not what she'd meant, and Fenella had only succeeded in looking like a know-all.

'Thank you, Fenella. Very illuminating, I'm sure. But what I was getting at was who was Mary married to at the time and what led up to her writing the book? Yes, Millie?'

'She was married to the poet Percy Shelley and was on holiday with him and a load of other poets and they had a sort of competition to see who could come up with the scariest story,' answered Millie.

From then on, Fenella tempered her contributions to the class to be more middle of the road and non-contentious. This frustrated her, however. She felt fit to burst a lot of the time, hemmed in by all the restrictions which seemed to exist to stifle the students, to stop them from expressing opinions, or even *having* their own opinions.

One morning, after another attempt at answering a question to everyone's satisfaction, this time in a history class, she began to get flustered and agitated. Over the next hour, she got so hot in her uniform that this escalated into panic. By the time breaktime came, she had stripped off her blazer and tie and made her way to the grounds. She had to clutch the wall several times on the way outside to steady herself, as her knees began to buckle. Her heart beat, beat, beat into her ribcage and dark stains flowered under her arms. Once she got outside, she ran. The grounds of this gothic building were well stocked with trees and intricately laid out gardens – a Victorian notion of academic inspiration. Fenella made for a far-off copse in the furthest corner of the estate.

Here she stopped, threw down her blazer and leant her back against a tall pine tree – slinking down it as she caught her breath – and sobbed. Her panic was replaced by anger. She fumbled with her thick grey skirt, reached for the top of her woollen tights and pulled them and her pants down. Angry tears trickled down her face as she squatted and peed at the base of the tree. Instantly, she felt better. She sorted her underwear and skirt and flung herself on top of her blazer, legs outstretched, staring up through the thick tall spikes of the Douglas firs to the clouds above. She started to laugh at the ridiculousness of what she had just done. It was a little protest against the restrictions of her new surroundings. It was an invisible protest, nevertheless, she felt a little surge of satisfaction, of marking her territory here.

As her breathing normalised and she grew calmer, she made a decision. This was just a temporary thing she would have to endure. She would go to school, pass her exams, do everything she was supposed to, but as soon as she could, she would go back to Africa. This school was a means to an end, and the end was Africa. And it was all very well reading about people who were interesting, brave and kind; if she followed her plan, she might also find a way to be these things herself. People told her that she was brave already, to have come through everything that had happened. But she didn't really believe them. She needed to prove it to herself.

The bus paused at Fenella's stop and she got off and crossed the road to the little supermarket. Every day, she picked up whatever order her aunt had phoned through that morning. Today, Mr Patel had put together a small box of groceries – milk, butter, flour, eggs, bread, bacon, celery, ham and cheddar cheese. Fenella shivered when she inspected the box. This combination of ingredients meant only one thing. Her uncle's dreaded celery wrapped in ham in a runny cheese sauce. She had no idea where he had learnt to cook this dish, but it was an abomination. Nevertheless, Fenella always ate whatever was put in front of her, grateful as she was to have been taken in by this lovely couple.

They had had no children of their own, so her sudden arrival had involved a huge adjustment for all of them. But they were gentle and kind to her, unquestioning, and they gave her the space she needed. This had been the best thing for Fenella, whose world had been so shaken she might not have trusted anyone again. They lived a simple life, running a pottery and art gallery for local painters and sculptors. Her aunt had been a rather glamorous artist, living first in Glasgow and then New York. Fenella's parents had discussed her in rather hushed tones. There had been some sort of scandal, which Fenella never got to the bottom of. Aunt Gabrielle (or Goo as she had always been called, the reason having been lost to family lore) had returned to Scotland when she married and, although still glamorous in Fenella's eyes, was now in far more humble surroundings. That didn't seem to matter to Goo, though. She and Uncle Andrew were clearly devoted to each other and they were part of a thriving local artistic community.

The pottery was a magical place to Fenella. Andrew's parents Donald and Claire, Fenella's grandparents, had started it and had now retired to a small cottage in the village, leaving the business to Andrew and his three siblings. Although Andrew's brother and sisters and a few of the next generation still intermittently worked at the pottery over the years, Andrew and Goo had really made it their own.

Donald and Claire had been Fine Art students at Glasgow School of Art in the 1960s, but instead of staying in the city to follow more commercial and lucrative careers, they moved north east. They had been on a holiday the summer after graduation, driving their old campervan around the east coast when they chanced upon this area, fell in love with it and, on a romantic whim, bought a derelict collection of unwanted council-owned fisherman's crofts five minutes' walk from the beach. They bought the cottages – which were completely uninhabitable – for just a few hundred pounds, funded by their meagre savings, a small loan from their parents, and wages paid in advance for manual labour carried out for a local sheep farmer.

The crofts were laid out in an L shape, surrounded by a high wall with an overgrown square of land in the middle. After a few days spent clearing this land of brambles, thistles and rocks, Claire and Donald, drove in, parked up and lived in the campervan whilst renovating the buildings, bit by bit, as time and money would allow, occasionally helped by visiting arty friends from university, who camped in any parts of the cottages that were dry and warm enough to sleep in. Evenings were spent cooking crabs or langoustines over fires on the beach, drinking strong homemade cider and putting the world to rights. Andrew was born in their second summer in the crofts, followed by three more children in the next three summers.

Once the crofts were completely habitable, they moved the campervan to a far corner and turned the land into a courtyard with a small vegetable garden in the south-facing section. Here, the family grew potatoes, onions and beans (nothing very delicate could grow in this sharp, salty climate) and Claire tried to prettify the garden with the begonias and nasturtiums that reminded her of more Mediterranean climes. What they lacked here were colourful pots to complete the continental effect. So, hearing of a potter's wheel and kiln going cheap in a house clearance near Leuchars, Donald and two of the children trundled off in the van and returned with, not just the wheel and kiln, but bags of clay, shelving racks, stools and even aprons. Putting their basic ceramics training back into practice, the couple set about experimenting with pots: seeing what would survive the warm summers and freezing cold winters of their garden. The children took great joy in sculpting tiny penguins, elephants and hedgehogs out of the spare clay. The tiny fingerprints squashed into ears and wings would be treasured forever.

Claire and Donald realised they might have a commercial business on their hands after more and more visitors fell under the spell of the 'Spanish garden'. They began to make pots as gifts for friends, then a local florist bought a few to display spring bulbs outside her shop and the word spread. The couple started to make smaller, more delicate items like milk jugs and cups, and business boomed. Donald had been doing farm labouring and signwriting to make ends meet and Claire had taken in sewing and looked after a couple of local children. Now they could focus more of their time on what was becoming a passion and growing venture for them both.

Into this environment in which Andrew had been raised, Goo had brought her more flamboyant artistic designs. She still had some useful contacts in the broader art world and had managed to bring the family's pots to wider and more lucrative markets, particularly in the States and China, who were charmed by their authenticity and evocation of their Scottish origins. Fenella admired the way the family had managed to maintain their creativity, ethos and their community spirit, whilst being able to bring in a good income.

'I'm home!' Fenella called through as she stepped up the little stoop and bowed her head under the stone arch of the gateway into the courtyard. Over thirty years on and Claire's courtyard looked as authentic as the garden of a Spanish hacienda. It always made Fenella smile. Even in the depths of winter, the colours popped from every corner of the yard. In front of the gate sat a huge trestle table, piled with giant bowls, ewers and platters, each painted in glorious deep colours. Shelving stacks made from old pallets and orange boxes were crammed three layers deep with garden ornaments. Plates were hung from the sides of the shelves, some decorated in geometric patterns, some with swirling fish, abstract boats or circles of houses, reminiscent of the fishermen's cottages in the village. A little garden waterfall bubbled in the corner, the pottery cat lapping from the gentle overspill. Being April, the descendants of those original begonias, busy lizzies and nasturtiums were already in full bloom, some long and twiggy, tumbling out of pots on high shelves, some young and stubby, newly planted in fresh pots. It was one of Fenella's favourite spots in the world – a little bit of sunshine.

She took the box of groceries into the kitchen and made herself a cup of tea. While the kettle boiled, she put the perishables in the fridge. Crackle, the latest in a long line of pottery cats, named for his unusual brindled coat, jumped up on the worktop to greet her and see what titbits she had brought him.

'Hi, Crackle. I'm sure Mr Patel will have sneaked something in here for you. Yes, ooh, a tin of sardines – what a treat, Crackle. Just one, okay.' Crackle batted her hand as she opened the tin, purring loudly and rubbing his chin along Fenella's arm, then forgot all about her as he demolished the sardine.

Kettle boiled, she fixed herself a red bush tea in her favourite cup – a fine portly mug glazed a delicate sea-green and scattered with tiny white birds. She poured out coffees for Goo and Andrew and carried them through to the studio, the local paper tucked under one arm.

'Lovely, Nella. Thank you,' said Goo, smiling but not moving her scalpel from a large Greek urn.

'Smashing, Nell. Any biscuits?' asked Andrew. Fenella and Goo exchanged knowing looks.

Biscuits dispatched, Fenella returned to the courtyard, mug and a new library book in hand. The sun seemed to illuminate the yard even on dull days and she found her favourite chair – an old wooden love seat so tangled with ivy and jasmine that it was now like a plant itself, rooted to the spot. Next to the chair was her grandparents' campervan, no longer roadworthy, but used as a spare bedroom for less discerning visitors, and packed with cushions and throws for use in the yard or when the family ate out on the beach. Nestled in the chair, and with Crackle curled up in a big blue bowl at her feet, she inhaled the calm of the yard. Sea air mixed with clay – the most comforting aroma she knew.

CHAPTER 22

EAST NEUK 2003

'NELLA – tea?' Goo called up the stairs. It was still early, and the sun seemed reluctant to rise. Goo was always first up. She enjoyed the solitude of that first hushed hour of the morning. She would pad about, checking the kilns, organising the glazes and tools required for the day, whilst sipping on a large black coffee. Fenella also woke early, but usually left Goo to her pottering. She would sit by the window and read for a while, looking up now and again to watch the sea. She never took long to get ready and, a habit from her self-sufficient childhood, she always got the next day's clothes ready the night before. So, on school days, she could have an unbroken hour to herself, reading or writing at the little desk by the window before joining the others for breakfast and heading out to catch the bus.

She always slept with the window wide open, despite the nippy Scottish climate; she felt stifled with them closed. The long sash windows of her fortress-like school had been painted so many times the latches were as immovable as limpets. Fenella couldn't bear the stillness of the air inside the classrooms, changing rooms and gym; the stale, still odours and the dust motes. After each ring of the school bell, she was the first to rush outside and gasp the air.

Today was not a school day, however. It was the start of the Easter break and for the next few weeks the pottery would be busy with the first tourists and day-trippers of the season. Andrew would have to hold the fort today, though, as Fenella and Goo had made a pact months earlier to take a day together in the break to go shopping in Edinburgh. Goo understood that Fenella, her day-to-day life so fundamentally altered, would need not just new routines, but things to look forward to, to work towards, so she could keep looking forward, not back at the familiarity and the sadness she had left behind. She and Andrew could provide a cocoon of love and shelter for her at the pottery, but it was good for Fenella to be exposed to bigger, busier places too. Goo herself had always enjoyed spreading her own wings, meeting new people, learning new things.

Fenella, for her part, privately hoped that these trips – this was the third such visit – would develop into a ritual for the two of them. Her grocery market visits with her mum, and her trips into town with her dad to hunt for supplies, had been special to Fenella. Such expeditions served not only as breaks from schoolwork and changes of scene from their camp, remote as it was, but they meant that, for a few precious hours, she had one parent all to herself. The memory of those lost times gnawed at her, piling more guilt and confusion onto her young shoulders.

Joanna had been the nucleus of Fenella's life: her teacher, her warrior, her home. The separation from her family had left her disorientated and she grieved for the things she had taken for granted as a child, particularly the fierce lion-love of her mother. When Fenella felt strong enough, she would squeeze her eyes shut, pushing back through the layers she had draped around her memories, revealing her mother in a singular powerful image. Joanna would be standing firm on the edge of a kopje, surveying the bush. Her hand shielding her eyes from the hot white midday sun, her wild red hair tangled in the warm breeze, catching on her lips. If she were to see her mother now, they would be the same height. Only a year had passed, but the balance would be tipped, the perspective altered.

She did not look for a parental replacement in Goo – she was too different from Joanna, which was a relief. The two of them had not even needed to fumble around in search of a relationship. They just connected from the moment Goo met Fenella off the plane. Goo had not questioned the request that they take Fenella in. It seemed to her the most obvious thing – they were family, they had room and they had no other children to consider. She and Andrew had gently and instinctively coaxed Fenella into some sort of routine and ordinary life. Although her new home was, on the face of it, nothing like Africa, it was quiet and rural and so was better than moving to a busy town or city. There was no possibility that her mother could cope with looking after her now, and her grandmother had her own grief and troubles.

The formidable Goo was in charge of the household – that was clear – but she was kind and sweet and funny and they had settled into a gentle relationship, happier than either of them could have hoped. Goo never asked any searching questions or expected much conversation. Neither was she embarrassed to bring up Fenella's parents in conversation. She talked about them without any hesitations or weighted emphasis. Fenella was not quite ready to do the same, but she appreciated Goo's efforts. She was easy company – a comfort, but with the touch of a lace shawl, not a smothering blanket.

Andrew drove them to Leuchars station to meet the nine o'clock train. Goo had never learnt to drive, there being no money as an art student and no need when she lived in big cities. They would have some errands to run – they needed a few supplies for the pottery that could not be obtained from the usual couple of suppliers. Fine gold-leaf sheets could usually be found from a favourite small art shop on the Lawnmarket, and an old family-run hardware shop in a quiet passage was a treasure trove of essential odds and ends. It amused Fenella how Goo, with all her glamour, could be gleefully occupied for hours over trays of screws and wires at Norton & Sons.

'So, where do you want to go today?' Goo asked as they settled into their train seats. She distractedly blew kisses to a waving Andrew as the train pulled out.

'Chambers Street Museum?' suggested Fenella.

'Of course.'

'Museum of Childhood?'

'Naturally,' replied Goo.

'After that, I don't know. What sort of clothes do I need for the summer? I haven't really got used to the seasons here.'

'Much the same as the winter, darling. Perhaps one less layer,' Goo replied dryly. 'Don't think you need to go clothes shopping. I know it's not really your thing. Bookshops are what you love, so let's do that. There's a lovely one near Norton's, so why don't we split up then and you can mooch on your own for a bit.'

'I'd love to do that. And I have a book token left from Christmas in my purse.'

'Perfect. That's the morning taken care of. You know what we've not done yet and I am dying to do with you?'

'What?' Fenella was a little nervous at the excited look on Goo's face.

'Go to an art gallery.'

'Really. Do you really think that's me? I don't know anything about art.'

'I don't believe that. I don't believe for a minute that Jo didn't talk to you about art.'

'Well, yes, she did. But I suppose she felt it was difficult to explain it if she couldn't properly show me. I mean, we had a few books, but I always found them a bit pompous and wordy. I'm afraid she despaired of me a bit when it came to art. She did love it so, and I think that was one thing she missed from life in Scotland. She had always taken art for granted, growing up surrounded by it, like you all have been. She painted a bit still, but we couldn't get paint easily. She would make up pigments of her own, from leaves and bark and things, but I know she craved proper paint and canvas.'

'Well, I think for your artistic baptism, we should head first to the National Gallery and then to a couple of art shops. I'll try to convert you. If you hate it, we'll go and do something you want to do, but will you please give it a chance?'

'OK, but don't expect me to say anything insightful and clever!'

'Agreed!'

The National Gallery was busy but, Fenella was pleased to note, it was not just full of men in cord jackets and Panama hats, or women in smock dresses and Birkenstocks. There were families wandering round, pushchairs laden with coats, sandwiches, juice bottles and protesting children. Students stood or sat on benches, hunched over sketchpads, frowning meaningfully at their chosen artwork. Fenella was unsure if their serious poses were affectatious or genuine. A tiny old lady was standing in front of what looked to Fenella like nothing more than a yellow square with a red dot, just off centre. The lady appeared to be quietly weeping.

Goo took her directly to a section on Pop Art, thinking this would be a gentle introduction. Fenella recognised a Warhol which formed the centre of the exhibition, surrounded by dancing Keith Haring figures.

'What do you think?' asked Goo, trying to play down her excitement.

'I'm sorry, but I just don't get it. It just looks mass produced. Like comic books or television.'

'Well, it's supposed to. The point is that art doesn't have to be highbrow, the things depicted don't have to be expensive or enjoyed only by the wealthy. A tin of soup is as worthy of our interest as a fine racehorse.'

'I guess, I understand that. But I just don't like it.'

'Fair enough, that's an honest response. I can't persuade you of the value of a Lichtenstein or a Hockney. But I'm sure there will be something here you will like. That's the thing – there are so many schools of art, so many interpretations of so many things, that everyone can find something they can find joy, or at least recognition in.'

They carried on walking through room after room, until Goo, with sudden purpose, swerved off to the right, grabbing Fenella and pulling her behind. 'I know! I know what you'll like! Oh God, at least I hope so. Come with me!'

She led Fenella through a few more rooms, checking signs and listings, until they reached a large room, seemingly randomly laid out with paintings and sculptures of all shapes and sizes. Colour infused the space, but not in the stark artificial way of the Pop Art room. This was subtle, dreamy, blurry. They slowed their pace and Goo pointed out Gauguin, Picasso and Matisse.

'This sort of art is called Primitivism,' explained Goo. 'It encompasses Western artists' desire to return to a simpler life, to reduce art back to simple forms and muted colours, like in the primitive art of Africa and South America. Some actually lived the life – like Paul Gauguin. He lived in French Polynesia for ten years.' But Fenella wasn't really listening to Goo. She was staring at an Henri Rousseau.

'Tiger in a Tropical Storm,' said Goo. 'I knew you'd like that. 'Look, they have several by Rousseau. And Frida Kahlo. Now there was an artist. She's a bit of a heroine of mine, I have to say. She was married to an artist, who was huge at the time, in Mexico and abroad. She was so modest and brave. She had a horrible accident in her youth – broke her back and lived the rest of her life in pain, trussed up in medical devices. She had so many demons and she painted them out of herself. You see, she is almost always the subject of her paintings. But she wasn't vain, she was painting her pain, her affinity with animals, her otherness. All the colours and textures she felt. Magical realism. You can *feel* her paintings. I always feel awfully strong and feminine after looking at her art.'

'I love it. I love her and… Rousseau, did you say?'

Goo nodded. 'Do they feel sort of familiar? Touch you because of your life?'

'I supposed that's what it is. Memories, colours I recognise. African art is like this.' She indicated a picture of a tiger attacking a buffalo. 'Not just the colours of the country itself. And I don't mean I saw paintings there, but actually, art is everywhere there. Everyone who has a shop or a little business makes it look as nice as they can, and they often illustrate what they do inside. The barber will have portraits on the wall of the styles he cuts, the grocer will have paintings of fruit and vegetables. There was even a butcher who had pictures of live animals on one side of his door, then arrows pointing to pictures of pieces of meat on the other side! The paintings were always good in their way. Illustrative and sort of rough and ready, if you know what I mean?'

Fenella suddenly felt utterly overwhelmed and started to cry. 'Sorry, I don't know what the matter is. I'm not sad. At least, I am sad, of course, but that's not why I'm crying.'

Goo said nothing, but led her to a café area they had passed outside the room. She whisked off and returned a few minutes later with two giant hot chocolates smothered with whipped cream and two iced buns.

'Tuck in,' said Goo.

Fenella looked down at her fingers, picking at her cuticles.

'They were so like Mum's pictures. I don't mean the skill, she was good, but not that good!'

Goo laughed softly.

'I miss it, Goo. I miss the heat and the leaves and the birdsong. I miss the elephants.' Fenella's voice lowered further; she couldn't look Goo in the face. 'I feel so out of place here. I love you guys – you've been so kind to me. I love the Scottish countryside and the pottery, but I just can't picture myself here forever, you know?'

'You are a child of Africa, darling.'

'I am. I understand why I was sent here. It was completely the right thing to do. Mum is ill, I know, and Bibi has her own grief to deal with, along with running the camp. And Dad, well, he's gone. But I want to go back so badly. It's home.'

They sat quietly, the hubbub of the café swirling around them like a speeded-up film. Then Goo spoke. 'Okay, then you need a plan of action. You can't go back now – you know all the reasons – but you can't see yourself anywhere else. So, what do you see? Think of older Fenella. I tell you what. Get up, let's walk around a bit.'

They left their drinks, but Goo wrapped up the cakes in some napkins and secreted them in her huge French basket. 'This way.' They returned to the Art Nouveau paintings in the Primitivist Room. 'Right, take your time, but try to think "If she were in one of these paintings, where would grown-up Fenella be?" Be objective. Think of Fenella as another person, but think where she belongs. Where she would be happiest?'

Goo let Fenella walk around on her own. She slowed down in front of a few of the paintings and stopped to admire a sculpture of a woman's face carved from a dark wood. She kept on walking, past a few Gauguins and a Victor Palmov. 'Ah!' It was an image that seemed at once dark and foreboding and bursting with colour. The adjoining plaque explained that this was 'The Dream' by Henri Rousseau, but it was not dreamlike, in that ethereal, passive way – not a cliché of a dream. The edges of the leaves were sharp, the colours solid and stark, the faces of the animals unsophisticated like those in Chinese silks or a child's scrawl. But the vivid image was not hard or frightening and Fenella was completely absorbed.

On the left of the painting, but definitely at its focus, lounged a woman, naked, on a soft brown chaise longue. Her arm was outstretched, reaching to what was beyond her, but her face was calm and serene, not anxious or overwhelmed by her strange surroundings. She was enclosed in her dream: tall tropical flowers and exotic fruits surrounding her, the moon above illuminating her in a cool golden light. Peering between palm fronds and thick grasses were animals – wild but gentle. Lions, birds, a snake, an elephant and, almost obscured by the shadows, a dark woman in traditional dress blew a flute or pipe – a charmer or a companion of the animals? These animals should be intimidating, but instead were cautious and curious. The sight of it made Fenella's throat feel dry and she felt a tingle behind her knees. Goo was watching Fenella and paused until she thought the moment was right to approach her.

'I think you would need more clothes on in the jungle!' Goo

joked, standing beside her to look. 'But, yes, it's perfect. Okay. We shall track down a print of this, or a postcard. There might be one in the gift shop. Then, when we get home, pin it on your notice-board in your room. You can look at it and write down what you think you need to do to turn you into that "Fenella".'

Nella nodded. She felt a little lighter, and ideas began flooding into her head – possibilities, choices. She was free in some ways, she realised. She really had no one to answer to but herself. Up to now, that had made her feel lonely, but now she felt almost empowered. The 'Fenella' in the picture was whatever she chose her to be and she could reach her. She knew she could.

Once they were home, Fenella pinned the postcard to the board, as instructed, and stared at it for a little while. She then got out a notepad that Goo had given her for Christmas. She had not yet written in it – it felt too special. It was feint-lined with gold edging on the pages and the cover was made from slices of cork, so thin and worked so carefully that it had the appearance of pale leather. This was as good a reason as any to begin using it.

She took out a ruler and opened the notebook at the middle. She made a rough sketch of the painting, then worked her way backwards to the beginning of the book. She wrote a title at the top of each page, spreading these out in the notebook, leaving space in each section for ideas and plans.

- Back to Africa
- Job with wildlife
- Training in zoology
- Degree environmental subject – zoology/ecology?
- Money for university?
- Highers – Sciences, Maths, Art?
- Standard Grade Options – Biology, Chemistry, Physics, Geography, Design and Tech, Computer Science?

Each title was written neatly and underlined with a box below entitled 'What I need to do'. Fenella sat back and flicked through her work so far. At last, she felt purposeful. She had moments of real happiness with Goo and Andrew, but she was a guest in their home; she was still only thirteen and could not really control any aspect of her life. But she had the power to change her future, if she really tried. She at least had a vague outline in which to colour in her dreams

She picked her shoulder bag up from the floor and reached inside. She had bought a second postcard in the gift shop – a print of Matisse's 'Icarus'. She pulled it out of its paper bag, turned it over and began to write:

> Dear Bibi
> Spent the day in Edinburgh today doing lots of Goo-type things. Went to primitive art exhibition – lots of jungles and tropical climates. Made me think of Africa and of you. How are you? You haven't written for a while. Is Hamisi back with you? You said that his wife had had a baby daughter. What have they called her? I am doing quite well at school. It was hard at first, but I think I know what to do to make it okay. Please write soon and tell me all the news. Is Hector the Hornbill still hanging around on the veranda? What happened to the baby warthog that Peter found? I miss you all so much.
> Nakupenda
> Nella

She found an envelope for the card and addressed it to her grandmother:

Mrs Barbara Chege
PO Box 456
Voi 30500
Taita-Taveta County
KENYA

CHAPTER 23

EAST NEUK 2008

'NELLA, put your case outside your room and I'll carry it down for you,' Andrew bellowed up the stairs.

The day had come. She felt numb. She had been happier here with Goo and Andrew than at any other time of her life. She owed them everything, for taking her in and for helping her to rebuild herself. She knew that it was now up to her to pick up and use what they had given her and sculpt it into a life, a life uniquely hers. Anyway, she'd tried pottery and she was awful at it.

The goodbyes at Leuchars station were full of weepy smiles and wet tissues. Promises to send pictures and make Facebook posts were made, and then she was on the train and their image gradually retreated: Goo clutching to her chest a little stuffed elephant Fenella had bought her; Andrew, taller by over a foot, standing behind Goo hugging her protectively with his bear-like arm.

She arrived at her digs a few hours later. The distance in miles had not been far, but getting around the city required focus and, after emerging from Waverley station, she took a little while to get her bearings again. She had often come to Edinburgh with Goo, but Goo was the sort to take charge and Fenella was the sort to let her. So, finding her own way in the city was a little daunting. Once she was up on Princes Street, though, she recognised the shops and cafés and it wasn't long before she was headed the right way.

The flat was in the Grassmarket at the foot of Edinburgh Castle, and only a 20-minute journey to her part-time job at the zoo. She had only seen a few photographs of the interior. The price was so reasonable, and location so perfect, she had paid the deposit without question before the landlord let it out to anyone else. It took up the top floor of a tall, narrow townhouse: an 18th-century building that had been sliced, floor by floor into one-person apartments, except for the ground floor which had housed the same quirky gift shop – Minerva's – for over thirty years. Fenella had loved going into this shop when she'd taken trips into the city with Goo. They had perfected a strict rota every visit, whereby they proceeded from the most educational (but still fun) to the most indulgent, peppered by pit stops: a museum or art gallery – coffee – second-hand bookshops – lunch – Minerva's – train home.

She was thrilled at the coincidence of the flat's location. The entrance door was around the back, away from the main street. She tried the door: it was unlocked and opened into a wide, dim hallway. Intricate bannisters encircled the stairway, which uncurled in front of a huge stained-glass window, doubtless installed to glamorise the otherwise drab view of the backs of other dwellings. Each floor had a half landing, at the end of which was a huge oak door – each one the entrance to a separate flat. Fenella's was number 7.

The key was held in a box outside. Remembering this, she fumbled in her bag to find the code she had noted in a small pad. Releasing the key, she turned the lock and stepped tentatively into the little flat. To her relief, it was clean and bright. The door opened directly into the main living room. A small sofa and an armchair, both lemon yellow, faced the longest wall, which had been entirely lined with shelving.

'Ooh, good, somewhere for the books,' Fenella thought to herself.

Andrew was driving down in a few weeks with the rest of her necessary belongings, ninety per cent of which was books. A square pine table was pushed up against the far wall, with two dining chairs, facing each other. It was spare, but it was co-ordinated and cheerful.

The bedroom was beyond the dining area. A double bed, unmade

(Fenella would make do with a sleeping bag until Andrew arrived with the bedding), took up almost the entire space, but that was fine and she felt very grown up, faced with the first ever double bed of her own. A little shower room and toilet were next to the bedroom – again, clean and functional although she would have to bend her head under the eaves to use the loo. Going back through the living room and off to the right, the kitchen completed the accommodation. It was in a galley shape, squeezed into the last few feet of space in the flat and separated from the living room by a half-height wall. It was tiny but deceptively airy as, despite this being a top-floor flat, which might have been poky, the windows were enormous and gave out to a full view of the square below, with all the colourful shops and cafés set into the ancient buildings.

In days long passed, this square had been both a livestock market and a place of execution. But like many cities, when times changed, people just covered up their old lives and built on. Edinburgh famously had miles of chambers and streets under the current city. Fenella thought that, although the Old Town still retained an antiquated feel, this had been partly obscured by attempts to Scotify the city for the millions of annual visitors. The Royal Mile and Princes Street felt like yards of tartan unfurled for the tourists who came for the Festival, Royal Tattoo, golf, and underground tours. By contrast, Fenella imagined that the Grassmarket and Lawnmarket had been swathed by a giant crocheted 'granny blanket' – randomly colourful, augmented through the years by hundreds of unrelated souls passing through, adding their individual touches to the district. Decades of artistic and student vibes had long since concealed any gruesome undertones. Beyond the tall buildings, Fenella had a good view of the hills beyond Edinburgh, and if she craned her neck to the left a little, there was the actual castle.

* * *

A few weeks later, on a rare morning without work or lectures, Fenella sat down at her little pine table to write.

Dear Bibi
I'm sorry that I haven't written for such a long time. I had exams and was very focused on doing well enough to get on my course, so couldn't think of anything else for a while. Of course, I also had my jobs – Saturdays at the shop at the gallery, and waitressing at The Lobster Pot – but I managed to fit it all in. Well, anyway, I got my results and here I am!

I'm writing to you from my little flat in Edinburgh's Grassmarket. I have been here for a month now. Term started two weeks ago and my job the week after that. Andrew and Goo helped me with all my stuff and I have got the place the way I like it now. Naturally, the shelves are full of books (and I don't need to worry about termites eating the pages!). I am taking the Wildlife Management and Global Ecology modules this term. I get to do a project in the third term and I am going to write about the differences in British and Kenyan lake ecology, so I have another excuse to read about my beloved home.

I have had my first week's induction at the zoo. My boss, Ian, seems nice, but a little bit grumpy. I think he just wants to be alone around the animals. He doesn't seem to like people much! I have found that the way to get around him is to talk about the animals as much as possible, he especially seems to like being asked advice, so I sometimes play down my knowledge just to get him on side!

In Freshers' Week I joined a book group and a walking group, but they both meet at times when I'm working. I hadn't really thought about what I would miss at uni by also having a job. It seems like no one else is in the same boat – everyone just sticks to being at uni or socialising in the city in the evenings. I have to say that by about nine o'clock I just want to curl up in bed and read. I don't really mind though, as I am doing a job I enjoy and a course which I hope will be the beginning of good things.

I do allow myself a treat every Friday – I go to one of

the places I used to go with Goo and buy myself a book, or a few beads or something. I have a strict budget (I think I take after you in my love of spreadsheets!) and with my savings from my old jobs and my job at the zoo, I should hopefully cover daily expenses, course fees and materials. I will need to work a few more hours after six months or so, but the zoo manager has told me that there is usually plenty of overtime and holiday cover available.

I do miss Goo and Andrew, but we speak often and they're not far away if I need them.

How are you? Have there been any dramas at the camp? How are Hamisi and Angel and their little girls? Has the eldest started school yet?

I hope that you are well. Please pass on my love to the animals.

Nakupenda
Nella

* * *

Fenella completed her first term and took a week off from her job to spend Christmas with Goo and Andrew. They met her at the station and took her straight out for dinner at a favourite restaurant in St Andrews for a catch-up.

'So, how's it all going?' asked Andrew once they had ordered and got comfortable.

'It's fine,' replied Fenella, a little absently. 'How about you, did you sell that huge platter you were making with all the sea birds on it?'

Goo could tell there was something wrong. 'It takes a while to settle in, Fenella. But, of course, you know that – you made a much bigger change when you came to stay with us. And you did brilliantly at that.' Goo smiled at her. 'Although, I do remember your shock at macaroni-cheese pies. And square sausage.'

'And the Loony Dook!' added Fenella. 'What sort of crazy people jump into the Firth of Forth on New Year's Day?'

'But you accepted us and our funny ways and you've become an amazing young woman into the bargain,' said Goo.

The three were silent for a few minutes at this. Fenella felt a little embarrassed. 'I'm not that amazing,' she mumbled. 'And actually, I'm not that fine. But I will be. Like you said, I've done it before.'

'Do you need any money?' asked Andrew. 'You know you only need to ask. We know you want to fund yourself, but that puts a lot of pressure on you to earn money, when you need to concentrate on studying.'

'I'm fine with that part, really. You're very kind, but I can manage. It's just a bit full on, that's all. I'm sure I'll be fine once I really know what I'm doing at work and get a rhythm going with the studying. At the moment, it's all so new, I'm on hyper alert all the time, trying to take it all in. It's pretty tiring.'

'Well, you know we're not far away if you need anything,' said Andrew, knowing not to push it further. 'Right, pudding. Clootie dumpling, anyone?' He looked over his menu at Fenella, grinning. She made a mock retching face in return.

When she returned to her flat in the New Year, there was a letter waiting for her in her cubbyhole. She grabbed it and heaved her case up the stairs (Goo had sent her home with enough tins of beans and packets of lentils to last the next term). She let herself in and went straight to the kitchen to put her feet up with a hot chocolate. Opening the letter with her keys, she waited for the kettle to boil. It was from Barbara.

> My Dearest Nella
> How wonderful to hear how things are going in Edinburgh! I am so glad to hear from you. Oh, how I have missed you. I am so sorry that I have not written more often. It is unforgivable really, so I will not insult you with excuses. It sounds like you are very busy and it all sounds very exciting! You are so clever to have got onto this course and you have worked so hard – I am very proud of you!

There is not a day goes by when I don't think of you and the others. I don't hear from your father very often, but I do occasionally get word of him. He wrote me a brief letter a few weeks ago and asked that I pass his love on to you and that he hopes you are well and happy.

I have been getting on with camp affairs. We had a film crew in last week, so that was very exciting. But they were surprisingly fussy about food and whether everything was organic – really we try, but there is a limit to what we can do about that. They were putting together a film about mongooses, so Hamisi and Paul – a local man with seemingly magical powers around wild animals! – had been acclimatising the mongooses for months before the film crew came. Apparently, it is a fine balance between getting the animals to not be so timorous that they scuttle away at the slightest sign of humans, and making them so tame that they do not behave naturally and are put at risk of being too confident around humans who might do them harm. It involves a great deal of slow and gradual interaction and some bizarre greeting rituals and noises on the part of Paul. He really is a wizard – I hope one day you can meet him.

Hamisi's girls are doing well. They came for the whole summer with Angel, and I took them up to the high kopje to watch the baboons. We have also seen a lot of Makena and her family. They are often at the waterhole below the escarpment, so I can see them from the house. Makena seemed to come to visit us more and more often after the incident. I wonder if she knew we needed her to help us with our sadness.

Please write again soon.

Kisses

Bibi

CHAPTER 24

EDINBURGH 2009

FENELLA approached the new term with vigour. She had already read two of the next unit's textbooks ahead of the start of term and, despite her hours at the zoo, attended every lecture, scribbling copious notes throughout. She went to the university library every week, to check through extra materials and scientific journals to help with her end-of-year project. Her enthusiasm began to wane, however, exacerbated by the long, grey evenings and bitter weather.

She got on well enough with her fellow students, stopping for the occasional coffee at the union bar during the day, but while they headed off to shared flats or to house parties at the end of the day, she got on the bus to work or back to her flat on her own. What began as a comfortable solitude was morphing into loneliness. Fenella, particularly since moving to Scotland, had enjoyed time alone; and Goo and Andrew had given her the space when she needed it. She'd had no school friends who lived in the village but, through her jobs at the gallery and café, she had developed friendships with locals, and occasionally she would meet up with a group from school to spend the day in St Andrews at the beach or shopping. In those five years, she had been able to put her past behind her for a while, and had found a sort of social equilibrium that suited her.

But here it was different. She was starting to realise that the choices she had made caused her to fool herself into thinking that she was in control. She had been planning ahead, aiming for what she wanted to achieve – to return home armed with an education to make a life back there. What she hadn't factored in was what she would sacrifice to do that. It wasn't just the hard work; it was enjoying the whole experience of university. Whereas she embraced solitude – felt that she managed it – loneliness had crept up on her without her permission, forcing her behind a wall, outside, looking in. She straddled a path of loneliness and solitude all the time. As she walked the tightrope between them, she kept tripping into loneliness more and more.

She wanted to have more friends at university, but felt she had little in common with her fellow students. Very few of them, it seemed to her, approached the course with any sense of ambition. Instead, they would chatter all through lectures, hand in work late, miss lectures. In some cases, she couldn't fathom why they were there at all, they seemed to care so little for their subjects. And yet, they inevitably got through their courses, passed exams and prevailed, seemingly effortlessly, whilst she would repeatedly be up late at night trying to complete assignments prior to an early shift at the zoo.

Waiting for a lecture to start one morning, she had grabbed a coffee at the bar and was now in the lecture theatre, reading through an article on invasive species, trying to get to grips with the abundant use of Latin in the text. In the row in front, two of her classmates shuffled into their seats, full of excited chatter. She acknowledged them with a smile, but they did not smile back, not seeming to notice her.

'Oh, I didn't tell you!' exclaimed one of the girls, pulling off her scarf. 'I've got that internship at Kilifi!'

'How exciting!' said her friend. 'Did that contact work out then?'

'I didn't need it after all. It turns out that the chap who owns the conservancy is an old pal of Daddy's, so he said 'Of course she can spend the summer here!' I get my own room and use of a jeep. And there's great water sports there and a spa for the days off. You know Jem? He goes sailing off there every year when he goes home. There will be loads of guys there.'

'You're so lucky!' said the friend. 'I'm just going to Greece with my sister. The folks have a boat moored at Mykonos, so I'm just going to lie on the boat and get a tan and go clubbing. I deserve it after this year.'

Fenella felt the bite of irritation. Some people just seemed to sail through life with advantages lobbed at them wherever they went. She knew she should feel proud that she was trying to make her own way, but sometimes it felt so unfair, that for all her hard work and dedication, there were people for whom social advantage would always carry them through.

She completed her first year and stayed in Edinburgh to work full time at the zoo over the busy summer season. Her boss, Ian, became marginally less grumpy, but he would not relinquish any of the more interesting or complicated tasks, leaving her to prepare food, muck out the animals and carry out the paperwork. She longed to be allowed to handle some of the larger mammals, to help with a birth or with acclimatising a new arrival.

With some reluctance, he had allowed her to apply to the zoo's ethics committee, which analysed the welfare needs of individual animals and the benefits of keeping them at the zoo. She had been accepted onto the committee, after proving her knowledge and commitment to the Chair. This work was enlightening, because she learnt a lot about zoo management. However, it also brought home some uncomfortable truths about zoos and what they were for. As the summer drew to an end, and visitor numbers dwindled, Fenella became more introspective about the job. She was learning a great deal about the animals in her care, but she became less and less comfortable about the morality of the existence of zoos. More than ever, she wanted to get back to the wildness of her home.

One evening, Fenella was sweeping up in the lemur enclosure. She could do this without much trouble, as the lemurs, being non-predatory, did not have to be shut away while she carried out jobs in their compound. The rhythmic, mechanistic sweeping allowed her to lose herself in her thoughts. There had been talk of bringing pandas to the zoo from China to attempt a longterm breeding programme. The staff were divided about the wisdom of this and talked of little else. As she mused and swept, she suddenly felt like she was going to burst into tears. The feeling came over her without warning and with such force that she threw down her broom and sat down suddenly on the ground. The clattering sent the lemurs scurrying for cover.

For a moment, she couldn't see, then she felt compelled to clutch her knees into her chest and bury her head into them. Her heart was pounding against her thigh, her throat dry and she was panting uncontrollably. Random thoughts seemed to race and collide into each other, stopping only when she took in a huge breath and tried to calm herself, still gripping her knees. After a few moments she dared to look up. The lemurs were peeking down from the high ropes above her head, looking at her curiously. She tried to stand up, but dizziness forced her down again. After what seemed like long minutes, she had the vague feeling that there was someone else there, so looked up again. Squinting against the overhead light, she saw Ian, looking down. She was vaguely aware of his voice – was she alright, was she hurt, why was she crying? She hadn't been aware of it, but now realised that tears were pouring out of her, soaking the knees of her trousers.

'I don't know… I… I'm not hurt, I just suddenly felt very frightened or something.' Her own voice echoed in her head.

'Can you get up?' asked Ian, bending down and offering a strong, gnarly hand for her to grab.

'Yes, thank you.' She wobbled a little, then found her balance and stood for a moment, embarrassed and shaken. Ian took her both her hands to help her to steady herself, then picked up the broom and led her through the small exit door. 'Go into the office and get a cup of tea. I'll finish up here. Then I'll drive you home.' Fenella started to protest, but Ian had already turned away.

They drove in comfortable silence for the first ten minutes. Ian wasn't much of a talker, which was one of the things she liked about him. But suddenly, Fenella found herself gabbling at him, thoughts and worries pouring out of her.

'I'm so unhappy, Ian. I am never anywhere long enough to make any friends. My uni friends all live in groups and go out together, the staff at the zoo think I'm above it all because I'm also a student. I study really hard, but I can't make sense of a lot of what I'm reading, so I just have to memorise everything. I'm up late studying, then up early working or heading off to lectures, I have nearly run out of money and second year hasn't even started yet. I just don't think I can do it all. If I give up uni, I give up my dreams; if I give up the job, I can't afford to go to uni. I just don't know what to do.' She inhaled raggedly, then let out a voluble single sob. It was met with a long silence. Ian had not looked at her during her tirade, but now carefully pulled over into a lay-by and stopped the car.

He turned to look at her. 'Right, Nella. No, you can't do it all. You're going to have to make an uncomfortable choice. Why are you doing the course?'

'To get a job in wildlife management when I'm older,' she sniffed.

'But why do you think the degree will get you there?'

'I suppose… I don't know, you need a degree, don't you?'

'Will you be doing a Masters or a PhD?'

'I hadn't really thought about that.'

'Well, I'm only a lowly zoo ranger, but as far as I know, the animals don't give a fig whether you have a degree. And any organisation taking on people in wildlife management will have more interest in your experience with wildlife, don't you think?'

'Perhaps,' Fenella nodded.

'So, it seems to me that there are other ways to achieve your dreams. You've got a year of your degree under your belt and a year of working at the zoo. I'll happily give you a good reference; you work hard and you're a natural with the small mammals. Why don't you apply to do a conservation project through the zoo? You know they run internships abroad, don't you?'

Fenella shook her head. 'I had no idea. Do you know people who have done them?'

'Yes, some of them come back and apply what they've learned back here, but most stay with the project or carry on elsewhere, doing similar things. What do you think?'

'It's definitely worth looking into.' Fenella sniffed back the last of her tears. 'Who do I ask about it?'

'See Jenny in HR. Tell her I sent you. She'll give you all the bumf. Right, that's that, then. Let's get you home.'

Fenella spent the next few days packing her things up to take back to Goo and Andrew. She would have to decide whether to renew the lease on her flat, but for now, she had a couple of weeks to mull things over. Bags packed, she had an hour before Andrew came with the car to pick her and her stuff up, so she sat down to write a letter to Barbara.

> Dear Bibi
> Thank you for your latest letter. I love to hear your stories about the camp. I picture it in my mind every night, remembering the sound of nightjars or watching the civet which used to sneak into the kitchen after supper.
>
> Have you heard any more from Dad? Where was he last? Is he even in Africa these days?
>
> I have made a decision about my course. I perhaps didn't let on how things were really going here. Perhaps I didn't even realise myself. Anyway, I have been struggling a bit and it all came to a bit of a head at work. I thought I was ill, so went to see the doctor on campus and it turns out I had a major panic attack. She referred me on to a counsellor who I saw last week.
>
> I've been told that I might have depression but that, for now, we will tackle just the panic attacks. She had given me some strategies to try and was nice and practical about what I can do to look forward. I think the trouble was I was being unrealistic about my goals and need to simplify things a bit. I've had the odd wobble since the bad attack, but I'm generally feeling a lot better.

I wish it could have been as straightforward for Mum. Do you think I've inherited something? I worry a little about that.

Nakupenda

Nella

PS I shall be at the pottery for the next fortnight or so, so you can reach me there.

* * *

Fenella spent a few weeks in the comfort of the pottery. Goo chatted with her about her options, while Andrew fed her up with increasingly experimental and revolting food. The time with her aunt and uncle gave her some perspective and she began to make alternative plans.

'Your boss made a lot of sense, you know, Fenella,' said Andrew one evening, whilst passing her a bowl of alarmingly cerise-coloured stew, before returning to the kitchen.

'What is this?' Fenella whispered over to Goo indicating the vivid concoction.

'God, I don't know. Borsht, goulash? It'll be fine.' The two women giggled.

'You can work towards your goal, rather than study,' continued Andrew as he handed Goo her bowl and sat next to her. 'You can always take courses as you go along. In fact, you might get some training paid for, which kills two birds with one stone.'

'I phoned work today,' Fenella replied. 'I've definitely decided to take a break from uni. I passed my first year, so it will continue to be transferable for several years, should I want to go back. I'm going to stay on at the zoo and work towards getting on their internship programme. Of course, my aim is to join a project in Kenya and this way I might get there much quicker than going the uni route.'

'You'll need an extension on your lease, then,' said Goo. 'We'll sort that out tomorrow. How about you and I go over to your flat a day early, then we can have a last blowout round the shops before you have to go back to work?'

'I'd love that, Goo. I've missed our little jaunts.'

The day before she returned to Edinburgh, she received a letter from her grandmother.

> Dearest Nella
> I am so sorry to hear about your panic attacks. I remember when you started at the school in Scotland – there were a few similar episodes, weren't there? It is all completely understandable, my darling. You had a great trauma, which we all tried to help you with, but perhaps, although we made sure you were somewhere safe and happy, we did not think to explain more about what happened or think about how shutting you out might affect you. For that, I am truly sorry. As for inheriting depression from Jo, I am not an expert, but I doubt that very much.
>
> Anyway, you are older now, so I shall attempt to describe a bit of what happened here after the incident; perhaps it will help. After you left to stay with Goo and Andrew, your dad stayed on here for a few months. There were many unpleasant legal and practical matters that had to be dealt with. I was in no fit state to face them alone, and he was my rock. Jo, as you know, went to Nairobi straight away. She just couldn't stay around camp. She was not herself and needed to get away from where it all happened and, to be honest, from us. She had to try to make sense of everything for herself. Please don't be angry with her. It must seem to you that she abandoned you, but really she had to be with friends who had more strength than I could muster. We do not hear from her much now, but friends tell us that she is managing. She has a part-time job at the university – Angel sees her occasionally.
>
> Your dad is, I think, in Asia somewhere, at least that's what he told me when I last heard from him. His whereabouts are always rather vague. As soon as I know more, I shall let you know.

Please let me know if you want to talk more about everything. I haven't been deliberately secretive. I suppose I just felt that letting you have a life away from here where you wouldn't be reminded of everything would be best for you. You are always welcome home.

I am glad that you have got yourself some help. You are such a sensible girl. Just make sure that you are kind to yourself.

Let me know what you have decided to do. I do hope that you can come home soon. We miss you.

Much love,

Bibi

CHAPTER 25

EDINBURGH 2011

'NELLA, it's Dad.' The shock of hearing his voice in this place was disorientating. At first, she didn't understand who was on the other end of the line, which was ridiculous, but his presence, even just as a disembodied voice, was so incongruous as to be almost comical.

'Dad? What on earth. It's been… what is it? What's wrong?' She realised, in a sudden rush of logic that only bad news would bring her father into her life now.

'It's Mum.' Fenella's head swam. Everything she had succeeded in shutting out now burst open.

'What? What's happened?' Her voice was someone else's.

'She tried to kill herself, Nella.' He replied quietly.

She felt dumb, like a small child at the dinner table, not understanding the conversation, not following what anyone is saying. A time delay, like a satellite phone between the words being uttered and her taking them in.

Her father's words kept coming. 'Her friend, Cecily, found her in the bath. She'd slit her wrists. She's been taken to hospital in Nairobi, but I'm arranging for her to go back to Scotland. To a hospital there. She's out of danger, Fenella, but she needs help and I can't help her.'

Fenella's bag slipped off her shoulder as she dropped into the chair. 'Out of danger. What does that mean?'

'They've patched her up. She lost a lot of blood, but they got to her in time and she's responsive. Well at least she's sedated, but not unconscious. I'm at the hospital now, but you know she won't want to see me. She won't want me to look after her. There's no one here I can expect to do that, it's too much. There's only you, Nella.'

'But, Dad. I can't. I'm sorry, really, but I can't. I can barely look after myself.'

'I don't mean that she should live with you. She's going to need a lot of professional care, but she just needs someone on hand to visit and keep her grounded. She's not been at all well, Nella, I should have seen it sooner, but we saw each other so little... and you know how it is.'

'You mean you're sending her to an institution?'

'I'm not sending her, Nell. You make it sound so Victorian. She has been assessed for psychiatric aftercare. She would be better getting that back in Scotland, for lots of reasons.'

'Okay, Dad. What do you need me to do?' Fenella stared at the Conservation Trust pamphlet she had just printed out. Smiling faces gazed back at her. A picture of a woman in a green smock, feeding a bottle to a baby elephant. This would never be her. She was stupid to think it.

Arrangements were made, and a month later her mother was flown to Edinburgh Airport. Fenella met her off the plane, but this was no emotional reunion. Joanna was unrecognisable, hair limp and greying at the roots, her laughing freckled face now creased in a permanent frown, not of annoyance, but bewilderment. Fenella offered kind words as she took her bags and walked her mother to the taxi, but they were strangers now, altered by time and grief. Fenella even called her Joanna, not Mum. A tangible silence accompanied the taxi ride to the hospital. Joanna, hunched up as far to the right side of the back seat as possible, stared blankly out of the window. Fenella, head reeling, tried to mumble a few pleasantries, but got no response.

The hospital was one of those large stately buildings that went one of two ways during the last century. Taxes forced their owners to pass them on to the National Trust or else they became residential care homes or private sanitoriums. This one was white and turreted; Fenella half expected a tweedy laird followed by a couple of fat gun dogs to emerge from the front door. Inside, it was far more clinical. Suits of armour and hunting trophies, which might have adorned the large hall, had been replaced by mediocre and apparently anonymous portraiture, presumably intended to soothe the patients. Rather than dark recesses and patterned carpets, the hall was painted a light colour and could have been any city hospital – all automatic doors, lifts and hand-gel stations. Joanna was checked in and an over-smiley nurse took one of her bags from Fenella and marched them upstairs.

'Well, we'll get you comfy and show you around. Here we are – number seven.' The same as my flat, Fenella mused.

They entered the room. It was pale and anonymous, but with far-reaching views, which heartened Fenella – at least there were big skies for her mother to watch.

'So, you've flown all the way from Africa to be with us,' wittered the nurse in a reedy, high-pitched voice, 'How nice. And you are her daughter, I understand. Don't you have fabulous hair!'

Joanna seemed to jolt at this, faltering in her steps, almost tripping, but grabbed the banister in time and composed herself. Fenella saw this and just managed a distracted 'Uh-huh' in acknowledgement.

Fenella closed her book and stretched to turn out the bedside lamp. As she did, the headlights of a car in the street below streamed into the room, picking out a photograph on the noticeboard above her desk: a family group standing in front of a whitewashed bungalow, flaming pink bougainvillea bowing over a louvre door. The photo presented a typical family pose: adults at the back, mother clutching a red-faced child who, evident from the blurry image, was wriggling uncontrollably; father resting his hand on the shoulder of an older girl in the foreground. She was not looking at the camera, but was distracted by something beyond the photographer. Fenella could not remember what or who it was, but she remembered the laughter. The sheer delight on the faces stood out for her in this picture, this moment. There was always laughter. Before everything changed. Fenella gazed at the picture, savouring its warmth, but a chill came over her and she snapped back to reality. She hugged her knees, and fell into a fitful sleep.

The next morning, she peeled the clammy sheets from her body and sat up, stiffly. An arc of pain gripped her forehead, foreshadowing the day ahead. She had two hours until visiting time. Enough time to shower, dress and eat, and to finish off her application form. The thought of this, at least, lightened her mood and spurred her into action.

Pinned next to the family photo, were the two other pictures which focused her days. The first was the front fold of a pamphlet for *Wild Guardians*, an environmental charity which arranged volunteering and education in conservation. The other was the Rousseau postcard Goo had bought her all those years ago at the National Gallery, perforated around the edges with dozens of drawing-pin holes. Months of worry about her mother had blown her off course. This and money worries had almost defeated her and she had all but decided to remain in her flat and find a second job. Fortunately, long telephone calls with her beloved Goo had steered her back.

'Where is that Fenella now?' asked Goo, when she had explained the previous week that she would have to give up on her plans. She had been poring over her notepad, trying to work out how her meagre salary could possibly stretch to a plane ticket to Kenya.

'She is broke, frustrated and living in a bedsit in Edinburgh,' she had muttered in reply.

'No, she is not. She is sitting on a kopje, watching elephants browse, congratulating herself on being so brave and resourceful.'

'I just don't think I have it in me anymore, Goo.'

'That's not the Fenella I know,' said Goo. 'The Fenella I know would hitch up her skirts like Elizabeth Bennet, kiss her mother and move forward with her life.'

'Would she?' Fenella had been doodling and realised she had drawn dozens of little butterflies all over her notepad.

'She would. Now here is the plan. Jo is not herself, but she is well looked after, and Andrew and I will visit her every week. You have my solemn promise that we will. You, on the other hand, will fill in that application form and get yourself onto that volunteer programme. We will lend you the money for the air fare…'

'Goo, I can't ask that of you, please, no. It's too much.'

'Nonsense. We have a bit put by. We got that commission from the hotel, so we will be churning out dinner sets like there's no tomorrow for the next few weeks. They paid us a nice advance, and we really don't need the money right now. So, you can pay us back when you can afford to. Please let us do this for you, Nella. You're the nearest thing to a daughter we have, and we have watched you work so hard. You deserve a break.'

Fenella's seed of a plan had been dormant and neglected for so long, she thought it could never be revived. With Goo's offer, she found a new purpose and dared again to plan a future – to imagine a life beyond this one.

Fenella walked the half mile from the bus stop to the hospital. By now, she was as skilled as any other local at negotiating the thick snow, leaning slightly forward as she walked, lifting each leg straight up, to avoid her boots filling up. Somehow, the snow underfoot felt warm despite the biting cold wind. She had never got used to the cold. No matter how she dressed, she always felt the cold in her bones. The sharp blue light, the clarity of the view ahead of her, seemed to accentuate the bleakness. There was never that hazy wobble of heat softening the view. She found the harshness unnerving – everything was too exposed and real in this light. The Edinburgh skyline, although admittedly historic and beautiful, was daunting and imperious. She felt less at ease in this city with each year that passed.

The softest sweep of a memory passed through her mind. It was of deep warmth, sandy colours, laughing voices. As gently as it came to her, it was gone again.

She arrived in the building and aimed right towards the stairwell, taking the four flights up to Munro Ward. Every single wall and door was painted an insipid lilac colour, chosen (she supposed) for its calming effect, but to her it just signified monotony, sickness, indifference. The atmosphere was solemn and melancholy. A palpable sadness stuck to her skin like a damp cloth. She would need to shower when she returned home, just to wash the misery off her.

She saw her mother through the smeared glass panel in the door. She was knitting. This was a development, as she had not been allowed knitting needles before, but she must have persuaded the staff that she would do no harm with them. She had given no one any call to suspect she would do so since she had arrived. She had been utterly calm and pleasant. She was making a sweater; Fenella could tell from the shape of the nearly complete piece.

Fenella knocked as she entered 'Hi, Mum, it's Nella.'

'Nella, love. Sit over there by the bed. I need the light by the window to see what I'm doing. It's been a while and I can't quite get the rhythm!' The yarn was cheap and synthetic and a lurid shade of mango. Not a colour her mother would have chosen, one of the nurses must have given it to her. But at least it was cheerful.

Fenella perched on the edge of the deep wingback chair. She didn't want to get comfortable, or even give the impression that she was. She would not be staying long. For a while, not a word passed between them. There was no need to fill the silence in the way strangers might do – silence between them was quite customary, but for Fenella it was loaded with anguish and things unsaid. She found with every visit she was less willing to stay. She had run out of mundanities and evasions, and resentment now simmered inside her. This had eclipsed the concern she had felt at being the only person who was left to take care of her mother. She had wanted to do the 'right thing' despite everything, but as she sat and watched her mother work, she knew that she was, little by little, coming to terms with the fact that her mother's condition was static. Her visits were making little difference to Joanna's progress, and if she did not do something to change her own life now, she never would.

Her mother's face was utterly expressionless. Fenella opened her mouth in an attempt to break the silence, she wanted to say something meaningful, otherwise what was the point? But she clammed up again, unable to articulate the rush of feelings. Instead, she looked out of the window into the bleak, piercing light. Birds circled above the city rooftops. She was unsure what birds they were – some sort of gull? The flora and fauna here did not really interest her. To her, these birds looked ugly and mean, there were too many of them and they were completely audacious, grabbing food from bins, even out of people's hands. Greedy and selfish; they pecked their companions and pulled food out of each other's beaks.

'It's for Evie,' Joanna said, not looking up from her work. 'She always likes bright colours.'

Fenella swallowed hard. 'Lovely, Mum. What else have you been up to this week? Did they get the cinema screen working again?'

'Evie likes orange and Nella likes green,' mumbled Joanna.

'I went to the HR office today, Mum. To ask about internships again. Jim at the zoo – he's from the large mammals' section – he says his son did this one-year placement and got a job researching pumas in the US. I'm never going to progress beyond the small mammals department or do what I really want without proper experience, and well, a place has come up. In Kenya.' She could tell that Joanna was not listening, lost in her own thoughts. She frowned slightly as she counted the stitches on her right-hand needle, shook her head and turned the piece to face her. Fenella noticed, however, that the little vein on her mother's right temple was pulsing – a sure sign of anxiety. It had been a warning when she was a little girl that she had done something to upset her mother, or that trouble was coming. She changed the subject again, small talk, safe ground.

'Well, I must be off to work, Mum. I'm doing the afternoon shift today, covering for Ian.' She got out of the chair, leant over her mother, but the kiss she attempted landed awkwardly in Joanna's hair. Her mother mumbled something about getting the nurse to iron the pieces she had knitted to keep them neat.

'Bye, Mum,' whispered Fenella. 'Sorry.'

She didn't look back. She balled up her hands, pressing the nails into the soft flesh under the thumb until the skin broke on her left hand. She kept walking at a brisk, marching pace – she had walked this way all her life – until she was out of the hospital and back on the street.

CHAPTER 26

EDINBURGH–NAIROBI 2012

FENELLA rushed into the departure lounge; her gaze searched the information screens. Her flight was there – all was well. The check-in queue was over to the left. She joined it and let herself relax for a minute. This queue was going nowhere for a while, so she sipped the coffee she had brought with her and allowed her thoughts to wander a little.

For Fenella, this was going to be a homecoming of sorts and one she had been planning for years, although she had put out of her mind much of actually living there. She'd often had little flashbacks, snatches of memories – a game of chase through grass taller than she was, a laughing woman in a gingham dress, a porcupine quill turned into a hairpin (which she still used), a particular combination of spices in a stew, the smell of which made her feel comforted and nourished before she even ate. These memories had grown in frequency and intensity as her plan had developed. She could see faces where before she had only blurry half-visions, full sentences where there had only been the tone of a conversation.

Her coffee drunk, she focused on her surroundings. The journey is the destination: wasn't that how she was supposed to feel? Only she could do without this part of the journey and she wished it was over, so she could get on with the actual experience. The airport was teeming with people and Fenella clutched onto the tall handle of her carry case to stop herself from crumpling onto the floor. She told herself that she would soon be out of here. It was not the flying that frightened her, but the cloying atmosphere of the airport. How can a place be so huge but so airless? It was like an indoor city – everyone anxiously trying to get somewhere fast, only to spend hours sitting in one place. The staff were, by necessity, controlling and unsmiling. Anything could happen. A fire, a bomb, a riot. These fears bubbled under Fenella's lungs and she tried to suppress them, pushing them down with each stifled breath. Her heart beat so fast, she could feel the rhythm echo in her throat. She obeyed the advice of her counsellor, she of the improbable name – Dido – and started to count, breathing steadily and deeply between each number. As instructed, she pictured her goal – a waterhole, surrounded by impala and zebra – closed her eyes and breathed.

A bump to her back knocked Fenella out of her meditation and she shuffled forward with the rest of the queue. They were boarding now. The Scottish sky came back into view as she neared the plane. Although distorted by the large, misty windows, smeared with dirt and a thousand lungfuls of breath, the light was still white and sharp. She wouldn't miss it – that cold sky. This place and her extended family – they had been a safety net. She had known kindness and sympathy here and there were people and places she did love, but it would never be home. She was not exactly sure what would happen when she disembarked from the plane and made her way to the camp, but she reassured herself with that tinge of excitement – the tiny warm pleasing feeling deep inside her that *she* was doing this – not her mother, not her counsellor – her. She was brave and anything was possible.

She tried to focus on one of the advantages of airports, that they contain every type of person one could imagine, and amused herself people-watching. That was something she used to do with her dad, she remembered abruptly – they would make up little back stories for passers-by. Her dad was better at this than she, and would invent ridiculous lives for people, each time outdoing the last. The thin, bespectacled man at the market was a botanist, just back from his travels to the Congolese jungles, and was buying apples for the first time in years. The woman in front of them at the ironmongers was a strong woman in a circus and needed screws for her dumbbells.

Her fellow passengers included a tall, slim African man, high-cheekboned and elegantly dressed in a long robe covered with brown swirly shapes, his head topped with a kufi cap. Fenella had only ever seen such hats years ago, when she was a child. There were several tourists, easily distinguishable by their attire – already clad top to toe in khaki despite the urban surroundings. But Fenella smiled at them. They were not to be mocked – they wanted to absorb the experience, and part of that is the dressing up. In front of her in the queue there was even a definitive British vicar, dog collar, waistcoat and all, reading a Bible. Perhaps he was a nervous flier seeking solace from his Creator.

She had managed to book a window seat, thankfully, and she found that the passenger seated next to her was the tall African. They exchanged pleasantries and Fenella waited anxiously for take-off. She gave her full attention to the flight attendant demonstrating the emergency procedures. Actually, this attendant had incorporated a little comedy into his presentation, perhaps to break the monotony of this routine for himself, but it worked as an attention-grabber. People watched and laughed along with his gurning and mincing and he even received a round of applause.

As they turned up and away from the high rises and motorways below, Fenella peered out of her window, suppressing an excited squeal which had been building up inside her. She settled into small talk with her travelling companion.

'Oh, I'm glad to be in the air,' he chuckled. 'I hate airports.'

'I do too,' agreed Fenella, exhaling loudly. 'It just takes so long. Are you going on holiday?'

'No, no, not at all. I'm returning to Nairobi University. I've been on a year-long sabbatical at the University of Edinburgh, teaching Environmental Studies. Seif Mutinda, how do you do?' Fenella shook his outstretched hand.

'Fenella, lovely to meet you. I love what you're wearing.'

He laughed. 'At home in Nairobi, I don't generally dress like this. I wear a suit and tie to work, but I have rather enjoyed being a bit more flamboyant on my sabbatical. I like to stand out, and surprise people. They don't know quite what to expect of me, but I catch their eye!'

'I bet you do!' laughed Fenella. 'You keep them on their toes?'

'Yes, I sometimes have to shake it up a little. In Kenya, the students have often had to overcome a lot of difficulties to make it as far as my class. They then expect their teachers to be smart and businesslike. On the other hand, I have found that my British students respond well to a little... erm, pantomime!'

When Seif asked politely about her destination and plans, Fenella was vague and non-committal. Something about an internship. She said nothing about it being the place of her birth. That didn't feel real anyway. That was the other 'Fenella', a girl in stories she told herself while getting ready for bed or dreamily stirring a soup.

They both settled down to read and while away the couple of hours before their stopover in Amsterdam. This was a place she had always wanted to visit. Sadly, she was to be stuck in the airport, so had to content herself with what she would see from above, when the plane would circle over the city briefly the next morning at first light.

Amsterdam airport, despite being a central international terminal, seemed less frenetic than Edinburgh and she found a quiet corner café to retreat to for a few hours. Despite herself, she bought a tourist guidebook to East Africa and scanned through it. She searched for the name of the town nearest to the camp she would be staying at – Voi. It was near the Nairobi–Mombasa highway and (most excitingly for her) was near the site of the elephant orphanage rehabilitation camp. This got a brief mention, most entries being about hotels and places to eat, but it made Fenella feel a little more grounded – that she was aiming for somewhere, a real place on a map, rather than just escaping.

The final boarding call came, and she braced herself for the longer part of her journey. She found herself coincidentally next to Seif again, which made them both laugh.

'Fate has brought us together again, Fenella. Now we must tell each other our life stories. It's a long way to Nairobi and time goes much faster in the company of a friend.'

Fenella's heart sank at this, as she didn't really have any stories to tell, or at least any that she wanted to share. This was partly the reason for her trip – to have an adventure, to make new memories for herself, beyond those that had got her to this point. Luckily, Seif was an excellent raconteur and she found herself sitting back and letting him regale her with funny tales about his students' shenanigans.

They arrived at Jomo Kenyatta Airport in the full heat of mid-afternoon. Her third airport of the day, this one was dark, apart from a few stark fluorescent lights hanging from sagging wires from the ceiling. Below them, tables sat at odd angles where suitcases were being flung open and rifled through. The walls were covered in flaking paint and the ground was concrete, scuffed to a dirty grey. There was a slight air of menace, of unease. Men in full camouflage, carrying machine guns, stood at all the exits and milled around the departure area. An Indian family had been pulled over to one side and a woman amongst them was quietly crying. The airport shops sold pots and bowls as well as, curiously, televisions and bedding sets.

The baggage collection queue dispersed quickly, and Fenella moved through all the formalities with relative ease. She said her goodbyes to Seif, who handed her a business card and implored her to keep in touch and let him know if she needed any help while in the city. Before they parted, he found a taxi driver for her and helped her out to the right exit. The kindness bolstered her confidence and she stepped out into the wide street outside. It was notably hotter outside than in, but the soft blue sky and trees lining the streets calmed her. Her driver bundled her luggage into his boot and asked her destination. 'The YWCA, please.'

The driver was chatty and gregarious. She was still on alert, not yet ready to relax, but laughed along with him and listened with interest to his views on the latest national political goings-on. Her patience was waning a little as they reached her destination, but only because she could now visualise a bed and shower and was keen to reach them. She dreaded the rigmarole of signing in at the hostel, but, in the event, the process was painless, and she got to her room quickly. This was a small dormitory, with two single beds dressed with pristine white sheets. So far, the room was unoccupied. Fenella flung her luggage on one of the beds and fumbled in her suitcase for a change of clothes and her washbag, ready for a quick shower and a rest before the evening meal.

While drying herself in the bathroom, she heard a soft knock at the door and a cautious 'Hello, are you decent?'

'Yes, it's fine, I'm just finishing off in the bathroom.' Fenella called through. When she emerged back into the bedroom, she encountered a tall, blonde girl, about her age, vigorously shaking a large khaki rucksack off her shoulders and onto the unused bed.

'Hi! I'm Bryndís.' Her rucksack strap was caught on her jacket collar and Fenella tried to help free it as Bryndís wiggled her arm back and forward. She got herself more and more tangled in the strap until eventually she just resorted to yanking her arm right out of her sleeve. The rucksack dropped with a muffled thud, taking a spinning Bryndís with it, collapsing face down on the bed.

'Well, that was dignified! I thought I was never going to be free!' she laughed. Her voice was husky, with a gentle accent Fenella couldn't place. Any tension she had felt about sharing a room dissipated. 'I'm Fenella, well, Nella. Nice to meet you.' Fenella returned to the bathroom to finish dressing and Bryndís started unpacking.

'How long have you been here?' Bryndís shouted through to Fenella as she pulled off her boots and hung up her jacket.

'I just flew in about an hour ago. I came straight here. You?'

'I have been up north – Samburu. I've been travelling for a couple of days and my bus broke down at Laikipia. Oh, my feet! We had to wait hours for another bus to take us on. So, I'm straight into that shower after you.'

They squeezed past each other and swapped places. Fenella unpacked as Bryndís chatted through the bathroom door.

'Where are you from?' she asked Fenella.

'Scotland,' Fenella replied 'You?'

'Iceland. But I've been in Africa for eight months. I was at university in Denmark, studying Economics, but I dropped out. I've been volunteering and working here and in Uganda. What do you do in Scotland?'

'I was working at the zoo in Edinburgh, but I've left my job to come here.'

A few minutes later, Bryndís emerged from the bathroom. 'Wow, that shower was actually okay. I've been in some shockers! I almost feel clean!' Fenella got a proper look at Bryndís now. She was pink-faced from the hot water and her damp hair was already drying with a slight frizz. Her face was mischievous, elfin. Fenella liked her already, but also felt slightly intimidated by her obvious self-assuredness. Bryndís tore into her rucksack, pulling out a pair of jeans and a tie-dye t-shirt that had been scrunched into a solid ball. She assumed an expression of mock disgust. 'So, we are both dropouts! Right – we both should rest for a while. Do you want to sleep? No, probably not, but maybe just lie down for a bit.' She sniffed the crumpled t-shirt. 'And I will sort out some washing I need to do.' Fenella tried to interject a few times, but Bryndís kept talking. 'Are you in Nairobi for long? I expect you want to see some of the sights. Or perhaps you are going to a job, or a tour of something.'

Fenella waited a few seconds before trying to answer. She had a feeling she was not going to get the rest Bryndís had suggested. 'I'm going to a wildlife research camp near Voi to work as a volunteer. The day after tomorrow, I meet with a guy from the camp who is going to drive me and few others down.'

'Fantastic! We can spend the day together tomorrow. I can show you round,' said Bryndís.

'Really, don't you have things of your own to do?'

'No, not really. I'm not sure what I'm doing next. Just waiting for a call about something.'

'I'd really like that, thank you. I am trying to travel alone, but I'm not very good at it. You see, this is really my first-ever trip. Well at least since I was a child.' Fenella was a little embarrassed, but was beginning to feel more at ease with her new friend.

'Good for you. OK, well I'm your woman. Let's go and find something to eat.'

'I don't think they start serving until 7.00'

'Oh, God, don't eat here – pigswill. I'll take you to a great kibanda – they do delicious chapatis and kebabs and things. Just right to fill you up after a long day. And very cheap! And clean, I promise.' Fenella was trying not to look horrified, but had clearly failed.

After a few more minutes sorting their belongings, the girls locked up and headed out into the city. The cool of the early evening signalled the end of the working day. Swarms of commuters headed purposefully from the office blocks and colleges to the main bus station. Colourful matatus were packed with people, space barely discernible between faces. These infamous minibuses were known for their vivid artwork and standout names – 'God Protect Me', 'Trojan', 'African Ninja'. The buses themselves looked cheerful and innocuous, but matatu drivers were notorious and, although their intricate spray paint art did a good job of camouflaging damage, if one looked closely, not a single matatu was unscathed.

Bryndís held Fenella's hand and pulled her through the throng. 'Come this way, don't buy anything from the hawkers. Just say no, don't even smile. Look confident.' Fenella was not feeling confident. She was terrified. But she did her best, balling her spare hand into a fist and trotting to keep up with Bryndís's wide strides.

'Jambo, Daudi! You're still here, man!' Bryndís greeted the man behind the stall with a fist bump.

'Bryndís, my best customer!' Daudi wore a chef's hat, teetering atop his impressive dreadlocks. He seemed to be simultaneously chopping vegetables, frying long, curled sausages and wielding a giant wooden spoon, which he was using to stir delicious-smelling stews.

'OK, good ladies. Here at Chef Daudi's famous restaurant, I have made for you maharagwe, githeri, served with chapatis and ugali or rice. 200 shillings for any meal. What'll it be?'

'Give me a bit of everything, Daudi, I'm starving. Fenella – same?'

'Erm, can I have that bean stew, is that the maharagwe? Yes, some of that with rice and a chapati, please, thank you. It all looks amazing!'

'Coming right up, ladies.' Daudi moved with the deftness of a circus performer, in time with an up-tempo beat booming from speakers under his counter.

'Who's the singer, Daudi?' shouted Bryndís.

'Osogo Winyo – best Ohangla musician ever – he's a legend.' He dished out this, stuffed that, sprinkled everything artfully with chopped chillies, cucumber and coriander, a grind of pepper and presented the final meals with a theatrical bow. Fenella almost clapped.

The food was warm, rich and spicy. They found a couple of bollards to lean on and ate their food with their hands, scooping up clumps of rice and ugali and using it to swab up the stews.

'So, you've been in Nairobi already?' Fenella was the first to talk after a few mouthfuls.

'Yeah, I passed through about two months ago, from Uganda, en route to Nakuru, then Samburu. I was with some friends, but you know how it goes, everyone sort of drifted off as they found their thing, or went home.'

Fenella didn't know how it was, but she nodded. 'Is it safe here?'

'God, no! Not for us. Solo female tourists? No. But as long as you keep to some ground rules, you're okay.'

'Such as?'

'Such as knowing who your friends are. Daudi is the brother of someone at the hostel and he has looked out for us more than once. Stay near his stall and you'll be okay. Never wear any jewellery or carry much cash. Same as anywhere, really, but just be a bit more careful.'

Night was falling fast and the passers-by had morphed from office workers to nightclubbers – young men loudly calling to each other from either side of the street, drawing looks from laughing women on tottering heels.

'They are heading for Florida Club. Can you see it?' Bryndís pointed at a shape jutting out from around a corner. The nightclub was in the form of a huge flying-saucer, hovering over the brightly lit streets.

'You know a woman designed it?' Bryndís grinned. 'The first woman architect in Kenya. It used to be called the Bonanza.'

'It's amazing!' said Fenella. 'I don't think you'd see something so wacky in Scotland.'

'Certainly not in Reykjavik!' laughed Bryndís.

A familiar fear built up inside Fenella with the rising hubbub. She felt it climb from her wobbly legs to her stomach. Her head was swimming and she began to get the dizzying sensation of being outside her body, looking down at herself. Dido's words come to her again. '*Just stop. Grab something solid. Sit down if that's better. Breathe slowly and let it pass.*' Fenella turned to face the bollard, grasping it with both hands, eyes screwed tight.

'Do you mind if we go back now, only I really need to get some sleep?' Fenella tried to make light of how she was feeling, but

Bryndís could tell something was not right. 'Sure. Let's go. You okay?'

Fenella felt she could put a little trust in her new friend. 'I… I… get these "episodes". I'm okay, I'm not ill, I just get very anxious all of a sudden. Sort of fear the worst and that I'm losing control. It's hard to explain.'

'No need. Come on, we haven't come far.' Bryndís grabbed Fenella's hand and led her back though the street. The crowd was swelling and pushing against them, but within a few minutes, the two women were at the entrance to the hostel and headed back in. To the left of the lobby was a little common room with an old battered vending machine listing at one end. Bryndís bought them both a bottle of water, as Fenella sought out a clean patch of carpet and sat there, hugging her knees.

'It's a panic attack,' she explained after a few minutes 'I used to get them a lot, especially in busy places. I'm amazed I haven't had one sooner on this trip. I've come close, but I've managed to hold it together.'

'Maybe it's because you've got a friend with you now.' Bryndís's words were reassuring and probably accurate. Up to now, Fenella had had no real choice but to get on with things on her own. Now she had someone she could put a bit of trust in and her body had succumbed to the relief.

'I just need to sit here for a while. Get my head together. So sorry. I feel such an idiot. I really shouldn't travel so far from home, but I so want to get to the camp.'

'Don't be stupid, dúlla. You're not an idiot, you're brave. It would have been much easier to stay at home, wouldn't it, but here you are.'

Fenella didn't want to explain that no, home was not easy. But she knew that Bryndís meant it kindly. She had no idea of what Fenella had left behind. 'What's this call you're waiting for? Have you got something sorted?'

Bryndís sat down on the floor next to Fenella, tipping her bottle back and forward. 'No, I've had a text from a friend of a friend about a teaching job in Kilifi. I've missed out on it because of that bus breaking down. So, I'm a bit stuck, to be honest.'

'Come with me! Or at least ask. The guy who's picking me up on Wednesday – he might know if they have some places available where we're going.'

'Where is it you're going?'

'Near Voi. It's on the edge of Tsavo East. It's about six hours from here. Of course, I paid to come. I don't know how you'd work that out.'

'Oh, there's usually a way in Africa!' laughed Bryndís. 'I'm all okay to work here – visa, insurance and health stuff and all that. And I have a little emergency money put by. It will just be down to whether they've got room, I guess.'

The conversation had helped to calm Fenella and she rose slowly to her feet, sipping the water and steadying herself on the worn back of an old armchair. 'I'm good now, thanks for helping me.'

'Happy to. Maybe you've helped me too. Come on, let's get some sleep.'

CHAPTER 27

NAIROBI 2012

FENELLA woke early, the sun rising at 6:00 am as it always did this close to the equator. The thin brown fabric at the windows did nothing to soften the bright morning sun. The street had been too noisy for the girls to open the window, and now the heat was stifling, and Fenella was desperate for a drink. She still had a little water left in the bottle from last night. She sat up and sipped that, checked her phone – no messages. She swung her legs over the edge of the bed and bundled her clothes into the bathroom to wash and dress. Bryndís, true to her word, had done a 'little washing'. Every surface was swathed in drying clothes – the shower rail, the shower itself, the open door, the hoop for the towel. The arid heat had allowed everything to dry, albeit rather stiffly, and Fenella gathered and neatly folded the clothes so she could get into the shower.

When she returned to the room, Bryndís was up and dressed. This morning she wore a long tunic in a dark blue, embellished with abstract leopard faces. Denim shorts and well-worn walking boots completed the outfit. She had tied a scarf in a bright orange print around her head in an effortless but stylish look that Fenella had always coveted, but could never achieve. She pulled her own hair back into its usual low ponytail, loose auburn curls evading the hairband. Her attire was composed of lightweight beige trousers, a blue vest top and a green fleece, remarkably similar to her zoo uniform, she suddenly realised. She had absolutely no idea about clothes and had always preferred not to draw attention to herself anyway. She envied those, like Bryndís, who could put random things together and look so interesting. She contemplated that her own clothes reflected her personality perfectly. Bland, nondescript, practical.

Well, it wasn't worth dwelling on that now. Excitement was building up inside her stomach. Tomorrow, she would get to where she had dreamed of for years, planned for months. And today – well they were in a place unlike anywhere she had ever been, and it was thrilling. Bryndís noticed her smile and smiled back.

'Excited?'

Fenella nodded. 'Hmm.'

The girls went downstairs to the main canteen for breakfast. It was typical international tourist fare, if on the basic side, reflective of the room price. Cereals, toast and jams, bacon and eggs, yoghurt. Nevertheless, this was exciting for Fenella, given her lack of experience of hostels, so she ate as much as she could manage.

'God, these eggs are awful! All salt and rubber. I think I actually have to pick them out of my teeth!' Bryndís whispered as she ran her tongue round the back of her mouth to dislodge the offending eggs. 'So – what shall we do today? I didn't have time to linger here last visit, so I'm up for anything. How about you?'

'Actually, I did have it all planned out, if you don't mind falling in with it. You see I have been planning this for a while and I had time on my hands to look into things. Anyway... well... You'll see'. Fenella produced a journal, into which she had sketched out a full itinerary for the day.

'Shut up! What is this?' Bryndís took the journal and scanned down the page. 'But you've got timings, and transport and everything on this. Wow!'

Fenella looked embarrassed. 'I'm just not very good at being spontaneous, and I wanted to make sure I could see these places while I had a spare day. But it will mean leaving in about half an hour.'

'No problem, dúlla. Let me just finish my coffee and I'm all set.'

Fenella sat back and scanned the room. 'You know there has been a YWCA here since 1912?' she told Bryndís. 'It was where the young women who wanted to start work in office jobs in the city took lodgings. It was almost a little community of its own. I should say *White* women.'

'I guess racial segregation was still pretty common then.'

'Yes, it was, but I've read a bit about it. It was pretty well ahead of its time. It became much more multi-racial from the mid-fifties. The last White woman to be Head of the YWCA was here until 1964. She was a bit of a pioneer and ensured that her successors were Black African.'

'Good for her! Is she in any of these photos?' Hanging in random groups all over the walls were photographs, mostly black and white, of women in smart clothes, many smiling and chatting. The older pictures were of more formal groups of exclusively White women, organised like school photos. Then, as time progressed, the pictures become more relaxed and showed more and more women of different racial backgrounds. Some had been taken at meal times or what looked like dances.

'I don't know. I don't know what she looked like.' There was a selection of images on the wall above their table. Some had little inscriptions scrawled at the bottom – 'Njeri Kennedy's birthday, 1953', 'Mrs Nimmo's retirement, 1942', 'Independence Celebration Dance 1963, sisters Barbara and Sheila.' There was something about the last photo that caught Fenella's eye, something familiar about the two girls. They were very similar to each other; one looked a bit older and more self-possessed. She had neat fair hair, tied immaculately into a chignon, the other was laughing wholeheartedly. Her hair was in a flicked bob, swept up at the front into an impressive coiffure like a blonde Jackie Kennedy. They had their arms around each other and weren't looking at the photographer, but pointing at something else in the room. Fenella smiled at them.

Coffee drunk, they got up to leave. Behind the desk of the hostel reception, stood the manageress, Lily – a large, ebullient woman, with the loudest laugh Fenella had ever heard. 'You're up early, baby!' she bellowed at Bryndís as they came out of the canteen. 'I normally have to bang, bang on your door to wake you up!' This was clearly hilarious to Lily as she followed her statement with peals of laughter.

'I'm trying a new thing, Lily,' replied Bryndís, mock squinting. 'I think it's called "mornings"!' More laughter from the exuberant Lily. A few minutes later they were in a taxi, which Lily had called for them, and were heading for the Nairobi Giraffe sanctuary on the edge of the city.

They edged the suburb of Langata, and drove up the long shady avenue to the entrance to the sanctuary. Fenella paid up and they waved off their driver. Before them stood a large wooden rondavel on stilts, completely encircled by a platform. The makuti straw roof of the structure shaded the platform and small groups of laughing people were gathered on it and on the ground below. Surrounding the building, behind a low fence, several giraffes were feeding from trays attached at varying heights to the structure, and from the cupped hands of the visitors. Although the giraffes seemed to have large grounds in which to roam, the gifts of sweet leafy branches and pellets proffered by the excited tourists ensured the giraffes stayed near the viewing platform. Bryndís and Fenella paid the entrance fee and made their way up to join the visitors.

'Can you see the big house over there?' asked Fenella. 'At the far end of the giraffes' enclosure? It was built by a Scot, Jock Leslie-Melville. He and his wife rescued a giraffe and the whole thing snowballed into a sanctuary. They turned the house into a hotel, where guests can stay and dine with giraffes poking their necks through the dining room windows.'

A smiling ranger called Samuel introduced the girls to giraffes Laura and Lee and their calves. They then spent a lot of time feeding them pellets, some mouth to mouth. It was rather like kissing a lippy, bearded man, but more pleasant.

Samuel explained about the different types of giraffe in Kenya. 'The ones here at the sanctuary are Rothchild's. They are our rarest giraffe and the work started by Jock and his wife, Betty, brought them back from the brink. We also have Nubian, Reticulated and Maasai. They are all becoming endangered. Their numbers are going down really fast now. We all need to help our giraffes.'

Fenella gazed at Laura, who nudged her for more tasty pellets. 'We didn't have giraffes at the zoo. This is a much better place for them. They're so beautiful.'

'Beautifully weird,' laughed Bryndís. 'They're just so odd, aren't they? I think that's why they're so beautiful. You can't stop looking at them.'

'They're very interesting, too,' said Samuel. 'Did you know that they don't blink, they lick their eyes to keep them moist, and their saliva is antiseptic. They also have four stomachs, a bit like cows, and they only sleep for twenty minutes at a time.'

'There's a baby there. How old is he? She?' asked Bryndís.

'She's nearly a year. She was already six feet tall at birth!'

'Wow!'

'Yes, well they have a long way to fall!'

'I suppose so!' laughed Bryndís. 'And when will she be fully grown?'

'It takes around five to seven years.'

'They're so elegant and gentle,' muttered Fenella, still captivated by the greedy Laura.

'They are, yes, but they can look after themselves too. They can be very dangerous – their kick can kill a lion and they can run fast, fast – fifty kilometres an hour for ten kilometres at a time, so they do not have many predators. Though I've seen a lion chance it once or twice. They are most vulnerable when they're drinking. Have you seen them drink?' Fenella didn't answer.

'No, I haven't,' said Bryndís.

'Well, their necks are too short, you see?' Samuel grinned.

'Really?'

'Yes, they have to splay out their four legs and tip forward. It's really not very elegant. They can't take too long over it because they have to keep their necks upright, or they constrict blood and oxygen. And, of course, they are vulnerable in that funny position.'

The girls kept feeding and murmuring to the giraffes, until an excited group of schoolchildren came up the steps and they let them stand in their place.

'The kids are here as part of our education programme.' Samuel had to raise his voice a little. 'We have school competitions every year. The schools submit artworks by the children and the best pieces are put on display, you see, over there?' He pointed to a glass-covered noticeboard, full of colourful, cheerful paintings and sketches.

'Each year, one boy and one girl with the best art pieces are chosen and awarded prizes. Their schoolmates then win a week's holiday at one of the local nature reserves.'

'That's such a great idea, and what great prizes!' said Bryndís.

'Well, it's really meant to get the children interested in their wildlife. You know, very few Kenyan children have ever seen even a lion or an elephant? They live in the cities, or so far away from the wild that they can't afford to go and see it. These children here today are actually from Kibera. Do you know what that is?'

'I've heard of it, but no, not really,' said Bryndís.

'We have the dubious honour of having the largest slum in the world, right here, outside Nairobi. We bring groups of children from there, show them around, give them a meal and tell them about their environment.'

'I had no idea what a wonderful place this is. Thank you so much for your time, Samuel,' Fenella said. Any anxiety she had felt the day before could not have been further from her mind now. This was what brought her joy and grounding – being around animals.

'You know, I worked in a zoo, back in Britain,' she explained to him. 'I loved my job and the animals, but it never felt right and real, if you know what I mean. I know that these giraffes are in a sanctuary, and your aim is to free them, isn't it?'

'Indeed, it is,' said Samuel. 'Not all of them will be, but, as far as possible, we translocate them in groups to protected areas and help them to acclimatise. Otherwise, what is the point? They do not exist for our amusement; they should be free, out there.' He swept his arm in the general direction away from the city.

'Absolutely,' agreed Fenella. 'Out there.'

* * *

The next morning, a young man was waiting for Fenella in the reception area. They had agreed to go out for breakfast before the long journey to discuss the details of the weeks ahead.

'Good morning. Is one of you Fenella?' the young man asked.

'That's me. This is my friend Bryndís.'

'Good morning, both! I'm Simon.' He showed them his company ID. 'Are you staying here, Bryndís, or would you like to come join us? We are just going to a little canteen I know.'

'I'd love to, thanks, if that's alright.'

The girls settled their bill at the desk and, leaving their bags with Lily, left the hostel and jumped into Simon's jeep. A few blocks up the road, Simon stopped and helped the girls out. He greeted the manager of the canteen and ordered up a full breakfast. As the food was placed on the table, their host explained each item.

'First, we have chai na mandazi.' Tea with pastries. He lifted the lid of a large steaming pot, 'Uji porridge.' And another. 'Scrambled eggs.' Then pointing. 'Toast, jams, honey. Enjoy.'

'What a feast!' exclaimed Bryndís. 'I love Uji. I ate it every day in Samburu.'

'Me too,' said Fenella absent-mindedly as she scooped up a hot spoonful of the porridge and expertly smothered it in brown sugar and cinnamon.

'When did you have it before?' asked Bryndís, her words steamy through her mouthful of Uji.

'Sorry, what?' Fenella fumbled, realising her mistake and burning the end of her tongue. 'Oh, no. I just mean I love porridge.'

'So, Fenella. How much do you know about our programme?' asked Simon once they had finished eating.

'Well, you are working with a lot of local farmers to help with HEC – erm… human/elephant conflict and you do de-snaring and monitor elephant numbers.'

'Yes, that's right. This project is specifically about crop and tree damage and sustainability, so we assess trees and crops for evidence of damage inflicted by elephants, and we observe local elephant behaviour and movement patterns to establish links – to check whether it is definitely the elephants causing the problems – and come up with possible solutions. We work with the local farmers. We then help with replanting and deterrents to protect the flora from the fauna.

'Do you have any spaces on the programme?' asked Bryndís. 'I find I am at a loose end for a few weeks and I'd love to join it.'

'Let me check with the office,' said Simon, 'I think it should be fine, but we'll need to do all the paperwork and things first. I'll go and call now if you like. Would you like to get some more coffee while you wait for me?'

'We'll sort ourselves out, thank you,' said Fenella. They watched Simon for a few minutes as he chatted on his mobile and turned to give them a nod and a thumbs-up. Fenella turned to face Bryndís. 'I'm so glad you're coming. And since we're going to spend a few weeks together, there are a few things I should explain about myself.' Fenella started to pick at her cuticles, then looked up shyly at Bryndís.

'Intriguing!' said Bryndís. 'I thought there was something going on. What is it, are you a crazy runaway heiress? An undercover spy? Spill it!'

'Nothing so thrilling. No, it's just that, well. This is not my first trip to Kenya, not at all, just the first on my own and to the city. You see, I was born here. I've come home.'

MAKENA

TAITA HILLS 1988

I HAVE led my family to this spot, as it is far, far from the wide tracks the humans have made. We keep our distance from them now. When I was younger, when our thirst was urgent, we would follow their flat empty trails to get quickly to a waterhole. Humans riding their noisy creatures would sometimes meet us, but they did nothing more than whisper and laugh and hold stones in front of their faces. Then they would move on and leave us. But then we had the dry time and the trees died and the shrubs grew brittle and the only humans who came had their loud sticks. We moved away from their tracks and their sticks, but the dead trees left no shelter anymore, there were no green branches to hide within. The humans did not stay on their tracks, but carried on through the empty bush to seek us out.

Today it is hot, hot. We are weak and slow. We can only move as fast as the slowest in our family. Today, as all days now, this is my mother, Flower. She is the kindest among us and always makes sure that the youngest get the most to eat, so she goes days and days without food, sometimes without water. And now she is thin and broken.

We hear a bumping roar behind us. It can only mean danger; they have found us. Humans sit in their giant moving creature, growling as it speeds towards us. We cannot outrun it and we scatter in panic. My grandmother, Fierce screams at them and slows, so they turn sharply and chase after her. I know that she has led them away on purpose to give the rest of us a chance to escape. We hear a loud snap which makes a flock of starlings burst from their roost. I see my grandmother drop to the ground. We run.

We do not stop until we reach the tall baobab and I check the group. We are still missing Muddy and Flower as well as Fierce. We stop and wait. No one comes. I mumble to the eldest of my sisters to stand with me. We shuffle close together and concentrate on standing very still. Then I begin the song. We close our eyes and, one by one, my sisters join the song with their own voice. Light Eyes is the most skilled. She has the deepest voice and I can feel her hum as it runs down her legs, through the parched solid ground and up through mine. We build our song layer upon layer, deeper and deeper, sending the sound through the dusty broken twigs at our feet, through the cracks in the soil, through the channels dug by mongoose and naked mole rats, through the roots of the trees more ancient than us, twisting through the earth, spreading our song. We begin to rock side to side, mesmerising ourselves into our gentle trance. This is our secret song. When we sing, no lions roar, no birds fly away, no antelopes run. No humans appear. We keep singing and waiting.

Then I can feel it. I feel a different song. A different pitch overlapping with ours. It is not far away. Dew Drop looks at me. We take a deep breath and sing again, deeper still. The sound is answered. It is a single voice. It is Muddy's voice. There is tension in it, so we slow our song to reassure him and to help him to follow our sound. His song stops and we sense he has moved. We wait. It is not long before we see his shape in the distance. He is moving quickly, jerkily. There is something wrong. I signal the group to stop their song and urge them towards Muddy. As we near him, he turns back on himself, so we follow. I can smell pain and blood coming from him; as I near him I can feel his anxiety and see a large angry stain on his rump. And then we see what he is leading us to. It is my mother, Flower. There is no blood on her. She is simply sitting on the ground on all fours, head leaning on her front legs. At first I think she has just knelt down to reach a low branch, although I know that cannot be true.

We close in and circle her. I shuffle forward and touch her cautiously with the very tip of my trunk, as though to tap harder would wake her. She still smells the same – of love and comfort. She is the delicate, sweet mother who fed me and taught me about the different leaves and smells and the breath of the wind. She taught me how to rub my skin against the wild sage trees to protect my skin from ticks. She and I would gorge on figs and I shared her hatred of baboons and frogs. When I was small enough to slot under her, she was the towering shadow that kept me cool on the long walks to water. The kindest of us all, she took Muddy and Pink Tail and all the youngest of our group to her heart. I have lost my protector and lifelong friend.

I am torn now between love and fear. There is danger around us, but I feel the pull to stay with my mother. I want to be with her and let her know that she is loved, but there is no time to linger. I look around me and the family are looking to me to make a decision. When the sun rose on our family we were led by Fierce. Flower was her daughter and closest counsel. The sun has not yet set, and I am now the head of this family. Two generations have gone in the time it takes the sun to arch over the land. I turn towards the setting sun and away from Fierce in the distance, and from Flower, here by our feet. We walk slowly, tightly, our heads low, until we reach a scrabble of acacias where we stop to rest.

The sun is up now and there is a strange noise overhead. Mousey and Trips-Up are squabbling as we rest under the wide acacia and I stop my chastising to look up into the white-blue sky to see a huge bird clip the top branches of our shelter. Although this does not smell like a bird and it is close enough for me to smell it. It smells hot and sour and the noise it makes is like the scratchy roar of the creatures the humans ride on their tracks. I suddenly feel panic rise through me. I kick the two youngsters further behind me. I have kicked too hard and Trips-Up yelps, but I am too focused on the strange bird to attend to him. The thing is higher in the sky, but still it circles, like a wheeling vulture. I keep my body low and covered in the knotty dry branches, but I still stare up at it. It tips and lowers slightly, and I see two shapes within it – two humans – but they do not hold their loud sticks, so I allow myself to relax a little.

By now, some of the herd have woken from their slumber and are immediately alert. They look to me to guide them, nudging me. They also sense the human presence and are on the point of panic. The rhythm of our group a few moments ago was a slow collective pulse; a wave of sonorous breathing. Now our feet shuffle agitatedly and we scratch furrows in the dirt as we fight the urge to run. But I sense that there is no threat in this visit – that these humans mean us no harm. The thing tips again, circles one more time, then leaves.

PART 5

CHAPTER 28

TAITA HILLS 1990

JOANNA woke up on the floor again. Despite the altitude making the nights cooler, she was hot all the time and could not sleep in the wide Lamu bed with all its fussy cushions and throws. She preferred the cold hard surface of the polished concrete. She was usually fine: despite her Scottish blood, she found the Kenyan climate, at least upcountry like this, suited her very well. But lately, at night, she was irritable, hot and itchy. Otherwise, her pregnancy had gone smoothly and, rather than feeling overweight and uncomfortable, she felt empowered and invincible. She was creating another human – she was amazing. More than just feeling healthy and strong, she had become so intrinsically linked with the wild creatures who shared this land, she felt she had the soul of a lioness.

Her auburn hair was sticking to her neck and shoulders in limp, wavy trails. She pulled herself up, grabbing the edge of the bed for support, and tiptoed out of the bedroom. An outdoor cubicle surrounded a shower (another Heath Robinson effort by Rob and Hamisi). This contraption comprised a tank, various tubes and pulleys, and a bucket, which formed the shower itself. Joanna filled the bucket with water from the adjoining tank and stepped in. She pulled the chain to release the water, which trickled out creating deliciously cool rivulets through her hair. She had to wash her hair quickly, as the water was limited and always ran out sooner than she expected. Just as she had finished rinsing, she opened her eyes. The noise of the running water had prevented her hearing anything else, so at first, she was startled. But she quickly relaxed. It was Makena and her young calf browsing on the shrub outside the bedroom.

'Good morning, Makena,' she whispered. 'You are so well-mannered, trying not to wake us!'

She stepped slowly out of the cubicle, a kimono swathed around her, straining to cover her nine-month bump. Makena took a few steps towards her and Joanna reached out, ready to accept her trunk in greeting. But the elephant did not respond in the usual way, with the trunk to Joanna's waiting palm and face, instead she reached gently towards Joanna's belly. Joanna's heart instinctively quickened a little, but she stood quite still and allowed Makena to investigate. The tip of her trunk brushed softly over the belly, scanning it, very purposefully, then stopping just below the belly button. Joanna felt a sudden, flicker inside her, as a tiny foot kicked out, enough to make a sharp imprint under her skin. Joanna giggled, but Makena did not flinch. She turned her trunk upwards to stroke Joanna's face and they held each other's gaze for a long moment. Joanna lifted her arm out to gently stroke Makena's trunk and the elephant slowly took a few steps backwards and turned towards her calf. The two of them ambled away in the direction of the riverbank, leaving Joanna exhilarated but utterly tranquil. She felt that this little moment of bliss had imparted some sort of magic on her unborn child.

After a moment, the episode already felt dreamlike as she heard the sound of people stirring inside the house. She shook her head, bringing herself back to the moment to set about preparing the breakfast. She didn't want to tell even Rob about what had happened. Not just yet. She wanted to hold the moment to herself just a little while longer.

Rob drifted into the kitchen, scratching the back of his head, smiling at Joanna stirring porridge, her body turned sideways, her bump precluding normal positions. His hair, always unruly, was particularly wild at this time of the morning, dark blond helixes springing out at all angles.

'Morning, JoJo.' He kissed the back of her neck, still cool and damp beneath the towel turban. 'What's the plan today?'

'I thought we should go north of the river; Hendrix has been hanging around there and it looks like the young male from the Painters family has been trying to hang out with him. I thought it might be interesting if we got to see them together.'

After a few minutes, they were joined by Barbara, who carried two folders to her place at the breakfast table, ready to peruse the day's tasks. 'Morning, you two. Joanna, you look bright as a button. How are you feeling?'

'I feel amazing actually. This thing happened outside the... never mind. I feel great, like I could climb a mountain. But this nesting thing never happened, did it?' She laughed as she scanned the chaos of their camp kitchen.

'I think I had it for you,' laughed Rob. 'I keep sorting the office, getting everything in order. Not sure how useful that is for the baby though!'

'Are you both out all day today?' asked Barbara.

'Probably. We're going to stop at Voi River, just on the edge of the conservancy. We're hoping to see Hendrix in action and maybe Miro,' explained Rob.

'OK, I'll need to ask Hamisi to help me then.' Barbara was pensive.

'Problem?' asked Joanna.

'Just some repairs, I went to check the two huts up on the top kopje and the plumbing needs looking at. I tried to do it myself, but I think I made it worse.'

'Young Sammy is probably better for that. Remember when the kitchen flooded? He knew just what to do.'

'Good point,' conceded Barbara. She had a tendency to refer all issues to Hamisi who had arrived the previous July, fresh from Nairobi University to research his postgraduate degree. On discovering he could turn his hand to many practical matters too, Barbara had come to rely on him for lots of things that were nothing to do with wildlife.

'I need Hamisi to go through his findings on the oestrus levels of the females in the western side of the conservancy. He's done a lot of work on it so far, and he's just finishing off his report. We need to get the data together to take to that district meeting next month.'

'You're quite right. He needs to be left alone. Sammy will be great. I'll have a word after breakfast.'

They finished their preparations and headed off to their day's duties.

Joanna spotted him first. Miro looked very despondent, almost hidden in a thicket of wait-a-bit thorn. They had passed the rest of his family back near the road behind camp. There was Makena and her calf again, with sisters Dora and Leonora. They were a young family. Makena was definitely only twenty-two, Rob could attest to this, having witnessed her birth as a child – his first proper memory. But she was already matriarch of the group, and was almost the eldest. They had put their ragtag family together themselves – a collection of orphans and hangers-on, after the awful drought and poaching of recent years.

This part of Kenya, flanked on either side by Tsavo East and West National Parks, had suffered very badly. Parts of the land were still parched and looked so innately desert-like it was hard to imagine they would ever recover. The local elephant population had been at breaking point, and indeed was really only starting to show small, hopeful upsurges now. But they were a strong and resilient family, this one. Teenage Miro had only recently been excluded, staying longer than would be normal with the female group, it was now his time to find his own way.

Rob had just begun to compile notes detailing the individual elephants. This was a technique devised by another distinguished elephant researcher. Identification of individuals was clear if you concentrated on the details of the ears. Joanna was the better artist and drew clear diagrams of each animal with measurements, behaviour traits, relationships with others in the group and with those in larger groups. Given the long, uneventful hours they spent in the field, Joanna liked to embellish these notes by adding a second page behind each sheet with more detailed sketches of the elephants. Sometimes, if she had time, and it was a special animal, she would use these sketches back at camp to paint portraits of the elephants. These canvases adorned the walls of their living area and study.

They continued along the dry bumpy road, the red dust billowing around them. The vegetation grew a little less sparse, twiggy trees scattered with hopeful leaves, curled upwards in readiness for rain, then the sight of a long tree-lined ribbon indicated that they were nearing the Voi River. A whining sound began to emanate from the radio. Joanna was sitting on the back of her seat to get as high as possible. She twiddled the radio's controls whilst simultaneously holding the aerial as high over her head as possible.

'Slow down a little while I get this signal set,' Joanna said. Rob slowed to a crawl and a definite repetitive beeping came over the airwaves. 'He's so close. Get the 'nocs out. See what you can see.'

Rob lifted the binoculars to his face and slowly scanned the view. 'Nothing yet. This bank, or the one opposite, do you think?'

'Hard to tell. Drive on a bit. God, my arms are killing me.'

They drove slowly towards a bridge. There was no option but to drive slowly over it. Intermittent floods and droughts had caused the bridge to disintegrate and crack all the way across. Every journey across was a gamble and a test of driving skill. The couple held their breath as the jeep stumbled its way over the bridge, and let out mutual sighs of relief when they reached the opposite bank.

'Oh, my goodness, right on cue, look!' said Rob. There he was: Hendrix. They could tell, from his body language, even at a distance, that he was tense. A continuous stream of liquid oozed from his temporal glands and his penis. He rocked from side to side and flipped his trunk around, clearly agitated. They stayed back; he was evidently in musth. This testosterone surge created an almost trance-like state in bull elephants, and even if, like Hendrix, he was used to humans being close by, his behaviour was entirely unpredictable and potentially dangerous.

'You really shouldn't have come today. I was stupid to let you,' said Rob.

'Let me? Give me a break!' said Joanna. 'I wanted to come. I wanted to see how he was. His collar looks fine from here. Are you getting a good reading from it?'

About six months earlier, Hendrix had been sedated in order to fit a radio collar. This enabled them to track and monitor his movements. There had been complaints from the local community that lone bulls had been raiding their farms. Though Rob and Joanna knew that there was as much disruption from illegal cattle grazing as from elephant invasions. But the elephants were an easy target. At the moment, Rob and Joanna were only monitoring. They had yet to work out if there really was a problem. If there was, there was little they could do. Fencing was expensive and fraught with difficulties and they absolutely refused to endorse any sort of cull. Numbers were only just beginning to recover after the decimation of the populations. For now, they settled into observing Hendrix.

'Pass me the flask, please, darling. I'm so thirsty.' Joanna felt a bit odd. She drank heartily, but it didn't really help. 'I'm getting a bit cramped sitting here. I'm just going to get out to stretch my legs.

'Okay, love.' Rob was looking though his binoculars and writing notes, fully engrossed in Hendrix's doings.

Joanna lowered herself down from her perch on the roof and into the back of the jeep. The back seat had been folded forward, so she stretched out as best she could. She left the canvas roof rolled back to give her more space and air, but it was still cramped, so she hopped out of the back door. Pressing her hands into her back, she straightened her spine, rocking from side to side. She was still staring at Hendrix and found herself following his lead, rocking in time with him. Suddenly, something changed. She had caught Hendrix's eye somehow and he was running right at them.

'Get back in, for Christ's sake!' yelled Rob. He made to turn the key, but the engine wouldn't start. Over and over he turned it, as Joanna pulled herself tight into the back of the jeep, curling protectively over her bump. Finally, the engine kicked in, but by then, Hendrix was upon them and smacked right against the front of the jeep. Rob reversed as fast as he could. He knew to always give himself an exit route and, though they had parked under the shade of a doum palm, he had taken care to stay on a flat, barren section of ground. The jeep squealed as it sped back, but Hendrix persisted and kept running and slapping his trunk on the bonnet. The jeep hit something behind it – a rock, or tree stump, and suddenly listed onto its left side. It felt like it was tilted in mid-air for a long minute, but it must only have been for a matter of milliseconds. Thankfully, it didn't topple sideways, but found its equilibrium, just as Rob put it into first gear and spun to the right. The sudden change in direction was enough to startle Hendrix and he stopped abruptly, as if released from a spell. Joanna looked back at him as they sped away. He looked bewildered, almost sorrowful.

She opened her mouth to say this to Rob, but instead of her words, an animal scream rose from her throat. Rob spun himself round to look at her. She was clutching her stomach and screaming.

'No, aargh, no, Rob. Stop the car. Stop. I need to get out.'

'I can't, love. Not here. We're still too close to Hendrix. Stay calm. I'll get us up to the main road. He drove on, feeling like he was outside, looking in, and that someone else was in control, driving, swerving and jouncing across the bumpy ground. He just focused on getting to safety. Voi was not far from here, if he could just get on a bit further.

'Please Rob, now. I'm having the baby now. You have to stop. I need you.'

Rob saw a clearing on the side of the road ahead and pulled over. He was shaking as he jumped out, but a surge of adrenaline seemed to rush up from his shoulder blades, through his whole body and he knew exactly what to do.

'Right, you need to get out, just for a minute. Grab me.'

He opened the back door of the jeep, steadying Joanna with his arm, then threw all the kit and general detritus onto the front passenger seat. Once he had made room, he spread out a tarpaulin and grabbed a couple of blankets. 'Here. Lay on this.'

'I don't want to lay down. I need to be on all fours,' said Joanna, clambering back in.

'OK, but just back up a bit so you're on the canvas.' Rob moved to the back of the jeep and opened the boot. 'Business end towards me.'

'Charmer.' Joanna tried to make light, but another contraction swelled through her like a tsunami and it wasn't so funny. Once that pain had passed, she complied and got up on all fours. 'Oh, for God's sake. How am I supposed to do this, fully dressed?' She fumbled with her trousers, actually Rob's trousers held up with braces, as hers no longer fitted. Between them, they clumsily removed these and she got herself ready.

'Just stay calm, love. I'm just going to the front to get you some water and some kit.'

'What sort of kit?' gasped Joanna.

'Scissors, alcohol, gloves.'

'Boy scout,' laughed Joanna. 'Ow, ow, ow!'

'You'll thank me later. Now just breathe. Steadily. In through your nose out through your mouth, okay.' Rob made the appropriate noises himself to help her focus.

As he walked to the front to reach into the glove box, he heard a rustling from the bushes beside them. His heart quickened. 'OK, got everything.' He tried to sound cheerful, but Joanna detected the strain in his voice. 'What is it, what's wrong?'

'Nothing. We just have a bit of an audience.'

'What? What the Hell? Get in here with me. Close the doors.'

Rob didn't need to be asked twice and ran to the back door, jumped inside beside Joanna and slammed it shut behind him. They both stopped and caught their breath for a moment. At first there was not another sound and Rob began to doubt himself, but then a trunk emerged, then another and another until the saw they were completely surrounded by elephants.

'What do we do?' Joanna squealed under her breath.

'I don't know. I don't… wait. They've stopped moving. They're just standing there.' The group were circled around thirty feet away on all sides, facing the couple, but they just stood and looked. There was a gentle grumbling coming from some of them, but no trumpeting, no agitated head twitching. Rather, an almost encouraging anticipation seemed to emanate from the herd.

'I think they just want to watch. Or make sure you're OK. Perhaps they're protecting you!'

'I don't think they… aaargh. This is it Rob. How's that medical training?'

'Basic and aimed at quadrupeds, but I'll do my best. Let me see how dilated you are… OK, there is a person coming out of there now, so let's not worry about dilation inches, hey? Okay… slow down… breathe in quick little shots… OK. I'm going in.'

'Don't joke, Rob.'

'Just lightening the mood, love.'

'Ha, ha, aarggh. I've got to push, Rob!'

'That's fine, I've got you. I've got the head. Another push.'

Joanna made an animalistic howl, but the elephants didn't flinch, they just stood, like sentries, utterly calm.

'The back's out, it's the easy bit now.'

'Easy bit, are you f… Aaargh!' A final push, and the baby was out.

'We did it! We have a daughter!' Rob cried.

Joanna burst into tears. Right on cue, the baby cried too. She blinked slowly and gently unfurled like a new flower as Rob passed her gingerly to Joanna.

'She has your ringlets.' Joanna managed through her sobs. A few damp curls clung to the baby's forehead, some already springing free in all directions.

'I like to think of them as manly coils, actually, But she's a fiery redhead like her mother!' grinned Rob. 'What a beauty.'

'Aren't you going to the cut the cord?' asked Joanna, sniffing.

'No, I think we need to get you girls to a hospital first.' Rob bundled the baby up in a blanket and wrapped another around Joanna. 'Are you comfortable enough?'

'I'm fine, but how long will it take. There's still the placenta, you know.'

'I think half an hour. Let's just get moving, but shout if you need me to stop.'

Miraculously, the engine started first time and they headed off, much slower this time. In the excitement, they had forgotten the elephants. They were still there, but had shuffled back a little and Rob was able to navigate through a gap between two large females. They still stood, purring their comforting support.

The onward journey was thankfully uneventful, and they reached the district hospital at Voi in less than twenty minutes. Rob pulled over and shouted to a passing nurse 'Can you help me, please. My wife just gave birth in the car!' A sudden flurry of activity followed as people poured out of the building to help, some pulling a wheeled bed out to the back of the jeep. Joanna and the baby were lifted gently onto the bed and into a clean white room, smelling strongly of iodoform and damp plaster. Joanna was taken care of and cleaned up. A nurse called Rob over to cut the cord and they weighed and checked the baby. All was well. She was quiet now, suckling happily, curled in the crook of Joanna's arm.

'Drama over. What shall we call her?' asked Rob.

'Fenella,' Joanna said firmly. 'It was my grandmother's name, so she has a piece of her Scottish roots always with her. And it's a pretty name. But I think she should have an African name too, to keep her African roots in her heart. Any suggestions?'

'How about, Ndovu?'

'Of course, "elephant"! And it's prettier than Tembo. Fenella Ndovu Chege. There won't be another one – she's unique!'

'Of course, she is.'

They spent the next few hours at the hospital, filling out forms, chatting to the nurses. They stayed the night, Rob sleeping in a chair beside Joanna's bed, and the next morning Joanna and Fenella were given the all clear to leave.

'I would recommend that you stay a while and rest. We can help you with the feeding and changing for a few days,' a kind nurse had said to Joanna.

'No, thank you so much, but I just want to get home. It's not far and I'll have lots of help. Thank you all so much for looking after us.'

The nurse took Joanna's hand in both of hers and gave her a squeeze. 'Well, you know where we are. If you struggle, just come back and we are here for you. God speed.'

CHAPTER 29

TAITA HILLS 1990

BARBARA had not moved from the office desk all morning. Rob had radioed en route to the hospital with the news of her granddaughter's birth, and again when Joanna had been admitted and all was well, but that was the previous day and now she sat helplessly awaiting news. She tried reading, planning the month's rotas, paying invoices. But she had to keep doing them all over and over; her thoughts scattered and unfocussed.

She gave up attempting to do anything practical, taking herself off to the kitchen. She poured herself a ginger tea and took it out onto the veranda. Sitting back in her favourite chair, she allowed her thoughts to settle and closed her eyes, reminiscing and wallowing in happy thoughts. Rob had been their only child. They had wanted more, but it had just never happened, so they poured everything into him. She felt overcome with pride at this moment and wished that Clive was home. Right now, he was in Nairobi, meeting with delegates ahead of the next CITES conference due to take place in Kyoto in two years. The great and the good of the conservation world would be meeting to discuss the status of thousands of endangered species. Richard Leakey and Joyce Poole were among the most important people in conservation in the country, and indeed the world, and Clive had been trying to set up meetings with each of them for months.

How different life would have been without Clive. She regretted that they had spent so little time together over the years, but when he returned from each trip, she looked forward to it with the excitement of a new bride, a lightness in her heart. She liked to get his favourite food in, fill the refrigerator with Tuskers and the house with flowers and they would talk long into the night about his trips and the goings-on at the camp. If she had married Maurice, as her parents had wished, and remained a wealthy suburban housewife, she would most likely be drunk and sad and probably out of her mind with boredom. Here she was making a difference, while also supporting the man she loved to do an important job.

Clive was the cleverest person she knew – as sharp as a knife, but measured and careful. When he voiced an opinion, he had truly deliberated the issue and come to a firm conclusion. His editorial pieces were well regarded, not just in Kenya, but by those in conservation groups internationally. He understood the responsibility he had to bring the truth of issues to the public domain. He held no truck with histrionics or over-sentimentalising. He unravelled the facts knitted up in over-complicated language at conferences and in government reports to bring them to the audience that mattered, that had the power to make changes, to be appalled or elated. People voted with their feet and their money.

He was proud of Kenya's anti-hunting stance, of the ivory burning, of her refusal to be kowtowed by other, more powerful nations. Corruption was still rife, of course, and his outspoken editorials often resulted in enraged threats when he sailed close to the wind. But he had never in his twenty-five-year career put a foot wrong. His word was true and firm and trusted.

Where Barbara could be stubborn and emotional, Clive was sensible and pragmatic. She knew that this was largely down to upbringing. She had had the luxury of a privileged, upper-class childhood with very few real worries. He had the burden of loss and poverty, family responsibilities and high expectations. She could be all the things she was because no one had really expected anything of her except to toe the line. No one except Clive. He had pushed her in her job at the Game Department, then, when Toby and Sheila had returned to Nairobi, signing over the farm to her and Clive, he persuaded her to put all her love and knowledge into developing it to become a well-regarded centre for researchers. With his support, she had talked other local landowners into communal agreements on wildlife protection, and together they had become a force to be reckoned with in the face of governmental pressure on the use of their land.

She looked again at her watch, then at the telephone. No, she just had to wait. She would hold off trying to contact Clive until they were home and settled. He was travelling at the moment anyway. Like so many times before, she would have to wait for him to contact her once he reached a hotel, or a newspaper office. She had become used to waiting.

Barbara had practically brought Rob up alone, but she had a loyal staff at the camp who helped with all the domestic duties, so she had been able to home school him throughout his younger years and have adventures with him in the bush, which might be the thing of storybooks to other children. He had been a shy child, but he grew in confidence with every year, surrounded as he was by all the bustle of staff and guests at the camp. He had lots of friends in the nearby villages, running around naked with them while Barbara saw to the running of the camp. He learned from them how to string beads, shoot arrows and play complicated games of hide and seek.

The main clientele at the camp had originally been wealthy European and American tourists, wanting to follow in the footsteps of the Adamsons, Alan Root and David Attenborough, beguiled by the recent upsurge in nature travelogues on television and in books. Rob, or Bobby as they had called him then, amazed guests with his precocious knowledge of the bush, taught to him by Jackson and Fidel, the camp's rangers, who had remained loyally at the camp for what was now nearly thirty years. In older childhood, he began to take an obvious interest in the work being carried out by visiting researchers, who were coming in greater numbers to stay for long periods and complete academic papers for PhDs or to carry out work for government departments. Bobby could sit for hours with them, watching birds or antelope, completely absorbed, listening to the quiet observances between colleagues.

When he was accepted to study zoology at Nairobi University, she and Clive had celebrated with Rob by hiring a boat in Malindi and spending the summer with him and a rotation of spirited young friends, sailing up and down the glittering blue coast of the Indian Ocean – a last family holiday.

They had all made sacrifices to be here and keep things going, and every day was hard work, but she wouldn't swap a minute of it. She and Clive had been a team of two, then three, then Jo had joined the family. Jo and she had clicked from the start. They shared a love of art and fashion and would take themselves off together for a few days for a change of pace if Rob needed to be left to finish a piece of work. She felt so lucky to still have her child and now his family living with her.

And now there was to be a third generation at the camp. The thought of that thrilled her. She allowed herself to bask a little longer in happiness and anticipation in the silence, as she waited for their return. When she finally heard the familiar rumble of the jeep in the distance, she nearly cried with relief.

Joanna sat on the veranda rocking gently, Fenella lying in the tilt of her knees, wrapped in a kanga. She was never still – starfish fingers clenching and unclenching, eyes scrunching, chin quivering. Joanna studied her, noticing every tiny detail of her body. Her nostrils were perfect, neat triangles set into her still rather puffy face. Her skin was a soft fawn colour; the colour of a lion cub. Joanna coiled her fingers into Fenella's delicate corkscrew curls, the way she sometimes did with Rob, letting them spring back into the soft mass. She could imagine nothing more beautiful than the sight of one of Fenella's copper ringlets brush her plump cheek. The birth had been dramatic, but a sense of total calm now came over Joanna and nothing else mattered. All pain and fatigue forgotten. If there was anyone else around, she was oblivious to them. There was only the two of them, rocking, soaking up the warmth of Africa. Joanna closed her eyes and tilted her chin to the sun. She had told someone when she was pregnant that she was a little sad about the prospect of giving birth, as it would mean sharing her baby with other people. But now she knew they would still have moments like this. Just the two of them.

Those early days were spent in a fug of sleeplessness and love. When Fenella developed bronchiolitis at three weeks, the bond between them was already so primal that it was to be the most stressful thing Joanna had ever been through. Rob had driven them to the hospital at Voi, then they endured a four-day marathon of blood tests, wires, needles, nebulisers, saline drips, kind but brusque nurses and distracted doctors. She was already so in love with Fenella, that this very real chance of losing her was terrifying. After they had left the hospital, she was so traumatised that for months she carried the baby around in a papoose, feeding her hourly and not leaving the house.

As the months passed, however, she began to loosen the ties and let Rob in. He would look after his daughter while Joanna took a break for a bath or to read for a little while.

'I feel a bit like a male elephant sometimes,' Rob said one day when Joanna passed a fractious Fenella over to him. 'I'm on the outskirts, making sure you are safe, but you don't really need me.' His tone was light, but Joanna could see that he felt hurt.

'I don't mean to leave you out. It is just so intense; I can't explain it and I certainly didn't expect it. You know I was never much of a baby person. I barely notice babies. But what I feel for Fenella is so powerful. I think it is to do with being out here too.

There are no baby groups, cuddly toys, music boxes. Nothing getting between us. There is just us. And the wild. We are part of this wild that surrounds us, and the sense of it overwhelms me. I'm sorry.' She looked up at Rob, tired and expressionless.

'I know what we should do,' said Rob suddenly, bouncing Fenella on his lap. 'Embrace the wild! Come on, forget your bath for an hour or so. Let's grab a sundowner over at the river. Makena was there a few hours ago; she might still be around. Let's introduce Fenella Ndovu to her elephant cousins.'

They filled a basket with fruit, beers and two hot flaky pies that the camp cook, Peter, had just taken out of the oven and wrapped for them in a small kanga. Joanna strapped the baby seat into the back of the jeep and the little party set off for the river, half a mile from camp. Sure enough, Makena was nearby. Not on the banks of the river any more, but in a cluster of acacias a few hundred yards up a hill from it. Rob got out, pulled the basket from the back seat and laid a kikoy over the bonnet of the jeep, placing their picnic on top. He had attached a 'tracker's seat' onto the front left corner of the bonnet for the guides to use on safari and Joanna bundled Fenella into her arms and perched on it.

'Here,' Rob passed Joanna a Tusker, then sliced up one of the pies and placed it where Joanna could reach it.

'Come on up, the engine's cooled down enough on this side.' Joanna patted the kikoy beside her. Rob jumped up behind them and stretched back to lean on the windscreen.

They sat in silence for a few minutes. Fenella snuffled and huffed and her tight, cross face loosened into a smile. Joanna propped her up on her knees to face her and played pattycake with Fenella's hands. This brought on a fit of giggles in both of them. Rob picked up a corner of her pie and fed it to Joanna, then took a big bite of his own and leant back to gaze at the view. The light had lost its crisp edge and had softened into watercolour hues of ochre and khaki, the sky a bruise of purples and yellows. A go-away bird was calling from a tree overhanging the river and there was an almost imperceptible swish of elephants walking in unison towards them through the thickets.

'Here's Makena and her little one,' Joanna whispered to Fenella. The elephants continued to trundle in their direction, lazily browsing on thorn branches as they went. Rob and Joanna watched Makena turn to face them and give her calf a little nudge. It, too, then turned, and the two of them approached the jeep slowly and nonchalantly. Joanna's instinct was to clutch Fenella tight to her chest as the pair circled the jeep to reach their side, but she unclenched as Makena stopped a few feet away, bowing her head in a gesture that held no threat. Again, she nudged her calf forward and he tipped up his head, weaving his trunk from side to side and snuffled at the air around the family. Joanna gently held out her hand and touched the tip of the little trunk, then led it towards Fenella's tiny soft feet. Joanna and Rob held their breath, watching as the young elephant reached out so tenderly, that only the tips of the hairs on the end of his trunk tickled Fenella's toes. The baby giggled in delight and her parents exhaled a collective sigh of relief.

The calf continued to sniff and nuzzle at the family and his mother joined him, holding her trunk out a little further from the group, so that Rob had to reach towards it to greet her. As she moved her trunk to Joanna, Rob reached over to get his camera from the picnic basket and leant back to photograph the group.

'Hello, dear Makena,' Joanna said softly. 'This is our baby daughter, Fenella. She is very thoughtful and gentle and she is going to have a wonderful time getting to know you and your family.'

CHAPTER 30

TAITA HILLS 1996

CLIVE, at fifty-nine, was near retirement from his job as senior environment editor of the *Daily Nation*, his service unbroken since the sixties. He would stay in Nairobi or go wherever the paper sent him – to Europe, South Africa, and – most frequently these days – Asia, where ivory markets were blatantly and relentlessly on the rise. He and Barbara had lived this way for over thirty years, and when he returned from his assignments for short, sporadic periods of time, it was always to great fanfare from the family. He'd arrive laden with gifts for his granddaughters and with news of current issues, national and global, from his investigations.

Fenella was three when her sister, Evelyn, was born, and they had become inseparable. They needed no books or games, the land around the camp had become their playground and their classroom. From knowledge passed on from rangers Jackson and Fidel, Fenella taught her sister all about the baboons, hoopoes and vultures. Clive loved to watch them from the high veranda which reached out from the bedroom he shared with Barbara. Together the girls would trip after dung beetles. Fenella explained to her wide-eyed sister that the relentlessly optimistic beetle would shape the dung ball, rolling its prize over seemingly impassable terrain, hardening its sides so that it could lay its eggs within. She showed her the way a trapdoor spider builds its underground lair entirely from web into a long tube, complete with lid. Bare-footed, they would squat, watching, until an unsuspecting cricket would pass over the lid, creating vibrations sensed by the waiting spider. The spider would then jump out and snatch the cricket, causing the sisters to squeal in horrified delight.

Jackson and Fidel, with apparent infinite patience and enthusiasm, would spend hours with the girls, taking them for long walks near the house. This afternoon, Clive sat back in a low-slung canvas chair looking down from the kopje. He could see his granddaughters walking hand-in-hand with Jackson. 'See the gerenuk over there?' he heard Jackson say quietly as he pulled the girls low to the ground. The girls nodded. 'The old stories say that they are a cross between a giraffe and a camel. They have the long neck of a giraffe, so that they can reach the highest, juiciest leaves. Then they get enough moisture from what they eat, so they never need to risk drinking down at the waterhole – so that is why they are like a camel.'

'And see this over here? This is called a "midden". It is where the local dik-diks poo.' Evie was particularly fond of these tiny, wide-eyed antelope. Jackson pushed through some dead branches and lifted them up, so that the girls could see what he had found. On the ground was a pile of droppings apparently deliberately arranged in an elaborate fan shape. 'It marks their territory and they keep it away from where they eat, so they don't pollute the bushes they feed on. They are very clever animals. Very clean. You see how dry the poo is?' The girls nodded, smiling in shy delight at all the 'poo' talk. 'That is so they do not have to drink. Like the gerenuks, they use all the water they can from the leaves they browse on. Their pee is also very thick!' The girls erupted into giggles.

These nature walks had become part of a set routine for the camp. In between early morning game drives and lunch, when they had to look after clients, the two rangers spent time with the girls. They taught them about which snakes to be especially wary of, the habits of the little hidden animals like pangolin and tortoises, the names of all the different starlings and hornbills. At mealtimes, the two men joined the family, as they had always done, to tell them stories of their own childhoods, of living in small, warm huts filled with woodsmoke and song, of ceremonies and festivals, of what it was like tending the animals, helping their parents and going to school.

Sundowners had become a nightly ritual. Makena and her family were sometimes there, sometimes not, but when they came across each other, greetings were always observed and a mutual understanding between the families grew. Soon Fenella was old enough to sit on the tracker's seat herself and her sharp young eyes could pick out the slightest movement in the scrub as the family 'bundu-bashed' around the conservancy, monitoring the wildlife and driving guests and researchers to the best vantage points.

Joanna helped Rob and Hamisi for a few hours each morning, then after their 'safari school', the girls would sit around the table on the veranda with Joanna to learn reading, maths, geography, science and history. The table was in the shadiest part of the house at that time of day and Joanna insisted that the girls get plenty of fresh air, but it was also fraught with distractions. These mostly came from the bold vervet monkeys who were so tame, they would sit on the wall of the veranda, waiting for Joanna's back to turn, when the girls would surreptitiously toss grapes or bits of toast for them to pilfer before being shooed away.

It was a golden time, a time when everyone at camp was doing what they loved. Clive remained in awe of his wife. Barbara was at the helm, ensuring that the camp retained its reputation for a quality of experience and care for the animals, and an atmosphere of community. She had no scientific training herself, but being a natural organiser who had spent her adult life surrounded by conservationists, Barbara took care of administration and recruitment of interns and volunteers who came to assist Hamisi and Rob with their research. Clive knew that she missed him, but she kept herself busy and distracted by looking after the guests, dealing with suppliers, sorting staff issues and the myriad tiny issues that beset them.

Clive's passion for the wildlife of his country had been further ignited when Rob attained his degree in zoology. They would talk into the night about the comings and goings of the local lions, elephants and leopards and discuss the bigger issues surrounding wildlife trade, tourism, hunting and the links with the funding of terrorism. Clive, with his experience of the wider world, served as a conduit between Rob and colleagues at the university. Clive's research into international trade, and Rob's behavioural studies, gave essential perspectives on the local and international issues surrounding conservation. And now Clive was deeply proud of their team: Rob, Joanna and Hamisi were developing solid statistics regarding the animals on the conservancy, particularly the elephants, and were building their standing within conservation circles.

Clive had just returned from a trip to China; he brought unwelcome news of an old adversary when the family were sitting down to dinner.

'Darling, do you remember Johan du Toit?'

Barbara hadn't heard the name for years. 'Of course, how could I forget? Our delightful farm manager. Rob, I remember telling you about him, years ago, but I don't think we have ever mentioned him to Jo. Why do you bring him up now?'

Clive turned to Jo to explain. 'Well, he had worked for Rob's Uncle Toby here when the conservancy was a large cattle farm. He had been running a nice little operation for himself on the side, paying local people to poach wild animals and selling them to buyers in Mombasa and Johannesburg. We managed to… apprehend him…'

'Your Babu was a hero, girls!' Barbara winked at the girls.

'What did you do, Babu?' asked Fenella.

'Well, he left very suddenly one day and Uncle Toby and I found evidence of what he had been up to and followed him to Mombasa. We traced his dealings to a convent school and had an… erm… encounter with him there.'

'Modest,' said Barbara. 'They were threatened at knifepoint by Mr du Toit and another man, but they got away and led them into a trap. It was all very exciting!' The girls turned dumbfounded from their Bibi to Babu.

'Yes, well, it was something and nothing. Anyway, the point is – he's… um… resurfaced.'

'What do you mean? Where has he been? It must be over thirty years.' Barbara had stopped smiling.

'After he was arrested and charged, he was deported back to South Africa. He was dealt with by the authorities there and was in jail for a while, but for less time than he might have got here.' Clive stopped talking for a few moments to eat, then continued. 'So, a man like him with a criminal record was not going to get a job back as someone's estate manager. I've heard his name mentioned now and again. Nothing definite, just vague remarks when there has been a container of goods go missing before they reach a port, or reports of large elephant herds being poached, or when a sudden flood of weapons has been noticed by police in pockets of the country. South Africa, that is. Nothing concrete, nothing leading directly to him. All the while, du Toit has been untouchable. He has built up a little empire, running his own farm, earning enough to make himself bulletproof, quietly bribing the authorities to turn a blind eye, or having police fully on his payroll. He has become quite powerful.'

'And dangerous,' mumbled Barbara. 'Well, at least he's far from here.'

Clive flashed her a look and a tiny shake of his head. She nodded back in recognition that he could not talk more without alarming the children. So, she changed the subject.

'So, girls, I bet you never knew your Babu was really James Bond! And we thought he was just a journalist. Now, Nella, can you go and help Peter with bringing out the pudding. And Evie, darling. Those monkeys are getting very close and they have their eyes on the papaya in the fruit bowl. Why don't you ask Peter to give you some scraps from the fruit salad and scatter them over by the pump. Make sure the monkeys see you!' The girls ran off, gleeful at all the excitement. Barbara turned back to Clive. 'So, he's here then?'

'Yes, he's here.'

'Living in Kenya?' asked Rob.

'It appears so. He has companies running out of Kisumu and Mombasa. Fish exporting. It's big business anyway, but there are also lots of opportunities to, let's say, augment your income when it comes to exporting fish. He has legitimate markets in Asia, the Middle East, the US.'

'And what else could he possibly be exporting to those markets?' added Joanna, sarcastically.

'Indeed,' said Clive. 'I'm digging around, but he's as clean as a whistle. But I won't let it go now that he's on my radar. One day, he will trip up and I'll be there to catch him.'

A brief silence was soon broken by the Evie breathlessly running back to the table, licking sticky fingers. She was followed by Fenella, walking solemnly, trying not to spill a large bowl of fruit salad.

* * *

Later that evening, once the girls had gone to bed, the family gathered in the living room, joined by Hamisi, to discuss Clive's news.

'So, what have you heard?' asked Hamisi.

'I was following a trail from Murchison Falls in Uganda, through western Kenya and eastwards to the ports.' Clive traced an imaginary road in the air with his finger. 'Uganda's elephant population has been decimated in the last twenty years, with all the civil unrest and poverty. They've been putting some protections in place recently, with improved law enforcement as the country has begun to stabilise. Elephant numbers have begun to improve. Nevertheless, old habits die hard and some members of the security and military organisations there have been caught swapping rifles for tusks.'

Barbara tutted and shook her head.

Clive continued. 'Investigations by the Ugandan Wildlife Authority had turned up a name – a fish exporter dealing with Nile perch from Lake Victoria and lobsters and mud crabs from the coastal mangroves.'

'Your old friend?' Rob raised his eyebrows. 'How big is his operation?'

'Hard to say at the moment. Discreet, but potentially huge. We have to tread softly at the moment. We can't connect the company with trafficking within Kenya yet, but we have our spies out. We have to be very careful about treading on toes.'

'You mean involvement in high places?' asked Hamisi.

'I mean when people in high places are turning a blind eye, or refusing to answer questions, you have to assume there is something at stake for them. I have no proof of any criminal involvement, but I know I'm close. So does my editor and it makes him nervous. A big exposé would unveil more than just the immediate criminal gang, so I have to be a hundred per cent sure of my facts and my sources and I have to time things right. I'm afraid I have to play the long game.'

'In the meantime, elephants are needlessly dying,' interjected Joanna.

'And weapons are ending up the possession of those who mean to use them,' added Rob.

CHAPTER 31

TAITA HILLS 1999

'KEEP up, Nella!' Fenella saw the backs of her dad's calves, tanned and taut, brown socks, one pulled up, one scrunched down – always the same. Boots scuffed and stained an ochre orange from years trudging through this parched dusty ground. She could easily keep up with him. She had learnt to match two of her paces with one of his long quick strides. 'Ssshh… there they are. Keep down.'

The matriarch elephant they had been monitoring had arrived at the waterhole with her family. She was first to emerge from the commiphora trees, just one ear visible, then the tip of a trunk, sniffing the air for several moments, checking all was well. Slowly, other elephants began to appear in strict order. First the other adult females swished through, a couple of little babies scuttering under the shelter of their legs, then the teenage females – all sizes – finally, one teenage male, straggling behind, anxiously whipping his trunk as he threw his head up and down and sideways. They all headed straight to the waterhole, taking long drinks by dipping their trunks in the water, tipping back their heads and squirting the cool brown liquid into their mouths. Two of the older babies jumped into the shallow end of the pool and began to play. One backed up on his heels, spinning his head. Unacquainted with his trunk, it flapped wildly like a hose turned on too suddenly. He seemed to hit himself in his own eye and, startled, fell back into the mud. A second baby jumped near him, drenching his playmate. An older female admonished them, pulling the first baby out of the mud by levering him up with her foot. Fenella imagined her actually 'tut' at them.

The scene was not new to Fenella, but it was still infused with magic. Her delight turned her tummy and burst out of her in a spontaneous 'Hah!' She threw her hand to her mouth and her father turned to reprimand her, but stopped himself. He knew she had not meant to make a noise and, besides, these elephants were perfectly aware of their presence, their senses being far more sophisticated than humans, but Fenella and Rob were familiar and trusted. As long as they didn't do anything too outrageous, they would be tolerated.

They sat and watched the elephants for half an hour or more. Squatting on their haunches, they had to be ready to react to any disturbance or danger. Other people might get stiff or cramped from doing this, but Fenella and Rob were used to it and had developed strong leg muscles and the patience of leopards. Rob made notes on his clipboard as they watched. He would later scan the area after the family had moved on to take urine and faecal samples to take back to his lab. A ring binder on his lap contained detailed notes on hundreds of elephants who lived in and passed through this area. Each one had its own page, with a sketch at the top, detailing its ears and tusks and the markings which distinguished each animal. Rob knew every elephant he saw as well as any human of his acquaintance, better probably. He had a terrible memory for names – Jo would have to mouth names to him if they came across fellow humans – but he knew the age, family, character and social habits of all his elephant friends.

Each elephant was named according to its family group. Rob or Hamisi would decide on any general theme which gave rise to lots of names – the Greeks, the Romans, the Trees, the Winds, Books, Music. Their individual names ranged from the beautiful to the ridiculous – Hamlet, Scirocco, Galadriel, Hendrix, Bilbo. It was a point of honour to come up with the most imaginative groups and names. Fenella's dad was not a stuffy sort of scientist who numbered everything and saw his subjects in some impassive, cold way. He and Jo felt very deeply for the elephants – to them they were people. They understood the complexities of their lives precisely because they had become so involved, and it really mattered to them when anything significant happened like an inter-family quarrel or, worst of all, a death. This group they were watching was the Planets family, headed up by matriarch Venus (naturally) and included Neptune, Jupiter and babies Mars and Mercury.

'Did I tell you that I saw Bowie last week, Nella?' Rob interjected, with real excitement in his voice. 'He was over at Kasigau Gate. Miles from anyone. Definitely in musth – his glands were pouring, and he was pacing around, rocking. I kept my distance this time!'

Bowie had been known to occasionally 'have a bit of a cob on' as her mother had understated it, chasing their jeep a number of times in a rage, one time ramming one of his enormous tusks right through the vehicle's spare tyre, sticking there and getting even more furious (and probably a more than little humiliated) as they tried to liberate him from the tyre and get the hell away.

Fenella had been seven months old when she had met her first elephants. She didn't remember the event, of course, but she had a photograph of the moment framed on her bedroom wall. Her mother was holding her in a folded kikoy, tucked onto her lap as she sat in the tracker's seat on the front of their jeep. In the photo, Joanna is offering out her left arm to greet Makena, her trunk reaching in return. Her calf is beside his mother, snuffling at Fenella's toes. The mother elephant's gaze is held by the baby who mimics her own mother, reaching out to this huge, gentle creature, just touching the tip of her long, smooth tusk. The intensity and trust of that look is captured for all time. Nine years on, Fenella still met Makena – they still greeted each other with an outstretched arm and a trunk and a loving gaze.

'It won't be long until they cast out little Pluto, there,' said Rob.

'Poor Pluto, he must be so sad. I know it's the way of things, but I still feel sorry for him,' said Fenella.

'Yes, I feel for the males really. It's brutal – tough love!' agreed her father. 'And it does seem a bit lonely for them sometimes, but he'll find other males to meet up with and he can still see his family now and again. It's just the best way to stop interbreeding and spread the genes around – they have to move on.'

Fenella looked seriously at the scene in front of her, wondering about the fate of Pluto when he got older. He kept running up to play with the teenage females, but they treated him like an annoying little brother who butts in when you are discussing serious grown-up girl things. He got the message and hung his head as they moved on from the waterhole in search of more sweet euphorbia shrubs.

'He's so handsome already, isn't he, Dad? And his tusks are so long,' mused Fenella.

'He is. They are extraordinarily long for his age and so perfectly matched. That's really unusual. Most adult elephants have one tusk longer than the other, sometimes significantly so, if it had been broken in a tussle with another elephant or in protecting its herd from a pride of lions.'

'Why do their tusks sometimes inter-cross? It looks so awkward. I don't know how they can use them properly when browsing the scrub or shifting logs to get to all the sweet grass underneath.'

'They just manage. They are used to the shapes of their own bodies, I suppose, just like us. You know there was a young bull elephant in the Rock Band family. You might have seen him – Slash?'

Fenella nodded.

'Well, he lived up to his name, unfortunately. He caught his trunk in a snare, about a third of the way up. He managed to free himself, but as he did, he severed the flesh half way through his trunk.'

Fenella bit her lip as she winced at the thought.

'Hamisi and I predicted a slow and painful death – we couldn't see how Slash would possibly drink. But he managed, through his own determination and help from Zeus and Titan. His wound healed without infection, but he has been left with a deep hole in his flesh.'

'How does he drink?' asked Fenella.

'He flicks water sideways from his very wonky trunk into his mouth, and still manages to pull branches down to eat from.' Rob demonstrated with a twist of his arm. 'He took a little longer than the others, but he must have doubled the strength of his muscles to do it.'

The elephants gradually peeled away from the scene in front of them until all that remained were egrets and a pair of jacanas. Fenella thought they were the perfect combination of the elegant and the comical – little monochrome wading birds with a striking mass of smooth copper feathers just around their middles and massive clown feet.

'That's me for the day,' said Rob, standing up and tipping back to stretch his spine. 'I got a good sketch down of Jupiter. I'll get your mum to redo it at home. Jupiter was always facing at an awkward angle before, but I got her face-on today. She has an interesting line on her left ear, can you see? Dead straight from top to bottom. You know tusks can break, trunks and eyes are not very different between eles, but ears are absolutely unique. They're what give each elephant their character. Sometimes they can actually depict an elephant's life. You know… if it's a wild bull with a penchant for fighting, like Titan, they can get torn and perforated.'

Fenella giggled, she knew Titan and his reputation.

'So, they can alter over time. But, things like the way they curl in at the top… Or like Hendrix – his look like Prince Charles's. They properly stick out! Those things don't really change. Just get used to looking at their ears first and you'll soon get to know who's who.'

Rob looked pensively back at the now silent tableau. 'Let's go home, I promised Mum I'd make my famous banana curry!'

'Why is it famous again, Dad?' laughed Fenella, a look of mock disgust on her face.

* * *

Fenella liked to rise early before any of her family got up. She always tried to creep out of the house just before dawn and sit on the porch chair for a few minutes, wrapped in her favourite patchwork blanket, ready for the sunrise, listening to the sounds around her. The birds always beat her to it, of course. This morning, the white-browed coucal, nicknamed the 'water-bottle bird', would make its hollow gargling call, the go-away bird urgently called 'g'way, g'way' and a symphony of warbler and starling songs rose through the air, passing through Fenella as she sat smiling, eyes closed.

She shivered a little in the cool of the porch, and slowly opened her eyes to the new day. Sunrise began as a soft, apricot glow infused the grasses and the tips of the trees. Before long, the sun's power would be strong, building until the unforgiving hours just after noon.

Their house sat on its own kopje a few hundred metres above the rest of the camp. Fenella, Evie and their parents shared the top right side of the house, and Bibi Barbara and Babu Clive had a large, cool room which took up the top-left corner of the house.

To Fenella's right was a succession of flat ridges jutting out from the mountain. On the lowest of these, a baboon sat in a patch of full morning sun. It was a big young male and it was assuming the same tranquil expression as Fenella, settled into a yogic pose while satisfactorily picking at its ticks. A small waterhole just within view, which attracted few but the bravest animals during the day, was at this moment host to a small group of Thomson's gazelles and a family of warthogs. The gazelles were taking it in turns to look nervously around while the others drank quickly. The warthogs, much more audacious, jostled amongst each other for the best position, squealing and snorting and sliding in the mud bank. It had been a very dry month so far and the animals, who would not often venture so close to camp, had been forced to drink here.

Fenella took a deep breath and tried to distinguish each individual scent. The cool, earthy tang of night gave way to the hot, dry, brittle smell of morning. There was the woody scent of the commiphora trees, the leleshwa (or wild sage) and thyme which had been crushed underfoot by night-time visitors, fresh bark (the scent left behind by browsing animals) and, yes, it was quite distinct, the warm, wet-straw smell of fresh elephant dung.

The silence was broken by the snap of Fenella's mother shaking the sleeping insects out of the kitchen rug. The warthogs turned tail and scuttled zig-zaggedly into the thick bush, followed by the skipping gazelles.

The natural smells now gave way to the comforting aromas of porridge and chai. The family guzzled down their breakfast wordlessly, Rob reading through his notes from the week's visits to the Sagana Dam. Today he would spend his time in the office – a quiet corner room in the house. Rob, Barbara and Hamisi shared the office, with Joanna occasionally joining them, although much of her time was spent back and forth with the girls. Now six, Evie still needed a lot of looking after. She was a very happy child, though, and amused herself much of the time with her soapstone animals and wirework cars, or moulding shapes from dough her mother made from flour and water. These had to be disposed of outside as, leaving them lying around, as they found to their cost, attracted unwanted dinner guests. So, Evie purposely formed little shapes – leaves, nuts, bananas – that she thought would be enjoyed by the ants and mice and would leave them in artistic displays on stone altars to be munched by the local minibeasts.

'Today – Ancient Rome, Fenella. What do you know about Ancient Rome?' Her mother was sweeping the last breakfast crumbs from the table and reaching for a pile of books and folders on the shelving that Fenella's father had fashioned from some orange crates, Perspex and chicken wire. They did their best to keep the cupboards and shelves sealed to keep out ants and termites, but now and again a new little hole would appear, only revealed when someone spotted a tiny convoy determinedly making their way across the kitchen or living room walls. Jo's precious children's encyclopaedia had more than a few nibbles along its papery spine.

'I know that they ate and ate until they were sick, then ate some more!' laughed Fenella. 'And I know that they threw Christians to the lions.'

The rest of the morning followed its usual rhythms, Barbara was meeting with Peter to discuss the week's menus, Rob emerged occasionally from his notes to get a drink and bounce ideas off Joanna. Schooling veered from Romans to fractions to French regular verbs. Lunch was fresh bread and lentil soup; which Joanna had been preparing while listening to Fenella recite her seven times table and gluing the head back on a favourite wooden zebra to allay Evie's quivering chin. Afternoons in this dry season were fiercely hot and Jo and the girls rested in bed for a couple of hours, Rob concentrating on a report his father had written about ivory markets in China.

Hamisi arrived at the camp in the late afternoon, having returned from a visit home to Nairobi. He called as he entered. 'Hodi!' The girls looked up from their schoolwork to greet him.

'Jambo, Hamisi,' Rob looked up at his colleague who had put down his rucksack and was stretching out his arms and un-cricking his neck. 'Can I get you a drink, Rob? I'm going to get myself something.'

'Let me do it, Hamisi, you've been driving for hours. And I could do with a breather.'

'I'm happy to come with you, I need to shake the stiffness out of my legs.' Then, in a whisper, 'So, what's the latest?'

Hamisi's tone seemed urgent, so Fenella pretended to carry on with her times tables but listened as the men continued to talk in the corner of the kitchen.

'Well. Have you seen Dad's latest article?' asked Rob.

'Where he names du Toit in that poaching ring?' said Hamisi. 'Yes, I got a copy yesterday. Where is Clive now?'

'In Joburg. I'm quite worried for him this time, you know. He's really stuck his head above the parapet. I think he couldn't stand the subterfuge any more and has just gone full throttle to flush du Toit out.'

'Risky.'

'Indeed. I'm actually a bit cross with him.' Rob set about boiling the kettle, and turned to Hamisi, who leant against the worktop. 'We are all easy targets if du Toit has a mind to take his revenge. It's not as if he doesn't know where we are.'

'I see what you mean. But they have arrested him, haven't they? And it should be enough to send him away for much longer this time. It was nearly a tonne of ivory.'

'I know. But he has friends in low places. And it won't stop him. He'll pay the fine, do a little time, then be out and do it all over again. I think he's the only reason Dad hasn't retired yet. He is determined to bring down his empire. But it's too far-reaching. Too far underground.'

'And in plain sight, I should think. Lots of people on the payroll.'

'Exactly. He knows how to get to people who are poor and desperate. And you know what it's been like here for the last year.'

'Poaching's definitely on the increase,' agreed Hamisi. 'So are charcoal burning and bushmeat trading.'

'And with the recent crop failures, they're all ideal conditions for someone with big promises and cash to flaunt.'

'We'd better warn the others,' said Hamisi, 'and get all the staff in. We should make sure everyone is behind us and no one has reason to take the bait.'

'As far as we can,' said Rob. 'People are people.'

'As far as we can,' agreed Hamisi.

CHAPTER 32

TAITA HILLS 2002

IT was still pitch dark when Fenella woke to hear her father moving around downstairs. She knew she wouldn't be able to return to sleep. So, she jerked a sweatshirt over her pyjama top and padded downstairs. Rob was filling a flask with tea, buttered toast jutting out of his mouth. 'Can I come with you to town, Dad?' Fenella asked her father, causing him to jump.

'It's so early, Nella, and I do have a lot to do. Most of it would be quite boring for you,' Rob replied. 'I have to pick up the new bed I was having made, and some paint, and I have a meeting at the bank which might take a long time.'

'That's okay. I have to run some errands for Mum. Now that Babu is back from the city she needs more food from the market and also some new pens and paper. And I could visit the book stall while you're at the bank.'

'Ok, if you're ready right now you can come. I need to be back early enough to fax a report out to London.'

They got into the truck and headed out on the half-hour trek to town.

'Who's staying at camp this week?' Fenella asked Rob.

'We have a group of volunteers studying elephants. They're from all over the world – England, America, France. They're here for three weeks to help the centre study the movements of the elephants within a fifty-kilometre radius of Kasigau. You know that Hamisi has been studying those elephants and identifying them?'

Fenella nodded. 'He told me it had taken nearly a year to get it right.'

'Yes, well, he thinks that he has established total numbers, the aerial count we did last month in Charles's Cessna confirmed his data, but he needs help in plotting each family's pattern of movement. You know that people have been saying that the elephants have been coming too close to the villages. Well, he wants to see how much of a problem it is and why they might have changed their habits.'

'And what if there is a problem?'

'Well, in the short term, the water storage tanks that we have been constructing in the west should help a bit. They are already proving popular with some of the lone bulls; the only problem has been making them accessible and safe for the babies. We've built tanks that are on top of the ground with metre-high walls, as that was the easiest and quickest construction. The big males and the bigger females don't have a problem drinking out of them, but the water is out of the little ones' reach. If we built the tanks into the ground, they could be dangerous for humans and elephants. We're trying to figure out a solution.'

'And in the long term?'

'Well, that's the real issue. The weather seems to be getting hotter and drier. The vegetation is not recovering quickly enough from elephant destruction. Normally, as the elephants digest their food very quickly, plants and trees are seeded from their dung. That way, in the past, although the elephants might have seemed destructive, they actually helped to spread the forests out as they moved around. Do you see? Where their droppings landed, new vegetation would grow. But with this drier weather, that's not happening, so they are still knocking down and pulling out trees, but not replacing them. The only solution to this is either to destroy the elephants or for us to replant the trees.'

'Surely you can't destroy the elephants! It's not their fault, is it?' Fenella was horrified at the prospect.

'No, of course it's not what I want or what the researchers want, but what can we do? It takes far more time and effort to replant the forests.'

They sat in silence for the rest of the trip. Fenella thought about how much she still had to learn about her father's work. She loved going out with him to watch the elephants, to count them and work out what was going on in their lives. To her they were like extended family. But she knew that hers was only one perspective; that there were far more complications than she had thought about. The reality of life for local people and animals was fraught with issues. People were hungry and poor in this area. They wanted short-term solutions because the short term was all they had. When your child is hungry, you can't worry about what will happen in five years' time. You need food now. The thought ate away at her.

'Here we are,' said Rob as they parked up in the main town square. 'Cheer up. No decisions have been made yet. And the rains might still be good this year. Come on. You get the groceries for Mum while I do my bits and I'll meet you at the Twiga Café at 8:00 for a quick drink.'

Fenella entered 'Mama Susie's Happy Store' and browsed the shelves, her mother's shopping list in hand. Tea, condensed milk, Omo washing powder, tins of pineapple, flour, rice and cardamom pods. As she left the store, she was blinded by the bright mid-morning sun. The shop which sold the pens her mother liked was across the street, luckily in the shade, so Fenella made her way over, weaving through the stalls, bustling people, loose goats and men on bicycles to get to the 'Useful Office Supply Shop'. Outside the shop, ladies were sitting on folded kikoys, shelling peas and tying up bundles of mchicha. They chatted amongst themselves and gave Fenella wide smiles as she passed.

Buying the pens was a nice quick job, which gave her a few minutes to browse the book stall – her favourite activity. As she cocked her head, searching the book titles, she spotted a book about elephants. She pulled it down from the shelf and began to flick through the fragile, musty pages. The book was full of photographs and had been written about twenty years ago, given the hairstyles and fashions in a few of the pictures. There were pictures of elephant family groups, individual babies, aerial photos of huge herds. Most disturbingly, though, there were images of elephants that had been poached for their tusks. These were too awful to look at and Fenella closed the book, her eyes stinging. She had enough money left from the shopping to pay for the book – she was allowed to treat herself occasionally in return for running the errands for her mother – so she paid the stallholder and tucked the book under her arm. It was nearly eight o'clock, so Fenella walked the few blocks to the Twiga.

She could see her father sitting at their usual table under a sunshade, reading the *Daily Nation*. When she was very little, they had used to go into town every month together, until Fenella's schoolwork and her desire to spend more time with her friends from the local village took over. She felt a pang of nostalgia for their trips. They always sat at 'their' table, he with a coffee and the newspaper, she with an orange juice and a book, enjoying a companionable silence or people-watching, inventing stories about the lives of the people whose faces they saw time and again, milling around the busy square. Fenella felt a sense of detachment this time as she looked at her father with different eyes and kissed him as she sat down to join him.

'Hello!' said Rob, a little startled, engrossed as he was in his paper. 'Did you get everything you needed?'

'Yes, thanks.'

They chatted over the week's events at home. Fenella showed him the book she had bought and they discussed the author, who was well known to Rob.

'Come on, let's head back.'

They drained their drinks, left the payment on the table and headed back to the truck.

Fenella read her book as Rob navigated the termite mounts and potholes on the road back to camp. A sudden chill came over Fenella and she looked up and gasped.

'What?' exclaimed Rob. 'Did I hit something?'

'No, no, it's… I don't know. Something's wrong. We need to get back. I just… please hurry.'

Rob sped up, but it was not easy in the truck, with all the wood in the back and several times they bumped fully into the air as they collided with rocks. When they reached camp, they were met with an uneasy quiet.

'Hello, we're back! JoJo?' Rob called out.

Fenella wanted to run to the house, but something made her legs feel like jelly. 'Mum, Bibi, Evie, where are you all?'

They entered the house, but no one was there. Insects had gathered on the table where Joanna had been cutting up a melon, the knife sticky, coated with flies. Coloured pencils were strewn across the wooden table, a picture half drawn. A kettle had boiled dry and was starting to smoke. Rob ran and turned off the gas burner, then ran back outside. 'Joanna, Mum, Evie! Where are you?'

He and Fenella instinctively ran towards the river, calling. There was a sudden rustle in the shrubs ahead of them and Hamisi emerged. He seemed to be traipsing aimlessly with a look of horror on his face. He did not even appear to have seen them.

'Hamisi, what's happened?' begged Rob.

Hamisi, woken from his trance, seemed to suddenly see them. He just shook his head. He opened his mouth to speak, but again shook his head; no words forthcoming.

Rob ran in the direction Hamisi had come, Fenella following. The dread which had begun on the journey home was now real, but she felt oddly calm and detached. Before long, bright colours were visible through the branches of an acacia tree. The colours became clothes, then people. The jumble of colours was heaped on the ground, though. Fenella couldn't process this. Why was there a big pile of clothes on the ground? Then the vegetation suddenly parted and there was their family, in a sort of mock tableau. It seemed unreal, like a play or a game. But then sound permeated Fenella's consciousness. It was animalistic – a wailing. She heard her mother shouting 'No, no, no, no, no', over and over. Her grandmother was squatting on the ground, her arms on Joanna's back, rubbing her. But what was on the ground?

Rob dived at the women, Barbara stood aside, but Joanna didn't move, as if she was totally unaware of his presence. Curled up in the undergrowth, covered in branches, leaves sticking to her cheeks and forehead, was Evie.

'I can't find Clive,' said Barbara. 'He was here, but when I call, he doesn't answer.' She sounded mildly irritated, as though Clive was just late for dinner. Rob seemed not to have heard her. He just stood and stared at Evie and Jo. Jo was cradling her daughter and moaning.

Fenella was still carrying her bag of groceries. She had been clutching it when they got out of the car, but now her hand slid open and the bag dropped, tins rolling down the small bank, the bag of flour exploding as it hit a sharp rock. Fenella skirted around the group and headed into the bush, as if pulled by a magnetic force. She kept walking purposefully, gaining speed. Some branches ahead had been recently broken – a track formed ahead, ferns trampled, a piece of fabric caught in a wait-a-bit thorn bush. Then a shape on the ground, colours, not as bright as before. There he was, her Babu. Face down in the dirt. Somehow also covered in branches. She looked up from the ground, eyes following the direction he had been facing, and she ran. She could hear the far-off sound of an engine, smell the diesel fumes. A large green bag was lying on the ground ahead, split open, its contents spilling out, wet and bloody. She could not make out who was in the truck in the distance, but saw that there were several people sitting in the cargo bed. They were pointing rifles at her as they sped away down a dirt track and turned towards the mountains.

* * *

Fenella turned back to see that Barbara had followed her. She was with Babu now. She had swept away the branches that had covered him and was lying prostrate on top of his body, her face nuzzled into the back of his neck. She was muttering something Fenella could not understand, but she knew this was private, she should leave them now. She didn't want to turn back to the others. She felt repelled by what was there, so kept walking forward, on towards the road. The bush cleared suddenly, revealing open ground and in front of her, leaning into the low branches of a yellow fever tree was a huge male elephant. His face had been obliterated; his tusks hacked off. Around his thick neck was a leather collar. It was Hendrix.

Now she screamed. She screamed for Evie, she screamed for Babu, she screamed for Hendrix.

MAKENA

TAITA HILLS 2002

I CANNOT rest tonight; I cannot feed or drink or stop. We felt rumbles earlier – warnings through the deep earth, telling us of I know not what. But I am alert. My sisters and I crowd around our family. Butterfly is here with me and helps me with the younger calves. She has her own baby now. We had to make our family from scratch, from young frightened sisters. I was the eldest and was the granddaughter of Fierce, who was known to be the wisest of elephants, so I am matriarch now. Now we are creating our own descendants and we are thriving. But there is something wicked in the air tonight. Our cousins have warned us through the ground and we step and grumble and worry. I insist that the others eat. Hyenas are fussing around us. There is a pride of lions nearby and the hyenas are waiting, waiting, but for sport they fuss around us, snapping at the little ones, forcing our circle tighter until we crowd together in a cluster under a sausage tree.

Suddenly, the hyenas prick up their ears and scatter. They stop their jibing and are totally silent, heads low, trotting lightly away. They are gone in moments, as though they were never there. This can only mean danger. Real danger, not just the lions they have been teasing but something much worse. Nothing silences a hyena. I keep completely still and make the others do the same. My baby stands under me and I suckle him to keep him quiet. There is a distant rumbling sound, but it is not other elephants. I know this sound, but I usually hear it in daylight. The night turns the sound into a menacing echo. It is nearing us. I shuffle back a little, forcing our little group even tighter under the tree. We are well covered here with commiphora and acacia. As long as we do not move.

Louder still and moving fast, although I still cannot see it. And then I do. There is a light moving towards us and the low sound of humans talking. They are not shouting or making the dust rise as they ride, but something is not right. I can feel the tension in the air. So can my sisters, but we stay quiet and still for the little ones, showing no alarm. We wait. The noise stops. The light goes out, but the humans are near; we can smell them on the light, dry, night breeze. We breathe as one, waiting and listening. Then there is a loud snap. I have heard that snap before, so have some of my sisters. They are terrified, but I urge them not to panic, to stay still. We are well hidden, we are downwind, if we stay calm, it will be better. I have seen before what happens when the loud crack makes us scatter. I have seen my aunties and cousins and my grandmother die like this.

There is another crack, then another, then it stops. There is more rumbling noise from the humans and banging and slamming. Then a different smell. And a thud through the earth. A message as before? No, it is just a thud, not a rumble. Not a warning, but it tells me everything I need to know in that moment. I can smell and hear death.

The sun is beginning to rise on the horizon. For a few moments there is silence. Sunrise is normally an electric time. The birds call to each other to greet the day, the frogs speak, the antelope and zebra are skittish. But not this morning. There is a heavy, thick hush. The noise from the humans invades the silence. There is more crashing, and another sound, breaking branches and a crunching. The sound continues, then stops suddenly. There is a shout, then another. A yelling and a sweet high scream. A sudden burst of crackling noises. The loud rumbling sound begins again, then passes us at terrible speed.

We wait a few moments, but all sound and smells of the humans have gone. The sun is up and we dare to loosen our circle and move out to the open grass. As we start to move, a strong smell hits us. We raise our trunks to search where it is coming from. I signal to the others – the older ones of our group are to come with me, the youngsters are to stay with the babies. We follow our senses to find the source of the scent. It does not take long. We see him leaning awkwardly on a tree, his face gone. Our friend and the father of my newest baby, gone. Not far from him is a human, lying on the ground. We inch over to their bodies to smell them. I know the human too. He is kind and gentle and I have known him all my life. We all run our trunks over his body and brush his face. I know he has not hurt my elephant friend, that he would never do such a thing.

My sisters and I cover them both with branches. As we do, I sense another smell and see another human body further back, behind the man. It is smaller. I know this one too. It is a youngster, not much bigger than my baby. We repeat our ritual, covering her with branches and sweet juicy leaves, so she will have sustenance and shelter. Then we leave. As we do, I trumpet loudly. We turn and go and I see that my trumpet has brought out the other humans, the ones who are family to these lost souls.

PART 6

CHAPTER 33

TAITA HILLS 2012

GIGI'S family had set off at nine o'clock for the six-hour trip to Bibi's Camp, stopping briefly at the halfway point – a place called Hunter's Lodge. Refreshments were served on a terrace overlooking a pristine lake, which shimmered in the midday sun. The terrace was shaded under a low fever tree and the air was cool, despite the hour. Relieved to be out of the car, Gigi paced up and down the bank for a while to steady her legs and stomach after hours driving through pitted roads. Dragonflies flitted over the mirrored surface of the lake and Fikiri pointed out a malachite kingfisher and a sunbird. Gigi thought she had never seen a creature so perfect as this tiny iridescent bird.

The second half of the journey was rife with roadkill – even a dead zebra – and potholes the size of cars. The toilet-break stops were indescribably revolting, but when the party arrived at the camp in the mid-afternoon, the welcome was cheerful and convivial – cold drinks and warm smiles all round. Fikiri took the family to their tents – they were to have three large tents between them, each with their own bathroom, porch and living area.

The tents were perched at the end of the camp, on a small escarpment, a steep climb from the main camp. When they reached the tents, Dan stopped so suddenly that Gigi thought he had come across a snake. But then the same thing stopped her in her tracks. What she saw gave her an actual lump in her throat. A stunning, vast patchwork of acacia and commiphora trees, as far as the eye could see, flanked by an emerald-green mountain range. No 'civilisation', no lights, no telegraph poles, just pure, wild bush. They all took a moment to drink in the view, saying nothing. Fikiri smiled – he loved that bit – the surprise, the utter awe that this landscape could still produce, even in him.

They turned to the tents behind them. They were made of thick green canvas, topped with a wooden roof, each with a couple of chairs and a table outside the front, facing the view. In a little mound of stones, between two of the tents, there were two small animals, huddled together, staring quite unashamedly at the group.

'What on earth are they?' asked Xander. 'They look like chinchillas or something!'

Fikiri laughed 'Those are hyrax – rock hyrax. They are all over the camp and if you leave any food out, they will have it! Do you know what is their closest relative?' He directed the question at Annie.

'Rats?' Annie asked, tentatively.

'Would you believe, it is the elephant? They come from the same ancestor, many, many thousands of years ago. But they became different things – one very big, one very small. Look at their feet. Can you see that one just poking out from under his chest? Their feet are the same – just the same. They have little flat round toes like elephants. They even have tiny, tiny tusks!'

'Well, I for one need a shower and a change of clothes,' Xander said as he aimed towards one of the tents.

'As it's sunset in just a few hours, I suggest you don't,' said Fikiri. 'Just put your bags inside the tents. I think you should make the most of the light, and things get interesting about now. There will be a couple of hours this evening before dinner when you can freshen up. Our sunset is bang on six o'clock, you know.'

So, with just time to catch their breath, the family jumped into the camp jeep. Painted on the doors and spare wheel cover were the symbol of the camp – a stylised elephant, its body and tusks forming the initials – BC of Bibi's Camp.

'Hi, guys. I'm Joseph. Get comfy and I'll give you a tour of the camp,' said a smiling guide.

'Thanks, Joseph,' said Dan offering a handshake. 'Nice to meet you.'

Their first stop was just metres from the mess tent behind a pile of wires, stones and other building detritus. Lying absolutely still in a small patch of water lay two Nile crocodiles, one of which was basking on the shore in the sun, the other was deeper in the water, with only its eyes and nostrils protruding out of the murky depths. They of course had that sinister knowing look of crocodiles, but Gigi had always had a soft spot for these creatures, as ancient as the dinosaurs, so beyond our understanding.

They continued their slow, bumpy drive, with Joseph explaining where the baboons fed, about the moths that eat buffalo horn, about the lions – 'Romeo's pride' – that frequented the area. Although nothing spectacular appeared, the family were beginning to learn how to look and how to find interest in the smallest or apparently dullest of creatures. There were so many things to be seen if one really looked, and a thousand stories to be told.

Dinner was due to be served at around seven o'clock. The family arrived together, all dressed in high boots to guard against scorpions, at Gigi's instance. They were welcomed at the bar by Fikiri and introduced to their fellow volunteers.

'Dan, Gigi, please sit here and have a drink. I shall get them for you. Beer, wine, a fizzy drink?'

'Oh, thank you, Fikiri. Can I have a ginger ale and, Dan, beer?'

'Mmm, thanks. I've been fantasising about a cold beer since we left Nairobi!'

'Well, you will need a Tusker. Our finest national beer!' said Fikiri 'And Xander – the same?' Xander flicked a quick look at his parents who quietly nodded back.

'Yep, sure, a Tusker would be great, thanks.'

'And Annie. You look like a fresh orange and lemonade sort of person!'

'Ooh, I've never tried that, but it sounds nice, thank you.'

As Fikiri headed to fetch their drinks, two more people joined the family at the table, introducing themselves as Allison and Jordan, film students working their way around East Africa. Finally, a tall, smiling man came over to the table. 'This, ladies and gentlemen,' said Jordan, 'is the incomparable Professor Gitonga who heads up all the wildlife research here.'

'Hamisi, please.' Hamisi extended hand to each of the new guests. 'You are my new assistants, I presume?'

'These are the Wedderburns, Hamisi,' Jordan replied for them. 'Dan, Gigi, Xander… yes?' Xander nodded.

'And the boss?' Hamisi nodded in the direction of Annie who was still chattering to Fikiri.

'That's Annie!' laughed Gigi. 'She makes friends wherever she goes.'

'How about you guys? What brings you here?' asked Allison.

'Would you believe we won a magazine competition?' said Dan.

'I would. I know the one you mean,' exclaimed Allison, her voice clearer now. 'Oh, you won that? Well done! I read that magazine online all the time and read the article about Barbara. I couldn't enter the competition, as I'm from the US, but the camp sounded like just the sort of place I wanted to film. I worked three jobs to cover my airfare, but it was worth it.'

'I'm so pleased. We're very excited about this trip. But we're very inexperienced. You will have to give us lots of tips,' said Gigi.

The family's first night's meal was full of chatter and laughter as the volunteers got to know each other. No one lingered, however, tired as they all were from driving or from being up very early that day. So, everyone headed off to their own quarters, ready for an early start in the morning.

That night, Gigi dreamed that she was showering in the tent bathroom, whereupon a huge male lion strolled in and attacked her. She woke abruptly just as she was about to be eaten, when she realised she could actually hear a real lion. The sound was so loud, long and deep, she could feel the vibrations in her bed. Dan had woken too and the two of them, lying in adjoining single camp beds, stared across at each other, hardly daring to breathe.

'That's a lion.' Dan stated the obvious.

'How close?' Gigi whispered back.

'I have no idea, but it sounds really close. What do we do?'

'How would I know?' Gigi giggled nervously.

They waited and, after a while, realised that the deep sonorous rumbles were not very close, just very loud, and so relaxed a little. The roars became less and less frequent, then stopped altogether. By this time, they were fully awake, Gigi could feel her heart fighting to come through her ribcage.

'Oh God, Dan!'

'I know! I have to say, this tent doesn't feel quite as robust as it looked at first!'

They resolved to keep quiet and get back to sleep, but the adrenaline was still pumping through Gigi's veins and she tiptoed outside to one of the chairs. This proved to be a bit stupid, as it was utterly pitch dark, freezing and Gigi jumped at the slightest sounds, so she backed into the tent again. Something scuttled across her foot. She jumped back into the safety of her bed, still warm and comfortable, and once her heart rate had returned to normal, she eased back into sleep.

CHAPTER 34

TAITA HILLS 2012

THE next morning the family had a huge breakfast of eggs, toast, sausages and fruit, then headed out for a walk near the camp for about an hour, looking down at what they could find underfoot – the native flora, elephant dung, termite mounds. Hamisi walked with them and explained in detail how termites constructed their homes.

'They use fresh dung, break it down to the rough ingredients, then carry it to their mound, which they build with holes at ground level and holes like chimneys above, can you see?' He pointed at all the elements of the construction. 'They need to keep their stored larvae at exactly thirty degrees centigrade. There is a strict hierarchy in their society – they have a king and queen which produce all the eggs – soldiers and workers.'

The complexity and ingenuity of this astounded Gigi. 'To me it just looks like a huge pile of earth, but it's quite incredible,' she said, daring to touch the top gently.

After they had walked off their breakfast and freshened up, they set out in the jeep to investigate all the nearby waterholes, checking which might most likely have elephants drinking there. Just below the camp was an enormous troop of baboons. They had to slow down to get past them, as the baboons seemed unmoved by the jeep and continued their bickering and roadside nit-picking. One of the troop's females had a tiny baby clinging to the fur on her back – back legs gripping limpet-like. Gigi noticed that the mother was missing her front left leg but she kept up with the others as though there was nothing wrong with her. As the jeep reached a clearing, the numbers of baboons doubled – they were spread out almost like grazing animals, feeding in the long grass, picking at something. Small groups were sitting together grooming each other in a circle; a nearby fever tree held a few more.

'That is their "sleeping tree",' said Hamisi. 'At night, they all sleep up that tree all together. They also rest and keep watch up there.'

'They sleep there every night?' asked Xander.

'For now, yes. But they will move on soon. They have to stay one step ahead of their predators.'

'Who are their predators?' asked Dan.

'Usually, leopard, but also lions. And cheetahs will take a baby if it is left by itself.'

The group drove on a bit further to find a good waterhole for watching elephants. As they continued, Gigi could tell that each waterhole had its own particular characteristics, some seemed welcoming, with small animals dotted around, relaxed, familiar; some seemed so desolate, you couldn't imagine anything visiting there. Hamisi and Fikiri sat together in the front, mumbling to each other at each stop about the pros and cons, elephant-wise. At one particular waterhole, Hamisi told Fikiri to stop and get everyone to get out and look around with him. The waterhole was about three hundred yards across, surrounded by thick acacia bush.

'Can you see why this place might be good for elephants, guys? Have a good look around. It's okay, there's nothing here at the moment, I promise!'

Everyone paced around, looking all about them, not really sure what to look for.

'Here!' shouted Annie, and everyone ran to join her. 'Look – lots of dung. And footprints and it's so muddy there on the bank. It's still so wet, something must have been here recently!'

'Fantastic spotting, Annie,' said Hamisi. 'Yes, there has definitely been a family here not long ago. See these branches too? They have been pulled down very recently, the ends are still oozing sap. So, an hour ago, this would have been a great stop for us, but sadly, they have eluded us, so – back into the jeep and we shall keep looking.'

They drove on a little further. Gigi felt brave enough to ask Hamisi about his work. 'How long have you been here, Hamisi? You seem to know the area so well. For me it just looks like a huge forest. I mean there are no signs, no proper roads. I can't imagine how you get your bearings in all this thick bush.'

'You become familiar with it like you do anywhere. I'm sure you could find your way around the town where you live without much thought.'

'Yes, of course, but there are landmarks – shops, signs, houses that you know.'

'Here too, but our signs are particular trees, the way a track bends, the direction of the sun at certain times of day. It's just familiarity. Of course, I got lost many, many times when I first arrived here.'

'When was that?'

'1989. I had just graduated from Nairobi University with a degree in zoology, but I wanted to study further – elephants in particular. I had met Barbara's son, Rob, at uni. He finished his degree at the same time and came back here – back home. He wanted to get things up and running here properly, to take over things from his parents. He did not want to do more research himself, but he had visions of this place being a great place to study the wildlife, as it is less populated by tourists than the big game reserves, almost unspoilt. So, he invited me to work on my PhD here in exchange for helping him with students and verifying the ecological importance of the conservancy.'

'And you've been here ever since?'

'I have indeed!' he laughed. 'How long is that? Twenty-three years. Oh, my goodness, I hadn't really counted it before!'

'You must love it here?'

'I do, but there is more to it than that. And also, I go back and forth to the city for a few weeks at a time. My wife, Angel, works at the university and our children go to school there.'

'Goodness, that must be hard. Being so far away from your family, I mean. How many children do you have?'

'Two girls. They are amazing.'

'I'm sure they are. Do you ever bring them down here?'

'In their main holidays, yes. They love it here. And Angel is a lecturer, so she can take a few weeks out in middle of the year too. It's always a very special time. And the girls help a lot while they're here. And learn a lot.'

'What a lovely life you have given them, lucky girls.'

'They're lucky, but then we're all lucky to have each other. Barbara is remarkable.'

'Is Rob not here, then? And does he have a family too?'

There was a few moments' hesitation. Hamisi mumbled something inaudibly. Gigi sensed there was something wrong with her question and felt embarrassed that she had interrogated this man she had barely met. A giraffe apparently found this an opportune moment to break out of the trees, causing Fikiri to slow, so that the group could admire it.

'I think he is pointing the way for us!' giggled Annie. 'Look, up ahead.' Off to the right of the road was a large waterhole, already busy with elephants and several antelope. Fikiri swerved in and found a spot under some trees, not too close, for the group to watch.

'Now,' said Hamisi. 'You all have a clipboard under your seat. Can you please fill out the form there with your findings? I need to you count the adults and young, observe the elephants' behaviour. Are they anxious, do you think, or relaxed? Do they all look healthy? Is it one family group or are there any hangers-on? We didn't see them arrive, but we can time them now and see how long they stay. Anything you can think of that might be important, write it down.'

Hamisi did the same, but spoke quietly to Fikiri in Kiswahili as he did it.

Gigi looked over at her family as they all watched and jotted things down. Dan smiled back at her, then focused on the job in hand. Xander was writing furiously in between brief but frequent glances up at the view. Annie just sat with her head perfectly still, resting on her crossed arms, leaning out of her window.

'Are you alright, Annie?' asked her mother.

She did not answer right away, then seemed to take in Gigi's presence. 'Hmm, yes, I'm fine. I will write things down in a minute. I just don't want to miss anything.'

Gigi rubbed her back and returned to her sheet.

When they had finished and the elephants had moved on, Hamisi asked them to read out their sheets.

'I noticed that there was one elephant who seemed in charge of everything,' said Xander. 'He was drinking less than the others; he broke up a tussle between two others and was pushing one of the babies around.'

'You're quite right, Xander, except in one important respect,' explained Hamisi. 'The only males in the group were a couple of the youngsters. You see, family groups like this are always made up of adult females. With one particular one in charge, like you said. She is called the "matriarch"; the rest of the group is made up of fellow females and their offspring. The males are thrown out of the family herds in their teens and become almost solitary, joining up with other males now and again. Some of the male groups are quite tight too, but never as large as the family groups. Perhaps only two or three males. Usually a mix of ages, so they are not really in competition with each other and the older ones teach the younger ones.'

'I never knew that,' said Dan. 'I feel a bit sad for them. What do you think, Xander? Would you like to go and live on your own forever?'

'Would I ever?' Xander mumbled jokingly.

The family drove back with Hamisi and Fikiri for lunch and a break from the heat of the afternoon, meeting them again for another drive in the afternoon; Allison and Jordan joined them.

'That last waterhole seemed lucky for us. I think we should go back there now,' suggested Fikiri.

Fikiri slowed the jeep up and backed into a patch of acacia trees. They waited, not talking. Absolutely nothing came for about an hour. Then there was a tantalising glimpse of an elephant ear through the bushes. Nothing more. Nothing happened for a full forty-five minutes, then a mother elephant and four young crept out to drink at the other side of the waterhole. They came closer to the vehicle, giving the family a brief look. The elephant family proceeded to eat right beside the human family. No one in the jeep dared to breathe. The elephants didn't linger at this patch of trees, but moved on to stop again a little further along, the adult turning to give the humans a meaningful glance as they passed.

All of a sudden, a large herd of elephants, led by a matriarch, poured in from the same direction, about fifteen of them in batches of around five. The adults drank, the babies played in the water and chased each other around. A new world was beginning to unfurl in front of Gigi. She began to see the elephants, not as something 'other', not as distant, obscure creatures. Their behaviour was suddenly recognisable, mannerisms familiar. Everywhere around her, elephants were doing 'stuff' – young friends tugged at each other's trunks, mothers nuzzled their babies, allomothers (Hamisi explained this was the name given to carers of other elephants' offspring) dunked younger elephants in the water.

After about twenty minutes, they seemed more aware of the human presence, and started to move towards the jeep. The matriarch neared the vehicle and stopped. She looked straight at Gigi. Their eyes locked. Gigi was transfixed by the watery, deep black eyes, framed by drag-queen eyelashes. Then the elephant turned and led her family to join the smaller group which had stopped to graze, just in view across the waterhole. As they moved off, a young male turned towards the jeep, slowly at first, then came running directly at it, stopping just short and trumpeting.

Hamisi chuckled. 'You have just had the privilege of meeting Makena and her ragtag family.'

'Who is Makena?' asked Gigi. 'Is she special somehow?'

'Special? Yes, yes she is special,' Hamisi said quietly. 'Some elephants have a sort of magic about them. Makena is one of those elephants. Barbara and her family watched her being born – that is very rare in itself. And we have been observing her all her life. No, "observing" isn't the right word. Makena is part of this place and we know what she is up to because we just know. Most of her family were killed in the eighties because of the drought and also when poaching got really bad around then, because people were desperate. But she has taken charge of so many little groups – other elephants who had lost their families – and made a new herd. Her herd didn't form in the natural way they are supposed to, of family members – she made it and she keeps them safe and together. She is probably the wisest and most loving creature I know.'

Peter had packed a small box of drinks and snacks for the group and tucked it under the passenger seat. Hamisi pulled out the box and passed the contents around, as the setting sun turned the colours of the landscape from the vibrancy of a photograph to the gentle hues of an oil painting. The group huddled in the jeep, quietly guzzling beer and nuts and whispering their thoughts on the group quietly guzzling in front of them.

CHAPTER 35

TAITA HILLS 2012

AFTER just a week or so, the family had settled into the rhythm of their days. Gigi was surprised at how little time it took them to adapt to their changed surroundings. She normally needed a few days to acclimatise, particularly when visiting hot countries, but she soon felt comfortable with the heat and change of pace. Time seemed irrelevant, they got up as it was getting light, sat for long periods monitoring the elephants under Hamisi's tutelage. They ate, rested, went out again. Time was regulated only by the pace of the day, and was slow, meaningful. Before long they were learning how the dynamics of each elephant group were different. A male group was not as playful or as alert as a family group but still played, in the way teenage boys box and fuss each other. A lone bull could be calm and contemplative or tense and unpredictable. Gigi and her family were learning how to observe and empathise. How to read the behaviour and understand its wider meaning.

True friendships were being formed around the dinner table and in their everyday encounters. Gigi had noticed that Allison and Xander in particular seemed to have hit it off from the start and had organised their own trip to a nearby village. Allison wanted to add some background to her piece on the camp and Xander had explained to Fikiri that he was curious about what school, in particular, was like in such a different place from the UK. So, Fikiri lent them a car and packed them a basketful of notebooks, pens and sweets to hand out to the children.

Annie had made a special friend of the guide, Joseph, and was helping him to set up camera traps around the waterholes and water storage tanks near the camp, to get a better idea of night-time activity there. Dan was interested in Hamisi's crowdfunding scheme and was helping him to draw up a proposal which he hoped to roll out on their new website.

Gigi was enjoying just taking a step back, no longer the centre of their hurly-burly family life, but an observer, watching how they each were growing and taking pieces of this experience and enriching their own lives. She felt inordinately proud of her little family. What she had not expected was the transformative effect the trip was having on Dan. At the back of her mind, after all her concerns about her mother's death, the children, her father, she knew deep down that Dan was crumbling. He had become noticeably hunched in recent years, as though he was truly carrying an invisible burden. His face, which she had always loved for its lopsided smile and the sparkle in his eyes, had become creased and serious.

They had weathered grief, job losses and serious money worries together and, while Gigi had friends to offload her worries onto, Dan, with his peripatetic and hectic life was frequently tired and rather lonely. It had been exactly the right decision to resign his job. She could see that clearly now. This trip was like balm for him – the physical warmth, the wonder of the animals and the detailed knowledge he was gaining about their lives; the companionship of their fellow campmates, the way he could offer useful financial knowledge to Hamisi – it had a physical effect on Dan. Gigi could see him walk taller, smile more.

Each morning, they rose early to spend a couple of hours before breakfast checking waterholes, looking for evidence of elephant and lion activity and noting down anything interesting. There was no attempt at anything constructive during the middle part of the days – it was simply too hot. Lunches were long but light and the camp's residents took that time to read, nap and chat. In the afternoons, they regrouped and spent the time sometimes driving around, but more often sitting at one waterhole and analysing the activity of the animals that visited.

Evenings were spent eating delicious meals magicked up by Peter and his assistant. Everyone who was not needed in the kitchen sat and ate together around the large table. Fikiri insisted on a rotation each evening, whereby one person had to sit at the head of the table and tell an interesting story. Hamisi was best at this, reeling off tales of angry elephant encounters, of bravery by mongooses or antelopes, the time he spent the night in his car when it got wedged in black cotton mud and became a curiosity for a pair of lion brothers parading their territory. Gigi dreaded her turn in the 'chief chair', as it became known, as she didn't think she had any interesting tales to tell, although she had some funny stories about the children, which seemed to go down well. Xander was a natural and was really very funny – Gigi loved to watch the reaction of the audience, as she saw her son in a new light – he was becoming so grown up, such a fully formed person, she was taken aback.

Gigi joined Xander for a visit to the nearby village, Kilenga. During his initial trip with Allison, he had got talking to John, the primary school teacher there. He was so in awe of what John had achieved, he asked him if he could visit again so he could find out more. Gigi wanted to get to know some of the local people better. So, Fikiri drove them there early one day, dropping them off and making the proper introductions, before heading off to Voi for supplies.

They had arranged to chat with John before school started, then Xander would stay with him for the morning and Gigi would spend the day with some of the women, learning about some of the crafts they produced. They were met by Freda who strode over to them, hands outstretched.

'Welcome back, welcome. So nice to see you back here so soon. You couldn't stay away, I think!' Freda's bellowing laughter made them feel instantly at home. 'Now, how is my dear friend Barbara?'

'She is very well. She's given me this to pass on to you, she thought it might come in useful.' Gigi pulled a large package out of her backpack, and handed it to Freda.

'Aha, she promised to send over something interesting. Why don't we peruse this over a cup of chai? John, would you and Xander like to join us later, when school is finished?'

'Absolutely, Freda. Good day to you both.' John started to walk away, directing Xander to the school, then called back, 'Shall we have lunch together in the schoolroom? I can ask Phyllis to make a few extra helpings.'

'If it's no trouble for her,' said Gigi. She still felt an underlying guilt at having anything done for her. She could not get used to the way that the people here had so little and yet were so happy to share their food and knowledge with them.

'She will be quite happy,' said Freda, tapping Gigi's arm gently and led her away to talk.

The package had been wrapped in a large kikoy, with a note pinned on it: '*As promised. Please let's talk through some ideas. Best regards, Barbara.*'

Inside was a large stack of magazines – American, English and Italian fashion and lifestyle publications.

'Barbara said that these get left behind by tourists all the time and she hates to throw anything away, a bit of a habit of hers, apparently.'

'Do the ladies here like to read them?' asked Gigi.

'No, not really. I didn't want them for the celebrity gossip and household tips!' laughed Freda. 'No, it's the fashion pages and the pictures of people's homes. Barbara has noticed that there is a trend for more natural fabrics and ornaments in the West. Between us, we have been thinking of ways the local women might make things to sell. We always sold trinkets and basic clothing to the tourists that came to Bibi's Camp, but she has changed the clientele a bit,' she winked at Gigi. 'So, we no longer have so many customers for such things.' Freda's voice trailed off a little as she flicked through one of the magazines. Then she looked up and smiled. 'But with change comes new opportunity!'

'Absolutely!' agreed Gigi, picking up one of the magazines. 'Did you have anything in particular in mind? What do the women make now that might adapt?'

'Beading and leatherwork, sewing, although we only have one machine in the village and it is very old. And the generator has such a big job to do, and it is always stopping.'

The women continued to flick through the pages and sip their tea.

'Ooh, look at this, Freda,' Gigi smoothed over the pages of a double page spread of a beautiful garden in upstate New York.

'Very pretty,' said Freda. 'So many flowers. We would never grow such beautiful but pointless things!'

'I've never thought of it like that, but you're right. I have quite a large garden and I just grow grass and flowers, never food. That seems ridiculous now.'

'Of course, it is not. You just have a very different life, that is all. And a different climate of course.'

'A better climate for vegetables. I feel quite ashamed!'

'Don't be. Anyway, I see what you mean. You are looking at the blankets and rugs, the napkins and things?'

'Yes. Here they are all pale linens – very sweet and old fashioned. But your fabrics here are very bold and bright. They would be great for younger people's homes – throws and bags and blankets. Do you have any of the items that you would normally sell here?'

'I do, wait a few minutes. I'll freshen up the teapot while I'm at it. Please feel free to have a wander around and chat to people.'

Emboldened by Freda's conviviality, Gigi stood up with her and made her way to a group of women, sitting with babies on their backs or cradled up to them feeding. Gigi approached the women quietly with her head bowed, muttering 'Jambo?' in a questioning voice. 'I'm sorry, do any of you speak English?' There was a ripple of laughter, then one of the women answered, 'We all do, some better than others!'

'Sorry, I wasn't sure. My name is Gigi, I'm here visiting Freda and my son is over there at the school, spending the morning with John.'

'Does your son miss school so much he needs to go here?' asked one of the women, jutting out her chin, so Gigi was unsure if she was joking. But the statement was quickly echoed by peals of laughter from her friends.

'Sorry, no! He has nearly left school. He will be eighteen soon. No, he wants to watch John teach, as he is very interested in it.'

'He wants to be a teacher?' asked another of the women.

'Well, he never did. He wanted to be an architect. You know, to design and build buildings, but I think he is changing his mind.'

This was the first time Gigi had said this out loud. She had been pleased by his obvious excitement after their first visit to the school. It was not like Xander to step out of his comfort zone like this. He was a confident person and very affable, but back at home he seemed frustrated. It was an age of big decisions, high expectations. The pressure on Xander and his peers was so intense – they were supposed to know what they were going to do for the rest of their lives by the time they were sixteen and the cost of further education meant once they had embarked on something, they felt they could not change course – tuition and living expenses put all but the wealthiest students into inevitable and sometimes enormous debt.

Of course, this was something which people seemed to annoyingly term these days a 'first-world problem'. These mothers would not waste their gardens growing flowers, nor allow their children to waste their education. Education was revered here, as it should be. We just took it for granted and even squandered it.

Xander's ambitions had seemed so certain before. He had

been so sure in childhood that he wanted to be an architect. Of course, this first manifested itself in his love of Lego, of drawing and problem solving. It seemed an obvious course for his life to take. But with the prospect of university actually looming and the many years of study this ambition would require, he had had more than a few doubts. He had preferred the part-time jobs he had worked in the weekends and holidays. He worked as a lifeguard and swimming instructor at a local swimming pool, as an occasional waiter for a friend's catering company, and did fruit picking in the long summer holidays. He enjoyed the company of people, and discussion and community. She hadn't considered that perhaps they had all become caught up in the one idea of what he should be, and not noticed the obvious.

Xander had packed his bag the night before. It sat expectantly on his desk, replete with school jotters and pens. His phone alarm went off at 4:30 am and he hurriedly switched it off before it woke anyone else. To wake them unnecessarily would be selfish, but he also wanted this time to be just his, alone. Opening his eyes just a crack, he set the phone torch on the desk and quietly dressed. The morning air was predictably cold, so he knotted a kikoy loosely around his neck like a scarf. He wore shorts, but kept his socks pulled up high, not only because of the cold, but because he had learnt from Hamisi to protect his legs from the scorpions which would be active at this time of the day.

He was up even before Peter, the cook, who was normally first up and last to bed; he must only get a few hours' sleep a night, thought Xander. Helping himself to a chunk of homemade bread, he heated up a whole tin of baked beans – a comforting after-school favourite from those days which seemed so far off to him already. Turning one of the dining chairs to face away from the long refectory table, he sat with his bowl of beans and hunk of bread to stare out towards the hills as he ate. There was still a full silvery moon above and the indigo sky shone with stars. It reminded him of a picture his little sister had made once. She had daubed glue all over a sheet of blue felt and then emptied an entire bottle of silver glitter on top. The sky was like she had tipped that picture up above their heads. It actually shimmered. Bird noises were already building from the trees down below. Part of him wanted to wolf down the meal, keen as he was to get to the school, but he forced himself to slow down and savour the unusual solitude and calm. He scraped up the last beans, washed his bowl and coffee cup, filled a water bottle and a flask of tea, and set off towards the jeep.

Driving down from the camp towards the track, he caught sight of a caracal, trotting alongside him. The little cat turned tail into a scrubby bush on the side. A few times, his headlights caught the reflection of eyes in the darkness. Sometimes he only caught a glint, sometimes, like the Cheshire Cat's grin, he could almost fill in the invisible face surrounding the staring eyes. Straight ahead of him at car roof height was a pair of huge eyes, so iridescent they were almost blue. They seemed unnatural, almost cartoonish. He drove slowly and the shape of the animal was revealed – a bush baby, clutching the branches of a euphorbia tree, utterly motionless. He felt a pang of guilt for frightening the little animal, but this was a well-used track and it was likely to have seen cars before. He continued to drive slowly, causing as little disruption as he could. The main road was still a good three miles away, but he had plenty of time.

The bush cleared suddenly, breaking out into a large flat barren area. In this part of the reserve, the wardens had constructed a large water tank for the use of the camp, but built so that the animals could also drink from it. Hamisi had explained that it had proved invaluable in times of drought, but was of course difficult to maintain. The elephants that used it also accidentally damaged its seemingly solid walls time and again. There was nothing to be done but to keep repairing it when this inevitable damage occurred. Even if they were to construct a well to be stored underground, elephants would find ways of digging down to reach the precious water. So, this cooperative approach was sensible.

There was a small group of elephants there now. The early morning was the busiest time for most of the animals here, they would rest and sleep more in the height of the day's heat. Lions were active – Xander could hear Romeo call from just beyond the escarpment. The morning's chill made predators more alert and more sensitive to smell, so all the smaller animals were clustered in edgy groups. Xander turned off the engine and sat for a while, absorbing the scene. After a couple of minutes, an aardvark nosed its way out of the scrub, crept up to a termite mound and nuzzled into the soft ground at its base. Xander dared to turn his torch slowly towards the elephant herd and watched them ripping into a euphorbia patch.

He really ought to get to the main road now. Engine back on, he headed out. The land was flat and clear now, with few trees as the small dirt track met the main road to Kilenga. The road was no less bumpy for being more used – in fact the trucks and vans that passed along here had gouged deep ruts in the tarmac. The dirt roads of compacted earth were often flatter and smoother. Heading east now, there was a definite slit of light rising from the horizon. Daylight and heat would come swiftly. A few cars were on the road now. Deliveries from the cities – ugali, vegetable oil, cement. They trundled into the small towns on vehicles designed to carry half their cargo.

Up ahead, Kilenga village came into sight. The settlement had a double line of defence. One thorny boma enclosed the whole village, keeping the community's livestock and people safe from marauding lions and leopards; a smaller one in the centre kept the livestock together at night. Surrounding their prized animals were the huts. There were about thirty of these, of various widths, head height, built by the women of the village to suit each individual family. They had been made using cow dung and straw, with an occasional tin roof, and were remarkably robust and clean. At the far end, at the foot of Kasigau Hill sat the primary school.

Xander parked up at the school and got out, stretching his arms behind his back for relief after his bumpy drive. The schoolmaster, John, was already inside, working through a lesson plan. John had been singled out for a scholarship whilst attending the secondary school in Voi and had gone on to study mathematics at Nairobi University. A promising career might have followed in a government department or within the growing private sector which was riding a wave of new investment in corporate Africa. However, John never took to city life, preferring to return to this, his home village, passing on his knowledge to the community he cared so much about. His teaching job involved negotiating for funding for resources as much as it did providing his students with adequate education – a fact that might have depressed him, but John seemed to be the most passionate teacher, indeed person in general, that Xander had ever met. It was the awe in which he held John that motivated Xander to help him at the school.

'Good morning, my friend!' John stood and extended his hand in greeting. 'Did you have a good drive here?' A good drive meant no flat tyres, incidents with pot holes, bashed wing mirrors.

'Very good, thanks. I took my time and did a bit of wildlife watching!'

'Great. Let me get us both a coffee and we shall go through the day's plan'

John's desk was as untidy as usual, piles of well-thumbed text books on everything from English for early readers to the geography of South America. Today was clearly going to be dedicated to evolution – John had an encyclopaedia open at a page about dinosaurs, and a précis of Darwin's *On the Origin of Species* sat opened face down, from which he had taken copious notes.

John's approach was simple – at least, it appeared simple but clearly took a lot of planning. As the ages of his pupils ranged from five to eleven, he taught around a theme, getting all the children involved in discussions and demonstrations, then set them all to work on tasks of different levels to determine what they had learnt. Xander helped the older children at these points, while John, with his necessary experience, patiently and methodically helped the younger ones, as well as a few children who struggled or had joined school late. It had been difficult sometimes to persuade the adults in the village that education was crucial if their children were to succeed in the wider world. Some of them had tended goats or helped with cooking and cleaning from a young age. Nevertheless, most parents had relented in the face of advice from their Chief, himself a well-educated man, who wholeheartedly supported John in his endeavours.

The coffee was delicious. Xander had not yet got used to the local method of making tea, which was made by boiling water and tea in a pan with goats' milk and palm sugar and was intensely rich and sweet. But if offered, he drank it as, like everything here, it was precious and the gift of it generous. To rebuff the offer would be rude.

The children started arriving in trickles from the village and a few shambas further out. Their loudening chatter gave Xander goosebumps. The thrill he got from helping these children was like nothing he had experienced before.

CHAPTER 36

TAITA HILLS 2012

VOLUNTEERING at the school became a daily event for Xander. He generally enjoyed doing things with his family and had been happy to join them on the elephant monitoring trips, but this experience was feeding his soul in a way he had never known he lacked. Despite the early starts, he rose each morning with his head buzzing with ideas and enthusiasm.

John had introduced Xander to Jonathan, a boy who really should be at secondary school, being only about five years younger than Xander himself. But Jonathan's parents could not afford to send him, and needed him to help take care of their goats and tend the maize and beans they grew on their small shamba outside the village. For a little extra money, Jonathan helped John at the school and was well-liked by the pupils. Indeed, without him, Xander was not sure he would have been accepted so readily by the other children.

Jonathan was shy, but perceptive and understanding. He knew all of the children so well and Xander felt a deep frustration that his circumstances were so restrained and he might never fulfil his obvious potential. He felt torn. On the one hand he wanted help the boy further, and thought about talking to his parents to try to find a solution. On the other, he knew that this matter was not his business: that with his personal privileges, his perspective could not possibly encompass all the nuances of Jonathan's situation. Nevertheless, he couldn't resist daily gentle persuasion to try to get Jonathan to see his own worth.

* * *

One hot, sticky morning, John and Xander were clearing the classroom as the children were having a quick snack under a fever tree, when a jeep pulled up. A man jumped out and strode over to John, a beaming smile and hand extended in greeting.

'John, jambo, jambo!' the man called, causing John to look up from his desk and out through the open door.

John jumped from his seat and met the man at the door, smiling. 'Simon, how are you? I haven't seen you for a few weeks. Everything cool?' He took his friend's arm and shook his hand vigorously. 'This is my friend, Xander. He has been working with me at the school for a couple of weeks.' Greetings and handshakes were exchanged.

'I've been in the city, doing paperwork and such, you know how it is,' his friend replied. 'Listen, I have some volunteers with me. They have been working at a camp near Kasigau, something got mixed up and now they have a day free. They wanted to do something at a school. I called Barbara at Bibi's Camp and she thought of you. I know that she often sends people your way, so I hoped you might be able to make use of them without too much trouble. I hope I'm not dumping them on you, but have you got something they could do?'

'Don't worry, Barbara does it all the time. We are quite used to it. And grateful for the help, or course!' he added hurriedly. 'I'm sure we can find them something. How many are there?' They started to walk back to the jeep.

'Just two. Let me introduce everyone.' He opened the back door of the jeep. 'Guys, come on out and meet my old schoolfriend, John and his workmate… Xander, is it?' Xander nodded as the pair jumped out of the jeep. 'This is Nella and Bryndís. They have been planting trees for two days straight and we thought – that is not tough enough – they need to really be put to work. They need to meet your kids!'

John laughed and beckoned the group over to the school. 'Come, guys – come and have a drink first, then we will come up with a plan of attack!'

Xander drifted to the end of the party and introduced himself again to the last girl. He was drawn to her striking red curly hair and shy smile. 'Hello, are you Bryndís or Nella?' he asked.

'I'm Nella. Xander, was it? Are you volunteering with a programme here too?'

'Sort of. I'm here with my family. We won a competition to spend a few weeks here helping out with various things whilst having game drives and learning about conservation issues. I came here to Kilenga with another volunteer and really fell for the village and the kids. I've been learning a lot from John about the running of the school.'

'But your family are doing something else while you are here?'

'Yes, they spend most of their time at Bibi's Camp, working with a guy called Hamisi, helping with animal monitoring mostly.' He saw Fenella's expression change; she had stopped walking. 'Are you alright?'

'You're staying at Bibi's Camp?' Fenella asked breathlessly. Xander noticed her clipped accent, a mix of Morningside Edinburgh and South African.

'Yes, have you heard of it? It's run by this formidable woman called Barbara. She's been there since the late sixties, I think, through thick and thin. Why are you laughing?'

'Oh, I'm sorry. Yes, she is formidable. That is the perfect word. You see, Barbara is my grandmother.'

'She is? But why are you with Simon and not with her?'

'It's a long story, but basically, I've been living in Scotland for ten years. I was working at Edinburgh Zoo and wanted to get myself on a volunteer programme in Kenya through my work. Perhaps it sounds a bit strange, but I needed to do it on my own. Get an internship, I mean. Of course, I know that Bibi is here. I wanted to find a way to get to her and surprise her.'

'She doesn't know you're here?'

'No. And we haven't seen each other since I left. But, actually, I grew up at Bibi's Camp. It's home.' As she said the words, Fenella felt a warm tingle that left her wobbly-legged.

Xander kept turning to look at her has they walked, she had the most beautiful faraway smile; a sort of serenity about her. 'Well, it looks like the stars have aligned for you,' he smiled. And thought, *And for me too.*

The group split up; Freda emerged and almost dragged Bryndís physically to her tiny office. 'You can help me to organise these fliers,' she boomed. 'They are for the local tourist camps, advertising our wares. I need them sorting into piles.' Bryndís meekly obliged and set about counting out the hundreds of pages.

John led Fenella towards the classroom. 'You can join Xander and me with the children. Did I hear you say you work in a zoo?'

'Yes,' Fenella nodded.

'Would you mind very much telling the kids about it?' asked John.

'Oh, I don't know that I would have anything interesting to say,' said Fenella.

'Oh, but I'm sure you would. You see, we of course have many animals out here, but the idea of a zoo is something they will not have heard much about before. And you can talk about animals from very different parts of the world.'

Xander saw that Fenella looked suddenly horrified, and whispered to her. 'If you like, I'll stand with you in front of the children.'

Fenella nodded in relief and they took their places at the front of the classroom.

The children filed in after their break and John stood up to talk. 'Eyes front, everyone,' he began. There was silence apart from two little girls who had been tickling each other and kept giggling for a few moments, oblivious to the hush surrounding them. John cleared his throat noisily and they looked up, startled, then shamefaced. 'Now, children. We have a treat for you this morning. We have a friend from Europe here today, Fenella. She is going to tell you all about her job in a zoo. What do we say to Nella?'

'Jambo, Nella,' chorused the group.

'Jambo watoto, mhali gani?' The greeting was met with laughter and smiles. 'My name is Nella and, back in Scotland, my job was working with small mammals in our city zoo. Can any of you tell me the name of some animals that come from Madagascar?'

'Lemurs!' shouted a tiny boy in the front row.

'And from South America?'

'Guinea pigs!' called another.

'Very good. And Australia?'

'Wombats!'

Fenella laughed. 'Absolutely! Now what two things do you think I spent most of my day doing?' The question was met with a lot of muttering as the children compared answers.

'Cuddling the animals?' ventured one quiet little girl.

'I did cuddle them very occasionally, but actually, we were not meant to touch them if we could help it.'

'Chasing them!' shouted a boy at the back.

'Not too often, thankfully. I actually spent more time than anything feeding them and cleaning up their poop.' This was met with raucous laughter.

'Why did you do that?' asked another girl. 'Why did they need you to clean it up?'

It had never occurred to Fenella that this was perhaps the main difference between looking after captive and wild animals. 'Well, they don't roam free like your animals here. They live in the same place all the time. And we don't have termites or dung beetles, to move things around, the dung doesn't feed the trees or serve any purpose. It just has to be cleaned up, or the animals would be at risk from bacteria, parasites and so on.' The children listened attentively. 'And of course, we have to feed them. The monkeys can't get their own fruit from the trees, the antelopes don't have large plains to graze from. It all has to be done artificially.'

'Why do they live in zoos? Do they like it better than being in the wild?'

'I'm afraid they don't have much choice. Zoos are meant to be there to help with saving species. They have breeding programmes, and my zoo and others are involved with education and reintroducing animals to the wild. But no, I can't imagine any of the animals would choose to live in a zoo. Your animals here are free and living in large families and they are in charge of when they eat or drink.'

'Unless there is a drought,' interjected a child.

'You're quite right. Unless there is a drought. And of course, there are a lot of dangers for the animals here. Traps, poaching, predators. Wherever they are, it's very hard to be an animal.'

The mood of the class was more contemplative now and John, clearly sensing a natural break, thanked Fenella for her very interesting talk and told the children to get out their chemistry jotters and put on their aprons, ready for an experiment.

'Thank you for that, Nella,' John said. 'The children don't hear much about animals, even their own. I'd love to get them to be more engaged with their own nature, but many of them have grown up fearing the animals or being told they are pests.'

'Do you think we could do something? At the camp, I mean?' asked Xander. 'Could they take them on safari?'

'That would be wonderful, but would take a lot of organising. And it's a big thing to ask of Barbara.'

'Barbara would be fine!' said Fenella, laughing at John's look of surprise at her remark.

'Let me find you an apron or an old shirt or something, Nella?' suggested Xander. 'Come with me to the store room. Then you can help John and Jonathan with the explosions!'

Once they were out of the classroom, Fenella turned to Xander and said, 'Could I come back with you this afternoon, if you are going back to Bibi's, that is?'

'Of course. I take a car here every day. Do you need any clothes or anything, though? You won't just come for an hour or so, will you?'

'No.' Fenella thought about this for moment. 'Let me check with Simon. Our camp isn't far if you don't mind a bit of a detour. Then I could pick up a few things. I'll quickly go and explain to him now. And to Bryndís – she's a friend, she'll want to know what I'm doing.'

The two of them agreed to set off at three o'clock to make the trip to Bibi's.

* * *

The volunteers' camp was just the other side of the Mombasa Road and only added half an hour to Xander's journey. After she had collected a bag of belongings from her banda and got back in the car, Fenella was silent. Xander could tell she needed to be left with her thoughts, and so waited for her to speak first.

'I'm so nervous. I don't really know why. Yes, I do of course, it's been so long and I have this fantasy about how everything will be, how Bibi will look. I want it to be exactly the same, I suppose. But it can't, can it?' All her thoughts came spewing out.

'I should think there will have been a lot of changes, from what I've heard,' said Xander. 'Barbara and Hamisi have put a lot of work into reviving the place over the last couple of years. But that doesn't matter. If it's magic you mean, then that's definitely still there.'

Fenella gave him a knowing smile. 'Magic,' she whispered.

* * *

As they drew up, the camp was full of the sounds of dinner being readied. Xander's parents were sitting on a long bench in the communal living room, chatting to Allison. Annie was squatting on the floor beside them, studying something. Fenella could sense

Xander turn as if to say something, but he stopped himself. She ignored the bustle of the communal area, rather, she was staring upwards, her gaze fixed as they got out of the car.

On the upstairs veranda, a peach-coloured muslin drape was twitching slightly in the breeze, revealing an open doorway. As a slight gust lifted the drape a little, Fenella could see beyond it a shape – a pair of turquoise legs. Then suddenly, Barbara emerged. She reached out to the wall of her veranda to survey the scene below. Fenella gasped and tears filled her eyes. It took a moment, but then Barbara saw the two people standing in the semi-dark looking up at her, silhouetted against the light from the dining area. Fenella's outline was unmistakeable and Barbara leapt back through her bedroom door and ran down the stairs. Fenella ran towards the house, giddy with anticipation.

They almost collided at the front door, but stopped a foot away from each other and simply stared as they took each other in.

'Nella, you've come home, my Nella, my darling.' Barbara threw her arms around her. Fenella had no words. She just tucked her face into the crook of Barbara's neck and sobbed.

CHAPTER 37

TAITA HILLS 2012

FIKIRI shoved a laptop bag and his rucksack into the passenger footwell to protect them from the heat, started up the van and set off for Kilenga. Barbara had packed him some pastries, fruit and bacon left over from the food for this week's guests, as well as a few shirts for the boys and some books for his wife Rosemary. He was due a week's leave after a full month at Bibi's Camp, but had promised to work on repairing the laptop. He needed to take it apart and work out why it was overheating, and that was more easily done back in his village where people were not constantly interrupting him and asking him for decisions. After ten years working for Barbara, he had proved himself invaluable; he was grateful for the stability, especially now, but he also felt trapped. Especially now.

'Jambo!' Fikiri called as he entered his house.

Adjusting his eyes to the dim light, he picked out Rosemary, lying curled up in front of a meagre fire. Two thin goatskins protected her from the solid mud floor and she was tucked into two woollen blankets, clutching them tight to her chest.

'Hi,' she croaked with a relieved smile. She was still beautiful. Her body was no longer more than skin and bone, but to Fikiri she was as beautiful as the day they had met. He crossed the room to kiss her. 'I've brought a few treats from work. Are you hungry?'

'Not at the moment. Come, come and sit with me for a while.' Rosemary pulled herself up to a crouching position and pulled her knees in under her chin. 'Tell me about work. I haven't spoken to anyone for two days.'

'Where are James and Patrick?'

'With Aunty. She said I should have a proper rest, so she has been looking after them at her house. Don't worry, all is well.' She stroked Fikiri's cheek and pressed the frown lines across his forehead with her thumb. 'Jonathan came looking for you this morning. I said you were back later today, so he might come by again. What is it about?'

'Oh, nothing, nothing, I am just helping him with something. Shall I go to Aunty's to bring the boys back?'

'No, leave it for tonight, let's just have a quiet evening, just us two. So how is Barbara?'

'She is very happy. Her granddaughter turned up out of the blue, from Scotland.'

'Nella?'

'Yes, you remember her?'

'Of course. She and Evie used to play with my little sister. How is dear Nella?'

'All grown up. She has been studying and working over there, but I think she might be home to stay.' Fikiri stopped to think for a few moments. He grabbed a log from a pile by the door and pushed it into the fire. 'She was not the same. You know, she used to be so full of life. She and her little sister were so cheeky, but she's not the same.'

'It must be ten years; she is older.'

'It is not just that. She seems sad and shy. She was never shy.'

'I'm sure that it will be good for her to be home then. Back with her Bibi, back with her people.'

'Not all her people.'

'Of course, poor girl. Of course, she is brave to come back. There must also be a lot of bad memories here. A lot of ghosts.'

The couple sat in silence, watching the flames lick around the new log.

'Indeed,' said Fikiri getting up. 'Now, I am going to make you a nice dinner. I have bacon, onions and I bought some sukuma from the ladies at the gate. Is there some pap in the cupboard?'

'Yes, a full bag. Let me help.'

'No, you stay there, stay warm. I am here to spoil you. I've brought some work home, but I can do it here at the table later and we can chat.'

'No, I need to get up and move around a bit. Let me just stir something. I am so stiff. And tired of being tired. I should be making you food after a month away.' Rosemary rose from the floor awkwardly and pulled one of her blankets around her shoulders. 'I am nearly going crazy here on my own all day. It was bad enough having to stop hairdressing. I know I couldn't have been on my feet all day any more, but I so miss the chit chat, you know?' She stirred the pan for a moment and looked up at Fikiri. 'But then, I'm sure you miss the boys. I wish I was still bringing in my salary too, not having to depend on you doing all the extra hours. I feel so guilty.' Rosemary's face hardened.

'Please, Rosie, don't do this again. It's not your fault. And I don't mind, really, I don't. I enjoy working at the camp and Barbara was kind to keep me on. We can manage. And I have a project on at the moment which will give us a real boost.'

'What sort of project?'

'Just a one-off thing. With Moses,' said Fikiri, immediately regretting it.

'Moses? That crook! Are you crazy? What project? Nothing that man does is ever on the straight and narrow.'

'It's really nothing. Just a bit of driving. Please, sit back down. The food will only be a minute, then I will tell you all about the plans that Barbara and these volunteers have got with Freda and her ladies. Perhaps if you are well enough, you can get involved too.'

* * *

'Daddy, Daddy!' He could hear the boys calling before they even entered the house. They toppled in through the door, chattering in unison, vying for Fikiri's attention.

'Aunty has a new puppy, Daddy. Her name is Susan!'

'I cut my thumb on a can and there was blood everywhere, Daddy!'

Aunty entered a few minutes behind them, rubbing her thigh. 'Eh, eh, tulia watoto! Give your Daddy a minute, then speak one at a time. One at a time, sawa, sawa.'

'It's fine, Aunty,' said Fikiri. 'I hope they didn't give you too much trouble.'

'They are little boys. Little boys are made of trouble. But they know they have to be extra good to make up for all the mischief, don't you, you monkeys?'

Patrick looked anxiously at Aunty who returned his look with a wry smile and a nod. Whatever passed between them was quickly forgotten and the boys ran over to their mother and cuddled in under her blankets.

Aunty took Fikiri to one side in the kitchen and whispered. 'You had another letter from the clinic this week. I didn't tell Rosie. I didn't want to worry her.'

'Thank you, Aunty,' Fikiri mumbled. 'But you should have just left it for me. I am dealing with it. Do you have the letter?'

Aunty dug into her bag for the letter and handed it to him. 'You are not dealing with it, Fikiri. I had no idea it had got that bad. Why didn't you tell me?'

'I am a grown man, Aunty,' Fikiri hissed. 'I am the man of this house. I appreciate all your help with Rosie and the boys, but this is my problem, not yours.'

'Well. Be that as it may. I've paid the bill.'

'You have what?'

'I have paid it. She is my niece. I am her family too.'

'You had no business… I'm sorry, Aunty. That was not fair, but it was so much money. Your money.'

'It is a loan. You can pay me back when you are able, not like that clinic's lawyers, threatening to take you to court. What would the worry of that have done to Rosie, eh, what then?'

Fikiri collapsed into a chair. 'I will pay you back, Aunty. Very soon. I have a job coming up. I mean an extra job. The money from it will come soon, soon. Thank you, Aunty. I'm so sorry, so sorry.'

'Let's not talk about it now. I bought a few cakes from Phyllis. Let me put on some tea for us all and you go and talk to your boys. Get James to tell you about his spelling test. He is bursting to tell you.'

Fikiri nodded and kissed her on the cheek. 'I am so grateful, Aunty, you know that. And I would do anything for Rosie. Anything.'

CHAPTER 38

TAITA HILLS 2012

GIGI woke first. There was something odd about the morning, a stillness and quiet that did not feel peaceful. She shivered. Dan stirred as she brushed her hair.

'What time is it?' he mumbled, disentangling himself from the mosquito net he had twisted around his arm in the night.

'Early. Six-ish. Go back to sleep if you like. I just felt like getting up.' Dan obeyed and was quickly fast asleep again.

Gigi made her way over to the mess tent, tripping a couple of times on some vegetation that was not there the night before. 'Elephants in camp again!' Gigi smiled to herself. The thought gave her a little thrill. As she neared the dining table, her heart started pounding. She felt slightly clammy as an odd sense of foreboding niggled at her stomach. Feeling the need to occupy herself, she took to the dining area and made a cup of coffee. Before long, she became aware that Hamisi was also up, dressed, and talking into his mobile phone.

'How many, do you think?' she heard him ask his contact. 'Who else is there now?' Pause. 'Okay, I'm on my way. Stay there and get Colin to mobilise the unit based at Voi. We'll need all the help we can get. Have you called central KWS to contact the other gates?' Pause. 'Yes, yes, do that now. We might still stop them getting further.'

He tucked the phone back into his pocket and turned around, colliding with Gigi as he went. 'I've got to go, sorry. We were meant to be up at the salt lick today, but there's been an incident.'

'What sort of incident?'

'Poaching. Elephants. A lot of them.'

'Can I help?' Gigi asked.

'No. It will be too distressing, and maybe dangerous.'

'Please, I will stay in the jeep if you like and won't get in the way, but perhaps I can help with calls while you drive. I'd really like to be of help.'

Hamisi relented, too distracted to argue. They jumped into the jeep, but before they could head off, there was a shout from the house and Fenella was running out.

'Please, Hamisi!' she panted, pulling on the sleeve of her sweatshirt. 'Bibi just heard the news from Colin. She wants to come. So do I. Please wait for just a moment.'

Hamisi frowned, but waited. Barbara and Fenella were as entitled to come as he was. Gigi climbed out of the passenger seat to make room for Barbara and clambered into the back with Fenella. Barbara had changed into a sweatshirt and jeans and looked distressed but calm as she neared the jeep and got in. 'Alright, Hamisi. Let's go.'

No one spoke as they headed out towards the Voi road. The sun had risen quickly. Gigi, even after her limited time in Africa, could tell this was going to be a particularly hot day. They drove in silence, interrupted only by sporadic updates back and forth on the radio. Twelve elephants killed, a matriarch and her family, including three babies. Gunned down, tusks gone.

The three women would be bound forever by what they saw.

For Gigi, all the romance and warmth of Africa seemed to vanish in that moment. Here was true brutality. The most awful thing that could be done, by people in the most need, for the least point. What need had anyone of ivory trinkets, of symbols of wealth and importance, when at its root was the most brutal act, carried out against the most innocent victims, by the most desperate people?

Barbara saw all she had tried to achieve vanish in that moment. All the care she had taken fostering friendships with the local people. All the times she had argued their case when government departments or commercial developers tried to push the people off their land. Years of love and dedication seemed to mean nothing when heartless, avaricious organisations could swoop in, offer money beyond the hopes of any of these people and make them do barbaric things.

Fenella felt all the strength she had tried to build through her disappearing childhood vanish in that moment. Ten years earlier she had watched the gunmen who had shot down her Babu and her little sister drive away after butchering an elephant. The grief that followed had torn through her family, sending her mother into a depression from which she had never emerged and causing her father to vanish for years without word. She had pushed this memory down and built layers of life on top of it. But in this moment, it all came back.

* * *

TAITA HILLS, 2002

Fenella returned to the family to explain what she had seen. Someone at the house must have alerted the local police: two officers had driven up in a police-issue pick-up and were pushing through the trees, accompanied by Hamisi who pointed them towards the little group. They nodded their thanks to Hamisi and approached Joanna and Rob.

'Hello, Sir, Madam,' the older police officer spoke gently as he stepped over towards Rob, who stood behind his wife and daughter. 'I'm so sorry, this is a dreadful, dreadful thing. But I must ask you to come up to the house and discuss what has happened.'

Hamisi had walked forward to join the group and tried to pull the officer away. 'Please, sir, I can explain if you will come with me. Please leave these people to be with their loved ones.'

The police officer was sympathetic and nodded his agreement

to Hamisi, but motioned to his associate to keep an eye on things from a polite distance. As the two men left, Rob leant down to grip Joanna's shoulders and was whispering something to her. He stroked her hair and tried to pull her up to standing but Jo would not let go of Evie. She sat utterly resolute, clenching Evie's little body to her chest, and flashed Rob a look like an angry cat. Rob left her for a few more moments, then he bent over her and gently prised her hands off the body. Joanna's arms dropped to her sides and she stood up brusquely, dipping herself away from Rob's attempted embrace, looking right through him. Then she stepped away, almost sleepwalking, past Rob, past the police officers, past Hamisi and upstairs to their bedroom.

She did not leave the bedroom for two weeks. She could not even be persuaded to attend the joint funeral they held in the garden, though Fenella had looked up at the window during the ceremony and seen the ghostly face of her mother, hair bedraggled, peering out, her head perched on her folded arms like a child daydreaming in a boring school lesson.

One night, a few days after the funeral, her father had gone. Just left in the night without word. Soon after, without explanation to Fenella, her mother had left in a taxi with a suitcase. Their goodbyes were wordless and surreal. In the weeks that followed, Fenella tried to understand what had happened, but Barbara's grief silenced her. The people who had bound them had been torn away and Fenella did not know how to break the shell of Barbara's sorrow. Barbara tried her best to care for Fenella, but it had been no good. She hadn't the patience to school her and was so bewildered and distracted that it had been Fenella herself who had asked if she could leave.

* * *

TAITA HILLS 2012

A ranger came over to them and spoke rapidly in Kiswahili to Hamisi. The man carried himself as professionally as you would expect, but Gigi could spot that he was trembling. Hamisi turned to her to translate what the ranger had said. 'The rangers at Voi heard gunfire at about 5:00 am. It was a hunter's moon, you know – full and bright. So, there had been no lights seen from their vehicles. The shooting lasted no more than a minute. Do you see how most of them have fallen, knees bent?'

'Yes.'

'They have been shot in the backs of the legs to immobilise them, then they've moved in and shot them in the head at close range. Then they've hacked off their tusks.'

Hamisi and the three women circled the scene. Barbara stopped and crouched down to each corpse in turn. Blowing a gossamer kiss and pressing her hand down on each back, before moving on to the next and the next.

'This one may have still been alive when they removed her tusks. You can tell from the blood loss,' Hamisi explained to Gigi.

'Do you know this group?'

'Of course. This is Makena and her family. Do you remember, we saw them all at the waterhole the other evening? Makena herself had only just had a baby a few weeks ago.'

A shot rang out that made Gigi jump. She turned to the source of the noise and saw a ranger draw down his rifle.

'One of them must still have been alive. Just.'

Gigi slowly looked over the scene. The smell of blood reminded her of the birth of her own children, brutal and primordial as that had seemed to her. But this smell carried with it a cold ferrous edge. Gigi expected to see vultures overhead, but there was nothing. Not a sound, not a creature. The air was still, and sweat ran from her brow and under her arms. 'It's carnage. How can people do this. How can people be so desperate?'

The question went unanswered. Gigi felt her gaze drawn to the far end of the pool. It seemed to her that something moved. She dismissed it. Then again. 'Hamisi – over there, something is moving. Perhaps it was just a bird hopping or something, but can we look?'

They headed over, circling around the edge of the corpses until they reached what at first looked like a pile of mud. The mud twitched. Then wriggled. Then Gigi could make out a small tubular shape resting on the stomach of a dead adult. Following the line of the tube, the form became clear – it was a baby elephant, mostly submerged under mud and the leg of its companion.

'That is Makena.' Hamisi pointed at the large elephant in a despondent, weary gesture, before running his hand over his head. She was probably shielding her baby. We won't be able to get it out'. Hamisi called to the rangers, shouting something Gigi didn't understand. Then, by the way the ranger carried his gun, she did.

'Oh, no, please. Can't we try to save it? It's just stuck, surely?'

'Yes, under a two-tonne elephant.' Hamisi's face was a picture of despair.

'Can we use the Landcruiser to lift the leg up?'

Hamisi frowned and bent down to examine the baby's position. It was weighed down by the adult's leg, but the soft mud cushioning it had allowed the baby to sink, rather than be crushed. The mud was sticky black cotton, sucking at the baby like tar.

'Well, okay, perhaps we can try. Can you drive a 4x4, Gigi?'

'Yes,' she lied.

'Right. Bring it around to this end so you're backing this way, stop, then I'll talk you through it. I'll use my panga to hack away some of these bushes. There are some KWS guys on the way. We'll radio them to say we have a live baby here. They might be able to get someone over from the Sheldrick place at Voi.

The rangers and Hamisi spurred into action like a crack military unit. Hamisi led the mission and everyone else knew exactly what they had to do. Gigi, for her part drove as instructed, driving and reversing in slow spurts, to avoid sinking the Landcruiser into the mud. Two of the rangers fetched rope and wooden planks from their vehicle and began to construct a makeshift ramp on which to lower the Landcruiser closer to the stricken elephant. Everyone in place, they next had to clamber over bodies and paw what mud they could from under the baby's chin and chest, forcing its head and trunk out of the dangerous, suffocating earth.

They lassoed a rope around as much of the baby as they could reach without strangling it. Another ranger had positioned himself behind the mass of animals and as the baby moved a little, its back end began to emerge, making a sucking noise and finally releasing from the mud with a loud 'pop'. There was a moment of brief levity as the elephant determinedly curled and twisted itself free. The ranger at the back took his cue and rammed a large plank under the baby's rear and pushed down to create a lever.

'Now, drive!' Hamisi shouted at Gigi who instinctively pressed down hard on the accelerator. 'Gently, pole pole… Stop!' The rope around the baby was straining at it was still caught somehow. Hamisi signalled to the ranger at the back to stretch over the baby and try to lift Makena's leg. To do this, the man had to lie on his stomach and use all of his strength to force the leg up at an unnatural angle and off the baby. 'Okay, drive… more, slowly…' The ranger held up the leg as the baby inched closer and closer to the car, then dropped it once the baby was clear, exhaling his held breath as he clambered back onto his feet, his khaki uniform now caked in blood-red mud. 'Keep driving forward, just a few more feet… okay. That's it, stop.' Gigi stopped but left the motor running and jumped out.

Hamisi was on the ground, next to the baby. A few of the rangers had fetched water from the waterhole and were washing off the mud, miraculously transforming the muddy figure into elephant form. Hamisi stroked the baby's face gently trying to keep its airways clear and eyes protected from the swilling water. 'Here, Gigi, take this.' He handed her a stumpy twig. 'Place that in the tip of her trunk, vertically, to keep it open while we do the rest.'

Gigi did what she was asked and afforded herself a little stroke of the baby, feeling the life emanating from its little body like electricity. She then stood back to let the experts do their job.

'Gigi, open up the back, please,' said Hamisi, the strain in his voice as he began to lift. The back ranger was now using the plank as a sort of stretcher, with another man holding the front, while Hamisi continued to attend to the elephant's head. They shuffled together in perfect time as if they did it every day. Gigi rushed to clear a big enough space in the boot, thrusting water bottles and coats into the seats in front in time for the men to lower the elephant gently onto the floor of the boot. More words of instruction followed and Gigi got back into the driver's seat, joined by an armed ranger in the front passenger seat, while Hamisi clambered into the boot with the elephant. A young ranger had run to their vehicle and was running back with something bundled in his arms. It was a shuka – a large red Masai cloth. Hamisi took it, nodding, shrouded the baby with it, and the young man slammed the boot shut.

Hamisi stepped over to the other two women who had sat on the bank, anxiously watching the operation.

'You think the baby can be saved?' asked Barbara weakly.

'She has every chance. She's Makena's baby, Barbara.'

She bowed her head and grabbed Hamisi's hand. They needed no more words.

'I'll take Barbara home with one of the other rangers,' said Fenella. Hamisi nodded, ran and jumped into the car, patting the door with his hand, which Gigi understood to be a signal to drive on.

'There is a track over there on the right that will take us to the main road, shouted Hamisi from behind her. We will take her on to Voi.'

Gigi exhaled. She felt like she hadn't breathed since she started their rescue mission and was now shaking, high on adrenaline.

'Are you alright, Mama?' asked her travelling companion.

'Yes, I am, thank you, I'm sorry I don't know your name.'

'I'm Stanley, Mama.'

'Gigi, hello, Stanley.' She burst into fitful tears, but quickly stopped and apologised.

'Please, don't be sorry, Gigi. You did very well there, you drove very well.'

Feeling a bit like a placated child, but still delighted at the compliment, Gigi returned her concentration to the bumpy drive and allowed her heart rate to settle a little as they made their way to the Voi stockade.

Hamisi had been quiet throughout the journey, allowing Stanley to help Gigi with directions. Stanley had also radioed ahead to the centre to let them know what time they would arrive and what state the baby was in. So, when they arrived, a stable had been made ready and a team of rangers was waiting at the gate to wave them through. Gigi drove the Landcruiser to a stop, then bolted out of her seat and ran towards some bushes, vomiting violently.

Before she could even get up to straighten herself out, there was a young man with her, holding out a wet flannel and a cup of water.

'Thank you so much, so kind,' Gigi managed to mumble to the man, taking the items gratefully. She swivelled and sat back on the ground, clutching her knees, wiping down her face and took a few sips of the water. Once she felt she could put some weight on her legs she rocked forward and gratefully accepted the proffered hand of her helper. The two of them walked closer to the scene of the elephant being removed from the Landcruiser. The keepers at the rescue centre had a proper canvas stretcher and a team of people was pushing and pulling the elephant into position.

A nod from Hamisi, and Gigi understood that he needed her to move the vehicle out of the way, so that they could manoeuvre the animal into its hospital bed. Landcruiser moved, she returned to watch. The men lowered the baby gently onto a pile of fresh straw and a senior-looking woman entered with what looked like a hospital bag, as well as various accoutrements Gigi assumed to be saline drips or breathing equipment. She must be a vet.

'We need to leave them for a while now, Mama,' said a kind young man. 'Just for a little while to see how she is and what we can do for her. Please, please come with me. I think you need sweet tea.'

'So, tea is the cure for everything here, too?' joked Gigi in an explosion of relief. The man didn't really understand her joke, but led her through to a cool dark room full of tables and chairs and she sat down.

Another man, in a torn greying t-shirt was already in the room washing some dishes. He removed a pot from a small stove and lifted the lid, stirred the contents and poured out a cup for Gigi. The young man went back outside to join the rescue team. Gigi took the tea from the man, who smiled, revealing one solitary tooth, and sat back in her chair. There was small window opposite and she watched the action, trying to discern from the body language and the tones of their voices whether it was good or bad news. When she saw Hamisi emerge, take off his cap and wipe around his face and head with it, she could tell that there was an expression of relief on his face. Her tension lifted and she took a big gulp. Tea had never been sweeter.

Hamisi joined her in the little room. 'Okay, well, it seems that she is alright. I mean that there seem to be no broken bones and she is breathing quite normally, but of course, it is only the beginning. The next twenty-four hours are critical and if she lives, she has a huge mountain to climb. What we saw today was effectively the end of her world.'

Those words cut deeply into Gigi, the elation of the successful rescue tempered by the realisation that, thrilled as she was to have been part of it, it was still a disaster.

CHAPTER 39

KAREN, NAIROBI 2011

THE sprawling red-roofed bungalows peeking from behind thick, manicured hedges and tall trees attempted a semblance of country-club sophistication and suburban serenity. The façade was exposed, however, by the interruption every few hundred yards of ugly concrete pillars supporting heavy wooden gates. Each gateway had a garish boarding nailed to it warning that this property was under the watchful eye of such-and-such security company. Large wire spiked coils topped each gateway, reminiscent of the snares Rob had removed countless times from the bush around Taita Hills. A different sort of prey.

He drove slowly towards the turning, reacquainting himself with the street. Sometimes the buildings visible from the road only hinted at the affluence within. These were merely the staff quarters; the main properties being completely hidden from view down long shady driveways. These were modestly termed 'villas' but occasionally resembled baroque castles or mock-Tudor mansions. One such gateway guarded nothing more sinister than a garden centre, but had the sort of security that, in the West, might only be reserved for high-status politicians. Rob mused how much paranoia had exceeded the likely occurrence of crime. He hadn't been into this part of the city for years; he never felt comfortable in its cloying Sleeping-Beauty-like atmosphere. He, for one, had never desired these desirable residences.

He found the house, and, as the gates jerkily parted, a smiling askari waved him down the drive. Cecily had come out to greet him, her partner, Marina, was presumably away on business. She pointed to a shady parking spot and held her arms open to him as he approached.

'Darling Rob, how are you? It's been years. Too long.'

'I'm okay, Cec. Long drive though. I've been at the coast.'

'Come inside. Please get freshened up and I'll sort out some drinks.'

When Rob emerged into the back garden, a veritable banquet awaited him. Cecily had a knack for throwing together the most elaborate feasts at a moment's notice. Of course, she had not done it, it was her cook Priscilla who was the magician. But Cecily accepted Rob's effusive thanks modestly as though it had been all her own work.

'Take a chair in the shade here, darling, and I'll explain everything.'

Rob sat down heavily and accepted a beer and a plate of 'bit-ings'. 'I got here as soon as I could, you do know that?'

'Of course, of course. Listen, I know how hard this has been for you and that you've had to be away. I just feel bad that I didn't realise how desperate she had got.'

'I'm so grateful she had you here to be a support for her, for all these years,' said Rob.

'Yes, well. It's not just me, there's Emma and Kate. Lots of the old gang from uni still live out this way, so we have all been keep-ing an eye. But it was me who has been closest to her, so I don't know how I didn't see this coming.'

'It was Evie's eighteenth birthday, you see,' Rob reassured her. 'And nine years since her death. She's now been dead as long as she was alive. Jo always had a thing about counting and anniversaries, symmetries and things, do you know?'

'I didn't know that about her. And I had forgotten that it was Evie's eighteenth. How remiss of me.'

'Please stop blaming yourself. Just talk me through what hap-pened.'

'Well, I went over on Thursday evening. We were supposed to have met in the afternoon at Westlands for lunch, but I had to cancel. She said she was going in anyway to get some shopping, so I thought she was fine, she didn't seem put out or anything. Anyway, she had promised to get me some fabric and pass it on to me next week when we were due to meet again, but I thought I'd pop in as I was passing and get it from her and make up a bit for cancelling lunch.'

'What time was this?'

'About seven. Jimmy was on the gate as normal, he let me in. Then, when she wouldn't answer her door, he came to unlock it for me. He stayed with me while I called for her. He knew she hadn't gone out again, you see, so we both ran around the house looking for her. Luckily the bathroom was unlocked and we got there in time. Oh, God…' Cecily's voice cracked and she took a moment before continuing. 'Jimmy was amazing, so cool and practical. I just went to pieces, I'm afraid.' Cecily sobbed loudly. Rob held her hand in both of his and waited for her to continue.

'We could see she was still alive, but God, there was so much blood, Rob. Jimmy grabbed a towel and ripped it up to make bandages, and handed me one, then we took a wrist each and tied up the wounds. She just kept looking me straight in the face, utterly bewildered, almost angry, but Jimmy kept talking to her in his lovely gentle voice and she stopped fighting us.'

'I'm so grateful, Cecily. Really, you were amazing.'

'It was just chance that I was there. I can't stop thinking about that. Anyway, the paramedics got there, I don't know how long after, not long. And I went with her to the hospital. They patched her up and gave her a transfusion. But she won't talk, Rob. She hasn't uttered a word.'

'I guess she doesn't need to explain. I guess we all know why. But I didn't think it was this bad, either, Cec.'

'Oh, but she might have explained more. There was a letter for you in her bedroom.' Cecily went inside for a moment, grabbing a tissue to wipe her nose and pulling an envelope out of a bureau drawer. 'I held the police off opening it until you got here, but you will need to take it to the station. I suppose if she'd died, it would have been evidence. Here.' Cecily passed it over to Rob, his name scrolled decisively in Jo's youthful loopy hand like a teenage girl's writing on a Valentine's card. This gave him a further pang of sadness.

Dearest Rob
I'm so sorry to do this to you. To Nella. I just can't seem to get any better. I have tried and tried to find a way out of this. Countless times I have tried to write to you or call you or Nella or Barbara, but I just don't have the strength and I feel too ashamed. I loved my letters from you. I have treasured them and your words did mean a lot to me, but I just didn't know how to reply. My silence has not been angry and recriminating, it has been just full of sadness and regret.

I can't condone my own behaviour – my shutting down and shutting you out. But now I cannot see what value I have to you or Nella and I need to go now. You two must find each other again. Please promise me that you will get her and bring her home – she belongs in Africa. We should never have sent her away to Scotland, but it seemed for the best. I know you wanted her to stay with Barbara, but she had so much of her own grief to deal with and I thought it would be better for Nella to be completely away from everything that had happened so she could build her own life. You both have so much love and you need to repair what I have unravelled. I know it will not be easy, but you are both stronger than I am, both have so much love. And Barbara too – she is a rock, an alpha mother like our beloved elephants. Please let her help.

I know I blamed you for not being there on the day that it happened, because I had told you not to go out– that we had a deadline to meet and you didn't need to go to the town. But I just needed to blame something or someone. I know that wasn't fair or true. I know that you also needed to find a way to make it better and that is why you left, you needed to find your own solutions and they did not include being a nurse for me. But please, can you make it right with Nella? I know that you are not to blame for what happened, I truly do, but I just long for my baby. It is something I cannot explain. It gets stronger every day. I long for Nella too, but I know that she needs to be free and out in the world. If she were with me, I would be stifling and controlling and that is not what she has needed all this time. She has needed love and space and I know that she will have had that. The longer it has been since I have seen her, the further away she seems.

Lastly, please look after yourself. Now and again, I hear word of you – just a whisper, someone has heard something, or there has been some big cache of ivory found and I know you are behind it, quietly vanishing into the background. But I know that you will have been putting yourself in terrible danger. I can make no demands of you – you have done so much good; you have nothing to prove. So please go home and go back to what you always loved to do, surrounded by the people who love you.

Forever yours,

Jo

Rob passed the letter on to Cecily, sipping his beer as she read. She returned it wordlessly and he folded it back carefully into the envelope and tucked it into the breast pocket of his shirt. They sat in silence for several minutes, until Rob looked up at Cecily. 'I don't know what to do, Cec. I have to leave in two days to finish this thing I'm working on. It's terribly important and if I don't do it, there will be huge repercussions for other people who are depending on me. People who have taken huge risks for me. The next few weeks are crucial. But I can't just abandon Jo.'

'What about her family back in Scotland. Can they help?'

'Her parents are elderly. Her brother and his wife are still there; you know they were the ones who took Nella in. They are very special people, but I can't ask this of them too. And Nella is only twenty-one, she can't be expected to drop everything and look after the mother she hasn't seen for nine years.'

'And your mother, Barbara, isn't it?'

'My mother is the most gorgeous person, but I have broken her heart and I can't face her. I certainly can't expect her to take Jo and just make her better. I just left; you see. Jo's way of dealing with everything was to hide away and shut down. For me, I had to leave. I had to leave her and my mother and my daughter and our friends. I only thought about getting revenge. It seems so stupid now. So pointless. But I had to make amends, to avenge Evie and Dad. And the elephants. When I say it out loud, it sounds ridiculously thoughtless, but I was utterly closed-minded about it. Does that make sense at all?'

'Listen, Rob, I know you, I know how much you love your family and it is not right to go on like this. I think that first, you should visit Jo. You can't make decisions about all this without doing that. I'll come with you. We shall go over in the morning. Then you need to think about the short term and the long. This thing you have to do – do it, and get Jo somewhere safe for now, but then you need to think about what your family needs in the future. You've spent the last nine years doing good things. I don't know exactly what – you don't need to explain it all to me. But perhaps now is the time for you all to try to rebuild bridges. A family as lovely as yours should not be apart, it's unthinkable. What good is it doing any of you?'

Cecily stopped talking, to see that Rob was curled forward in his chair sobbing, his fingers white-knuckled in the curly mass of his hair. She fetched a kikoy and wrapped it over him, filled up his glass and ran her hand softly over his fingers, leaving him to let out his grief.

CHAPTER 40

MOMBASA, KENYA 2012

THEY were to meet at a new office complex in Mombasa. Rob had been up all night, still recovering from a bout of malaria, his third in the last few years. For now, he lay in his motel bed staring at a spider scuttling on the ceiling fan. The room was stark and dirty, bats were roosting in the roof; guano had dripped from a gap in the ceiling tiles leaving a sticky slick across the bathroom sink. But at least it was north-facing so he had escaped the worst of the heat. He showered and dressed, packed his canvas shoulder bag and set out.

He had built up a reputation as 'gamekeeper turned poacher' and this latest meeting was with Johan du Toit. Du Toit's latest metamorphosis was as a fixer. Clive's investigations as a journalist had peeled away many layers of poaching activity, Rob's had got to the core. There were actually very few subtleties in the business of poaching, for a 'business' it was. Everything was kept nice and simple. There was only one person in Kenya who was central to all the orders received and who communicated these orders to poaching gang leaders. This person had all the numbers, all the names. And this person was Clive's nemesis.

Rob had tried to get a meeting with du Toit for five years, having to build up his own identity with a reputation as a serious buyer – a Mr Taylor from London – in order to be granted an audience. The pretence wasn't so hard; not really. These last ten years had changed Rob almost entirely. Before, he had been sensitive, curious, gentle; but over the years, he had grown a shell around his heart, protecting him from fear and grief that might otherwise consume him. He had learned how to slip in and out of groups of people who would have been alien to him ten years ago – traders, poachers, money men – without drawing attention to himself. He trusted no one. His own safety came second to achieving his aims – to protect and avenge those he had loved.

He felt an oppressive guilt about what he had done. It was very likely that elephants had died because of his involvement in the trade; he had to turn a blind eye on many occasions in order to maintain trust and not arouse suspicion. But now, this meeting was the culmination of years of work and regret and Rob had to make it succeed.

His canvas bag was strapped across his chest. He fiddled with the side pocket, checking for the twentieth time that the lens was twisted into the brass eyelet riveted into the fabric, making it invisible, the slim body of the camera sewn inside the lining of the pocket. His afro was ideal for hiding a microphone and he checked it as he walked through the busy market, playing the calls of the market vendors back to himself.

The office complex was clean and smart – the sort of place where serious people made serious business. He had dressed smartly for the occasion. Rather than his usual checked shirt and khaki shorts, he wore a crisp linen suit, a white short-sleeved shirt and blue silk tie, hair smoothed down and tied as best he could – the very image of an elegant and wealthy man.

He checked in at reception – they had booked a meeting room on the second floor. He was a little early, allowing himself time to sit for a few minutes to help calm his nerves. His bag was opened and inspected by the guard, but there appeared to be nothing more sinister than a ring binder and two notebooks.

A huge man in a dark suit arrived in the foyer and quietly requested his presence at the room upstairs. Inside Rob felt like a small child scuttling after a grown up as he followed the man up the stairs and into the room. Two more men stood by the window. Thin blinds were drawn but failed to cut out the piercing light.

The man he had come to meet sat directly in the window, a

deliberate act, thought Rob, silhouetting himself against the light, adding to his enigmatic aura.

'Good to meet you at last, Mr Taylor, please sit, sit. We shall have a drink and then we shall talk. How is everything with you? How is life in Hong Kong?' His voice betrayed his age and he spoke quietly, so that Rob had to lean in to hear him. This man had no need to shout.

'Life is very good, thank you. When I've finished my business here, I'm heading to my boat, moored at Malindi, then I shall take a short cruise over to Zanzibar.'

'I am glad to hear it, the sea is so good for the soul, isn't it? Now, to business. I understand you have the funds in place to make the transfer?'

'I do. Just as soon as I see the merchandise.'

'All in good time, all in good time. Please join me for a whisky. It's a 1969 Kinclaith, very rare. I wonder where we both were in 1969? And a cigar.' One of the standing men leant in with an elaborate ivory cigar box and opened it for Rob. He would have to pretend to smoke.

'I trust that you have everything ready? I need to know that we both understand the transaction,' said Rob, picking tobacco shreds from the end of his tongue.

Rob needed him to say the words, but du Toit just nodded and said, 'It is all there.'

Rob tried again.

'To be clear. What quantities have you set aside for me? My people need to know that we are paying a fair price.'

This seemed to work. 'One hundred and eighty kilos of ivory, forty kilos of rhino horn, and one hundred and twenty-five kilos of pangolin scales.'

'May I see it?'

One of the men looked to du Toit and, receiving a nod, moved over to three large chests in the corner of the room, covered with a blanket. His colleague crowbarred the lids off to reveal the contents. Rob got out of his chair and reached into the first chest, pulling out a short stumpy tusk. This was not a broken piece, but a fully formed tusk. It had to have been from an elephant no more than five years old. Rob felt bile rise up to his mouth, but managed to turn his disgust into a smile. He had all he needed. He just needed to get out of there.

'Great. That all looks in order. I'll phone the office and tell them it's all go.'

Du Toit sat smiling in anticipation, liver-spotted fingers wrapped around his whisky glass. 'Very well. And we shall check out at this end that the funds clear.'

Rob made his call. 'Hello? Okay, we are all set. Please go ahead. Thank you.' He waited. No one on the other end of the line spoke. Something was wrong. His line was supposed to be their cue to storm the room, but there was nothing, just silence. Rob felt sick. Sweat rose from his stomach up to his underarms, and his heart thudded. 'I'm sorry, there seems to be a bad line, just give me a moment.' He tried to sound casual as he redialled. The line rang and rang, but this time no one even picked up. He needed to get out of that room. Now. He tried to keep the panic from showing on his face, but du Toit continued to smile placidly.

'I… I'm sorry. Something is not quite right. I'll need to make a few calls.' He felt his forehead begin to perspire; he knew they could see it. 'Is there a room I could use to speak to my people and try to find out what has happened?'

'Of course. Gentlemen, please escort Mr Taylor into the room across the corridor and make sure he is comfortable.'

Rob stood shakily and was led firmly down the corridor. A door was opened and one of the men threw him into the pitch-black room. He heard a lock turn and voices on the other side discussing what to do next.

He stood where he had been thrown, pressed up against a far wall, motionless for several moments, his heart beating so hard he thought he would choke. Adrenaline began to course through his veins, and he tried to calm his breathing – tried to order the dozens of thoughts that filled his head. How had this happened? There had to have been a split in the long chain of people he had put his trust in. After all this – all these years.

He took a deep breath and wiped his brow with the sleeve of his jacket. No – he was not going to let one slip ruin the whole scheme. Everything he had done in the last decade had led to this one moment. Perhaps not all was lost. Mike should be outside and he trusted him completely. They were not in the jungles of Angola or downtown Johannesburg. This was market day in Mombasa, the town was full of people. All he had to do was to get out of this room and outside.

His eyes darted around the windowless space, beginning to adjust to the light provided by a small slit under the door. He realised he still had his phone in his hand. It dropped to the floor, slipping from his sweaty palms. They hadn't taken it. They must be in a hurry to have done something so careless. He rubbed his palms on his trousers then, picking up the phone and pressing the torch button, he shone a light around the room. There were a few chairs stacked up in a corner. He pulled the top one off the pile and slammed it against the door, ramming the back of it under the door handle, just as a key turned in the lock and the handle wiggled.

He scanned the torch around again. Opposite was a door, presumably to a cupboard. He ran over and tried the handle: it wasn't locked. The sound of low voices again in the corridor, then an almighty thump as they tried to dislodge the chair. There was no time to lose.

Perhaps there was some way out through the cupboard. A childishly hopeful thought of the wardrobe leading to Narnia passed through his mind. That was fanciful, but these office blocks weren't all that solid – all thin frames, stud walls and polystyrene tiles. Perhaps if he just gave the ceiling tiles a thud with something? Fumbling around, he found a broom and, quietly as he could, thrust it upwards at the tiles – success. He hung his bag across his body, grasped the sides of some metal shelving inside the cupboard, and clambered up through the hole he had just made. He carefully shimmied along the ceiling structure above the next room.

On loosening a tile he saw a similar cupboard below, but this was empty and filled with daylight. He heard the men breaking through into the room next door, and, fuelled by fear and adrenaline, he pulled his body along, booted a tile out of the ceiling and scrambled into the other cupboard. Once his feet found the floor, he dashed out and into the corridor. There, to his relief, he saw a gaggle of women laughing at the entrance to the lift.

'Ladies, ladies! How are you today?' Rob boomed at the women, as he walked over to them, hitching up his bag and dusting off his suit. More giggling as the group pressed together and into the lift. 'May I join you?' Rob said in the manliest voice he could muster. 'I'm at a loose end, you see, and you ladies look like you're having a lot of fun.' Rob and the women continued to chat and laugh out of the office building and down towards the Old Town, just as two large men emerged from the stairwell.

Rob carried on walking with the women as they turned to enter a restaurant. Figuring that he was as well to stay in plain sight surrounded by people, he followed them.

'I don't want to gatecrash your lunch, ladies,' he said in a more modest tone. 'I'll take a table upstairs. Have an enjoyable meal.'

He ran up to the second floor of the restaurant and found a table by a window, overlooking the market square. From here he phoned his contact at the police department.

'Hey, Mike, where were you?... Yes, I got out, but the stuff is still there. He is still there. You need to get in now! Okay. No, I'm in a café across the square, watching now. Yes, two of his heavies are out there, looking for me… No, no, I'm fine, there's lots of people… Yes, I can see your guy now. Tell him to make his way over to the spice stall outside the government building. One of the men is there… um, let me check… Yes, the other one has joined him again, they are walking back to the office block. Du Toit can't have got far yet. You'll need to block the car park exit now, right now!… The merchandise is in three metal chests. Du Toit's men can't move them quickly. Send someone up to the second floor to get them… Look, I'm on my way down. I don't want to miss this.'

Rob hung up and ran out of the restaurant, apologising to the waiter who was just moving towards him. Back in the street, he could see a commotion ahead as he pushed through the market. He drew level with the policemen and, nodding to one of them, followed them into the office reception where he had been, just a few minutes earlier.

Just then, another police officer ran into the building. 'They're round the back!'

Rob and the officers ran back out into the street, turned where the policeman pointed, and saw du Toit and his men about to get into a car. Rob ran at them and launched himself at du Toit, slamming him against the side of his car. The officers caught up with him, one grabbed one of du Toit's men, the other pushed Rob aside.

'I'll take it from here,' he said, giving Rob a grateful nod.

The second of du Toit's men tripped on the kerb in his haste and landed splayed out on the road, quickly grabbed by a policeman. Rob stepped away, back towards the office block to let the police handcuff and caution the men.

Backing himself up against a wall, Rob slid his body down, panting, head bent, clutching his knees until he stopped trembling. Then he looked up and took in the scene. Tears pricked his eyes. This was it. After all these years, all the chasing, all the near misses and the pretending and the false hope, finally he'd done it. He allowed a few tears to fall as he continued to watch as an officer pushed down on du Toit's head to guide him into the police car. Du Toit turned to look in Rob's direction. Rob rubbed his eyes with the heel of his hand, stood back up and walked over to the car. He stooped over the open back door, still shaking from the adrenaline rush, his mouth dry, but his voice calm.

'It was for my father, Clive Chege,' he said. 'And for my daughter. Rot in hell!' Du Toit gave a wry, twisted smile as the car door slammed.

The police car did not drive off straight away, but waited while two more officers came through the office doors with a large chest propped on a sack barrow and wheeled it towards a waiting van. Mike, the superintendent, came running towards Rob and stopped, panting, then placed a hand on Rob's shoulder.

'That's it. We've got him. You got him. Now leave the rest to us. He's going nowhere.'

'What happened? Why didn't Steve answer my call?' asked Rob.

Mike shook his head in bewilderment, straightening to refill his lungs. 'I don't know. There's no sign of him. He was in place outside the office doors as he should have been, ready to take your call, but he vanished.'

Mike's phone rang. 'Hang on a second, Rob.'

He spoke to the caller. 'So you've found him? Where was he?… I see… Yes, I'll be there in a few minutes. Cuff him and put him in the car. I want to speak to him myself.'

That was my sergeant. They caught Steve trying to get a cab out of town. Looks like he was in it with them. I don't know how or why.'

'I'm sorry he's let you down. He seemed such a good man.'

'There's a lot of money floating around this deal; a lot of temptation. Many a better man would sell his soul.'

'Not you though, Mike?'

'What use would I have with a few extra millions of shillings?' he joked. 'Right, Rob, please go home to your family. Stop this now. You've done it, my friend, you've done it.'

Rob watched as the vehicles drove off, loosened his hair and walked away.

CHAPTER 41

TAITA HILLS 2012

FIKIRI was staring up at the ceiling. Another sleepless night. He turned to look at Rosemary sleeping the deep sleep of the innocent. She was so gentle and good and it was so unfair. That was the worst of it; she had done nothing but good all her life. What use was a good life, if this was your reward? He tiptoed out of the bedroom and out into the yard. The cloudless night might have been cold, but Fikiri didn't notice. He didn't hear the chattering of nightjars or the lonely scops owl that had nested outside the house. He didn't hear Rosemary shuffle up behind him; so tiny and fragile and silent now that, when she laid a hand on his shoulder, he jumped.

'What is it, Fikiri? What's the matter? There's something going on, I know it. You are so tense and jumpy these days.'

'Nothing. Nothing's the matter.'

'You think I don't know my own husband. What's wrong?

'I can't tell you.'

'Well, you have to. Has something happened? Is it your job?'

Fikiri shook his head. 'Rosie, please. I can't… I've done something bad; I can't tell you, not to your face. I can't see the look in your face.'

'You're my husband, Fikiri. We've been together for over twenty years; you cannot have any secrets from me. It's as simple as that. Tell me now.' Some of her old strength was back in her voice.

Fikiri stood still, avoiding her gaze, staring instead at the giant baobab tree in the distance – guardian of the bush – standing sentry, silhouetted against the bright moonlight. Finally, he nodded, his voice flat and impassive, still directed towards the baobab.

'There's something I have to do.'

'What do you mean? Something for work? What is it, Fikiri?'

'I can't...' Fikiri faltered. 'I have to go.' He grabbed his keys and made for his truck, then turned. 'I'm sorry, so sorry, Rosie.'

He walked back to the front door where she stood; he couldn't bear the look of confusion on her face. He held her, felt her tiny, birdlike frame through her cotton nightdress. He had resolved not to weep.

Rosemary stood back to hold his face in her hands and looked into his eyes, seeking answers, but he pushed her away gently, turned back to the car. He jumped in and started the engine, driving away without a backward glance. Rosemary watched as the truck vanished through the dust, then she returned to the house.

Making for the kitchen, she saw a piece of paper on the dining table, neatly folded, her name written across it. Opening the paper to scan the contents, she ran her finger across the first few lines. These were written in Fikiri's usual neat, deliberate hand, but as the letter went on, the writing became more and more untidy, words scored out, smudges – tearstains? The last few lines slanted as if desperate to leave the page, the pencil darkening and scoring the paper nearly right through like cat scratches. There was no signature, no valediction, no words of love. A feeling of dread engulfed her as she smoothed out the paper on the kitchen table and sat down to read.

It is night, but the moon is bright enough for us to see clearly – a hunter's moon. Moses shouts to me, 'Fikiri! Stop driving now! I can see something. Stop!'

I ram down hard on the brake, my foot slipping on the cold pedal. There is no grip left on my thin rubber flip flops. We sit and wait for a few moments and, even though the night is cool, I can feel sweat trickling down between my shoulder blades, soaking through the waistband of my shorts. Moses is right. There is movement ahead at the waterhole. We were right to wait in this part of the reserve. Moses knows his stuff.

Our ragged breathing seems louder than the noises the elephants make. I look behind at the rest of the men, sitting back in the truck bed. Jonathan is looking down at his lap, mumbling something to himself, maybe he is praying. Eliud's lip is bleeding as he grips his rifle tight against his chest. Moses is staring ahead, waiting for the right moment. We wait for his signal. We need to be quiet, stealthy. If we charge in too soon, the group will panic and disperse, then our job will be harder. We need to hold back and take them unawares.

Moses shouts 'Go!' and I floor the gas pedal. Eliud is screaming and ululating. The three of them are poised with their rifles pressed to their cheeks as I drive us right up to the first elephant in the herd. She swings round on her back leg and stares at us, raging.

That moment alone I can never forget. It runs through my head, over and over.

She makes her body big, flaring out her ears and throwing herself forward at us, screaming with fury. It takes a shower of bullets to bring her down. Then everything speeds up and I only remember the sounds, I don't know if I have closed my eyes, or I have just shut out the vision as it is easier that way. I hear crashing, high-pitched shrieks – from the men or the elephants – I don't know; it all echoes in my ears. The weight of their bodies as they drop seems to send tremors through the ground. Water splashes. A few more bullets… two more, one… then the only sound is Eliud's hollow screaming.

I turn off the engine and the men pile out of the pick-up, running towards the animals, still clutching their weapons high in case any are still alive and can run at us. There is no movement though, and the men swing their rifles onto their shoulders. There is silence. I reach to the back of the truck bed to a roll of green canvas – an old army-issue tent. Wrapped up in it are the tools we need for the rest of our job. I pull these out and pass them round. We spread out and find the biggest animals. All we need are the tusks. We work from the largest to the smallest, focused, working at speed. We are efficient, practised. Adrenaline is coursing through me, making my heart thump hard against my ribs. The ferrous smell burns my nostrils. I turn to carry my hoard into the pick-up, and pass Moses bending over the first elephant, the one who turned and tried to protect her herd.

I freeze. I realise that I know her. I have known her all my life.

Rosemary stood up slowly, steadying herself on the table. She walked out to the yard, clutching the letter. The sun rose through the branches of the baobab tree.

CHAPTER 42

TAITA HILLS 2012

XANDER drove up to the school, got out and wandered over to the kitchen, where he always met Jonathan for a cup of tea before John put them to work. There was no sign of him. Or of John. There was something the matter, he was sure of it. He went through to the back room of the kitchen and found Phyllis, her back to him, scrubbing cassava over a bowl of water. She turned and he could see she was crying.

'Phyllis, what is it, what's happened?'

Phyllis grabbed a corner of her apron and dabbed her eyes with it. 'The police. They came here. They took Jonathan.'

'What do you mean? Took him? Why?'

'I don't know, there was a lot of shouting from the police and from John. John is with them. Jonathan would say nothing. He just looked down all the time, like he couldn't look them in the face. Oh dear, I don't know what could be wrong. He is such a good boy. I can't understand it.' She sobbed into her apron again and Xander went over to help her into a chair.

'Oh Phyllis, I'm sure it's nothing. A mix up. What could he possibly have done?'

Just then a small boy put his head around the door. He was silent, but he looked at Xander and Phyllis as though he wanted to say something, but was finding it hard.

'Solomon, come in,' said Xander. 'Did you need something? I'm afraid John's not here right now. I'll come to the classroom in a minute and speak to you all.'

'Excuse me, Mzee, but it is to do with the elephants?'

'I'm sorry?' asked Xander.

'Jonathan and the police. Is it to do with the elephants?'

'Come, sit here, Solomon.' Xander held out a stool for the boy to sit on, and Phyllis handed him a cup of water. 'Now, Solomon, do you know what has happened? What's this about the elephants?'

'The ones that were killed.'

'What has that to do with Jonathan?'

'I don't want to get him into trouble.'

'Please just tell us if you know anything. Perhaps we can help Jonathan.'

'I saw some men, when I was walking home from school one day. My family's shamba is far, far. Jonathan had gone over to meet them. On the Rukinga Road, you know?' Xander nodded and Solomon continued. 'One of the men was from your camp. I know him because he lives in the village and his sons come to the school. And the other men, I knew them too. I know one of the men used to work at the game reserve over that way.' Solomon took a slow sip of his water. 'They were shouting at Jonathan, making him cry.' Solomon was starting to cry himself. Xander knelt down to face him and put his hands on the boy's lap.

'Could you hear what they were talking about, Solomon? Anything at all?'

'They were talking about elephants.'

'Right.' He stood and took Solomon's hand. 'Do you want to help Jonathan? Can you be very brave for me?' Solomon nodded. 'Let's find Freda and tell her that we are off on a mission. She will need to take the class today.'

After a quick explanation to Freda, Xander helped Solomon into his car and they drove off in the direction of Kasigau and the police station.

* * *

After returning Solomon to his shamba and explaining to Freda what had happened, Xander returned to the camp. John was staying in town to be near Jonathan and, between them, they thought it best to close the school for the rest of the week. Fikiri's confession and subsequent arrest had caused a further layer of melancholy to shroud the camp. Barbara had stayed in her room ever since they had discovered the butchered herd.

Xander found his parents in the mess tent, reading. 'How is everyone?' he asked.

Gigi put down her book and took his hand as he sat down. 'Sad. More than anything, just sad. No one has left camp since it happened. We all just mooch around here aimlessly.'

'I'm sorry. How awful for you to see it,' said Xander.

'Yes, it was awful. But worse for Barbara – they were like family to her. And I think it's made her relive something else. Did you know what happened here ten years ago?'

'No. To Barbara?' asked Xander.

'I knew her husband had died; it was mentioned in the article when I entered the competition,' replied Gigi. 'But, you see, he was killed, along with her granddaughter.'

'Nella's sister?'

'Yes, here,' his father replied. 'They heard noises behind the house and Clive went to see what had happened. Some poachers had shot a male elephant and hacked away his tusks. Then they shot him – Clive – and Evie had followed her grandfather and they shot her too.'

Xander sat back to take in what Dan had said. 'God. That's horrendous. And the family? What happened to everyone?'

'Hamisi told me,' replied Gigi. 'Joanna, Nella's mum, went to Nairobi to get away from everything. I think she has ended up in a clinic in the UK. They sent Nella to live with family in Scotland, and Rob – he's Barbara's son, Nella's dad – well, Rob sort of vanished. They hear from him now and again, but he more or less went to ground. I don't really understand it.'

'One act of violence and so many lives ruined,' said Xander.

'Yes,' agreed Dan. 'And Hamisi seems to think their deaths may not have been entirely incidental.'

'You mean they *meant* to kill Clive and the little girl? Surely, they were poachers, just out to kill elephants.'

'That was how it all seemed,' explained Dan. 'They caught them and jailed them, but apparently there was some connection with a guy named Johan du Toit. He worked here a long time ago and did something that caused him to be sent to jail. Clive was somehow behind that. So, Hamisi has always thought that Clive was the real target. Revenge.'

'So, it was really a murder, dressed up as poaching?'

'No one could prove it. Du Toit didn't pull the trigger and he has so much power over people that he walks away from things like this smelling of roses.'

'While the poor locals are driven to do these awful things and get thrown in jail,' mused Xander, shaking his head. 'I've just come back from Kilenga. They've charged Fikiri and the other poachers, including poor little Jonathan. It's just so unfair. I don't condone what they did, but God, who am I to judge them when there are people like du Toit in the background? Jonathan was stuck in the village with no hope or future. He was told by those men that he would earn 100,000 shillings for his part in the killing. That's about £700. That's an enormous, life-changing amount of money for him. So, he thought he would save his family and their farm, by doing this one thing.'

'Fikiri's wife is very sick,' explained Gigi. 'He never told anyone here, but Freda told me. She has cancer but can't afford treatment. And they have two little boys. Fikiri was trying to pay for the treatment, but it all got too much.'

'One of the other men had been a ranger,' added Dan. 'They are only paid about $100 a month and apparently even that can be pretty sporadic. They sometimes don't have sufficient uniforms, let alone weapons, yet they're expected to protect the wildlife at all costs against people with AK47s. It's no wonder some of them turn.'

'The issue is so complicated,' Dan went on. 'Do you remember the site of the ivory burn we saw in Nairobi? Well, for a lot of Kenyans, that act was a real source of pride, but for many others it just showed a lack of understanding. Wildlife rangers have families to feed, and, like I said, they are often paid very little, so they occasionally take a bribe, turn a blind eye, or even participate in poaching. Then when their government burns millions of dollars' worth of ivory in front of the world, it looks like an empty gesture, or just something to placate tourists or show off to other governments. While at the same time as showing the world that they can afford to make this gesture, they fail to pay the very people who are there to protect the elephants, it's no wonder the people on the ground become cynical.'

Xander added, 'And if your crop fails over and over and you have taxes and school fees and bills to pay and then your crop is destroyed in one day by marauding elephants, it becomes logical to kill what you see as pests, and you'll be paid extraordinary amounts of money to do so.' Xander shook his head. 'We see elephants as marvellous and perilously rare, but if you live here, they are part of everyday life and not necessarily a blessing. I do think there's more than one perspective. More than anything, I just bloody wish I had the power to change things.'

CHAPTER 43

TAITA HILLS 2012

THE group was travelling the twenty or so miles from camp to the elephant reintegration centre. Gigi was driving, joined in the front by Barbara and Dan; Xander and Annie sat across the middle bench. Gigi felt the brisk, warm air flutter over her face as she navigated the rocks and bushes which scattered the roads. She looked dreamily in the rear-view mirror at her children. It was impossible, surely, this idea that was forming in her head? But they all seemed so comfortable and happy here, didn't they? Of course, everyone does that – that thing when you relax and think: 'I could live here. I could give up my dull, complicated, futile existence and live here with the sunshine, the birdsong, the true stuff of life – do something worthwhile with my days.' But why not? Was it really a pipe dream? They could give it a try.

She looked beyond her children to Fenella chatting in the back seat with Bryndís. After their volunteering project had finished, Fenella had invited Bryndís to visit Bibi's camp. Gigi felt a pang of jealousy, which surprised her but jolted her into a realisation. There was no real reason why they couldn't do it. They weren't as free as Bryndís, but they could make a few changes and make it work. Xander could finish his exams by correspondence or stay with her father for his last school year. Annie could go to school here. Dan had already left his job; she had no real commitments apart from looking in on her father. Perhaps he could come out here too – a final big adventure. She smiled to herself at the thought.

This was it; the thing she was good at – she considered as she dropped gears, dodging a skittering dik-dik – navigating a ship through stormy seas. She had run a household for eighteen years – balanced money, time and commitments. She had been cook, nurse, teacher, accountant. She had pushed her children to work hard and her husband to believe in himself. She had supported everyone through life's disappointments and catastrophes, and cheered them through their successes. She had been their ship's captain and their safe harbour.

Before all that, she had worked in business, negotiated contracts, compiled statistical reports. Somewhere along the line, she had doubted her worth, but all those skills were not insignificant. She was bursting with ideas about how they could help with the camp – business sponsorships, school links, sourcing buyers in the UK for Freda's project in Kilenga, student internships. The more she thought about it, the more ideas she had, and she resolved to talk to Barbara about it back at camp.

'This is the furthest I've driven here!' she shouted across to Barbara. 'It's definitely not like bumbling around the Cotswolds!' It makes me a bit nervous, I have to say. I don't miss the school run traffic, but I suppose there is less risk there of tearing the canvas roof on a thorn bush or whacking the side mirror on a termite mound.' Just as she said this, they lunged sideways, the jeep righting itself with a bounce.

'Or wrecking the suspension in a lugga!' yelled Bryndís from the back.

* * *

Fenella smiled to herself, remembering that woman on the bus complaining about the Scottish roads.

'So what do you think so far?' Fenella asked Bryndís shyly.

'I think you need to bring me up to speed. Why did you not tell me about your grandmother and about being from Africa?'

'I had a lot of stuff I needed to do at my own pace, I guess. I never liked talking about it in Scotland and I suppose it became a habit. But okay, Barbara is my Bibi and I lived here until I was twelve.'

'I feel a bit stupid, making out that I am the seasoned African traveller, when you were from here all along.'

'Oh but you are. I couldn't have travelled around like you have, on my own, just happily taking up with strangers along the way. And I never went into the cities here, so Nairobi was genuinely strange to me. Really, it was quite a sheltered childhood.'

'Where are your parents? Are they still alive?'

'Yes, but… well, it's complicated, but mum is in a hospital in Scotland and Dad, well, I don't actually know where he is. I hear from him now and again. Anyway, now I'm home I've decided to stay.'

'Don't suppose your Bibi needs an extra pair of hands helping out around here?'

'I'm not sure. Why don't you speak to Hamisi tonight over dinner?'

* * *

'Is this it?' Gigi asked Barbara.

'Yes, just keep on this track a bit longer,' Barbara replied. 'There – do you see that flat area on the left? Park there.'

Sitting a little further up on a slight hill, the main area of the reintroduction centre resembled a small farmyard. A row of wooden huts backed onto a steep kopje. These were painted a utilitarian dark green and looked neat and well maintained, given their wild surroundings. Their tin roofs extended over narrow verandas, creating a pleasant shady corridor. It was really very homely. There was currently an atmosphere of industry as, from one of the huts, crate after crate of white plastic bottles was being brought out and lined up in the shade. A man who had been carrying one of the crates caught sight of the group and beckoned them over.

'Ah, Barbara, so good to see you, my old friend.' He clasped his hands over one of Barbara's and held it for a moment, looking straight at her. Barbara nodded and mumbled something, returning the handclasp. Fenella looked over to her, her heart hurting for her. She gulped back the sharp pain that had lodged in her own throat for days. The man turned to the rest of them. 'Good morning! We've been expecting you. Of course, you were due to visit soon anyway, but now you have a very special reason. Would you like to look around?'

'Yes, please,' said Gigi. 'If it's not imposing.'

'Not at all, we like to show people what we do here. I can introduce you to some of our orphans, then in about half an hour, the big babies will be coming back from the bush for their supper. Come, come this way. My name is Lembara, by the way.' He led the family to a door at the end of the row of huts.

'The first thing I want to show you is rather shocking, I'm afraid. You see, we spend a lot of time with the orphans, but actually, the larger part of our day is spent de-snaring. Just to warn you, it can be upsetting.' He yanked open the tall green door to an unlit room. The room was about ten square feet, and every inch of the floor was covered in wire rings. These were piled up, reaching the ceiling in tall coils. 'What you see here has been gathered in just the last two months.'

'But there must be hundreds of them!' exclaimed Dan.

'More like thousands. They are all different sizes, made for trapping elephants, buffalo, giraffe, zebra… down to dik-dik and other small mammals. We can collect sometimes three hundred in a day. We only find them by finding animals in them.'

'Dead?' asked Dan, cautiously.

'Out of those three hundred, perhaps only five or six will be alive and able to be helped back at the base here.'

Fenella watched as Annie turned to her mother and nuzzled against her side, clutching her little fists.

'Are you okay?' Gigi whispered.

Annie nodded. 'I'm angry.'

The group stood in silence a little while longer, but the nauseating atmosphere of the room drove them out one by one. Lembara closed and locked the door. They followed him up the shaded path, working their way along the row of huts, peering inside each one. All the huts were like stables, dark and cool with a concrete floor cushioned with fresh straw. The first one held a tiny dik-dik. It had been found that morning in a snare, which had slashed it across the eyes, blinding it.

'Will it live, do you think?' whispered Annie, clearly shaken at the sight of the tiny, vulnerable antelope.

'Perhaps not. She has been very badly hurt and this is a strange place for her. She will miss her kind. Dik-diks pair for life you know and she might have had a partner. But we can try a little food and kindness. If she lives, she will have to stay here, as she can no longer survive in the wild.'

The next hut housed a livelier animal. A baby zebra, still with its juvenile coat of brown and white, stood with its head over the lower stable door, bold and curious about the visitors.

'This is Ngulia. She wasn't hurt, but her mother was killed by poachers. She was found by a group of tourists just walking around by herself. Their guide brought her here, as we have milk and the facilities. So, we're helping her to grow.'

'Can she be wild again?' asked Xander.

'Possibly. We do reintroduce the fitter animals back into the wild, using the same methods we use for the elephants. The ungulates sort of club together to make little herds of their own. It looks a bit unusual, but in the wild, big herds of zebra, wildebeest and antelope stay near each other, so it's not so strange. Ngulia here is quite bossy, so she has a few animals under her wing. Then we have a grown-up zebra called Lualeni who was raised here, but now lives nearby. He comes to visit her.'

'How completely lovely,' mumbled Annie, giving the nuzzling zebra a scratch behind the ear. The group then turned to the source of a growing commotion, coming from the forest below.

'Go – sit over there on that little wall,' said Lembara. 'You'll be better sitting down when they come.' They followed this ominous advice and perched on a low wall to the left of the compound. A group of about fifteen young elephants started trooping up, in single file. They were clearly excited as they scampered up towards the keepers but there was still some order to their movement.

'That one – the one at the front, that is Nyiro, he is three and he's my favourite!' said Lembara. Nyiro came running towards them, virtually knocking Annie over, before greeting Lembara, then attempting to give Xander a big wet kiss and fumbling with his trunk to grab the phone he was filming with right out of his hand.

'A friend for life now!' laughed Lembara. 'Come, come and watch them have their supper. I know you've been to our Nairobi centre and seen the little ones, but these guys are like wrestlers!

'Also, they're red, like the eles near our camp,' said Annie.

'You're quite right!' laughed Lembara. 'They are caked in our beautiful, red Tsavo mud.'

'Where will they go to sleep tonight?' asked Annie.

'These elephants are older than the Nairobi orphans, so don't need the rangers to be substitute mothers in the same way,' explained Lembara. 'We're getting them used to being with each other, then eventually to mix with wild elephants, so, rather than sleeping in the stables, they sleep in the large pens. Little by little, they spend time out in the wild on their own, until they leave entirely.'

'Now, this lady over here is Emily. She is nine,' explained another keeper, Jonah.

'Isn't that quite old to live here?' asked Bryndís.

'Yes, it is. She has been at this centre for six years, but she shows no sign of leaving. We've tried to habituate her in the wild, but she prefers it here. Instead, she is a surrogate mum to the babies, especially the newest arrivals. She sees the keepers as her family. In fact, she recently saved some of the keepers who were walking the babies in the forest. They were suddenly surrounded by a group of six lions. Emily circled the lions, trumpeting loudly until they got scared and ran away.'

'What a brave girl!' Annie was delighted and, unlike her parents who held back a little, completely unafraid of the older elephants. She stroked Emily on the trunk.

'I think you know our newest resident.' Lembara came back over to the family, joined by Barbara and Fenella. Lembara walked them all back to the stables, to the last hut in the row. His voice lowered and he stepped aside, so that the group could get a look inside. Lying on a thick bed of straw and covered in a faded red and green blanket, was Makena's calf. The group fell silent and they could hear the baby's quick, uneven breath as she slept. There was an occasional whistle from her trunk which almost woke her up, causing her to flail her trunk around as if swatting a fly, then settle into sleep again.

'How is she?' whispered Dan.

'It's early days. She wasn't hurt… physically, you understand. But what has happened to her was very, very traumatic. Elephants are very emotional, you know.'

'Yes, we've been watching elephants here,' said Xander. 'We've only been here for a few weeks, but we've already seen how close the families are.'

'The next few days and weeks will be crucial, then it will be up to her. We do all we can, everything is here for her. Her keeper, Jonah will be with her day and night, trying to make her feel safe. But sometimes, they just die of unhappiness, you know?'

'Were we right to try and help her, do you think?' asks Gigi. 'Only, maybe it would have been kinder to, you know…'

'Yes, yes, you were quite right. They all deserve a chance and she could very well make it. You've seen the older ones.' The group turned to see the orphans guzzling down their supper of milk and sweet branches. 'Many of them, in fact most of them, have a story like hers. But they thrive here and we rewild them very successfully.'

As the young elephants fed, a large male wandered up from the direction from which the others had come.

'Good evening, Elliot,' Lembara greeted the elephant. 'Come and meet our new friends. Folks, this is Elliot. He is eleven years old now and he was an orphan like these guys. He came here as a one-year-old; his family had also been poached and we found him sitting with his mother. We patched him up and let him go and for the last five years, he has been part of another family. He is just beginning to grow away from them and he often comes here.'

'Erm... he is big, isn't he? Just eleven, you say?' Dan stood next to Elliot but barely reached his shoulder. He walked briskly away from him when the elephant tried to investigate the top of his head with his trunk. 'I don't think I'll ever get used to their size,' said Dan. 'It's a cliché, but seeing them on television just isn't the same. Until you're next to an elephant, you can't imagine how big they are.'

Fenella had stood back from the rest of the group up to now – just watching – vicariously enjoying the thrill that people get when they encounter Africa's wildlife up close. She loved to witness that moment when someone connected with a fellow creature – broke through the wall that we think surrounds us humans. This was her Africa. Nairobi had been too frantic, the tree-planting with other volunteers had been fun and felt productive, but this was what she missed – this was what her soul needed.

She walked slowly towards Elliot, head bowed, holding out a branch of young, sweet acacia leaves. Elliot took the gift willingly, curling his trunk around the branch and chewing contemplatively while looking down on Fenella with his liquid chocolate eyes. He edged a little closer to her and dropped the branch in order to touch her cheek with his trunk. She stood still and calm and hummed a little under her breath. Her skin prickled and she felt a flood of emotions, memories racing through her brain – touching Makena's trunk tip with her baby fist, waiting for trapdoor spiders to snap a cricket into their lair, sitting on her Babu's knee, reciting the names of all the different starlings, clutching the hand of her little sister as they giggled about dik-dik poo. Elliot purred in her ear and slowly, gently, wrapped his trunk over her and pulled her in close.

'Our baby needs a name,' Lembara turned to Barbara. Fenella looked at her grandmother. Despite the smile, the grief she shared with Fenella showed on her face. There was no mistaking the sadness that lay beneath every word, every gesture – a constant burden, a weariness of having to pick oneself up over and over. Barbara had been rejected by her family, lost the man she adored and her little granddaughter, been estranged from her son and separated from her daughter-in-law and granddaughter. Time and again, the raw nature of life in Africa had dealt her blow after blow. And yet, Barbara had strength and resolve beyond anyone Fenella knew. She watched her grandmother straighten, tilt her chin up and smile as she reached a hand towards hers.

'I think perhaps Fenella might have an idea about that.' They shared a knowing look.

'Can she be called Evie?' Fenella asked.

CHAPTER 44

NAIROBI 2012

CECILY and Marina waved him off and he headed back to the Mombasa Road. Only, this time Rob was not destined for Mombasa.

The legal process had been hastened by political expediency. A large haul of illegal animal parts, intercepted before they even reached the border, had been a coup for the police and a blessing for the government. For a country which prided itself on its anti-hunting stance and an international reputation as a paradise for tourists, a legal hard line taken against such a big player was an important move. Plenty of public mileage was made of the seizure and the condemnation of du Toit and his network. Rob preferred to keep his profile low and refused to speak to any reporters about his part in the affair. He was just glad it was over.

During du Toit's trial, Rob had given his evidence, although it was hardly needed, given the incontrovertible physical proof. And du Toit, old as he now was, would spend the rest of his life in prison. His reputation as a player was also tarnished, influential contacts who might have helped him before, could see no benefit in doing that now, given that the matter was so public. No – this time, Rob could definitely close the lid and move on.

Nonetheless, this task that Rob had set himself had taken over his life. Now that he had completed it, he obviously felt lighter, gratified, but also a little bewildered. A decade of his life had been obsessively dedicated to avenging his daughter and father, to acting for the animals who had no voice of their own, to proving to his wife, mother and older daughter that goodness prevails, that love is what matters. But had he done that? His wife was mentally traumatised, perhaps permanently, his mother had been left to run their camp without him, his daughter was estranged and living her own life in Scotland. A new burden now weighed down on him. He had to try to make amends. His first stop was Taita Hills.

* * *

After their visit to the rehabilitation centre, a new sense of purpose prevailed over the camp. Gigi and Dan and their family should have left several weeks earlier, but had agreed with Barbara to stay on. Xander would complete his A levels by correspondence, basing his final Geography project on educational architecture and social infrastructure provision in Kenya. Dan and Gigi had joined Hamisi on a trip to Nairobi to discuss proposals for providing grants and land leases to local people, ensuring sustainable farming and conservation methods. Bryndís took on some of Fikiri's work, assisted by Jonathan, the charges against whom had been dropped, following Fikiri's and John's testimonies.

Fenella was spending a couple of hours with Hamisi each day, going through the report he had written with her parents, adding some of the recent findings made by visiting volunteers and students, and updating some of the conclusions. She had driven out many times with Hamisi, and on her own, getting reacquainted with her home. Every day she had to stop herself from actually laughing out loud in delight, so happy was she to be back.

Having Fenella around was balm to Barbara. The loss of Makena and her family was devastating, but Fenella could see her grandmother's resolve resurface; she would not let the poachers and their buyers win twice. Together they redoubled efforts to promote the camp and its reputation as an important and valuable venue for both serious researchers and those seeking an authentic wild experience. Now, more than ever, this place was essential and Barbara would not be defeated.

* * *

It was Annie who saw the car first. She was with Joseph again. He was explaining the complicated reproductive behaviour of spotted hyenas. He seemed unsure how the conversation had started and perhaps wished it hadn't, but Annie would not be wavered from her questioning. 'But what is a pseudo-penis and why has the girl got one?' Joseph sweated and stammered his way through the explanations, so was clearly delighted when Annie's persistence was broken by the arrival of the unknown visitor.

He got out of the car and stood for a moment, looking around as if taking in the scene; a little confused. In front of him was the old house that seemed unchanged – but everything else was new – makuti-topped huts, a large mess tent, an open-air living area full of chairs, benches, cushions and books. Today, it was a scene of synchronised busyness – cooking, hammering, people with clipboards walking from one building to another. He had to shout to proclaim his arrival: 'Jambo! Jambo! Hello, I'm looking for Barbara Chege, is she here?'

'I know Barbara,' said Annie, jumping from her seat to greet him. 'Who are you? I'll go and find her for you.'

'I'm Rob… but, please, don't tell her that. Can you just tell her that there is an old friend come to see her?' Annie looked a little uncertain, but Rob gave her a reassuring nod and she ran to find Barbara. She found her in the kitchen with Hamisi and Peter, working out a menu for a birthday party.

'There's a man to see you, Barbara,' Annie reported. 'He said he's an old friend. He looks nice. He's quite old. Not as old as you. Like Daddy.'

Barbara chuckled. 'Not as ancient as me, huh? Let's see who this old friend is then, shall we?' She took Annie's hand as the little girl led her to the visitor. They stepped out into the afternoon sunshine, temporarily blinded.

'Mum?' Rob gasped.

Barbara dropped Annie's hand and flung her hands over her mouth. 'Oh, my goodness, is it you? Is it you? Bobby!'

'It's me, Mum. I'm home.' He ran over to her and engulfed her in a tight embrace, grasping her tighter as she shook. 'I'm so sorry, Mum. I'm so sorry for everything.'

They stood for a long while gripping each other, until Barbara pushed away. 'It's alright.' She sniffed and jutted out her chin, still clutching his arms. 'You're home now. And I do know why you had to go. I've seen what you did. You are your father's son. Your Baba would be so proud of you. I am so proud of you.' She wiped her eyes and stood back from him, drinking him in. He stood with his head bowed, like a little boy, trying not to weep. 'Someone else is very proud of you, too. Stay here a moment. It's my turn to surprise you!'

She vanished inside. He stepped back towards his car and made small talk with Annie, who stared smiling at him, fascinated.

Then she was there.

This time Rob could not hold back his emotion. He gasped and his legs went from under him; he had to lean on his car for support.

'Nella?' he breathed. 'You're here?'

Fenella walked towards him; her eyes brimmed with happy tears. She pulled him to her and held him, she had strength enough for both of them.

* * *

They arrived at Jomo Kenyatta Airport together and this time Fenella felt no anxiety, she was simply excited. They were being met at Edinburgh by Andrew and Goo who were also putting them up for a fortnight.

'Okay, Dad?' Fenella asked him.

Rob stared out of the tiny window at the city pulling away from them and nodded. 'Okay. I'm excited to see her, but… well… I'm ashamed, Nella. I shouldn't have left and let it get like this. I guess I told myself she was strong and capable, that she wouldn't need me.'

'What happened wasn't your fault, or any of our faults. I don't know if things would have been different if you hadn't left, but she is well looked after and Andrew and Goo see her every week. Goo writes to me and texts and she tells me she's definitely getting stronger. She takes messages and pictures from us and shows them to Mum, and she has been getting the occasional smile out of her. Oh, I am so looking forward to this. And if I'm honest, I didn't used to look forward to visiting her. Like you, I felt sad and guilty and powerless.' She grabbed his hand. 'But come on, let's not dwell on that. Let's just be ready to bring her some joy.'

They were waiting in the arrivals area. Goo couldn't contain her elation, and despite her outwardly sophisticated appearance – a long, white wool coat and raspberry cashmere shawl, tossed over one shoulder – she was actually jumping up and down on the spot when they caught her eye.

'Nella! Here!' They ran to each other, grinning and squealing.

Andrew took Rob by the hand and pulled him in for a hug, patting his back. 'It's been too long, Rob. So nice to see you. Good man. Come now, we thought we would grab an enormous Indian takeaway here and then gorge on it at home. You guys can unpack and get comfy and then we can hear all your news over a feast.'

The next morning the group drove to the clinic and Andrew and Goo dropped Fenella and Rob off while they took a walk. 'Give her our love,' said Goo, 'Oh, and this.' She reached into her pocket and pulled out a ceramic elephant, tiny but perfectly detailed.

'A matriarch.' Fenella smiled. 'Thank you, she'll love it.'

The room was filled with spring sunshine, and Jo sat on her chair by the window. She had put on weight since Fenella had last seen her. Her hair had regained some of its copper glow and there was a new quickness in her eyes. Fenella walked in alone and reached out to her mother. 'Mum. How are you? I'm so happy to see you. You have no idea.' She leant over and kissed her mother on the cheek. Jo reached up to stroke Fenella's face.

'I'm glad, darling, I'm so pleased to see you.'

'I have a little gift for you, from Goo.' She passed her the tiny elephant. 'It looks like Makena, doesn't it?' She looked at her mother, willing for a reaction.

'It does, it does. It has her kind expression.' She ran a finger over the elephant, examining every detail. 'Did you know you met her before you were born? I never told anyone about that. It was our little secret. She pressed her trunk up against my belly and you kicked. It was magical.' Fenella laughed, crouched down and hugged her. 'Oh, Mum. I do love you.'

They embraced for a few moments, then Fenella gave Jo a quick kiss on the nose. 'You look great! Listen, I brought someone.' She stood up to face the door; Rob took his cue and appeared in the doorway. He gazed across at Jo, anxious and hopeful.

'Mpenzi wangu, njoo hapa,' Jo said quietly, 'Come here, my love.'

Rob ran and threw himself at Jo, kneeling at the foot of her chair and sobbed into her lap. Fenella put her hand on Jo's shoulder, then Rob's and left them.

* * T H E E N D * *

Glossary

Words in the left-hand column are Kiswahili unless marked otherwise.

Acacia	Common East African tree species
Asante sana	Many thanks
Askari	Guard
Baba	Daddy
Babu	Grandpa
Banda	Sleeping hut
Baobab	Type of tree – very large, looks upside-down
Bibi	Granny
Boma	Secure enclosure, usually circled with thorny branches
Bundu-bashing	Off-road driving through the bush
Chapati	A flatbread, eaten in India, East Africa and southern Asia
Dhow	Traditional East African trade sailboat
Dik-dik	Tiny antelope
Dúlla	Icelandic – 'sweetie' common between female friends
Eh, eh, tulia Watoto	Hey, hey, calm down children
Emergency	(Eng.) Term used for the political situation in Kenya in the 1950s
Escarpment	(Eng.) High steep cliff
Euphorbia	A tall, succulent tree, balloon-like shape
Githeri	Kenyan traditional meal of maize and beans
Habari yako?	How are you?
Harambee	Pulling together
Jambo	Hello, hi

Jambo Watoto, mhali gani?	Hello children, how are you?
Kanga	Light cotton wrap
Kibanda	Street food business
Kikoy	Cotton sarong used as wrap, sling, towel
Kikuyu	Largest Kenyan ethnic group
Kiswahili	Language spoken by the Swahili people
Kopje	Small, isolated rocky hill in a mainly flat landscape
Kwa heri	Goodbye
Lala Salama	Sleep tight
Maharagwe	Spiced coconut bean soup
Makuti	Coconut palm thatch
Mama	Mother, Madam
Matatu	Local private minibus
Mau-Mau	Anti-colonial resistance movement – took place in 1950s–60s Kenya
Mchicha	East African spinach and curry dish
Mpenzi	Sweetheart
Murram	Clay road surface
Muezzim	Man who calls Muslims to prayers from mosque minaret
Musth	High testosterone state in bull elephants, making them aggressive
Nakupenda	I love you
Ndovu	Elephant
Ni Kijana	It's a boy
Nzuri sana	Very good
Ohangla	Dance music genre originating from Luo tribe
Panga	Broad, heavy knife, similar to a machete
Pap	Porridge made from meal or bread
Pole pole	Slowly

Rondavel	Traditional circular African house with thatched roof
Sasa	Now
Sawa sawa	Alright, okay, no worries
Shamba	Small subsistence farm
Shuka	Thick cloth, worn by Maasai or used as blanket
Sukuma	Wild collard greens
Sundowners	Refreshments taken at sunset
Tembo	Elephant
Tilapia	Freshwater fish common to Africa
Ugali	Maize meal porridge
Uhuru	Freedom/independence, denotes self-governance in Africa
Ululate	Wail made with the tongue to express strong emotion/cheer
Watusi	Dance popular in the 1960s
Yellow fever tree	Tree named for growing where malaria was common

Acknowledgements

MY father, **David Swinfen**, has been my greatest champion from the beginning of writing this book, supporting me throughout. He read every draft, making notes and encouraging me, even when I felt like giving up. The book truly would never have been finished without him.

My mother, **Ann Swinfen**, was a writer all her life, but could only really focus on it in later life, which she then did with gusto. She was ahead of her time, setting an example to her five children, especially her three daughters, that a woman doesn't have to be defined by her gender and can achieve great things with perseverance and hard work.

My nieces **Hazel** and **Heather** have been cheerleaders from the start. They were early readers of my manuscript and gave me lots of detailed and helpful feedback. They epitomise the care and support women can give each other, and are working in their own ways to make the world a better place.

A new, and now dear, friend **Marietta** read my first draft, despite us being strangers at the time. Something told me to be brave and reach out to her. I was right to follow my instincts and now we are friends for life!

My editor, **Eleanor Abraham**, has gone above and beyond with her help and suggestions, giving this novice writer advice on how best to craft and mould my story. She has enormous skill and patience and I am pleased that my story made her cry (in a good way!).

My husband, **Pascal**, knew I wanted to write before I did and even refurbished an old desk as a present to provide me with the means to do it. He puts up with my indifferent attitude to tidiness and my incurable book-buying addiction. While I wrote this, he made me nearly as many cups of tea as I made him.

When you change your life to have a family, the supposition is that you lose something of yourself. Our three sons, **Julius, Raphael** and **Theodore** have made my life richer and more meaningful and made me much stronger and braver than I ever was before. It is a privilege to be their mother. I hope we can make just one trip to Africa together before they all leave home!

A final word must go to those who work tirelessly to protect and preserve our planet's wild places, often at huge personal risk. Kenya is full of such committed conservationists. Wildlife crime is a huge issue, carried out by global syndicates with links to drug and weapons trafficking. According to a recent report by the World Wildlife Fund for Nature, "the illegal wildlife trade is the fourth largest illegal trade behind drugs, people smuggling and counterfeiting, worth an estimated £15 billion annually. It has heavily depleted some populations and has brought others to the verge of extinction."

My character, **Hamisi**, is based on a real person who had a huge impact on me; I met him twenty years ago and he continues to work for wildlife. **Dame Daphne Sheldrick** spent her entire adult life in the care of elephants and other wild orphans. She died in 2018, leaving a 45-year legacy in the form of the **Sheldrick Wildlife Trust** to her family and the team of dedicated staff. Their lives revolve around the love and care of animals, against a constant barrage of habitat destruction, greed and drought.

The Sheldrick Wildlife Trust has saved nearly three hundred elephants, and a further fifty have been born to those who have been reintegrated into the wild.

You can support their crucial work by sponsoring a baby elephant, rhino, or giraffe at www.sheldrickwildlifetrust.org.

About the Author

Nikki Swinfen was born and brought up on the east coast of Scotland. The daughter of two writers, she grew up surrounded by thousands of books. After a career in human resource management, dealing with adult misbehaviour, she gave it up to concentrate on bringing up children who, on the whole, were more reasonable.

In 2002, she won a competition to study elephants in Kenya, and so began a love affair with Africa and its wildlife.

She lives in rural Leicestershire with her husband, three sons and a dog. She is still surrounded by thousands of books, mostly about Africa. This is her first novel.

Printed in Great Britain
by Amazon